EVERY INCH A KING

EVERY INCH A KING

HARRY TURTLEDOVE

BALLANTINE BOOKS / NEW YORK

2007 Del Rey Books Trade Paperback Edition

Published in the United States by Del Rey Books, an imprint of The Random House Publishing Group, a division of Random House, Inc., New York.

DEL REY is a registered trademark and the Del Rey colophon is a trademark of Random House, Inc.

Originally published in hardcover in the United States by ISFiC Press, Deerfield, Illinois, in 2005.

ISBN 978-0-345-48736-0

Printed in the United States of America

www.delreybooks.com

1 2 3 4 5 6 7 8 9

Book design by Susan Turner

EVERY INCH A KING

'm Otto of Schlepsig. Ah, you've heard the name, I see. Yes, I'm *that* Otto of Schlepsig. Some other people claim to be, but I'm the real one, by the Two Prophets. I'm the one who was King of Shqiperi. I ruled the Land of the Eagle for five whole days.

No, I wasn't born blueblooded. By my hope of heaven, I wasn't. As a matter of fact, I was born in a barn. Truly. Literally. It was either that or make a mess of my parents' traveling caravan, and my mother—a trouper among troupers—would never have done such a thing.

I could lie to you and make out that Mother and Father were more famous than they really were. Why not? You'd never know the difference. But what's the point of telling a story if you don't tell a true story? So . . . They were sideshow performers, and that's the long and short of it. I grew up among more or less trained monkeys and bearded ladies and sea snakes and drunken, down-at-the-heels sorcerers and flea circuses and demons and all the other strange odds and ends that might make a mark want to part with some silver—or, a lot of the places where we played, with some copper.

I daresay it warped me for life. But I've had fun.

In the forty-odd years—some of them odder than others—since my mother waddled off to lie down in the hay, I've done a lot of things. I've been an actor. People still talk about the way I played King Clodweg in *The Maiden with Seven Boots*. Sometimes they don't even throw things when they do. I've climbed all 287 steps on the way to the top of the Temple of Siwa—and I met another traveler from Schlepsig when I got there.

I've been an acrobat. I've rescued a princess. That she didn't particularly want to be rescued wasn't my fault. I've served not one but two hitches in the army of the Hassockian Empire. (Whether that says more about how desperate I was or how desperate the Hassocki were, I leave for you to decide.)

And I've been King of Shqiperi. That's what I want to tell you about.

No, I didn't set out to be a king. Who does, except a crown prince? I was in a third-rate circus rattling around the Nekemte Peninsula in the middle of the Nekemte Wars. First-rate outfits never go down there: not enough money to be made. They stay up in Schlepsig and Albion and Narbonensis and Torino and the more civilized parts of the Dual Monarchy. The second-rate companies had cleared out when they heard dragons shrieking and crossbows being cranked. That left . . . outfits like mine, I'm afraid.

Dooger and Cark's Traveling Emporium of Marvels was just as bad, just as pathetic, just as hopeless as the name would make you guess. The roustabouts drank. When the tent went up, it went up sideways as often as not. The fortune-teller couldn't have seen a roc falling out of the sky. The sword-swallower coughed. That wasn't Max of Witte's fault, but it sure didn't help his act.

We were in Thasos the night everything got started. Thasos, most of the time, isn't a bad town. It's a bigger place, a fancier place, than Dooger and Cark's miserable little outfit usually gets to play. But, after belonging to the Hassockian Empire for something close to five hundred years, it had changed hands, quite suddenly, in the Nekemte Wars.

Frankly, it looked like a place that had just been sacked. The walls were battered. About every third building had a chunk bitten out of it, and fires had burned here and there. It smelled like a place that had just been sacked, too. Once you get a whiff of the smell of death, you never forget it. Mix it with old smoke and fear, and that's what a sack smells like.

And Thasos *felt* like a place that had just been sacked. A lot of the Hassocki pashas and beys had got out of town when their army ran off to the west, but most ordinary Hassocki—tinsmiths and ropemakers and butchers and what have you—hadn't had the chance to flee. The ones who were left alive sat glumly in their coffeeshops, robes drawn tight around them, turbans perhaps a bit askew, long faces somber. They drank tiny cups of sweet mud and sucked on the mouthpieces to their water pipes and tried to pretend the whole thing never happened.

Meanwhile, the Lokrians in Thasos were out of their minds with joy. Thasos has always been a mostly Lokrian town, even though Lokris lost it all those years ago. Now it was back under the Green Dragon, and men in short skirts and women in long ones danced in the streets. If you're not a Lokrian, the kind of music they play sounds like skinning a live cat with a dull knife. If you are . . . you dance. When they weren't dancing, they jeered at the surviving Hassocki.

After the sun went down, Lokrian warships in the harbor (junk Schlepsig and Albion didn't need any more) shot off fireworks. I hoped they were fireworks, anyway.

You're wondering why anybody in his right mind would want to bring a circus into a mess like that. You've never met Dooger and Cark, have you? One of them is from the wilder parts of the Dual Monarchy. The other speaks every language under the sun, and all with the same weird accent. If they had any idea what the demon they were doing, they wouldn't have touched the Traveling Emporium of Marvels with a ten-foot pole. Since they owned it . . .

Since they owned it, we got to Thasos a bare handful of days after the Lokrian and Plovdivian armies did.

Hassocki wizards should have planted salamanders under the roadbed and in the fields. That would have slowed down the Lokrians and probably the Plovdivians (who are wild men), and would have stopped civilian traffic in its tracks (although only Eliphalet and Zibeon know what Dooger and Cark would have done). It didn't happen. By then, the Nekemte Wars were going so badly for the Hassocki that they didn't think about much except running. The only places where they still held out and held on were in the fortress of Edirne, which guarded the approaches to Vyzance, and off in wild Shqiperi, where nobody was trying very hard to push them.

But that's another story. I hadn't even thought of the Land of the Eagle yet. To tell you the truth, I wouldn't swear I'd heard of the Land of the Eagle yet. I'd been a lot of places in my time, but nobody in his right mind went to Shqiperi. So I thought then, anyhow.

Our wagons rattled and thumped down that unsalamandered—I hoped—but potholed—I knew—highway to Thasos. I sat next to the roustabout driving mine. In my spangled shirt and tight trousers, I wanted to be seen. I combed my mustaches, trying to make them as splendid as I could.

Behind me, in the wagon, Max of Witte coughed. He's had a cough for as long as I've known him, and we go back a ways. Sometimes I ignore it. Sometimes it starts to drive me crazy. This was one of *those* times. "Stop that, Max," I said.

"I'd love to," he said in his foghorn bass, poking his head out to look around. Max is a lot taller and a little skinnier than people have any business being. His joints show more than your usual fellow's, too, so watching him is like watching a not very graceful marionette. He coughed again.

"One of these days, you'll do that while you're performing," I warned him.

"Only way I'll ever make the journals," he said dolefully. "First person in the history of the world to cut his own throat from the inside out. Something to look forward to."

"If you say so," I answered. Max isn't Max unless he's complaining about something.

We pitched our tent in a vacant lot not far from the Grand Temple of Thasos. That temple is all Lokrian; it was there for a thousand years before the Hassocki took the city. You could see the two spires piercing the sky whenever you turned your head that way. (The Lokrians, of course, are Zibeonites, and built his spire taller than Eliphalet's. Being a modern, tolerant man, I pass over in silence the ignorant heretics' errors.)

The Hassocki had built a fane to their Quadrate God next to the Grand Temple. It gave them a place to worship in Thasos. Other than that, I have to say, it wasn't a success. The four low domes on its roof aren't so much of a much compared to those two spires, even if the wrong one was taller. (No, I was going to pass over that in silence, wasn't I? My apologies, kindly reader.)

I got the feeling the lot hadn't been vacant very long. Whoever'd cleared the rubble from it had plainly won the contract on lowest bid and made up for that by *not* clearing a good bit of it. Bricks, broken bottles of arrack (if there'd been any unbroken bottles, the rubble haulers had taken care of those—oh, you bet they had), and roof slates argued a building had lived there not very long ago. Crumpled papers might have come from it, too, or from anywhere else in Thasos. They blew by, now in flurries, now in blizzards.

And we added our own papers, as if Thasos didn't have enough. We pasted flyers for Dooger and Cark on anything that didn't have a mouth and ears. There are at least half a dozen languages in the Nekemte Peninsula. Dooger and Cark, being too cheap to have wizards use the law of similarity to reproduce them in every relevant speech, solved the problem by not using any. Probably Cark's idea; he's the one who was born speaking no known tongue.

So our flyers showed a pretty girl wearing not very much (have you ever known a circus without one, or more than one, to give the marks something to stare at?) turning cartwheels, a lion and a unicorn on their hind legs like the supporters of the arms of Albion, a two-headed man (actually, José-Diego quit a while ago, after he got into an argument with himself), a clown brawling with a well-hung demon, and, soaring above them all, an acrobat doing an obviously death-defying flip.

Me. Yours truly, Otto of Schlepsig. Star of Dooger and Cark's, Prophets help me.

I lugged a pastepot while Ilona carried flyers. She's the pretty girl on the poster—a redhead from the Dual Monarchy with a temper like dragon's breath. "Hurry up!" she snapped at me, as if I were her slave. Well, I've heard ideas I liked less.

"You're carrying paper," I pointed out. "I've got this bloody heavy bucket, and my arms will be as long as a forest ape's by the time we get this job done."

Ilona said something in Yagmar, the language she grew up speaking, that should have set the flyers on fire. We'd been using Schlepsigian up till then. It's my birthspeech, and Ilona knows it because the Dual Monarchy crams it down everybody's throat in school, like it or not. Almost everybody in the circus business picks up some of it—except the Albionese. They think other people ought to speak *their* language.

Ilona wasn't in costume. She would have caused a riot if she'd gone out on the street wearing what she almost wore when she performed—and not a friendly kind of riot, either. Hassocki can have harems, but they start pitching fits if they see more of a woman in public than her hands and her face. You figure it out—I've given up. And Lokrians, probably because they've had the Hassocki next door for so long, are almost as straitlaced.

Costume or not, she still got stares. She's a damn good-looking woman—I already said that. And she has red hair down to about the small of her back. In a place like Thasos, where just about everybody's swarthy, she stood out like an honest man in parliament.

A fellow in a skirt and tights said something in Lokrian. Seeing us look blank, he tried again in Hassocki: "You're . . . circus people?"

Hassocki I speak—a lot better than he did, in fact. They beat it into you when you join their army. "Of course not, sir," I answered politely, adding my best bow. "We're in the chicken-giblet business. I can give you a fine bargain on gizzards."

It didn't faze him. Nothing much fazes Lokrians—either that or they start pitching fits. He jerked a thumb at Ilona. "Sell me *her* giblets."

"What does he say?" she demanded. Without waiting for an answer, she called the Lokrian something that made what she'd said before sound like love poetry. That didn't faze him, either. He swept off his broad-brimmed straw hat and bowed almost double. She turned her back on him. Considering some Lokrians' tastes, that might have been ill-advised. But this fellow just sighed and went on his way.

Such is the glamorous, romantic life of a circus performer. Makes you want to run away and join, doesn't it?

Actually going out and performing is always a relief. You may hate traveling. You may hate shilling (although nobody in his right mind hates Albionese shillings—they're the soundest money in the world). But if you hate performing, you wouldn't be out there in the first place.

With the usual jitters, I watched the crowd filter into the tent. If the house is lousy, the owners have an excuse for stiffing the crew. Of course, the owners will try to stiff the crew if the house is full, too—especially if they're Dooger and Cark—but at least then you know you're getting screwed.

Things looked pretty good. The portable stands on either side of the ring were filling up. Roustabouts steered Lokrians to one side, Hassocki to the other. Why borrow trouble? You get plenty even when you don't borrow it.

Hassocki complained they couldn't see the lions as well as they wanted to. Lokrians complained they couldn't see the clowns as well as they wanted to. Everybody complained about how much we charged for wine and pistachios. Hassocki aren't supposed to drink even a drop of wine. That doesn't stop them, or not very often. They flick out a drop from a cup, as if to say, *There, I didn't drink that one*, and then they go on. Sometimes I think they enjoy wine more because they don't just get drunk—they get to feel guilty, too.

Out swaggered the ringmaster, in an outfit that would have made an Albionese duke at a coronation feel underdressed: top hat, tailcoat, white tie, knee breeches with silver buckles, shining white hose, and patent-leather cambridges with even bigger silver buckles. And Ludovic had a whip—how can you be a ringmaster without a whip?—and he had waxed mustachios just as black and just about as long. Ludovic is a piece of work, all right.

He cracked the whip to draw everybody's eyes to him. Good thing the locals didn't decide the war had started up again, that's all I can tell you. "Ladies and gentlemen, welcome to Dooger and Cark's Traveling Emporium of Marvels!" he said, first in Lokrian and then in Hassocki. At least I assume the Lokrian was the same as what I could understand.

People applauded. They really did. Like I've said, we hadn't played Thasos before. For all the locals knew, we really were marvelous. Unfortunately, they'd find out pretty soon.

"And now," Ludovic called in a voice that filled the big tent without seeming strained, "I give you the famous Madame Ilona and the unicorn. Madame Ilona, ladies and gentlemen, direct from the court of the Dual Monarchy!"

The only court in the Dual Monarchy Ilona had ever seen was the one that gave her a sentence for vagrancy. Nobody from the royal and imperial court at Vindobon (royal *and* imperial, mind, not just one) was likely to show up and give us the lie, though, so why not?

Out she came, doing flips across the unicorn's back and cartwheels and somersaults all around the beast. Everybody stared at her. Well, Ilona is worth staring at anywhere she goes. But all she had on was skin-tight emerald satin that covered her from just above *those* to right around *that*, and women in Thasos *don't* dress that way, not where anybody can see them they don't.

Hassocki and Lokrians all gaped as if they'd never set eyes on a woman before. The shock value probably made Ilona look even better to them than she would have someplace where people don't have a stroke when they look at a leg.

Ilona knew what she was doing to them, too. There's a little—or more than a little—demon in Ilona. In between the tumbling runs, she threw in some wiggles that weren't gymnastic but sure were entertaining. You never saw such an . . . attentive audience in all your born days.

And the unicorn only made it that much more agonizing for the poor, prudish locals. Everybody knows about unicorns and virgins. Now, Ilona may possibly be virgin in her left ear, but I wouldn't bet more than a hemidemisemilepta even on that. She didn't try to *ride* the unicorn, of course. She just did flips on it. The unicorn put up with that. The other? Give me leave to doubt it.

She was good. Not only that, she was *riveting*. The marks couldn't take their eyes off her. I've seen plenty of acts with amazing talent that nobody wanted to watch. If you've got a choice between good and riveting, take riveting every time. You'll go further.

Our lion-tamer was good. He could get the big cats to do things . . . Well, if their mothers asked them to do some of that stuff, they would have bitten them. But poor Cadogan *wasn't* riveting, not even close. He made it all look too easy. Working with lions is supposed to seem dangerous. Curse it, working with lions *is* dangerous. A lot of trainers end up slightly dead, because one mistake is all you need. The crowd is supposed to sweat when you're out there. If it doesn't . . . If it doesn't, you end up playing with an outfit like Dooger and Cark's Traveling Emporium of Marvels. And Eliphalet and Zibeon have pity on you if you do.

Ilona came out again, this time doing flips on a mammoth's back. Maybe the mammoth got as many oohs and ahhs as she did—they don't live anywhere close to Thasos—but maybe it didn't, too. Clowns tumbled and brawled all around the parading beast. Some of the thumping and pounding that was part of the act probably wasn't just part of the act, if you know what I mean. Two of the men in whiteface and odd-colored wigs had fallen out over one of the women. When they slugged each other in the stomach and walloped each other with brickbats, they bloody well meant it.

It made the act go over better. There was an edge they wouldn't have had if they were just going through the motions. People can tell, even marks. As long as one of them didn't stick a salamander in the other one's drawers backstage, the show was fine. And they were both troupers. The show mattered to them.

Ludovic reappeared. One of the clowns larruped him with a brickbat, collapsing his topper. The clown scooted away, but not fast enough. The ringmaster's whip lashed out. It snatched the clown's green wig right off his head. Under the green wig, he had on a fire-red one. That's always good for a laugh.

"And now, ladies and gentlemen . . ." Ludovic speaks more languages than I do, and speaks most of them better than I do. ". . . Now the amazing, the astounding, the magnificent Grand Duke Maximilian of Witte!"

That was Max. I happen to know his father was a brewer. From an early age, Max showed himself much more enthusiastic about drinking ale than about making it—which is, no doubt, part of the reason he was making a poor but not too honest living with Dooger and Cark's.

Out he came, to more silence than I would have liked. Most places, his tall, thin, shambling frame stuffed into a general's uniform with twenty pounds of epaulets and medals and cloth-of-gold threadwork and crisscrossing scarlet sashes (also gold-trimmed) and the gaudiest scabbard in the world is good for a belly laugh all by itself. I knew right away what was wrong. In Lokris and the Hassockian Empire, generals really *do* wear outfits like that. The locals couldn't see the joke.

Max's face is one of those long, skinny ones that look sad even when the fellow who's wearing it is happy and go downhill from there. He looked out to the audience, to the Lokrians on one side, to the Hassocki on the other. The more he looked, the more lugubrious he got. If not for his other talent, he would have made quite a clown.

He made an extravagant gesture of farewell—so extravagant, he almost fell over. Then he made as if to cut his throat, but stopped halfway with another gesture, one that said that wasn't good enough. And then, throwing his head back, he swallowed the sword instead.

I've seen a lot of sword-swallowers, but Max of Witte is the best I know, or know of. Being so long and lean, he's got a lot of space between his mouth and vital points south, so he can swallow more blade than anybody I've ever seen. He outdid himself this time, too. He was just about ready to swallow the hilt; that's what it looked like, anyhow. Then he coughed.

That cursed cough is one of the reasons Max performs for Dooger and Cark's and not a circus really worthy of his talents. And those talents really are formidable. By then, people in both sets of stands were staring and pointing and shouting—and clapping like maniacs, too.

What's the other reason? Well, I don't exactly know. Max tells it different ways on different days, depending on whether he's drunk or sober or on which way the wind is blowing. Most of the time, it involves the wife of a prominent promoter. Sometimes, it's his mistress. Sometimes, it's his daughter. Once, it had something to do with the promoter's dog— but Max was *very* drunk then.

He coughed again. He'd joked about cutting his throat from the inside out. With that much steel still inside him, it wasn't a joke any more. He drew out the blade—probably a lot faster than he'd had in mind at first—and brandished it like a professional duelist. He bowed almost double as the crowd went wild.

Then, for good measure, Ilona came out again. She was carrying a long, thin loaf of bread. Max bowed to her, even more deeply than he had to the crowd. He kissed her hand, and kissed his way up her arm. The farther he got, the louder the audience squealed. No, you don't do those things in public, not in Thasos you don't.

At last, when the squeals were turning to screams, Ilona clouted him over the head with the loaf of bread, using it like a clown's brickbat. That seemed to make poor Max remember what he was supposed to be doing. He bowed to her again. She held out the loaf at arm's length.

And Max sliced it. *Flash! Flash! Flash!* went the sword. Slice after neat slice, every slice of bread flew off the loaf, till the blade paused about an inch from Ilona's hand. More cheers from the crowd—loud ones. There are always your half-smart marks who go, "Oh, but that blade hasn't got an edge on it anyway." Oh, but that blade bloody well *had*.

They cheered him then. He'd earned it, and he got it. He bowed himself almost double again, and had to make a wild grab to keep his hat from falling off. His hat? I haven't said anything about his hat? Well, what would *you* say about something so garish, it made the rest of his outfit look normal by comparison? It didn't glow in the dark, but I'm switched if I know why not. His ears stuck out from under it, too.

"And now, ladies and gentlemen, for your entertainment and amazement, the king of acrobats!" Ludovic bawled. "Ladies and gentlemen, the one, the only, the magnificent . . . Otto of Schlepsig!"

I was on. I bounded out there into the center of the ring and bowed every which way at once. I got polite applause. I hadn't expected anything more—I hadn't done anything yet, after all. But even that little spatter of handclapping gave me what the drunk gets from his brandy and the opium smoker from his pipe. I was out there. I was in front of people. They saw me. They liked me. I was *alive*.

I waved again. I bowed again. I ran up to one of the two big poles that supported the tent canopy and hurried up the rope ladder attached to it—big tents are rigged as elaborately as men-of-war. About two-thirds of the way up, there's a tiny platform. A tightrope stretches from it to the one just like it on the far tent pole.

As soon as I stepped out onto the rope, I heard the gasps. Some came from women's throats, some from men's. I teetered, deliberately, just to hear them again and make them louder. "He's going to fall!" somebody exclaimed in Hassocki.

"Yeah!" Several voices said that. They sounded eager—hungry, even. There are always people who *want* to see the sword-swallower cut his throat, who *want* to see the acrobat fall down and smash himself to strawberry jam, who *want* to see the demon get loose, who *want* to see the lion maul the tamer. It happens everywhere you go. You can't do a thing about it—and if you could, and you did what you wanted to do, wouldn't you be just like *them?* Better not even to think about that.

And better not to think about falling down, too. If it's in your mind, it's liable to be in your muscles, too. Actually, though, a tightrope is more forgiving than a slack one. And I wasn't trying anything new. Only the same old things I'd done ten thousand times in practice. Don't think. Just do.

Anyone who's known me for a while will tell you I'm pretty good at not thinking. Ask either of my ex-wives, for instance. Trudi and Jane don't agree on much, but they wouldn't argue with that.

So. Leap, right foot forward. Leap, left foot forward. Handstand rolling into a somersault, coming down on my feet. The rope *was* good and tight. I'd made sure of that beforehand. You don't trust the roustabouts when it's your own personal, private, irreplaceable neck. Not more than once, you don't, assuming you live through the once.

Out to the middle of the tightrope. Bounce up and down once or twice. Listen to them ooh and ahh down below. Listen to them scream when you spring out into nothing but empty air. Then listen to them ooh and ahh again, three times as loud, when you catch the glass trapeze rod. I live for that.

From down below, they can't see the trapeze at all. Magic kills the reflections. Magic also strengthens it—having it snap from my weight could be downright embarrassing. The first time I hit it in any show always worries me. The wizards Dooger and Cark use have the same sorts of troubles as everybody else in the troupe. One of them drinks. One of them built a bridge that didn't stand up. One of them—well, never mind about him. I don't let him have anything to do with the trapeze rod, that's all, and you can take it to the bank.

Once I was on the first trapeze, swinging and twirling from it to the next to the next was easy, in the sense that anything is easy if you've practiced it long enough. If I do say so myself—and I do—I showed the locals some moves they wouldn't have seen anywhere else this side of a forest ape.

My last flip was from the last trapeze to the tightrope. I caught the rope, used my momentum to swing up into another handstand, and went from that back to the upright. Some people would have cut more capers on the rope then. Me, I figured enough was enough. I went across to the far pole, took one bow on the little platform up there, and then came back down to the ground. The hand I got as I descended and when I finished my bows in the center of the ring said I'd gauged it right.

"That was the magnificent Otto of Schlepsig!" Ludovic boomed. I took one more bow. Who wouldn't feel magnificent with applause washing over him like sweet, pure rain? The ringmaster went on, "And now, Ibrahim the Wise conjures spirits from the vasty deep!"

Ibrahim the Wise is the twit I won't let near my trapeze rod. He's a fat little Torinan. His real name is Giuseppe; backstage, we mostly call him Joe. He dresses in robes that look vaguely Hassockian, to go with his alias. He *does* look wise, or at least impressive, when he wears them, which proves clothes really do make the man.

If only he'd stick to the handful of things he knows how to do, he'd be fine. But he's one of those mages who never saw a new spell they didn't like. He half learns them, and trots them out before he's got them under control. One of these days, he'll summon up a water elemental and drown us all. Did I tell you he smokes hashish? That doesn't do anything to make him think he's *less* powerful, believe you me it doesn't.

Today, though, everything went all right. I recognized his spell right away. He's called up that golden-winged monkey-griffin fairly often—often enough to get the hang of it, anyway. The green smoke that flared when the demon appeared was new, but it wasn't a bad effect. And the monkey-griffin put on a show, rearing up on its hind legs till it was twice as tall as a man and roaring like a lost soul.

Its tongue was long and green, too—so long that it almost stole the hat from a fat Lokrian in the first row who looked like an olive-oil merchant. The fat man let out a yelp even louder than the monkey-griffin's roars. His fellow Lokrians were sympathetic. The Hassocki in the other set of stands laughed at him.

To close things out, of course, Ibrahim the allegedly Wise had to de-manifest his demon. He did it, to my relief, and even threw in another cloud of smoke, this time red. He bowed. People cheered.

I got a better hand, though. You'd better believe it.

. . .

Afterwards, we did what people do afterwards: we unwound. And while we unwound, we kept a wary eye on Dooger and Cark as they counted the take. If they said we didn't bring in much, they'd be setting us up to cheat us. Like I said, it wasn't anything they hadn't done before.

We were all a little more nervous than usual this time. If we squawked, they were liable to sack the noisy ones and leave us stuck in Thasos. With the Nekemte Wars still sputtering behind us, with soldiers and brigands and pirates prowling the routes back to civilization, this wasn't really a place where we wanted to get stuck.

And the real pisser is, Dooger and Cark are *rich*. They don't worry about where their next copper's coming from. Screwing the people who work for them is like a game, as far as they're concerned. Or maybe they've been doing it so long, they can't *not* do it.

There are always signs. When they start muttering and sighing and shaking their heads, when they look like a coal wagon just ran over poor old Aunt Griselda, that's the time to start worrying for real.

When they didn't start doing any of that stuff, we all breathed easier. When Cark actually smiled, we broke out the arrack and the slivovitz and the schnapps and the genever and the cognac and the water of life. Joe—excuse me, Ibrahim the Wise—got a pipe going and probably doesn't remember any of the next three days.

Dooger? Dooger didn't smile. But that didn't bother us, because Dooger never smiles. Never. I don't want him to, either. I'm not ready for the world to end.

I washed off most of my makeup. I left a little on, so people would know I'm a performer. That always impresses local girls, or some of them, anyhow. A bottle of arrack came by. I took a swig and passed it on.

"Pretty good show," somebody said. Eliphalet's holy whiskers! That was Max. He's usually as cheerful as the Hassockian Atabeg's strangler. He must have been pleased—either that or he'd sucked in some smoke from Joe's pipe.

Trying to make the moment stretch, I said, "You did a nice job playing up the gloom when the people didn't laugh at your getup."

"Oh. Thanks." Max looked surprised. He also looked ridiculous. He still had on his Grand High Supreme Exalted Marshal's tunic, and under it his skinny, hairy legs stuck out from drafty drawers that needed mending. "Most of the marks, they're too dumb to laugh at funny. Give 'em something pathetic and they'll laugh themselves sick."

"Isn't that the truth?" I said, and told him my thought about the ghouls in the crowd.

Max gravely considered it. Max considers everything gravely. At last, he gave me a nod. "Well, I'm not going to tell you you're wrong," he said. "Some of those people, after I swallow the sword, they want to see it come out my—" A bottle of slivovitz interrupted him. After a show, a bottle of slivovitz will interrupt almost anybody. He gulped and sent it my way.

After he gulped, he coughed. This time, I didn't fret about him. For one thing, he didn't have a foot and a half of honed steel down his throat. For another, a good slug of slivovitz will make anybody cough.

Ilona let out a screech like a cat with its tail in a pencil sharpener. A moment later, I heard running feet. One of the locals must have been peeking into the wagon while she changed. Her window scraped open. What sounded like a bottle shattered on the ground—or possibly on the local's head. The window slammed shut. Ilona said something in Yagmar that had to mean, *That'll teach him!*

Ludovic brought in a copy of the *Thasos Chronicle*, the journal for foreigners in town. It's written in Narbonese, not because more foreigners in Thasos know Narbonese but because Narbonensis used to have closer ties to the Hassockian Empire than any of the other great powers did. Now that Thasos belongs to Lokris (unless Plovdiv takes it away), who knows how long the arrangement—or the journal—will last?

"Any news about the show?" three people asked at the same time. A natural question—and a dumb one. I don't care how fast the law of similarity lets you turn out copies. A scribe wouldn't have had time to write his piece, get back to the office or send it by crystal ball, and get it to the wizards. Not only that, the news-sellers wouldn't have had time to get it on the street. Magic is one thing. Miracles are something else altogether.

The ringmaster shook his beefy head. "I was looking for war news, for when we leave town. It's still sputtering to the north and west. The Hassocki aren't giving up there." He paused and turned to an inside page. "And it says Essad Pasha and the Shqipetari have asked the Hassockian Empire to send them Prince Halim Eddin to be their new king." He paused again. "There's a picture of the prince, copied by crystal from the original portrait in Vyzance." He held out the journal so we could all see.

It was my face.

II

Oh, the resemblance wasn't exact. Halim Eddin waxed his mustachios into points, where I let mine stay bushy. He plucked his eyebrows, the way Hassocki nobles do. I'd never let tweezers get near mine in my life. My hairline receded a little more than his. When I went up for a closer look, I saw that his eyes were bright blue, where mine are gray.

But we were about the same age. We both had brown hair. We both had long faces with strong chins and formidable noses. We both had high, proud cheekbones and wide mouths. We certainly could have been brothers. We might well have been twins. They say every man has his double. I never expected to meet mine staring at me off a journal page with a pound and a half of Hassocki medals on his chest.

Everybody in Dooger and Cark's Traveling Emporium of Marvels hurried up to gape at the picture—and at me. Now I know how the freaks and demons in the sideshow feel. Everybody started talking at once, using several different languages. Ilona—by then she'd come out of her wagon—looked at me sidelong and said, "There were things you weren't telling me, darling."

"There were things I wasn't telling *me*, darling," I answered.

Max bowed deeply. He looks like a carpenter's rule with big ears when he does that. "What is your command, your Highness?" he asked, sounding more like an undertaker than a courtier.

"Why don't you go soak your head?" I told him.

He bowed again. "With pleasure, your Highness." He grabbed another bottle—it was genever this time, I think—and got a long start on soaking, anyway.

All the rest of the night, the troupe called me *your Highness* and *your Majesty*. They wouldn't let it alone, even after the joke got stale. For a while, it annoyed me and made me angry. Then I started to accept it as nothing less than my due. That put some new life in the joke—except by that time I wasn't joking any more.

No, I'm not ashamed to admit it. That was how the idea caught fire in me: there at a drunken party for third-rate circus performers in a second-rate town that had just changed hands between a senile empire and a kingdom that wanted to revive an empire not just senile but centuries dead. Strokes of genius are where you find them.

I've acted on the stage, as I say. I've won applause in cities far grander than Thasos ever dreamt of being. Why I wasn't still doing that then . . . is a long story, and not altogether my fault. You can ask anyone who was there when things went sour. You'll hear the same thing—or perhaps you won't. Some people are nothing but natural-born liars.

But never mind that now. A role onstage is one thing. A role on the stage of the world, on the stage of history—that's something else again. The role of a lifetime! Liable not to be a very *long* lifetime if something went wrong, but nothing ventured, nothing gained. If only I could bring it off, I'd drink out on it for the rest of my days.

If. I couldn't do anything about it that evening. I couldn't do anything about anything, not as drunk as I got. An acrobat with a hangover is the most pitiful thing the Two Prophets ever saw, the only problem being that no one will pity him. Try doing flips and spinning through the air high above the ground when your head wants to fall off. Try not losing your lunch on the audience—it will get you talked about if you do. Try . . . Never mind. Try drawing your own unpleasant pictures.

Yes, I knew it was going to happen if I drank much more. And I drank much more anyhow. It was my own fault. I knew that, too. Come the next morning, knowing didn't help.

I staggered out of my wagon wishing I were dead. My mouth tasted the way the gutters in Thasos smell. A demon drummer twenty feet tall pounded the top of my head every time my heart beat. If I opened my eyes too wide, I was sure I would bleed to death through them. It might have been a relief.

Right at that moment, I probably didn't look much like Prince Halim Eddin. As I say, followers of the Quadrate God don't drink, or at least they're not supposed to. There are exceptions—oh, indeed there are—but I couldn't have told you if the prince was one of them.

Thinking of him, though, helped steady me on my feet. I ate some raw cabbage: the Lokrian hangover cure. I ate some tripe soup: the Hassocki hangover cure. I had the hair of the dog that bit me: my personal hangover cure. Put them all together and I was at least within screaming distance of my old self—if a bit on the flatulent side—by the time Max emerged.

He looked as bad as I'd felt a little earlier. He had his head in his hands, as if afraid he'd lose it. He didn't just have the hair of the dog. He had the tail and the ears and one of the hind legs, and a little tripe soup to go with it.

Everybody has to find his own cure for the morning after. Max of Witte's worked for him, and faster than mine worked for me. One of the things that proved is, his liver is made of sterner stuff than mine. He gave me a sepulchral smile—almost the only kind he owns—and said, "And how are you this morning, your Majesty?" He was joking, the way everybody had been the night before.

I took a deep breath. "Max," I said, "how would you like to be the aide-de-camp to the new King of Shqiperi?"

He looked at me as if he thought I'd gone smack out of my mind. "I think you've gone smack out of your mind," he said.

"Why?" I grabbed the copy of the *Thasos Chronicle* Ludovic had brought in. I opened it to the story about how the Shqipetari were looking for a new king. Sure as sure, that was—or might as well have been—my face looking out from the page. I tapped it with my forefinger. Then I tapped the end of my own nose. "They're looking for Prince Halim Eddin, the Hassockian Atabeg's nephew. And, by the Two Prophets, we'll *give* them Halim Eddin!" I tapped my nose again.

Actually, the Two Prophets had very little to do with becoming King of Shqiperi, except in the negative sense. Like the Hassocki, most

Shqipetari follow the Quadrate God. That was why they were interested in Halim Eddin and not one of the nine million unemployed princelings from Schlepsig or Narbonensis or Torino. I didn't think the other kingdoms in the Nekemte Peninsula would be particularly thrilled at that. Like the Lokrians, Vlachia and Belagora and Plovdiv and Dacia all reverence the Two Prophets, even if they are Zibeonite heretics.

Max looked from me to the journal and back again. "All right, you look the part," he admitted. "But how much Hassocki do you speak?"

"Enough to assure thee that thou art the bastard child of a poxed camel-driver and an innocent sheep he deceived and debauched," I answered in that tongue. One hitch in the Hassocki Army was enough to make me fluently obscene. By the time I finished the second term, I was just plain fluent. Languages have always come easy for me—easier than steady work.

His eyebrows leaped. "That's pretty good—thou shriveled and flyblown horse turd." Max knew some Hassocki, too. I thought I'd remembered that. It would help.

"Are you game?" I pushed him. "If you turn yellow on me now, you'll never forgive yourself, and you know it. If we pull this off, people will still be talking about it a hundred years from now."

"And if we don't, the Shqipetari will murder us. Or maybe the Hassockian soldiers still in their country will beat them to the punch." Max was not an optimist. But then, as I've found since, nobody who's ever had much to do with the Land of the Eagle is an optimist. Taken all in all, the Nekemte Peninsula is a backwater. Well, Shqiperi is a backwater even by the standards of the Nekemte Peninsula. It's mountainous. It's isolated. The Hassocki garrison there was long since cut off from any hope of relief or rescue. The national sport, as far as anyone can tell, is the blood feud.

But I could be a king!

I looked down my nose, so much like Prince Halim Eddin's nose, at Max. Well, actually, I looked up it at him, since he's about six feet eight. In my toploftiest tones, I said, "I don't think you've got the nerve."

If he'd had only the hair of the dog, he probably would have laughed and told me I was right. With a good deal more than that aboard, though, his pinched, sallow cheeks turned red. "Who hasn't?" he growled. "I'll go anywhere you go, Otto, and you know it cursed well."

And I did. We'd been some strange places together, Max and I, and who was watching whose back wasn't always obvious. "All right," I said, roaring as gently as any sucking dove. "All right. The first place we need to go is a public crystal."

"Why?" Max asked. "So we can tell the world we're sticking our head in the dragon's mouth?" He opened his mouth very wide and bit down. The effect would have been more dramatic if he didn't have a missing front tooth. It somehow impaired his ferocity.

"No, no, no," I said. "What are the Shqipetari and Essad Pasha going to need before they think Halim Eddin is on his way?" Essad Pasha was the Hassocki general in command of the garrison there. Before the war, he'd been the Hassocki governor of Shqiperi. He had fingers in so many pies, he probably had about four hands.

Max looked at me. "I was going to say a hunting license, but I don't suppose they bother with them there."

"Funny man! You should do vaudeville and music-hall turns instead of this," I said. "What they'll need is a crystal message from Vyzance saying he's on his way."

"And how do you propose to get them to send one, thou great lion of the perfumèd bedchamber, thou running rabbit on the blood-filled field?" Max dropped into Hassocki again. It's a good language for being . . . charming in.

I just grinned. I hadn't served those two hitches in the Hassocki army for nothing—though with what the Hassocki pay, it often seemed that way at the time. "It so happens that I'm friends with a certain Murad Bey. He was a lieutenant when I was a sergeant. These days, he's a major in the Hassockian Ministry of War."

"And he'd send a message like that?" Max shook his head. He does dubious very well. "Wouldn't he sooner send one ordering us arrested and handed over to the torturers?"

"I know this man, I tell you. It's possible he'll say no, if he thinks the Empire's honor is touched," I said. "But if he says he'll send the message I need, he'll send it. He *likes* practical jokes. Did I ever tell you about the time when he had three different officers thinking they'd got the colonel's courtesan pregnant?"

"The joke'll be on us if the torturers *are* waiting," Max pointed out.

"But it'll be a bigger joke if it's on Essad Pasha and the Shqipetari," I said. "Torturing foreigners is easy. It happens all the time. Making one of your own generals look like a fool, though . . ."

Max didn't answer right away. Instead, he went to work on the dog's other hind leg. After he set down the jug, he got to his feet. "This had better work," he said. "If it doesn't, I'll never forgive you."

If it didn't, he'd probably be too dead to forgive me. Of course, I'd probably be too dead to need forgiving. I stood up, too. "Let's get moving," I said.

Lokrian soldiers swaggered through the streets of Thasos. They were little dark men in green uniforms. They had kepis and neatly trimmed mustaches. There were also soldiers from Plovdiv, off to the northwest, in the streets. They were bigger and fairer, and wore tobacco-brown uniforms. They had floppy hats and big, bushy mustaches.

They didn't look as if they much cared for Lokrians. The Lokrians didn't look as if they much cared for them, either. Lokris and Plovdiv had been allies against the Hassocki. Of course, everybody in the Nekemte Peninsula—except the Shqipetari, mind you—had been allies against the Hassocki. Now, here in Thasos, you could watch the thieves fall out.

That round of fighting didn't start till later, though, so I'm not going to talk about it now. If you talk about *all* the wars, you'll never get around to anything else.

Both the soldiers from Lokris and the soldiers from Plovdiv looked as if they didn't much care for Max and me. I did my best not to notice, or not to be noticed noticing. Blithe ignorance tends to fray, though, when somebody aims a crossbow at your brisket. After a moment, when Max and I just kept walking, the Lokrian lowered the cursed thing and grinned as if he'd been joking. Maybe he had. But not even Dooger and Cark would hire a clown with a sense of humor like that.

"Nice fellow," I remarked in Schlepsigian. If the Lokrian soldier spoke my language—not likely but not impossible—he couldn't have proved by my tone that I was being sarcastic.

"Sure is," Max said, just as heartily. Neither one of us is usually such a good liar so early in the morning.

The Dual Monarchy has a post office in Thasos. Narbonensis has one. So does Albion. So does Schlepsig. And so did the Hassocki. It was their city, after all. Now that's a Lokrian post office. The Green Dragon flies above it, not the red lightning bolt on gold.

Right next to what's now the Lokrian post office is the local Consolidated Crystal headquarters. Consolidated Crystal doesn't belong to any one kingdom. They say their services belong to people from all the kingdoms—people with the money to pay for them, of course. Actually, in a lot of ways they're above all the kingdoms. Because what they do is so important, any kingdom that tried to interfere with them would end up in trouble with all its neighbors. Nobody talks about that, but everybody knows it.

We went in. Max held the door open for me. "Your Majesty," he murmured—and then let go of the door so it swung shut and got me in the seat of the pants.

"Some aide-de-camp you turned out to be," I said. "I should have asked Ilona."

"There's a difference between aide-de-camp and camp follower," Max said loftily. He was lucky Ilona wasn't there to hear that. She would have followed him, all right—with a knife.

Inside the CC headquarters, you never would have known that Thasos had changed hands not long before, or that fighting still sputtered not far away. Everything was peaceful and orderly. People—Lokrians, Hassocki, an Albionese merchant in baggy tweeds, us—waited in line for the next available crystallographer. Lots of places in Thasos, lines just sit there. They don't move. Not at CC headquarters. Perish the thought. Those people know what efficiency means.

We got to the front of the line pretty quick. "Good morning, gentlemen," the clerk said in fluent Schlepsigian. I'd already heard him use Lokrian and Hassocki. A man of parts, plainly, and smart parts at that. I look like Halim Eddin—and I had the picture to prove it!—while Max could be anything under the sun except handsome. But this clever young fellow pegged us.

The crystallographer he sent us to also spoke Schlepsigian, though with a Hassocki accent. "To whom do you wish to send your message, gentlemen?" he asked.

"To Major Murad Bey, at the Ministry of War in Vyzance," I answered.

He blinked. "I hope the Lokrians' sorcerers will pass it," he said. "Lokris and the Hassockian Empire are still at war, you know."

"Really? I hadn't noticed," I said. He was a swarthy man, but his cheeks went pink anyhow. I went on, "I suppose they'll use the intent test. They're welcome to, for I mean no harm to Lokris."

"Ah. Good. Excellent, in fact." He blinked again. "You know something of this business."

"A little something, maybe—no more." I knew a good deal more, but that wasn't the crystallographer's affair. It's a long story. In fact, I wasn't even there when they thought I was. If I was there, I didn't do it. If I did do it, I didn't mean it. And if I did mean it, the bastard had it coming. But I digress. Back to it: "Here is the message." I gave it to him, finishing, "Please acknowledge at CC office Thasos."

"I'll send it. They will vet it," the crystallographer warned. I shrugged. He bent low over the crystal on his desk. In places like Albion and Narbonensis, crystallographers wear turbans to look mystical. In Thasos, ordinary people wear turbans. The crystallographer probably wore one himself when he went off duty. Here, he had on a homburg to look modern.

He murmured the necessary charms, and the eight-digit number that made sure he reached a particular crystal in Vyzance and not one in, say, Lutetia. Nobody in the capital of Narbonensis needed to know anything about this. No, not yet.

Light flared in the heart of the transparent crystal sphere. As it faded, I saw the tiny image of another crystallographer. He too had a homburg on his head. Vyzance, sure enough.

Our crystallographer recited the message. The other crystallographer read it back. His voice sounded as if it came from very far away. As a mat-

ter of fact, it *did* come from very far away, even if the crystal sat right there
in front of it. When the men on both sides of the connection agreed they
had the message straight, they broke the arcane link. The crystal on the
crystallographer's desk went back to being a bocci ball for ghosts.

"You told the truth—I had no interference from the Lokrians," our
crystallographer said. "If there is a reply to this . . . communication, it will
be delivered to you at the carnival."

"Circus!" I said indignantly. Eliphalet help me—Zibeon, too—there
is another step down from Dooger and Cark's. I've played in carnivals. I
hope I never have to do it again. It's not honest work, and that's the best I
can say for it.

The crystallographer would have had to cheer up to seem unimpressed. "Go in peace," he murmured. "North and south, east and west, go
in peace." Yes, he followed the Quadrate God.

"North and south, east and west, peace to you as well," I said in Hassocki. His big, dark eyes widened. He didn't hear that every day from an
obvious follower of the Two Prophets.

Max and I had to stand in another line to settle the tab for the message. Anywhere in Thasos but here, we could have dickered to our hearts'
content. We could have drawn up chairs, ordered some thick, sweet
Hassocki-style coffee, taken a few puffs from the mouthpiece of a water
pipe, and told the clerk what a thief he was. Lokrians are as mad for haggling as Hassocki. But not at Consolidated Crystal. One price per word,
all over the civilized world and in as many of the barbarous parts as they
reach. They don't even charge extra in Tver, and if that doesn't prove my
point, nothing ever would.

"Now what?" Max asked as we left the CC offices. "We wait to find out
whether this Murad Bey is as daft as you are?"

I wouldn't have put it precisely like that. Since Max had, though, I
swept off my hat and gave him my grandest bow. "What else?" I said.

"We could make our funeral arrangements now," he suggested. "We'll
probably be too busy dying to do it later." Before I could find something
suitably devastating to say to that, he shook his head. "No—wouldn't
help. No undertaker here is going to have a branch office in Shqiperi."

"Think on the bright side, for heaven's sake," I said. "You're going to be aide-de-camp to a king. You'll help make decisions of state. And you'll brag about it afterwards as long as you live."

"Twenty minutes' worth of bragging. Oh, joy." Max is a good fellow in a great many ways, but he's convinced every silver lining has a cloud.

We stopped on the way back to the circus and bought sausages skewered on sticks and then dipped in maize batter and fried: a local delicacy indigestible enough to satisfy the most ambitious dyspeptic. The sausage-seller was a Lokrian—probably not named Kleon, worse luck. He tried to charge us some outrageous price because we were foreigners. I couldn't tell him what I thought of him in his own language, but figured he was likely to understand Hassocki: "Thou dog and son of a dog, thou wouldst steal the silver set on the eyes of thy mother's corpse."

"May the fleas of a thousand camels afflict thy scrotum," he returned amiably. We haggled in Hassocki, though some of the gestures we used had nothing to do with numbers. I finally argued him down to something approaching reason.

Max bit into his sausage. The batter crunched. Grease ran down his chin. He nodded approval. "Not bad. They'd go good with a seidel or two of beer."

Now, what passes for beer in Thasos is a far cry from what we brew in Schlepsig. Much of it, indeed, tastes as if it *has* passed—through the kidneys of a diabetic donkey. Still, as they say, any beer is better than none, and the food had plenty of flavor to make up for what the drink lacked. We found a beer cellar. We found its product . . . adequate.

Having swallowed the last bite of sausage, Max swallowed the stick, too—after his sword, it hardly made an hors d'oeuvre. The tapman's eyes almost bugged out of his head. I hoped—and so, no doubt, did Max—he'd be astonished enough to give us our next seidel free. He wasn't. He didn't. Bit by bit, naïveté leaks out of the world.

I was looking forward to Shqiperi. I was sure naïveté lingered there. It must have, or the Shqipetari wouldn't have believed a king would solve their problems. Or maybe Essad Pasha, being a Hassocki general, thought a king of his own blood would solve *his* problems.

When we got back to the circus tent, we started practicing for the evening show. Max had no trouble. I discovered doing trapeze flips with one of those sausages in my stomach was every bit as enjoyable as if I'd swallowed a thirty-pound catapult stone instead. If I had a weak stomach, I never would have turned acrobat in the first place, but I don't think I ever put it to a sterner test.

I was upside down in midair when I spotted the messenger boy in the blue CC uniform. "Are you looking for Otto of Schlepsig?" I called in Hassocki as soon as I was right side up again.

"That's right, sir. Are you he?" The kid spoke with a Lokrian accent, but we could understand each other.

"I am no one else but the king of acrobats, Otto himself." Hard to strike a pose while hanging from a trapeze, but I managed. If a man will not blow a blast from his own horn, it shall remain unblown forever.

I cut the rehearsal short to see what Murad Bey had to say. No one else was likely to send me a crystal message, not unless some of my stubborner creditors had finally found out what show I was playing in. I gave the messenger boy a couple of coppers and sent him on his way.

My thumbnail cracked the wax seal on the message. I unrolled the paper and read the transcription. It *was* from Murad Bey. *That which you asked me to accomplish, my brother, it is accomplished,* he wrote. *Go, then, and may good fortune attend you.*

"Ha!" I said, and, "Ha!" again. I turned a couple of backflips. Suddenly the sausage seemed to weigh nothing at all. I carried the message over to Max. "Here! Take a look at this!"

He made a gurgling noise. He had some considerable length of steel down his throat. In due course, it came out again. He wiped off the blade—swallowing a rusty sword is probably not something he wanted to do. Then he took the message and scowled at it. "What's it say?" he asked. "I speak some Hassocki, but I don't read it."

"Some aide-de-camp you'll make," I muttered, and translated what Murad Bey had said. Right about now, another messenger boy in a blue Consolidated Crystal uniform would be delivering not one but two messages to Essad Pasha in Shqiperi. One of them would purport to come from the Hassockian Atabeg himself, and would say, *Prince Halim Eddin is coming. He has supreme command over all troops present in Shqiperi.* The other would pretend to come from the high command of the Hassocki

Army in Vyzance, and would say, *Prince Halim Eddin is coming. Immediately turn over supreme command in Shqiperi to him.*

Max clapped a hand to his forehead. It happened to be the hand holding the sword, but he didn't cut himself. "You *are* out of your mind," he said.

"Yes, my dear, but I have fun." I pulled him down to my height and kissed him on both cheeks. He said something in Hassocki I won't repeat, even in translation. I laughed. Why not? The plot—a really pretty little plot, if I do say so myself—had started to move.

Another show down. Like most shows, it was measured more by what didn't happen than by what did. Ilona didn't come out of her costume. The lions didn't eat Cadogan, or even sharpen their claws on him. The mammoth didn't squash Ilona or any of the clowns. Max didn't cut his throat, from the inside out or otherwise. And I didn't splatter myself in the middle of the ring.

The marks ate it up anyway. Maybe we were better than usual. Maybe, what with everything that had happened to Thasos lately, they were starved for anything that might be amusing. I know which way I'd bet.

After the performance, I caught Max's eye. He tried to pretend he didn't see me: he made an elaborate production of lighting up a stogie that would do his cough a world of good. I walked over to him. "Come on," I said. "The time has come. You're not going to back out on me, are you?"

He looked as if he would have liked nothing better. But then, if you wait for Max to look enthusiastic, you'll wait till the Final Prophecy comes true, and twenty minutes longer. Puffing a cloud of noxious smoke, he unfolded himself from his stool. He towered over me, and I'm not short. "Let's get it over with," he said, as if about to call on the toothdrawer.

Side by side, we went up to Dooger and Cark. They were side by side, too, behind the table where they counted the take. As far as they were concerned, money counted for more than a couple of performers. Eventually, though, since we didn't go away, they had to notice us, or to admit they did. Dooger looked over at Cark. "We're at 2675," he said.

"Yes, 2675," Cark agreed in that nameless accent of his. They both wrote the figure down. The important business temporarily suspended, they could deal with the likes of us.

"What is it?" Dooger demanded of me. *It had better be interesting*, his tone warned. I don't *think* he sleeps in a coffin, but I wouldn't swear. I know bloody well he doesn't sleep with me—and a good thing, too, says I.

Max coughed. It had nothing to do with the stinking cigar. It just gave him an excuse not to talk. Me, I never need an excuse *to* talk. "Boss—bosses—we quit," I said. "We want our pay up through tonight."

"You can't do that," Cark said. If what he gave us wasn't the evil eye, I've never seen it. He's a squat little toadlike fellow who doesn't blink much at the best of times. When he's angry, he doesn't blink at all. It's unnerving. It really is. You start wondering when you last paid a temple a proper visit.

I stood there and waited. Max stood there with me, Eliphalet bless him. Obviously, we could walk out whenever we cursed well pleased. Whether we could get paid . . . That was a more intricate question.

Dooger tilted his head back so he could look down his nose at me even though I was standing up. "What are you going to do?" he asked. "Run off and be a king?" He laughed at his own joke. Even Cark let out a couple of dry little croaks that might have stood for amusement.

I bowed to each of them in turn. "How did you guess?" I answered. "And since you're making free with the royal treasury . . ."

"We ought to throw you out on your arse, *your Majesty*." Dooger turned it into a title of scorn. As if by real sorcery, a couple of hulking roustabouts appeared behind him.

Wheep! Max's sword slid out of the scabbard. The blade glittered in the torchlight. I was so used to thinking of it as a prop for his act, I'd almost forgotten about it as a weapon. So, plainly, had Dooger and Cark. But any sword that would slice bread would do a pretty fair job of slicing circus proprietor, too.

"I think perhaps you might want to reconsider." As usual, Max sounded as if he couldn't care less whether he lived or died. That made him more scary, not less.

Dooger and Cark went back and forth in a nameless tongue, possibly Cark's birthspeech. Cark gestured to the roustabouts. They vanished into the shadows as fast as they'd shown up. Maybe Dooger really had conjured them out of thin air. I wouldn't put it past him.

He glared at us now. "We'll pay you," he said heavily. "We'll pay you, all right, and we'll blacken your names from Vyzance to Baile Atha Cliath."

I laughed in his face. "As if telling anybody we had to work for Dooger and Cark's wouldn't do the job."

Dooger said something in Yagmar. Off behind us, Ilona let out a yip of surprise and possibly horror, so it must have been choice. Without a word, Cark slammed coins down on the table. They came from all over the known world: Lokrian leptas and fractions, Hassocki piasters, dinars from from Vlachia, dinars from Belagora (which are heavier), a thaler or two out of the Dual Monarchy, a couple of livres from Narbonensis, some Schlepsigian krams, and a few shillings from Albion.

"Happy now?" Dooger growled when Cark stopped doling out silver.

"Let me use your scale," I told him. That made him growl some more, and Cark, too. But they passed it over. When I got everything balanced, the alleged pay was light. Not by a lot, mind you, but light. I didn't say anything. The scales spoke for themselves.

Muttering, Cark tossed a big silver cartwheel onto the left pan. The shekel from far-off Vespucciland almost made the scales balance. A sixth-dinar piece—silver so thin, you could almost see through it—evened things out. "Happy now?" Cark croaked.

"Delighted," I told him. And I was, too. We had money, we had a plan, and the worst that could happen to us was death by torture. What was there to worry about?

I used the scales again, this time to make sure Max and I came out even. That sixth-dinar piece and a couple of others nearly as light proved handy for getting things right.

"You're really leaving?" Ludovic said when we'd settled our business with the proprietors. "I don't know whether to be angry or jealous."

Cadogan looked glum enough to let his lions eat him. "I wish I could go, too," he said, sounding almost as somber as Max.

"Why don't you?" I asked.

He stared at me the way people always stare when you've asked a really stupid question. "Don't be silly, Otto. Who'd take me if I left this outfit?" It wasn't that he was wrong, either, poor bastard.

Ilona came up to me. Like Ludovic, she asked, "You're really leaving?" When I nodded, she kissed me hard enough to make every hair in my mustache—among other things—stand on end.

Once I could see straight again, I wheezed, "Eliphalet! Why didn't you ever do that before?"

She batted her eyelashes at me. "But, darling, you might have thought I meant it." Before I could either grab her or slug her—Ilona usually made you want to do both at once—she adhered to Max. I don't know how else to describe it. She kissed him even more thoroughly than she had me.

His eyes lit up. He wiggled his ears. He really did—the mammoth couldn't have done it better. Color—veritable pink!—came into his sallow cheeks. All things considered, he looked amazingly lifelike. When the clinch finally broke—and he milked it for all it was worth and then some—he leered down at Ilona and murmured, "Well, sweetheart, are you a sword-swallower, too?"

She slapped him just as hard as she'd kissed him. The party went on from there.

It got drunk out, though not quite as drunk as it had the night we played our first show in Thasos. A good thing, too. I'm getting too old to do that as often as I used to. I don't like to believe that. I don't want to believe it. But my carcass reminds me of it more forcefully with each year that goes by.

Even Dooger and Cark, having finished counting their more or less ill-gotten gains, came over to hoist a few. Dooger put an arm around my shoulder. I kept my eye on his other hand, to make sure he didn't try filching what Cark had been so pleased to pay me.

He affected not to notice. "Ah, my boy!" he said, sounding tiddlier than he was. "I love you like my own son!"

"Do you?" I said. "Is that the one you sold to the Tzigany?"

He laughed, though I hadn't been upwards of two-sevenths kidding. "A funny man, too!" he said. "You should put on a clown suit and go on with the rest of that troupe. Otto the Impossible! You'd have star billing!"

"No, thanks," I said, which is what anyone in his right mind should say when Dooger starts scheming. If saying *no thanks* doesn't do the job, running away quickly may still save you. Since I was going to run away anyhow—for once in my life, not running away *to* join the circus—I went on, "I'd hate cleaning white greasepaint out of my mustache every night."

"Shave it off." As usual, Dooger had all the answers. Also as usual, most of them were to the wrong questions.

He and Cark tried to raise a stink about letting Max and me sleep in our wagons one more night after we'd left the company. Everybody else screamed at them. Even some of the roustabouts sided with us. And so, with poor grace, the proprietors backed down. I had the feeling they'd take it out on the rest of the company first chance they got.

The wagon's springs creaked when I settled myself in my cot. I expected I'd wake up with a headache in the morning, but not with the galloping horrors I'd had not long before. Most headaches are soluble in Hassocki coffee.

I don't know how long I'd been asleep when the springs creaked again and the wagon shifted. Somebody besides me was in there. Roustabouts? Were Dooger and Cark going to throw me out after the rest of the company had gone to bed? Not without a fight, they weren't. I reached out—and touched warm, smooth, bare flesh.

Ilona giggled. "If I'd done this before, darling," she whispered, "you might have thought I meant it." The springs did considerable creaking after that, let me tell you. I didn't have a headache the next morning, either. Did she visit Max, too, before me or afterwards? To this day, I don't know. I'm sorry for him if she didn't, though.

III

Max and I even got breakfast the next morning. If Dooger and Cark didn't deduct the cost of our rolls and honey and coffee from the company's share, they were missing a trick, and they don't miss many tricks like that. And speaking of a roll with honey, Ilona was sweetly impersonal to me and to Max both. Her manner said nothing had happened in the nighttime—and even if it had, it hadn't.

She did kiss us goodbye, on the cheek; she stood on tiptoe and Max bent down so she could reach his. Then, duffels slung over our shoulders, we were on our own. Max looked as if his rowboat had just sunk in sea-serpent-infested waters. I felt a little rocky myself, to tell you the truth. Not having the troupe at my back was daunting. These were the people who were always ready, when things seemed bad, to tell you why they were really worse. They were also the people who would try to pitch in and make them better. And now we'd turned our backs on them.

"Well," Max said lugubriously, "what next, your Majesty?" He didn't make that as noxious as Dooger had the night before. From him, it felt more like *you sap.*

I'd been thinking about what next, in the odd moments when I wasn't thinking about Ilona or about almost getting skinned by Dooger and Cark. "We're playing roles, right?" I said. "Roles, yes, except on the stage of life, not the one where they throw cabbages if you blow your lines."

"They'll do worse than that if we blow our lines," Max said.

Ignoring him, I went on, "If we're playing roles, what do we need?"

"Better sense?" he suggested.

He was getting harder to ignore, but I managed. I am a man of many talents. "We need costumes," I said. "If I remember rightly, Prince Halim Eddin is a colonel in the Hassocki army. And if you're going to be my aide-de-camp, you should be a captain or something."

"If I'm going to be your aide-de-camp, I should have my head examined," Max said.

"Did anyone candle thy skull, he'd doubtless find it empty," I said in Hassocki.

"Better empty than full of thy madness, the which is worse than a dog's and more assuredly fatal," Max replied in the same language. His accent was improving with practice.

He didn't ask me where we would come by Hassocki officers' uniforms. The atabeg's officers—and men—had done everything they could to escape when forces from Lokris and Plovdiv converged on Thasos. *Everything* included shedding their uniforms and sneaking away in civilian clothes—or, for all I knew, naked. All the tailor's shops in Threadneedle Street displayed discarded dusty-brown Hassocki military togs. We could pick and choose.

Or I could, anyway. I am a good-sized man, but neither enormously tall nor enormously wide. The second tailor we visited had exactly what I needed, right down to the boots and the belt buckle and the epaulets. We haggled for a while. He even knocked off another piaster and a half when I noticed a very neatly repaired tear in the back of the jacket. It was about what a rapier would have made going in.

No sign of a bloodstain around it, even on the inside of the material. Cold water will soak them out if you're patient, and who ever heard of an impatient tailor?

But when I asked about a captain's uniform for Max, this fellow bowed and shook his head. "My liver is wrung, O most noble one," he said in Hassocki, which we'd been using, "but I have none fit for a man of his, ah, altitude."

"No, no." Max shook his head. "Otto is his Highness here."

The tailor scratched his head. I made as if to kick Max. Without moving a muscle, he let me know that wouldn't be a good idea. I turned back to the tailor. "Know you, my good man, if any of your colleagues might have attire suitable to his stature?"

"I know not, I fear me. It is written, Seek and ye may find."

I'd always heard it as *Seek and ye shall find.* Considering how Max is put together, the tailor's version made better sense. "Verily, it is so written, or if it be not written so, so should it be written," I said. He was chewing on that as Max and I left his shop. Max looked as if he was also chewing on that, or possibly on his cud. By the time we'd walked into the next tailor's shop, I was chewing on it myself. It certainly sounded as if it ought to mean something, whether it did or not.

We ended up walking into every tailor's establishment on Thread-needle Street. Every tailor without exception took one dismayed look at Max, rolled his eyes, shook his head, and threw up his hands. "I'm not cut out to be an aide-de-camp," Max said. "Maybe I should go as your stepladder instead."

"Did Eliphalet lose heart when he faced the Tharpian King of Kings?" I demanded. "Keep your chin up, man."

He did. It made him look even taller. He must have known as much, too, for he said, "Eliphalet wasn't six feet eight."

"Not on the outside," I said, and cribbed from a hymn: "In spirit he was ten feet tall."

"Nobody ever tries to put your spirit in a uniform," Max said, which was true but so resolutely unhelpful that I pretended not to hear it.

Right next to Threadneedle Street is Copperbottom Alley. That's not where the tinkers and potmakers work; their establishments are along the Street of the Boiled Second Stomach—a Hassocki delicacy that loses something in the translation and even more, I assure you, in the in-gestion. No, Copperbottom Alley houses secondhand shops and houses of the three gold globes and other not quite shady, not quite sunny enter-prises. I was sure we could buy Hassocki captain's uniforms there; I was fairly sure we could buy ourselves a couple of Hassocki captains, if for some reason we happened to need them.

Whether we could find a uniform to fit Max . . . Well, I wasn't so sure about that, but I wasn't about to admit I wasn't so sure, either.

When we walked into the first secondhand shop, the proprietor, a round little Hassocki, shook his head. "I am wounded to the very heart of me that I find myself unable to aid my masters," he said, "but perhaps they will seek the place of business of Manolis the Lokrian. North and south, east and west, by the strength of my bowels no one else in Thasos is more likely to possess that which, should you acquire it, would make your spirits sing."

Manolis the Lokrian proved to run a house of the three gold globes halfway along Copperbottom Alley. Luckily, he wrote his name on the window in Hassocki characters as well as his own. A bell above his door jangled when Max and I went in.

"Gentlemen, I am at your service. Ask of me what you would," he said. He bowed and straightened and bowed again.

I didn't ask him anything at once. I was too busy staring. I saw at once why the roly-poly Hassocki had sent us to him. He had to be an inch or two taller even than Max. The two of them were also staring at each other. Very tall men aren't used to running into people their own size. They need to decide who's bigger and how surprised they're going to be about it.

"Have you by any chance a Hassocki captain's uniform to fit my friend?" I asked.

He broke out laughing. "I do," he said. "I do. By Zibeon's forelock, I do. I have the very thing." I reminded myself he was a Lokrian, and so unlikely to know better. I also reminded myself how big he was. Taller than Max! Who would have believed it? He went on, "During the, ah, late unpleasantness I purchased this from an officer desirous of decamping in such secrecy as he might—though when a man is of his stature, or mine, or your friend's, secrecy is hard to come by. Later"—he preened his mustaches between thumb and forefinger—"I had occasion to wear it, to personate the fled Hassocki and lure his comrades out of a strong and safe position. This I accomplished." He stood even straighter than usual.

So the uniform had already been used in one masquerade, had it? A paltry scheme next to mine—but still, I took it for a good omen. I said, "May we see this famous outfit?"

Manolis bowed once more. "Certainly, my master. Certainly. But what ails your friend? Can he not speak for himself?"

"No," Max croaked. "I never learned how."

The Lokrian broker scratched his head, tugged at his mustaches again, and disappeared into a back room. He returned with a neatly folded dust-brown uniform. Unfolded, it did indeed prove suitable for a man of Max's inches. The sleeves and trouser legs were slightly too short, but only slightly. It fit Max a good deal better than it would have Manolis, who was not only taller but wider through the shoulders and had the beginnings of a paunch. Imagining Max with a paunch is like imagining a nightingale with a bagpipe. I doubted the Hassocki who saw Manolis in disguise were inclined to be critical. Anyone who could wear that uniform without turning it into a tent had to carry conviction.

I spoke next with a certain amount of worry: "Ah, how much might you want for such an item, O most heroic and valiant one?"

"Well, I had not really purposed selling it at all," Manolis replied. "My thought was to save it for my grandchildren, a token of the time when Thasos passed out of slavery and into freedom." Half the city's populace would have juggled nouns and prepositions there, but never mind. He continued, "If I were to sell it, I should need to be suitably compensated for the future loss to my heirs and assigns."

"What do you reckon suitable compensation?" I inquired, more cautiously yet.

He named a price. I did not faint. I do not know why I did not faint. I merely state the fact. He added, "I suspect you may encounter a certain amount of difficulty finding such a uniform here or elsewhere."

I suspected he was right. No, I knew too well he was right. Nevertheless, I said, "And I suspect you are a saucy robber. Dust-brown cloth is cheap as pistachios in Thasos right now. I could have a tailor *make* me a uniform for half what you ask." That would still cost too much and take too long, something Manolis did *not* need to know.

He scowled down at me. A fearsome scowl from such a giant would have put most men of ordinary size in fear for their lives. I, however, am bold beyond the mean—and used to Max scowling down at me. Again, the hair of the dog that now could not bite me. Seeing me unafraid and unabashed, Manolis named a more reasonable figure. I named one in return. "Why, thou brazen son of a poison-tongued serpent!" he cried.

"Impute to me not thy parentage," I said sweetly.

"Thou admittest thy brazenness, I see, which is as well, for thou wouldst prove thyself liar as well as cheat didst thou seek to disclaim it." Manolis scowled again, and clenched his big fists. When I still failed to wilt, he came down some more.

We haggled through the morning. Just after he called me something too infamous even to repeat, he poured coffee for Max and me with his own hands. Both the insult and the coffee were politenesses of the trade. As noon approached, we struck a bargain. It was more than I wanted to pay but less than a tailor would have cost me: not perfect, but good enough. In this sorry world of ours, good enough is . . . good enough.

Manolis' sigh would have sailed a schooner halfway to Vyzance. "Thus vanishes a part of Thasos' history, and a grand part, too." My silver also vanished, into a stout cashbox he kept under the counter. So much for history, at least to the Lokrian.

As for me, I had all I could do to keep from jumping in the air and clicking my heels together as we left the house of the three gold globes. Manolis might have thought he was making history with the tall Hassocki's uniform, but Max would really do it. (Of course, he would be but a footnote to my reign, but even so. . . .)

His own view of all this was rather less exalted. "Nice to know I'll be properly dressed for my execution," he remarked.

"If you get any more cheerful, I don't know how I'll be able to stand the joy," I said.

He raised an eyebrow. "Is that what they call sarcasm?"

"I wouldn't know. I've never heard the word before. What does it mean?" I said.

Max pondered that. It seemed to satisfy him, for he nodded. "Where now?" he asked.

"Why, the port," I said. "Unless you'd rather go to Shqiperi by land, that is."

"I don't much want to go to Shqiperi at all," he said.

Normally, this is a sentiment with a great deal to recommend it. In fact, almost the entire world has wanted to avoid the Land of the Eagle throughout its history, which is how the Shqipetari have ended up living there. Nevertheless, going by land, through the sputtering remains of the Nekemte Wars, struck me as an idea singularly bad even by the standards associated with Shqiperi. "The port," I said again, and set off toward the sea. Max? Max followed me.

People write poems about the open sea: the waves and the wind and the soaring gulls and I don't know what all else. I'm a showman, not a poet. But I do know one thing: nobody in his right mind pens poems about a harbor.

For one thing, it's hard to wax poetic about stinks. The open sea smells fresh and, well, oceanic, at least till you go belowdecks. The port of Thasos, on the other hand, smells like the Darvar River, which runs into it. And the Darvar River, not to put too fine a point on it, smells like sewage.

Along with this ruling theme, there are grace notes: bilgewater from the ships tied up at the quays, essence of unwashed sailor, cheap perfume from the joy girls the unwashed sailors seek, the occasional dead dog or dead body, and other stenches, reeks, and miasmas. My asthma would have been very bad there, if I'd had any to begin with.

Shqiperi's chief port—indeed, for all practical purposes, Shqiperi's only port—is the grand metropolis of Fushe-Kuqe, which is every bit as famous and magnificent as the fact that you've never heard of it would suggest.

The harbormaster was a lean, weathered Hassocki named Bayezid. He looked like a recently—perhaps too recently—retired pirate. A big gold hoop glittered in his left ear. His right earlobe was oddly scarred and shriveled, as if a big gold hoop had been removed from it by force. He, unlike you, had heard of Fushe-Kuqe; his job involved knowing the ports around the Middle Sea, even the sleepy and obscure ones.

When I said we wanted to go there, he raised an elegantly plucked eyebrow. "You *do?*" he said. "North and south, east and west, my masters, *why?*"

"To put on a performance—a special performance," I replied, which was true enough. All the same, Max choked slightly.

Bayezid affected not to notice. "You will know your own business best, I am sure," he murmured, and I've never been called an idiot more politely. He gathered himself. "There is, I fear, no way to book passage straight from Thasos to Fushe-Kuqe. Commerce between the two cities . . . Well, to be candid, there is no commerce between the two cities."

Max brightened, no doubt hoping he was off the hook. I contrived to tread on his toes, not too hard. "There is bound to be a direct route from Thasos to Lakedaimon," I said.

"Oh, yes." The harbormaster nodded and looked pained at the same time. I might have known he would: Lakedaimon is the capital of Lokris, and he could not have felt too kindly toward Lokrians just then. He proved as much, in fact, continuing, "Had you come here a week later, I daresay you would have found a man from that other kingdom"—he wouldn't even dignify Lokris by naming it—"in my place. He might have been able to find Fushe-Kuqe on a map, assuming he could read. But as for getting you there . . ." That elegant eyebrow climbed again.

"Since we are lucky enough to have you in his stead, your Excellency, perhaps in your sagacity you will be able to assist us." Hassocki is almost as good for flowery compliments as it is for insults.

Bayezid bowed. "I am your slave." He pointed to a pier a furlong or so to the west of his cramped and tiny office. "Yonder lies the *Keraunos*. The name means *Thunderbolt* in that kingdom's tongue. She sails for Lakedaimon at the fourth hour of the afternoon, and is due there at the same time tomorrow." His eyebrow went up once more. "She will be late. I hope she will not be too late to keep you from catching the *Halcyon*, which sails for Fushe-Kuqe at midnight from the Quay of the Red-Figure Winecup."

He checked no references, no schedules or almanacs or anything of the sort. He *knew*. I didn't envy the Lokrian who would replace him, even if the man was good. Bayezid was a lot better than merely good.

"What if we're too late to catch the *Halcyon*?" I asked.

"North and south, east and west, all is as the Quadrate God wills," the harbormaster said, which told me less than it might have. But he went on, "Three days after that, my master, the *Gamemeno* sails out of Lakedaimon from the Quay of the Poxed Trollop. After, ah, several stops, she too will put in at Fushe-Kuqe." Again, no books, but he knew.

That sounded inauspicious. Max summed up just how inauspicious it sounded by asking, "Is she a smuggler or a pirate, the *Gamemeno?*"

"Yes," Bayezid answered.

"Well," I said as brightly as I could, "we'll just have to hope the, uh, *Keraunos* won't be late."

"Good luck, my friend," Bayezid said, plainly meaning, *You'll need it.* He added one word more: "Lokrians." From everything I've ever seen, Lokrians are not the most punctual people in the world—and, as a man of Schlepsig, I ought to know a thing or two about punctuality. From everything I've seen, though, Hassocki are the one folk who might out-delay Lokrians. I somehow doubted the curse of tardiness hovered over Bayezid's head, but it does afflict his countrymen.

When I tried to tip the harbormaster for his trouble and his help, he turned me down flat. Truly he was a man in a thousand. I don't think I'd ever met a Hassocki who wouldn't pocket a little baksheesh before. Come to that, plenty of Schlepsigians wouldn't have been sorry to listen to a few extra coins jingle in their pockets. But he told me no—Eliphalet be my witness. If the Lokrians sacked him, their new man would have made them sorry in short order.

Max and I walked up the quay to the *Thunderbolt.* Bird droppings dappled the planks under our feet. A pelican glided by overhead, looking like a gull apprenticed to a dragon. Seeing something that size on the wing made me glad I had a hat.

"Ahoy!" I called when we got to the ship. I must say its appearance didn't live up to its name. It was beamy and weary-looking, with untidy rigging and a crew who couldn't have been more than two steps up from pirates. Half of them wore earrings to put Bayezid's to shame.

The skipper, however, had on a uniform with more plumes and epaulets and tassels and—rather tarnished—gold braid than the Grand High Admiral of Schlepsig's. Old Forkbeard, of course, commands ships of the line and frigates by the score, whereas this fellow had the *Keraunos,* Prophets help him. He looked down at us with no great liking from under the brim of his three-cornered hat and asked, "What you want?" in fair Narbonese.

"Passage to Lakedaimon, sir," I answered in the same language.

He sized us up. I did the same with him. He was a sour, pinch-faced fellow heading into middle age and no happier about it than anyone else. Calculation glittered in his eyes, which were set too close together. *Judging what the traffic will bear*, I decided. The fare he named showed he'd misjudged it—either that or greed had got the better of him.

I bowed. "Good day to you, sir, and may your voyage be prosperous," I said. "We are not murderers on the run, to take passage regardless of the price. Let's go, Max." We started back toward the harbormaster's office.

"Thou wouldst suck seeds from a sick sow's turds," he said in Hassocki, before adding, "Do not go," in Narbonese.

I spoke in Hassocki, too: "An I did, I'd kiss thy mother." I did wait, to see what would happen next.

Those close-set eyes widened. For a moment, I thought he'd turn his cutthroats loose on Max and me, but he decided it was funny instead and laughed his head off. "The foreign gentleman took me by surprise, knowing this language so well," he said, speaking Hassocki far more fluently than he did Narbonese. He added something in gurgling Lokrian that probably meant, *Do you understand my language, too?* I just dipped my head the way Lokrians will when they mean yes and looked wise. He could make whatever he wanted of that.

He didn't haggle so hard in Hassocki as he would have in Narbonese. My knowing one of the local languages made me seem less foreign to him. I wasn't someone who existed only to be gouged. We got a cabin for a pretty good rate.

The sailor who led us to the cabin spoke some Hassocki. "Is crowded space. You two fit?" He sounded genuinely anxious for our comfort, no matter how villainous he looked. I don't know if he was, but he sounded that way.

"If I don't break my skull on these cursed beams beforehand," Max grumbled. The *Keraunos'* corridors and passageways were not made for a man of his inches. In fact, they weren't made for a man of *my* inches, and I own fewer than Max. He had to walk stooped over whenever he was belowdecks, and the crossbeams or whatever you call them were a special hazard. No matter how careful he tried to be, he banged his head two or three times before we got to the cabin.

"Is all right?" The sailor opened the door. We ducked inside.

It *was* crowded. *No room to swing a cat,* I've heard sailors say. Why anyone would want to do that to a poor harmless cat is beyond me, but never mind. Next to the room we don't have in a circus wagon, though, that little cabin might have been a palace. As a matter of fact, it was nearly as grand as the Shqipetari royal palace, but I didn't know that yet.

I reached into my pocket and gave the sailor the two coins I pulled out: a piaster and a semilepta. He bowed like a folding jackknife. "Zibeon's blessings upon you, my master!" he said, and scurried away. I would rather have had Eliphalet's, but in that part of the world you take what you can get.

You also do your best to make sure other people don't take what they can get—or, rather, that they can't get it. I had the lock that kept light-fingered strangers (and, no doubt, light-fingered acquaintances, too) out of my wagon when I wasn't around. I wasn't worried about taking it. Whoever Dooger and Cark hired to replace me would have a lock of his own. I put it on the cabin door now. It was cold iron, so I hoped it would be proof against wizardry as well as lockpicks.

"Do you suppose it's the fourth hour of the afternoon yet?" I asked Max.

He looked out the little round window—all right, the porthole; I'm no sailor, and I don't pretend to be one—to gauge the sun. "Getting close, anyhow," he answered.

"Does it seem we're about to leave the harbor?"

He shook his head. A ship's crew always goes a little mad when they set sail or weigh anchor or do whatever they need to do to start. I don't know why they need to weigh the anchor; isn't knowing the bloody thing's heavy enough? But when they do it, people run every which way and shout like men possessed. If the wind isn't favorable, and it usually isn't, the weatherworker stands at the stern to call it into the sails.

In the old days, you just sat there if the wind wasn't favorable. You could sit there for weeks if luck went against you. And if the wind died while you were at sea, at sea you'd stay. Weatherworking is one of the marvels of the modern age, but most people take it for granted. It's a good thing the Two Prophets lived long ago; nowadays, everyone would yawn at the miracles they worked.

No weather was being worked at the stern. Sailors weren't running back and forth above our heads. I know the sound—it puts me in mind of a herd of shoes. Nobody was shouting. As if to prove the point, a tern a gull had robbed of a fish screeched furiously.

"Maybe we ought to see what's going on," I said.

"I *can* see what's going on," Max said. "Nothing, that's what."

Sometimes Max can be annoyingly literal. "Maybe we should find out *why* nothing's going on," I said. Max only shrugged. I asked him, "Do you really want to get stuck in Lakedaimon for days?"

He jumped to his feet—and banged his head. After rubbing the latest bruise, he said, "Lead on—carefully, if you please."

I carefully locked the cabin door behind us. We made our way to the steep stair that led us up on deck. Max hit his head once more, but only once. Considering how low the ceiling was, that amounted to a triumph of sorts. By then, though, Max was thoroughly out of sorts. He breathed a sigh of relief when he could unfold himself on deck.

The captain was drinking coffee and smoking a pipe with a long stem and a bowl carved into the shape of a leaping dolphin. It looked very nautical. Anyone who didn't know better would think he'd got it from some clever, grizzled Lokrian craftsman who'd taken weeks to shape it especially for him. Unfortunately, I did know better. Any Schlepsigian would. We use the law of similarity to turn out those pipes by the tens of thousands for home use and the export trade. About every fourth man in Schlepsig smokes one. So it goes.

He seemed surprised to see us. "Is something amiss, my masters? Your cabin does not suit you? It is the best we had left."

I daresay it was, too: a judgment on the *Keraunos*, I fear. But that, for the moment, was beside the point. "Our cabin will serve," I said. "Is it not yet the fourth hour of the afternoon, however?"

He set a languid glance toward the hourglass set in front of the wheel. As languidly, he dipped his head in agreement. "Why, yes. I do believe it is."

"And is not this ship scheduled to sail at the fourth hour of the afternoon?" I asked with such patience as I could muster. A Schlepsigian ship would have sailed when scheduled, come what may. To my people, schedules are as sacred as if Eliphalet and Zibeon wrote each and every one. The wagons roll on time in Schlepsig, let me assure you.

Other folk, I fear, have other notions. "Oh. The schedule," the skipper said, as if he'd forgotten such a thing existed. He probably had, too. He shrugged one of those elaborate shrugs that are only too common all over the Nekemte Peninsula. What those shrugs say is, *You're cursed well stuck, sucker, and you can't do a thing about it, so scream as much as you please—it won't do you any bloody good.* He waited, no doubt hoping I *would* start screaming. But I've seen those shrugs before. Indeed I have. I waited, too. He sighed, balked of his sport. "Well, my master, we will sail—pretty soon."

Pretty soon, in those parts, can mean anything from a couple of hours to a couple of months. "What seems to be the trouble?" I asked.

"Oh, this and that." He gave me another shrug, even more melodramatic than the first. "You are so anxious to be gone from Thasos?"

I knew what that meant, too. He wanted to know if soldiers or gendarmes or an outraged husband with a blood feud were on our trail. If he could soak us for more silver to make a quick getaway, he would. But he couldn't, not this time. "No, by no means," I said truthfully. I have paid for a quick getaway or two in my time, but not that day. Max and I were honest—or no one could prove we weren't. I went on, "I just wanted to make sure you understood."

His bushy eyebrows came down and together in a frown. "Understood what?"

"You're going to be late."

He didn't laugh in my face, but the look on his said he was about to. Around a yawn whose studied insolence he must have spent a long time practicing, he asked, "And so?"

"Well, if you're late, I'm afraid you'll make my friend here *very* unhappy." I nodded toward Max. He was standing extraordinarily straight, no doubt in relief from being doubled over belowdecks like a pair of trousers in a small carpetbag. It made him seem even taller than usual—an obelisk with ears, you might say.

The captain of the *Keraunos* looked him up and down and then up again. "And so?" he repeated—he had style, in a reptilian way.

Max drew his sword. The captain stiffened. So did I. Murdering the man before we set sail might get us talked about. But Max didn't slice chunks off him, however richly he deserved it. Instead, he examined the blade and then took two steps over to the rail. He began carving strips from the wood. The strips were very long and very thin—so thin, you could almost see through them. They came off effortlessly, one after another.

The captain eyed them as they fluttered down to the deck one by one. So did several sailors. You could almost hear the wheels going round in their heads. Here was an uncommonly large man with an uncommonly sharp sword. If they were lucky, they might bring him down without getting hurt themselves. If they weren't so lucky—which seemed a better bet—one or more of them would end up skewered. *Shashlik*, they say in that part of the world.

One of the sailors said something in Lokrian. I know what I would have said in his sandals. Assuming he had said it, I nodded pleasantly to the captain and spoke in Hassocki: "Yes, I think we ought to sail about now, too."

He started to tell me something with a bit of flavor to it, but then his eyes went back to Max, who was still slicing strips from the rail. He seemed ready to cut right through it—or anything else that got in his way. The skipper coughed a couple of times, swallowing whatever he'd been about to say. What came out instead was, "Well, perhaps we should."

I bowed. Always be polite after you've won. "Many thanks, kind sir. I knew when I first set eyes on you that you were a reasonable man." Like anybody else, I defined *a reasonable man* as *a man who does what I want*.

When I first set eyes on the *Keraunos*' weatherworker, what crossed my mind was, *Be careful what you ask for—you may get it*. Had he been a circus performer instead of a wizard, he would have worked for an outfit like Dooger and Cark's. Since he was what he was, he sailed on the *Keraunos*. The captain of any better ship would have booted him off the stern. Man and tub, they deserved each other.

He might have been a good man once, or he might have been one of those dissolute wrecks whom trouble shadows even before they have fuzz on their upper lip. He'd been pickling in his own juices—and the ones he poured down—for a lot of years since then. The whites of his eyes were almost as yellow as the yolks of poached eggs. He swayed in the slight natural breeze as if it would blow him away. His hands shook so badly, he couldn't light a cigar. One of the sailors finally did it for him. He puffed on the cheroot—a nasty weed flavored with anise (a Lokrian vice)—and then coughed like a dying consumptive.

At a gesture from the captain, another sailor fetched him a flask. He tilted his head back. The flask gurgled. So did his stomach, when the nasty stuff in the flask hit it. "Ahh!" he said—a pungent exclamation, because the rotgut was flavored with anise, too. His eyes crossed for a moment. But when they focused again, you had a better picture of the wizard he used to be. Then he took another pull at the flask, and you knew why he wasn't that wizard any more.

The captain shouted to his crew as if there was no time to lose. And there probably wasn't. They raced up the masts like monkeys. Could the weatherworker get us out of Thasos harbor while the popskull still fueled him and before it knocked him for a loop? We'd find out.

Down came the sails from the yards. The weatherworker gathered himself. He began the chant that would call the wind into the sails. To my surprise, the words were in Schlepsigian. That probably showed where he'd studied magic. Where he'd studied looking up at the bottom of an empty bottle, I can't tell you. He'd got full marks in it, wherever it was.

For the moment, though, he stood precariously balanced between a hangover so devastating as to make any I've had seem a mild annoyance by comparison and drunkenness complete and absolute enough to make him forget his own name, or even that he had one.

"Poor bastard," Max murmured, recognizing the signs. I nodded. No, it wasn't hard to see how this weatherworker had wound up on the *Thunderbolt*.

For the moment, the balance held. I could *feel* the power flowing into him and then flowing out through him. When he pointed to the sails with a commanding gesture, his hands hardly trembled at all.

And that gesture, by what would serve for a miracle till a real one came along, did what it was supposed to do. A weatherworker operating alone can't change much weather. One man—or woman—isn't strong enough. It takes great teams of them for that, teams usually put together only in time of war. But one weatherworker can raise enough wind to fill a ship's sails, and from a direction that will take the ship where the skipper wants to go.

At first flapping and then taut as the silk over a well-built woman's bosom, the *Keraunos'* sails filled with wind. The masts and yards creaked, taking up the strain. The weatherworker didn't creak, but he was pretty plainly feeling the strain, too. He swigged from the flask yet again. That might help him for a little while now, but he—and maybe we as well— would pay for it later.

Still, later was later. For now, we began to move, in the beginning so slowly that I wasn't even sure the motion was real, but then faster and faster. The quay disappeared behind us. The captain stood at the wheel, guiding the ship away from Thasos. The weatherworker kept on chanting. Our wind kept on blowing. The *Keraunos'* sails kept on billowing. Thasos—indeed, dry land itself—faded and shrank in the distance.

"We're on our way," I said to Max. "We're well and truly started."

"Talk to me when we're on our way *out* of Shqiperi with our heads still attached to our shoulders," he said. "*Then* I'll be impressed."

If poetry were wine, there wouldn't be enough in Max's soul to sozzle a squirrel, and what there is has mostly soured to vinegar. He has his virtues, Max does, but his flights of fancy stubbornly refuse to grow feathers.

Thasos sits between two long, fingerlike, south-facing peninsulas that shield its harbor from most storms. By the time the weatherworker began to sway as if he were in a high breeze, we'd cleared them both. We were out in the open sea—or as open as the Mykonian Sea gets. It's full of rocky, jagged islands, as if one of the ancient Lokrian gods had pissed out the ocean and passed a swarm of god-sized kidney stones while he was doing it.

Little fishing boats bobbed on the wine-dark water or scudded this way and that with their lateen sails. They went by the real breeze, the true breeze, and if it died they would lie becalmed. Fishing boats can't afford weatherworkers. By all I can tell, most fishing boats can't afford a bloody thing. Fishing has to be a harder way to make a living than performing in a circus, and I know of nothing worse I can say about it.

For a while, the *Thunderbolt* cracked along, all sails set, all sails full, the weatherworker raising enough wind to keep even Max from being too gloomy. It seemed too good to be true—and it was. The weatherworker had been gulping that anise-flavored swill every few minutes to fuel his wizardry. I don't care how long you've been calcifying your liver; you can only do that for so long. And after a couple of hours of it, it was so long for him. He nodded in vague surprise, broke wind instead of raising it, and bonelessly crumpled to the deck.

The breeze died. I wished the weatherworker would die, too, but that was bound to be too much to hope for. The sails went as limp as a granddad's try for a third round. The *Keraunos* stopped creaking and started crawling. Her skipper stirred the weatherworker with his foot. The man never moved. "Oh, thou hellbound, swinish sot," the captain sighed in Hassocki: as resigned a curse as I've ever heard. Then he started shouting in Lokrian. His crew hopped to it; I will say that. They must have been through this many times before. They shortened sail and swung the yards to take what advantage they could of the world's wind. But we were going to be late, late, late to Lakedaimon.

IV

Once upon a time, the Lokrians were the most civilized people in the world. All the history books insist on it. And if that isn't proof we've made progress over the past couple of thousand years, Eliphalet curse me if I know what would be.

Scholars go on and on about the purity of ancient Lokrian sculpture, the magnificence of ancient Lokrian poetry, the innovation and insights of ancient Lokrian drama. For some reason or other, no one talks a whole lot about the ancient Lokrians themselves. And I'll bet I know why: they must have been just as annoying and insufferable as modern Lokrians are.

That was what I was thinking when the *Keraunos* finally got into Lakedaimon most of a day later than the miserable ship should have. We sailed into the harbor in fine style. The weatherworker was working again. He'd come out of his stupor, and he'd had enough anise-flavored firewater afterwards to remind him life might still be worth living. In between his spells of consciousness, we'd had to make do with fitful true breezes, but did he care about that? Care? He didn't even know!

Even now, Lakedaimon is a pretty town. The ruins on what they call Fortress Hill remind you of what a splendid place it was in the glory days of Lokris. Back then, of course, Lakedaimon tried to lord it over all its neighbors, and the other Lokrian city-states responded by trying to stick a stiletto in its back. Typical Lokrian politics, I fear. Two Lokrians will have three opinions and four faction fights. Lokrians will ally with an enemy's enemy even if they know that fellow will turn on them as soon as he's settled the first enemy's hash. They think, *Well, I lasted two days longer than he did and I got to gloat while he suffered, so who cares what happens next?*

Charming people.

And they've always been like that. Take a look at ancient history if you don't believe me. No, not the pretty stories—the history behind them. Yes, they held off the Sassanids all those years ago. Yes, they were heroes. Some of them were, anyhow. But an awful lot of city-states went over to the Great King. They fought on his side, and some of them were heroes, too. If he'd won, nobody would remember Lakedaimon.

When Lakedaimon fought Pallas for all those years, didn't she have a couple of civil wars, too? Wouldn't she have had a better chance of winning if she hadn't hated herself worse than she hated her enemies? Seems that way to me.

One more. When the Aeneans conquered Lokris, how did they do it? Weren't the Lokrians squabbling among themselves and with the Kingdom of Fyrom to the north? (The Lokrians claim the Fyromians were really Lokrian, too—just country cousins, you might say. These days, Fyrom is split among Lokris, Vlachia, and Plovdiv. Factions again, which argues that the Lokrians might be right.) Didn't some Lokrians invite the Aeneans in to help their side? And didn't the Aeneans pay them back by gobbling up all of Lokris one city-state at a time? If you look at it the right way, didn't the Lokrians have it coming?

I asked our peerless skipper where the Quay of the Red-Figure Winecup was. He shrugged, which made the gilded fringe on his epaulets bounce up and down. I asked a couple of sailors who spoke Hassocki. One pointed east, the other west. It didn't matter. The *Halcyon* was bound to have sailed. Since it was crewed by Lokrians, too, normally I would have assumed it was also running late. But that would have been convenient for us, so I didn't believe it for a minute.

Then I asked the captain how to find the Quay of the Poxed Trollop. He gave me excellent, precise, detailed instructions. Somehow, I was less than astonished. If anyone was likely to know all there was to know about poxed trollops, our captain was the man.

"The *Gamemeno* isn't supposed to go out for a while," Max said. "You should ask him to recommend a hostel."

I didn't care for that. "No, thanks," I said. "I want to go to a place where I won't need a mage to kill bedbugs and fleas—and maybe crabs, too—afterwards." I remembered the trollop one more time, and what might go with her.

We took our duffels off the *Keraunos* and got away from the misnamed ship as fast and as far as we could. Two large men—and Max is almost two large men all by himself—are safe enough by daylight almost anywhere. We waved down a cab. The hackman spoke some Narbonese. "Best hostel?" he said when I inquired. "The Narbo, without a doubt. But you pay there, sir—you pay."

"What's pretty good and costs a third as much?" was my next question.

We ended up at a place called Papa Ioannakis'. It was three blocks away from the Narbo. The big, fancy hostel blocked its view of Fortress Hill. But it was clean, it was comfortable, and you didn't feel a vampire sinking its fangs into your purse and sucking out your silver.

The real Papa Ioannakis was a priest who fought the Hassocki and ended up dead before his time for his troubles. I neglected to point this out to Max. If he stayed ignorant of the fine points of Lokrian history—well, he did, that's all. I preferred ignorance to babbling about evil omens, which is what I would have got if he knew that.

"Not bad," I said, sprawling out on my bed.

"It would be better if we had some money coming in," Max said.

"We've got enough." Odds are I sounded irritable. I *felt* irritable. "If you want to go stand on a street corner and swallow your sword in front of an upside-down hat, go right ahead. I don't feel like turning backflips just so I can buy myself an extra mug of wine—thanks all the same. If this goes off the way I hope it will, I'll never have to turn another backflip as long as I live."

"If this doesn't go off the way you hope it will, you'll never turn another backflip, either," Max pointed out. "But you won't live long."

I didn't argue with him. Life was too short. As a matter of fact, I wished that phrase hadn't occurred to me so soon after his raven's croak of doom. I wasn't about to admit that, though, either to him or to myself. And I was glad all the way down to my toes that I hadn't told him the story of Papa Ioannakis.

The hostel named for the late, lamented Lokrian priest had a pretty fair eatery across the lobby from the front desk. The waiter, a fussy little man in an ill-fitting formal jacket and a cravat that looked as if a strangler had knotted it, spoke enough Narbonese to get by. He beamed when we ordered local specialties: Max chose capon cooked with lemon, while I had grape leaves stuffed with ground lamb and rice. Mine were quite tasty, and Max turned his capon into bones fast enough to persuade me that he enjoyed his. The menu offered foreign dishes, too, but the native fare was half as expensive and probably twice as good. The cook knew what he was doing with it; he wasn't trying to imitate some other kingdom's style.

After a much better night than the two we'd spent aboard the *Keraunos*, we climbed Fortress Hill to look at the famous ruins there. Yes, it's something everybody does. Yes, practically everybody we saw up there was from Schlepsig or the Dual Monarchy or Narbonensis or Albion. (The Lokrians take their ruins for granted. They'd have a lot more of them if they hadn't torn some down to reuse the building stone.) But when were we going to be in Lakedaimon again? If the Two Prophets were kind, never.

And, even if everybody goes to see the ruins, there's a good reason: They're worth seeing. Take Cytherea's temple, for instance. You can't see the thirty-five-foot gold-and-ivory statue of the love goddess the Lakedaimonians put in it; one gang of barbarians or another stole it a long time ago. But the temple itself still is—and deserves to be—famous for its lines. You've all looked at woodcuts or those clever little spells that make a pair of pictures join together in your sight so you see not two pictures but one with real depth. Well, the difference between those and the real thing is about the same as the difference between a journal story about a pork-and-cabbage casserole and a big helping of the casserole itself.

Would you give a dog a woodcut of a bone?

The famous Lokrian sun and sky don't translate well in descriptions, either. All I can tell you is they don't make weather like that in Schlepsig, and I wish they did. It was warm without being sticky. The sky was a deeper, purer blue than my home kingdom ever knows. Up at the top of Fortress Hill, you thought you could see all the way to the edge of the world. Yes, I know the world hasn't got an edge. You thought you could see it anyway.

Even Max was moved. He took off his hat, fanned himself with it, and said, "Nice view." He really did.

And yet like I told you, you hardly see any Lokrians up there. Oh, they have a few guards, to keep you from sticking a temple in your hip pocket and taking it back to your hotel, but that's about all. Wait—I take it back. There was also a Lokrian woman up there. Her lines were almost as fine as the temples', and she dressed to emphasize them. Her eyes were dark as two sloes, but it was obvious she was fast.

"Is it that you speak Narbonese?" one of my fellow foreigners asked her, tipping his hat. After seeing so much marble, he was after something livelier.

He got it, too. She gave him a slow, sidelong smile. "Sir, my mouth will do anything you like," she purred in the same language. After that, he couldn't take her down off Fortress Hill fast enough. I only wished I'd spoken to her first. By the way Max's eyes followed her, he was wishing the same thing. No, he wasn't wishing that I'd spoken to her first. . . . Oh, you know what I mean.

Now we both looked around for something of more recent vintage and softer curves than the famous stonework. We were out of luck, though. That miserable Narbonese seemed to have snagged the only woman of, ah, enterprise who'd gone up there that morning. No wonder we're hereditary foes with Narbonensis, by Eliphalet's whiskers.

Since Max and I had no pleasant excuse to go back to Papa Ioannakis', we tramped every inch of Fortress Hill. I got a little piece of classical marble in my shoe, and had to park my fundament on a bigger one so I could take off the shoe and shake out the pebble. It fell to the ground with a tiny click—a bit of ancient history returning to anonymity.

Max, meanwhile, was peering down into the city. "Something's going on down there," he said.

"Well, so what?" I said. "Lakedaimon's a fair-sized town. Why shouldn't something be going on?"

"No, not something like that," he said. "Something nasty."

Now, Max's imagination can turn a wedding parade into a funeral procession. I've seen him do it. Actually, it's impressive, if you like that kind of thing. So before I believed him, I stood up and had a look for myself. Damned if he wasn't right. When people start chasing one another through the streets with clubs and spears and crossbows, something's come unglued somewhere.

Yes, we'd landed in Lakedaimon just in time for the Scriptural Riots. Thank you *so much*, *Thunderbolt*.

Everybody in the civilized world knows the Scriptures were first written in ancient Lokrian. Some sarcastic sage said a few years ago that the Goddess learned Lokrian just so She could write the Scriptures—and learned it very badly, too. But, while everybody knows this, nobody— nobody normal, I mean, leaving priests and sages out of the bargain— thinks about it more than once every five years, if that often. If you want to read the Scriptures, you read them in your own language. If you're feeling especially holy and you've got more schooling than is good for you, you'll look at them in Aenean.

But if you happen to be a Lokrian . . . If you happen to be a Lokrian, you read the Scriptures in ancient Lokrian. There's only one problem with that. Modern Lokrian is closer to ancient Lokrian than Torinan, say, is to Aenean. But it's not a whole *lot* closer. If you know modern Lokrian, you can sorta, kinda read the ancient language, with the accent on *sorta*, *kinda*.

So somebody got the bright idea of finally—Lokris kicked out the Hassocki a long lifetime ago—translating the Scriptures into modern Lokrian. And he published his book. On the day we were there, he published his miserable book. If we'd sailed away in the *Halcyon*, we never would have had to worry about it. If the *Keraunos'* weatherworker'd been sober, we never would have had to worry about it. The weatherworker was drunk. We didn't get to sail. We had to worry about it.

I have no idea whether this fellow's translation was good, bad, or indifferent, mind you. I read even less Lokrian than I speak, and I don't speak any. What I do know is that half the people in Lakedaimon seemed to think he was a hero, and the other half wanted to dip him in boiling butter—or, being Lokrians, possibly in olive oil instead.

I know all this *now*, you understand. I've pieced it together from journal articles and such. What I knew *then* was that way too many people in long skirts and short ones were running around assaulting one another with intent to maim, or maybe to dip in boiling butter. Somehow, I didn't think they would refrain from mayhem on my person just because my clothes said I was no Lokrian. If anything, both factions might decide that kicking in a foreigner's ribs was the one pleasure they had in common.

"How are we going to get back to the hostel?" Max asked. "They already seem pretty hostile down there."

In lieu of braining him with a chunk of classical marble, I nodded. "Don't they just?" I said. "I suggest we go . . . cautiously."

"Good luck," Max said. And we would need it. We were obvious foreigners. I'm a good-sized man, and I seem bigger next to Lokrians, who run short. Max is enormous next to anything this side of a temple steeple. The only way we could have made ourselves more conspicuous was by going naked. The idea did not appeal. We might have got by with it in ancient Lakedaimon, but not now, not now.

The idea of staying up on Fortress Hill didn't appeal, either. Fortress Hill has some of the most glorious stonework in the world. And that's *all* it has. No beds. No cafes. No nothing, unless you felt like chewing rocks. I didn't. "Let's try it," I said. Max made a horrible face, but he didn't say no.

We had no trouble going down the steps to the bottom of the hill. I knew why, too—the Lokrians didn't feel like climbing them. There have to be more than there are at the Temple of Siwa, even if those are a lot steeper. But when we got to the bottom . . . The first thing we saw was a woman's body. Someone had smashed in her head. Flies buzzed around the pool of blood. Max and I have both been through wars—but there wasn't supposed to be a war here.

Fine. That poor woman got killed in peacetime. It didn't make her any less dead.

My nostrils twitched. Then I coughed. You always smell a lot of smoke in a city, from cookfires and hearthfires and what have you. But you don't get a gust of wind with smoke as thick as if you were smoking six pipes at once. "They're trying to burn the place down," Max observed. "*That's* clever of them, isn't it?"

"Brilliant," I said. If the Hassocki had set fire to Lakedaimon, it would have been a fearsome atrocity. Everybody would have screamed and made them stop. Since the Lokrians were doing it to themselves, everybody would yawn—except for the people who got roasted. *They'd* scream, all right.

A band of a dozen or so rioters came tearing around a corner and started to rush right at us. They slowed down in a hurry, I must say. The sight of somebody Max's size will do that to the most riotous rioter.

Max bowed to them. Since he's so long and lean, he folds up amazingly. As he straightened to show them that, yes, he really was as tall as they thought he was, I bowed in turn. And I kept right on going, turning the bow into a handstand. If I'd been wearing a short skirt like most of the Lokrians, that might have played hob with my modesty. Or it might not—*do* they have drawers under those things? Trust me: I never tried to find out.

As things were, I had on ordinary civilized clothes: tunic, cravat, jacket, trousers. My hat fell off, but that was about it. I walked around on my hands, and waved to the Lokrians with one foot. If they were confused enough, I figured, they might go on leaving us alone.

After I'd stopped waving—and it isn't easy to do if you've got shoes— Max grabbed my feet. We impersonated a drunken wheelbarrow and its even more pixilated operator. I've never played a drunken wheelbarrow before. Putting your shoulder to the wheel is hard when your shoulder *is* the wheel, or at least the brace that holds the wheel on. But what's the point of performing if you can't improvise?

As well as a drunken wheelbarrow could, I kept an eye on the Lokrians. I knew I might have to play an all too sober sprinter any moment now. Some of the rioters were really fricaseed. But the sozzled ones stared with the others. Whatever they'd expected, a street show wasn't it.

After eight or ten of the longest heartbeats I've ever had, they decided they liked us. They crowded closer, laughing and clapping their hands. Some of them even tossed coins into my hat, which had landed crown down. I bet they thought I planned it that way. If I were as smart as that . . . If I were as smart as that, wouldn't I have been on my way to Shqiperi?

Hang around Max for a while and he starts to rub off on you.

Because they liked us, we had to play our parts longer than we'd planned on—not that we'd done much in the way of planning. Max took some liberties with me that a real wheelbarrow would have slapped his face for. I would have slapped him myself, except our audience thought he was the funniest thing in the world, and they would have done worse than slap us if they hadn't. The customer is always right, especially when he's armed and dangerous.

At last, the wheelbarrow got rebellious and started kicking in the traces like a restive mule. One of those kicks almost made a mule out of Max—trifle with *my* dignity, would he? The crowd ate it up. I wiggled myself free of him and flipped to my feet, and we both took our bows.

Instead of mutilating us, the Lokrians pounded our backs, clasped our hands, and gave us nips of what had inflamed them. Not only that, when I picked up my hat I found we'd made damn near five leptas in silver. One of the rioters spoke fragments of Schlepsigian. When I made him understand we were staying at Papa Ioannakis', he and his pals undertook to escort us back there.

The hostel was closed up tight, with shutters over the ground-floor windows and an enormous padlock on the front door. Riots are a fact of life in Lakedaimon. People get ready for them, the way they get ready for earthquakes. They do less damage that way.

A clerk came out on a second-story balcony. He shouted down at the crowd. They shouted up at him. So did I—he spoke Narbonese. He came down the fire escape to the first-floor balcony, then lowered a cast-iron stairway to the ground. Max and I went up the stairs. None of our riotous friends followed. I don't know what the clerk told them—maybe that he'd turn them into prawns if they tried. He would have needed something interesting and memorable to keep them down on the sidewalk. Whatever it was, it worked.

As soon as we got up to the first balcony, he hauled up the fire escape after us. Only then did he allow himself a sigh of relief. Cadogan the lion-tamer would have been proud of him. He hadn't shown fear in front of the wild animals. They'll turn on you every time if you do.

"Thank you," I told him.

"Not at all," he answered politely. "We would lose our reputation if we lost our customers." Around the corner, a woman screamed and kept on screaming. The hostel clerk winced. "This uproar, it is a misfortune." In Narbonese, things don't sound so bad as they really are. Max knows several languages, but that isn't one of them. It doesn't fit in with the way he thinks.

"A misfortune, yes." I admired the understatement, and the cool way he brought it out. "What will you do about the, ah, uproar?"

"Myself? Try to stay safe. In aid of which, shall we go up?" The clerk led Max and me to the second-story balcony, and then in through the window to the room it adjoined. As he did, he went on, "My kingdom? My kingdom will wait till things subside, then catch a few ringleaders and plunderers and hang them. And after that?" He shrugged a resigned shrug. "After that, we shall start getting ready for the next time things turn—lively."

I nodded to the stout middle-aged woman whose room that happened to be. Max gave her one of his deep and startling bows. Then we were out in the hall, for all the world as if nothing out of the ordinary had happened. And so it seemed—except even there the air smelled of smoke.

"Tonight's supper specialty"—the clerk took a certain somber pride in making five full syllables out of that—"is lamb with garlic and rosemary. I trust you will find it to your liking." He was working hard to pretend everything was normal, too.

"I'm sure we will," I said, and I was—nothing wrong with Papa Ioannakis' kitchens. But I couldn't ignore the riots, however much I wanted to. For one thing, that poor woman was still screaming, loud enough for me to hear her in the hallway through a closed door (and, by now, probably a closed window, too). For another . . . "How long do you expect the, ah, uproar to last? We have a ship to catch in a couple of days."

"As for the uproar, one never knows. It could peter out tonight, or it could go on for a week. Such is life." He shrugged again. "As for the ship . . . Which is it, and from which quay does it sail?" When I told him, he did more than wince: He blanched. "The Quay of the Poxed Trollop? Sir, even without the disturbances you would do better to stay away. That is no place for honest men."

In that case, Max and I were better suited to the quay than he suspected. With a shrug of my own, I said, "We have to get to Shqiperi, and that seems to be the fastest way."

"To Shqiperi?" Lokrians don't like Shqipetari. I mean, they *really* don't like Shqipetari. I'd just put us beyond the pale. "On your heads be it— and it will." The clerk stalked off.

"What was that all about?" Max asked. I didn't much want to give him the gist, but I didn't see what choice I had. After I translated, he gave me one of those looks you should only get from a wife. "You didn't listen to *me* when I told you we were putting our heads on the block. Will you listen to him?"

"If I didn't listen to you, why should I listen to some clerk at a hostel?"

"Because he knows what he's talking about?" Max is full of uncouth and unlikely suggestions.

"If he knew what he was talking about, he'd have too much money to be a clerk at a hostel," I said firmly. "In fact, if he says something like that, it's a pretty good sign he *doesn't* know what he's talking about." My logic impressed me.

For some unaccountable reason, it failed to impress Max. "Hmm," he said. "And just what do you know about the Shqipetari that makes you such an expert?"

"I know they need a king," I answered. "And I know their king needs an aide-de-camp. Are you coming or aren't you?"

"Oh, I'll come," he said, doleful as usual. "If I didn't, you'd just drag somebody off the street—though where you'd find anyone this side of that Manolis fellow to fit into that captain's uniform is beyond me." He shook his head. "If you went and got someone who didn't know you're a maniac killed, I'd feel bad about it afterwards."

"How about if I went and got myself killed?"

"Well, that, too—a little."

The riots eased off before we had to go looking for the good ship *Gamemeno*. From everything I've learned since, this was more luck than design. The constabulary didn't help much, because half of them were on one side and half on the other. And the King of Lokris didn't dare call out the army, because half of *it* was on one side and half on the other. Like I say, Lokrians form factions the way Schlepsigians form drinking clubs, the only difference being that Schlepsigian drinking clubs don't usually go after one another with cutlery.

So if the charming people of Lakedaimon wanted to go on murdering and raping and burning down chunks of their town, Eliphalet only knows what would have stopped them. Something else caught their fancy—a scandalous new dancer, I think it was—and they quit.

That clerk was on duty when we checked out. He rolled his eyes—partly, I suppose, at our getup. "I hope I don't read about your case in one of our journals," he said. I've had more encouraging good-byes. All things considered, it was lucky he and Max couldn't talk to each other. They would have got on much too well.

Our getup . . . If the Quay of the Poxed Trollop was as charming a place as everybody said it was, we had two ways to approach it. We could try to blend in with the local lowlifes and seem invisible. Or we could be so gaudy and ostentatious that nobody—I dared hope—would presume to bother us.

Max blended in with the Lokrians the way oil blends with water. Come to that, I look about as much like a Lokrian as a camel looks like a unicorn—er, as a unicorn looks like a camel. You get the idea.

Since we couldn't blend, we had gaudy forced on us. I put on my acrobat's rig, while Max wore the Super Grand High Panjandrum's uniform that was so much more effective in places where real generals didn't dress like escapees from comic opera. The uniform did help us flag a cab. By the way the hackman bowed and scraped as he opened the door, he probably thought we were the Schlepsigian minister to Lokris and his military attaché. He was apologetic for knowing only a bit of Narbonese—that and Albionese are the foreign languages a Lokrian is most likely to speak.

"Quite all right, my good man," I said in Narbonese, and he brightened. Then I told him, "Please be so kind as to take us to the Quay of the Poxed Trollop."

Have you ever tossed a big chunk of ice into hot fat to congeal it on the instant? If you haven't, you won't understand what the hackman's face did when I said that. "The . . . Quay of the Poxed Trollop, sir?" he wheezed. By the way he sounded, an invisible man was doing a pretty good job of strangling him.

"We have a ship to catch," I said, wondering what kind of horrible scow the *Gamemeno* would turn out to be.

The hackman was thinking along the same lines. "A garbage barge?" he muttered. He slammed the door shut with what I thought quite unnecessary force, climbed up to his seat, and cracked the whip over the horse's back. Springs creaking and big, iron-tired wheels clanging and bouncing over cobblestones, we set out.

Next to no one was on the sidewalk. Street traffic was drastically down, too. The riots had ended, but the locals feared they might pick up again any minute now. That was how it felt to me, too. When I said as much, Max looked at me and said, "I suppose you'll tell me there's a bright spot to all this, too."

"Well, there may be," I said. His expression could have frozen the ice to congeal the fat I was talking about before. "There may," I insisted. "If anything will keep footpads at home beating their children, it's the chance of getting caught in a riot."

"You're reaching," Max said, and said no more.

Some of the people who *were* out and about didn't have homes or flats any more. I say that partly because they looked as if they'd been wearing the same clothes for days—and they had—and partly because the cab rattled past the burnt-out ruins of quite a few homes and flats. Maybe the arsonists who started those fires hadn't managed to turn all of Lakedaimon into a roasting pit, but nobody could say they hadn't tried. The sour smell of old smoke hung in the air like an unwelcome guest who couldn't figure out it was time to leave.

Shops had gone up in flames, too. Here and there, shopkeepers or hired guards patrolled the ruins to make sure nobody greedy went digging through the ashes. "The cradle of civilization," Max remarked—and if that isn't a judgment on a lot of things that have happened since the glory days of Lakedaimon, it will do till a nastier one comes along.

As we went down toward the waterfront, the neighborhood got worse. Back in ancient times, Lakedaimon's port was a separate city. Nowadays, it's just a slum. Even the good parts—like the quay from which the *Halcyon* had sailed—weren't very good, and the bad parts were horrid. I would have taken the three gold globes for the harborside emblem if not for the profusion of wine jars and jugs of spirits over the taverns and the similar profusion of houses—if that's the word I want—with red lanterns out front. It was the sort of place where cats didn't eat rats. They got fat off protection money instead.

The hackman had the accursed gall to charge us three times as much for going from Papa Ioannakis' to the harbor as the other fellow had charged for going from the harbor to the hostel. When I squawked, he suddenly stopped understanding Narbonese. "What's going on?" Max asked. *Wheep!* Out came his sword, the way it had when Dooger and Cark tried to cheat us.

Maybe *Wheep!* is a word in Lokrian. Maybe the sight of the blade glittering in the famous Lokrian sunshine jogged the hackman's memory. All of a sudden, Narbonese made sense to him again. So did the notion that he might—by unfortunate accident, of course—have tried to charge us too much. He was glad to accept the fare I proposed. He was even gladder to hop back up onto his cab and get out of there as fast as he could.

If I were a hackman, I would have been glad to get out of there, too. I don't think Max noticed, but three or four men who, if they weren't ruffians and robbers, could certainly have played them on the stage sidled towards us while I had my little . . . conversation with the driver. When his sword left the scabbard, they discovered they had business elsewhere. Coshing a very big man isn't much harder than bopping anybody else over the head. Coshing a very big man who's liable to run steel through your liver is a different sort of affair, one for which they had less appetite.

When Max started to sheath the sword, I set a hand on his arm. "Maybe you should leave that out," I said. "It, ah, persuades people."

He looked down at it, coughed, and shrugged. "However you like," he said.

I didn't like much about the Quay of the Poxed Trollop. I didn't say anything about not liking it. We had to be where we were to get where we were going. That didn't make it a garden spot. If I'd grumbled, though, think what Max would have said. I thought of it, and decided I didn't want to hear it.

After the would-be highwaymen hit the highway (actually a foul-smelling, muddy alley where better than half the cobblestones were only memories), several poxed trollops came up to us. Well, I don't *know* they were poxed, but the odds seemed good. Trollops they definitely were, in tawdry, tight-fitting finery and with painted faces more mercenary than any mercenary's. They greeted us with endearments and obscenities—did they know the difference, or care?—in everything from Hassocki to Albionese.

I swept off my hat and bowed to them. After I nudged Max, he did the same. As always, his deep bow produced stares of astonishment, at least from the soiled doves who weren't eyeing his crotch. Come to that, they looked more than a little astonished, too; the trousers on that ridiculous uniform fit snugly.

"My ladies," I said (two lies in two words—can't do much better than that), "can you tell me how to find the *Gamemeno?*" I stuck to Narbonese. More of them seemed to use it than any other, er, tongue.

Maybe I was wrong. The question sent them into gales of laughter. "Right here, pal," one of them said, striking a pose that almost made my eyeballs catch fire.

"No, try me!" Another one twisted even more lewdly.

"Now what?" Max said, though he could scarcely have had much doubt.

I did. "I'm not quite sure," I muttered, and went back to Narbonese: "The ship called the *Gamemeno?*"

"Oh, the *ship,*" the trulls chorused, and they giggled some more. That was when I found out what *gamemeno* means in Lokrian. Why anyone would want to call a ship that . . . Well, you find peculiar people everywhere. I used to know a Schlepsigian who named his sailboat the *Rottweiler* because he wrote doggerel aboard it. He had other troubles, too, believe me. One of the strumpets pointed down to the end of the quay. "That's it."

That was the only ship tied up at the Quay of the Poxed Trollop. I had feared that would be it and hoped that wouldn't be. As usual, fear had more weight in the real world. The *Gamemeno* made the *Keraunos* look like a potentate's pleasure yacht. If you'd ever seen the *Keraunos,* you would know how badly I just insulted the ship Max and I now approached.

A few sailors eyed us as we came up. You know the romantic tales of pirates on the high seas they used to tell? Well, forget them. These fellows looked like pirates, and like the sort of men who gave piracy a bad name in the first place. They hadn't shaved. They hadn't bathed. They looked at us the way a dog eyes the meat in a butcher's window.

The gangplank was down. I went up it, Max right behind me. And I felt like a man who was walking the plank, too. Up close, the *Gamemeno* looked even grimmer, even more ill-cared-for, than she had at a distance. She took after her crew. By the look of them, someone should have taken after them—with a club.

"You sail for Shqiperi soon, is it not so?" I asked in Hassocki, the language I knew that I thought these cutthroats most likely to speak.

"Who wants to know?" asked the biggest and ugliest of them—a dubious distinction indeed. He wore the ugliest hat, too.

Before I could say anything, Max brandished his sword. Max was bigger than the sailor, though not uglier. He still had both ears, for instance. And he had a great load of righteous indignation in his voice as he exclaimed, "Have a care how you speak to the king!"

"The king?" The sailor—he turned out to be the captain—must have thought Max was a madman. Telling someone six feet eight with a sword in his hand that he's a madman, however, requires that you be a madman yourself. What he did say was, "Why, thou most credulous fool, the Land of the Eagle has no king."

"A horse's cock up thine arse, thou loggerheaded and unpolished wretch, for assuredly it has one now," Max replied. "Behold him!"

The fellow beheld me. If I seemed royal to him, he concealed it remarkably well. Laughing a laugh he'd surely bought secondhand from a carrion crow, he said, "He's no more king than he can kick the hat off my head."

Max bowed to me. "Your Majesty?"

I bowed to him. Then I walked up to the sailor, measured him with my eyes—he was an inch or two taller than I was—and bowed to him as well. "At your service," I said—and threw myself into a backflip. When my feet were over my head, I kicked out with one of them, caught the brim of the hat without kicking him in the face (too bad!), and sent it flying to the filthy deck. I landed on both feet, straightened up, and bowed to him again. "At your service," I repeated. "And you, I trust, at mine."

He stared at me. He stared at Max. He stared at Max's sword. And he stared at his disreputable hat. He picked it up and jammed it back down onto his equally disreputable head. "I don't know what your game is, *your Majesty*"—he freighted that with enough irony to sink it—"but I'll play along. Aye, we sail for Shqiperi. Would you honor us with your company?"

"I would," I said grandly—even royally. And so I set forth for my kingdom.

V

I expected the *Gamemeno* to have a weatherworker who made the poor drunken blundering idiot aboard the *Keraunos* look like a genius of thaumaturgy. I wondered what would be wrong with him. Mere drunkenness didn't seem nearly enough. Would he smoke hashish? Would he be haunted by a parrot's ghost that sat on his shoulder, invisible except by the light of the full moon, and croaked words of evil omen into his unwashed ear? Would he decide he was a dolphin and had to swim in the sea instead of standing on the poop deck? Only a fluke, or the lack of two, would save us from being stuck with the world's wind.

I turned out to be as right as a blizzard is black, which is one of the things we say in Schlepsig. They don't know much about blizzards down in Lokris, though they do in the mountains of Shqiperi. To give myself what due I can, I realized I'd made a mistake as soon as I set eyes on this fellow. Except for being swarthy and sharp-featured, he reminded me of nothing so much as the officer candidates at the royal military academy in Donnerwetter. He was all business. I don't think I'd ever seen a Lokrian who was all business before. I didn't know such a breed existed.

He nodded to Max and me, said, "Good morning," in perfect Schlepsigian, and started talking with the captain (whose name, I'd found out, was Tasos). Tasos might have been as snotty as a two-year-old with a cold to us, but he bent over backward (or maybe Lokrians bend over forward—I don't know) to stay friendly with his weatherworker. Well, we were just passengers. He'd have to work with the other man again and again.

And there was more to it than that. I saw why pretty cursed quick, too. Speaking of cursed, Tasos swore in half a dozen languages when he ordered his bandits to cast off the lines that held the *Gamemeno* to the Quay of the Poxed Trollop and set sail. I understood most of the bad language. The Lokrian I had to figure out from what the sailors did.

As soon as the lines were coiled on deck and the sails unfurled, the weatherworker—*his* name, I learned a little later, was Stagiros—got down to that business of his. I thought the sailors had spread too much canvas, not just for the size of their tub but for the likely powers of their weatherworker. Well, shows what I know, doesn't it?

Eliphalet and Zibeon, doesn't it just! Stagiros summoned up a mighty wind, a wind that could have taken a Schlepsigian ship of the line into battle against Albion. The sails here didn't sag and belly and slowly fill. No, not this time. They went taut all at once—*boom!*—and the *Gamemeno* left the Quay of the Poxed Trollop behind as fast as you'd want to leave a poxed trollop behind, or even a poxed trollop's behind.

The pace we set! There were Lokrian Navy ships in Lakedaimon harbor, frigates and schooners and sloops built for speed. Naturally, those ships are going to have good weatherworkers aboard them, to get the most from their sleek lines. We showed 'em our probably poxed behind, and I mean with ease. The way things looked from our deck, somebody might have nailed them to the water. I'd never seen such weatherworking in my whole life.

What was a weatherworker like that doing on a ship like this? I couldn't ask Tasos in quite those words, not unless I wanted him to pitch me over the side. So I asked, "How did you find such a fine man?" and pointed toward the busily incanting Stagiros.

"I paid him more than anyone else," he answered without the least hesitation.

Was that sarcasm? I examined it up, down, and sideways, and decided it wasn't. No, he meant every word, all right. This from a man who plainly clung limpetlike to every hemidemilepta he saw. Why?

More often than you'd think, asking the question makes the answer come. Why would Tasos and the *Gamemeno* want a weatherworker who had to be one of the best in the world? Because they needed to go from hither to yon and to get out of ports like a scalded cat? Why *else* would you want a weatherworker like that?

And *why* would you need to be able to run and scoot, to need it so badly that you had a first-rate man on a fifth-rate ship? I almost asked Tasos what he was smuggling, but that was a question I could ask myself, not one that would make me loved by our swashbuckling captain (ha!) and his jolly crew (ha! ha!).

I could legitimately notice we were sailing along to the southwest, not eastward as a lot of ships heading for Shqiperi from Lakedaimon would have done. "You care not for the canal?" I asked.

The Trans-Peninsular Canal is one of those places that almost have an ancient history behind them. The ancient Lokrians, not being blind, noticed that the secondary peninsula where a lot of them lived was connected to the rest of the much bigger Nekemte Peninsula only by a skinny little neck of land—a neck rather like that belonging to the present Hassockian Atabeg, as a matter of fact. They also noticed they would have themselves a demon of a shortcut if they cut through it.

One small problem: they couldn't. That was partly because the project needed cooperation, and the Lokrians gave the world examples of how *not* to cooperate, as they did of so many other important things. And it was partly because the ancient Lokrians, while brilliant in any number of ways, were, when you get right down to it, pretty lousy wizards.

And so were the Aeneans. When it came to sorcery, as with most things, the Aeneans learned everything they didn't know from the Lokrians. Even so, Emperor Otho had a crack at it. He assembled half the wizards in the Empire and about a quarter of the men who could carry a shovel, and they all converged on the little neck that separated the small peninsula from the bigger one. And they got started, and they went along for a couple of furlongs . . .

And Otho got bored.

Otho was good at getting bored. He was better at that than at most other things, though he did love his mother (which is another story, one you can look up for yourself). And so he went off and decided he was going to be a sprinter or a boxer or a god or whatever he felt like being instead of a fellow in charge of a canal. Or rather, part of a canal. A small part of a canal. The money stopped coming in. So did the food. The wizards went home. Some of the diggers did, too. Quite a few of them starved. Nobody knows just how many, because Otho was too bored to count them.

For almost the next two thousand years, nobody bothered with the canal. The Aeneans had tried and failed, so other people said it couldn't be done. Then, about thirty years ago, a Narbonese company had a go of it with modern magery. They got about halfway and ran out of money. A Lokrian firm bought them out and finished the job. It took two modern companies twelve years to dig that canal, with proper wizardry to placate the local earth elementals and stabilize the bedrock elementals (the Aeneans had never even heard of, or from, them). No wonder Otho couldn't hack it . . . through.

Tasos, I'm sure, cared as much for the history of the Trans-Peninsular Canal as he did for the history of the rutabaga. Whether he went through it or not was the only thing that mattered to him. "No, we will round Lokris instead," he told me. "We have certain . . . stops to make along the way."

"Uh-*huh*. I see," I said. And I did. I wondered what he'd be loading and unloading at those stops. Spirits flavored with anise? Tobacco flavored with anise? Hemp flavored with anise? Wanted criminals? Criminals looking to do something wicked enough to make them wanted? A black wizard or two? Crossbow quarrels? Copies of the Scriptures done into modern Lokrian? Anything that was expensive but didn't take up much room fit his bill just fine.

Like Max and me, for instance. Considering what he'd gouged us for a cabin to Fushe-Kuqe, we had to be at least as valuable as a few jugs of dragon spit. That was about how Tasos treated us, too—as cargo, I mean. As long as we didn't rattle around and cause him extra work, we were fine. If we did . . . Well, that might not be so much fun.

I just stood by the rail and watched the land and sea flash by. Fishing boats that worked by the world's wind bobbed in the water. Men with bushy eyebrows under short-brimmed black wool caps stared at us as we shot past. They were almost no sooner seen than gone. Stagiros really was amazing. Did he know how much he was worth? Could a shabby smuggler like Tasos possibly pay him that much? I found it hard to believe, but here he was.

The *Gamemeno*'s skipper posted a man at the bow to sing out warnings when we neared other vessels. Those fishing boats couldn't move fast enough to get out of our way. Some of them, with their sails furled and with nets in the water, couldn't move at all. *We* had to do the dodging.

As for Tasos himself, he kept a weather eye—I think that's the proper seagoing phrase, isn't it?—on the coast to our left. To port, I should say, shouldn't I? "What are you looking for?" I asked innocently. "Pirates?"

He jerked. He twitched. He grabbed my arm. "Where?" he demanded. "What do you know? What have you heard?"

I didn't know anything, not about pirates. I didn't even suspect anything, and I certainly hadn't heard anything. Well, no—all that wasn't quite true. Now I knew one thing about pirates, anyway: our magnificent captain was scared green of them. "Why are you worrying?" I asked him. "With your wonderful weatherworker there, you can outrun any pirate ship ever hatched."

"Would that Zibeon and Eliphalet gave me a pile of stones, of conformation like unto thy brainpan, that I might build me of them a rock garden in the courtyard of my home," he sneered.

"Go to kennel, thou who wast born betwixt two stockfishes," I replied. "Why revilest me so?"

"Should a fool not be reproved for his folly?" Tasos said. "We may outfly any pirate ship, aye. But catapult darts or stones? Fireballs? Arrows? Should one smite the weatherworker—" His hand twisted in a gesture designed to turn aside the evil omen.

"Oh." I did feel the fool. If any of those misfortunes befell Stagiros, the *Gamemeno* was, well, *gamemeno*'d. I rallied as best I could: "Surely you will have another man aboard who can call the wind."

"Surely I will. Surely I do," Tasos said. "But, while many men can work the weather, how many can work it like Stagiros?" He spread his hands, waiting for my answer. I had no answer to give, and I knew it. Tasos' second-best weatherworker wouldn't match some pirate's best. And so . . . he watched the jagged coast. Every time we darted past a headland or the valley where some stream came down to the sea, he muttered and played with worry beads while sweat ran down his face.

So much for honor among thieves. I wondered what a Lokrian Navy cutter would do if it came across the *Gamemeno*'s crew battling it out with cutlasses and crossbows and cantrips and counterspells against pirates. I know what I would have done if I were the skipper of a Lokrian Navy cutter. I would have laughed and closed my eyes and sailed away, hoping they slaughtered each other till not a man survived on either side. The more who fell, the better off the kingdom would be.

But I wasn't a Lokrian Navy cutter captain. I was, Eliphalet help me, a passenger on this miserable Lokrian smuggler. And so, whenever we passed a headland or a little valley, I muttered while sweat ran down my face, too. I had no worry beads, but found I was able to worry quite well without them.

We put in for the night at a village called Skilitsi. I've looked for it since on a map. I've looked for it on several maps, as a matter of fact. As far as mapmakers know, it isn't there. I wonder if the King of Lokris knows anybody lives in Skilitsi, or even that there is such a place. What you don't know about, you can't tax. The folk of Skilitsi struck me as being less than enthusiastic about contributing to their kingdom's general welfare.

If you blink while you're going by, you'll miss the place. That's what the people who live there have in mind. A big rock in the sea and groves of olives and almonds screen it off from the casual eye. If you don't already know where it is, you won't find it. And if you don't, nobody in Skilitsi will care.

Tasos knew it. As soon as we skimmed between that big rock and the mainland, Stagiros let his wind die. The *Gamemeno* glided to a stop. Tasos shouted orders. The anchor splashed into the sea.

Rowboats approached from the shore. Tasos turned to Max and me. "Why don't the two of you go below?" he said pleasantly. "What you don't see, you can't testify to, and no wizard can pull it out of you, either."

It sounded like a polite request. It was a polite order. Tasos had several burly sailors behind him. None of them was as large as I am, let alone Max, but they made up in numbers what they lacked in beef. "I think we'll go below," I said, sounding cheerier than I felt. "Don't you, Max?"

"Just what I always wanted to do," Max agreed, as excited as if he'd got an invitation to his own funeral.

Down to our cabin we went. Belowdecks on the *Gamemeno* left all sorts of things to be desired. The ceilings weren't tall enough for me, let alone poor Max. Several nasty odors filled the air. Some had to do with cooking, others with foul heads and unbathed men. Still others . . . I don't know what all the *Gamemeno* was smuggling, but some of it smelled bad.

Poor Captain Tasos was a busy man. I didn't want to upset him by reminding him that our cabin, while it didn't have much, did boast a porthole. And, since we were on the right side of the ship (oh, fine, the starboard side, which happened to be the correct side, too), we could watch what was going on as well as if we'd stayed on deck. We could, and we did. Poor Captain Tasos.

It was a lot less exciting than one of Ilona's tumbling routines, believe me. Lokrians rowed out from Skilitsi with crates and jugs and barrels. They rowed back with barrels and crates and jugs. I presume they sent the ship *this* and took away *that*, but I couldn't prove it.

As it got darker, we had a harder time seeing what was going on. We would have quit if Tasos hadn't wanted to keep us from watching. And how many times have *you* done something because somebody told you not to?

Oh, more than that. You must have.

For whatever it was worth, we finally got our reward. We saw something more interesting, or at least more unusual, than jugs and barrels and crates. I stared as a bigger boat than most came up to the *Gamemeno*. "Is that what I think it is?" I whispered.

"I don't know. What do you think it is?"

"A coffin."

"Well, it could be," he said cryptically.

And it was. The obscenity and blasphemy from the deck came in eight or ten tongues, and would have fried the beards off both Prophets if they'd been alive to hear it. The oarsmen in that big rowboat added their fair share, too. I wouldn't have been surprised if the corpse sat up and tossed in his hemilepta's worth.

At last, once the shouting died down to aftershock levels, they rigged a block and tackle on deck and hauled the coffin up from the boat. *Thud!* It made a dreadfully final sound when it came down on the planking— right over our heads, by the sound of things.

Max cocked a wary eye at our ceiling, which went on creaking. "If that comes through—" he began.

I shrugged. "If it does, we'll be too flat to worry about it."

"You always did know how to relieve my mind," he said.

We looked out the porthole again, but the coffin proved to be the grand finale. The boat that had brought it took back a load of illegal, immoral, untaxed . . . stuff. It grounded on the beach. The rowers unloaded it and dragged it ashore. No more boats came out.

Max closed the porthole. There were mosquitoes outside. As soon as he closed it, we discovered there were mosquitoes inside, too, but there were more of them outside. "So much for the exciting life of a smuggler," he said. "It's like watching grass dry."

"Or paint grow," I agreed. "What have we got for supper?"

He rummaged through his kit and pulled out what looked like a flexible billy club. "Mutton sausage."

"Better than nothing," I said, giving it the benefit of the doubt.

And it turned out to be quite a bit better than nothing. Say what you will about the Lokrians—and I'm one of their most sincere unadmirers—they do make good sausage: another tradition going back to the golden age of Lakedaimon, if you remember your comic poets.

Full darkness fell, fast as a drunk tumbling down a flight of stairs. Twilight lingers romantically in Schlepsig. The sky goes through every deepening shade of blue and purple toward black. Stars come out one by one. You can count them if you like, and you don't have any trouble keeping up.

Nightfall in Lokris isn't like that. The sun goes down. It gets *dark*, and wastes no time doing it. You look at the sky and you don't see any stars. Ten minutes later, billions and billions of them are up there. Where were they hiding? How did they all come out at once? You can see more of them in Lokris than you can in Schlepsig, too. The air isn't so misty— and, except when they're having a riot, it isn't so smoky, either. But I think our stars are more intriguing. You have to earn them. They aren't just *there*, the way they are in Lokris.

You'd think the moon, seen through a porthole, would fill that round window with its round self. You'd think so, but you'd be wrong. The moon looks so big hanging there in the sky, especially when it's just rising or about to set. But if you hold a kram or a livre out at arm's length be-tween your thumb and forefinger, you can make the moon disappear be-hind it. I was surprised when I found that out. You will be, too. Well, actually, you won't be, because now I've told you, but you would be if I hadn't. Of course, if I hadn't, you wouldn't have tried such a silly thing in the first place, would you?

Up on deck, one of the sailors was—praying? I wished I understood Lokrian. But it might not have mattered here. With the porthole closed, the rhythm of his speech came through better than the actual words. I did think I heard Zibeon's name a few times. That was . . . interesting. "A pious smuggler?" I murmured.

"Probably asking for blind customs inspectors," Max said.

If I were a smuggler—and I have been, on a small scale, a time or three—I would ask for something like that, too. (And if customs inspec-tors aren't blind, silver has been known to weight down their eyelids.) But a prayer like that is a businessman's prayer, not one that comes from the heart or the belly. Somehow, the Lokrian sounded more as if he meant it. I don't know the language, but the tone came through.

When I said so, Max only shrugged. "Maybe he's slept with someone's wife here. Or, since it's Lokris, maybe he's slept with someone's husband. Do that and you'll pray like you mean it." He yawned. "Whatever he's praying for, it's got nothing to do with me. I'm nobody's husband—and nobody's wife, either. What I am is somebody who's about to go to sleep." He yawned again, wider than before.

We got out of our fancy duds, put on our nightshirts, and made ourselves as comfortable as we could in the short, narrow berths. Mine wasn't big enough for me. Max's was much too small for him. Most beds are. He has two choices. He can fold himself up like an inchworm or he can let big chunks of himself part company with the mattress. He twisted and wiggled. After a while, I heard a foot thump on the deck, so I knew he wasn't imitating an inchworm tonight.

Along with being short and narrow, my mattress was lumpy. That was of a piece with everything else I'd seen on the *Gamemeno*—everything except Stagiros, who was in a class by himself. But I didn't want to sleep on the weatherworker, or even with him. My tastes along those lines are boringly normal.

After some little while, I was able to keep my eyes closed without having their lids jump and twitch, the way a child's will when he's pretending to be asleep. Max still wiggled not far away, but I'd heard him do that before. I've fallen asleep in the middle of a barracks hall full of Hassocki soldiers who'd had a supper of beans. After that, one oversized swordswallower with a cough wasn't so much of a much. Before long, I stopped hearing him or anything else.

I don't know how long I'd been asleep when someone knocked on the cabin door. I did my best not to hear that, too; for a moment or two, I turned the noise into a dream about woodpeckers. One of them was pecking on my wooden leg, which would make better sense if I had a wooden leg. Like most circuses, Dooger and Cark's has a wise woman who will take your money and tell you what your dreams mean. Ask yourself this: if she's so wise, what's she doing at Dooger and Cark's? If you really need to find out about your dreams, pay a little more and go to a mage who might actually know.

Then the woodpecker said, "Otto? Wake up, you bloody bonehead!" I didn't think a woodpecker ought to say something like that, even in a dream. Wouldn't an angry woodpecker call me *blockhead* instead?

I opened my eyes. That wasn't a woodpecker looming over me there in the darkness—that was Max, breathing sausage breath into my face. And somebody *was* knocking. I breathed back at him: "Do we ignore that, or do we open it and break something over the stinking whoreson's head?"

"If I could have ignored it, I'd still be sleeping," he said. If *I* could have ignored it, I'd still have had a woodpecker drumming on the wooden leg I don't own. There are worse things, I suppose, but lots more better ones.

With a sigh, I got out of bed and advanced on the door. Some advance—it must have been a good pace and a half. Even on ships a lot fancier than the *Gamemeno* (which is to say, most of them), cabins are cramped. Ours there had more room than a coffin built for two—I had to be thinking about the one that came aboard a few hours earlier—but not much.

Even as I reached for the latch, the knocking stopped. Whoever was on the other side, he *knew* I was reaching. How did he know that? I opened the door, and I found out.

There he stood, in the narrow little passageway. He was perfect—but then, he would be. Ruffled shirt. Cravat. Tailcoat—he might have been about to sit down at the harpsichord. He might have been, but he wasn't, because . . . Bloodless face. Red, glowing eyes. Oh, yes, and the obligatory fangs, too.

Vampire.

I should have known. So should Max. The Nekemte Peninsula has more undead than just about anywhere else. Vlachian vampires. Yagmar vampires (*not* Ilona, a warm-blooded wench if ever there was one). Dacian vampires, including the famous Petru the Piercer. Not so many Lokrian vampires. Lucky us.

Those terrible eyes grabbed me and wouldn't let go. "May I come in?" he asked in some language I could understand—I didn't so much hear his words as *feel* them in the middle of my head. They have to be invited in. They can't cross the threshold unless they are.

"Yes," Max and I breathed together. Under the spell of those glowing eyes, what else could we have said? Nothing at all. A vampire needs an invitation to come in, sure, but that doesn't mean he won't cheat to get one. "Yes," we breathed again.

But the vampire didn't come in. The light in his eyes went out. He gagged and hacked and coughed. If you've ever seen someone who's never smoked before take an enormous puff on a strong cigar, you have some small idea of how the vampire acted. He fled down the corridor as fast as he could go, silent as the ghost of a cat. I wondered if he'd make it back to his coffin or fall over somewhere and lie there till the sun came up the next morning. I knew what I hoped.

I turned to Max at the same time as he was turning to me. We both started to laugh. Up in Schlepsig, we flavor lamb and mutton with mint. I think I said that once before. The Lokrians use garlic. The Lokrians use garlic, lots of garlic, in almost everything. They'd put garlic in apple strudel if they made apple strudel.

"Well," I said, "shall we go back to bed?"

"Just a minute." He rummaged in his wallet, took out some silver coins, and stuck them in the crack between the door and its frame.

"I thought silver kept werewolves away," I said.

"It can't hurt," Max answered. "And how do you know this miserable scow isn't smuggling werewolves, too?"

I scratched my head. He was right. I wouldn't have put smuggling anything at all past Tasos. Just by way of example, he was smuggling the King of Shqiperi and his aide-de-camp into the Land of the Eagle, wasn't he?

Maybe the silver worked. Maybe the vampire had just had a noseful of us. Either way, he didn't bother us again. If he drained the rest of the crew dry—well, we'd have to figure out some other way to get to Shqiperi, that's all.

When we came up on deck the next morning, we were chewing on more sausage—just in case, you might say. Captain Tasos seemed surprised to see us. Then he got a whiff of our breakfast, and he didn't any more. "I trust you had a pleasant night?" he said, a certain gleam in his eye. After the vampire's glowing gaze, Tasos' gleam wasn't anything special.

"You're a trusting soul, then, aren't you?" I pointed to the coffin. "Chain that up. Put roses and garlic on it. We want no more visits in the nighttime."

"He is a paying passenger," Tasos said. "He pays better than you do, in fact—he pays in gold." So maybe there was something to Max's silver coins after all.

Whether there was or not was something I could worry about later. "Whatever he's paying, it's not enough to let him suck the blood out of your live customers."

Tasos stirred, as if he wasn't so sure about that. Whatever he might

have said, though, he didn't. Max was wearing his sword. I wasn't sure
he'd ever sliced anything more dangerous than bread with it, but Tasos
wasn't sure he hadn't. For an overgrown bread knife and theatrical prop,
it was proving mighty persuasive.

"Chain it up till he gets where he's going," I repeated, and pointed to
the coffin again. Then I took a step towards it. "If you don't chain it up, I'll
open it. Why should you care? You've already got his passage money."

Tasos tossed his head, where someone from another kingdom would
have shaken it. "I don't dare open it," he said. "If I did, *they* would know,
and *they* would have their revenge."

He sounded as if vampires were some sort of secret society, like what
they call Our Thing in Torino. He also sounded as if he knew what he
was talking about. We don't have vampires in Schlepsig, except for the
few who've settled there to take advantage of the longer winter nights. We
have werewolves and unicorns and trolls and dwarves and elves and
gnomes and cobolds and all sorts of other wildunlife, but not vampires. I
can't say we feel the lack, either. Even though I've traveled around a good
deal in kingdoms where they don't live, I don't know them the way somebody like Tasos would—he grew up with them, you might say.

"All right. If you won't open it, you won't. But chain it up and ward it,"
I said, adding, "If you don't, and if anything happens to me and my aide-
de-camp, the Shqipetari will find out, and they'll have *their* revenge."

That was inspiration, nothing less. Tasos flinched. Lokrians think
Shqipetari are passionate, faction-ridden feudists, bushwhackers and
bandits and thieves, grifters and liars and cheats—pretty much what the
rest of the world thinks of Lokrians. From everything I saw in Lokris, I'd
say the rest of the world has a point. From everything I saw later in
Shqiperi, I'd say the Lokrians have a point, too.

Max smiled his most sepulchral smile. "Would you rather have your
throat punctured or just slit? Would you rather have your blood drunk or
just spilled?"

"Zibeon!" Tasos muttered. I would have called on Eliphalet myself,
but they're both holy. Holy enough to ward against vampires? Of course,
if you believe enough. But then, if you believe *enough*, almost anything
turns holy.

He shouted for his crew. When they gathered, he harangued them in Lokrian. I don't know just what he said. Whatever it was, it turned the trick. At first, they stared at him as if they couldn't believe their ears. When they decided he meant it, they whooped. They hollered. They danced in a circle around the coffin. They kissed him on his stubbly cheek. Men do that a lot in the Nekemte Peninsula. I think it's to keep the kissee from noticing the kisser is about to stick a knife in his back.

After the sailors finished celebrating, they went to work. I don't know where they found so many chains aboard the *Gamemeno*. Maybe Tasos sold slaves when other business was slow. Maybe someone had peculiar tastes in bed. If so, his lady friend must have been an octopus. Otherwise, he never would have needed so many. Wherever the sailors found them, they used them.

And once they'd used them, they covered the coffin with so many roses and so much garlic, it looked like a collision between a florist's and a Lokrian kitchen. The only thing missing was the olive oil. I'm sure the garlic came from the *Gamemeno*'s galley. The roses? I asked a sailor who spoke some Hassocki.

He looked at me as if I were even dumber than he'd thought, and he'd already pegged me for an idiot. "Thou hast not so much brain as ear-wax, plainly," he said. "We brought them back from Skilitsi yesternight."

They knew what they had on board, all right. I remembered the one sailor praying. Did they tell their passengers? It is to laugh. If we lived, all right. If we didn't, well, Tasos had our fare, too.

Once the coffin was warded, the sailors swarmed into the rigging with higher spirits than I'd ever seen from them. Stagiros stood on the poop deck and whistled up the wind. The sails filled with wind faster than a politician on the stump. The *Gamemeno* left Skilitsi behind so fast, you almost forgot it was ever there. I'm sure the people who lived there were just as happy to keep it forgotten, too.

Off to the west, islands poked out of the sea. Some of them had little towns and fields and olive groves. You could live out your days in a place like that and never go more than ten miles from where you were born. Some people think that's a life. Not me, by Eliphalet's wind-whipped whiskers! Here I was, on a fast ship, heading for my kingdom!

I made the mistake of saying something along those lines to Max.

One of his eyebrows acted as if he'd pulled on a string attached to his hairline. "Here you are, on a sneaking smuggler with a vampire's coffin on the main deck, heading for a place where they'll either assassinate you because you're the king or execute you because you're not."

Some people haven't got the right attitude.

I've tried explaining that to Max. He has an easier time swallowing cold iron than common sense. Arguing one more time seemed pointless. Instead, I reached up as far as I could, draped my arm around his shoulder, and crooned, "And here you are with me."

"Well, someone has to do the worrying." He shook me off like a unicorn whisking away flies.

Some of the islands out there on the blue, blue sea were too small or too dry to keep a town alive. They had goats, and a herdsman or two to keep track of them. You could live out your days in a place like that, too. It would make a hamlet on one of the bigger islands look like Lakedaimon, but you could do it. Not many of your goats would be much smarter than you were.

And some of the islands were just rocks like the one in front of Skilitsi, but farther out to sea. Maybe a tree or bush would find enough soil in a crack to take root. Maybe a pelican or a gull would perch and look out at the sea all around. Maybe the rock would be—a rock, grayish or golden, useless for anything except smashing a ship that didn't see it soon enough in fog or storm.

Then there were the almost-islands, rocks that *would* have been islands if only they'd finished their suppers and drunk their milk when they were young instead of running out to play. They can't quite poke their noses out of the water now, and they resent it. And they get even by using those noses to rip the guts out of ships that try to sail over them.

Thanks to Stagiros, we were going at quite a clip. I hoped Tasos knew exactly where we were. Discovering he didn't might prove—embarrassing. The *Gamemeno* made a couple of small swerves. One was around a place where waves boiled even though you couldn't see anything that would make them do it. The other stretch of sea looked ordinary enough, but he dodged it anyway. We didn't hit anything. I approved of not hitting anything.

The wind of our passage ruffled my hair. I patted it back into place.

As I did, I glanced back toward the coffin. If that wind was making my hair blow, what was it doing to the roses and garlic that helped hold the vampire inside? As a matter of fact, it wasn't doing anything. The sailors had thought of that before I did. They'd stuck the stems and the strung-together cloves through the links of the chain. The wards against the vampire weren't going anywhere at all.

Which I couldn't say about us. The *Gamemeno* was as unsavory a ship as ever soiled the sea, but she didn't waste any time. Whatever Tasos was paying Stagiros, he got his money's worth. We hustled along. We would have hustled faster yet if we hadn't stopped at small islands and in little hidden coves to unload this and take on that. Most of the time, I couldn't tell what this and that were. Once, though, *that* was a pair of veritable Klephts.

Lokrians sing songs about Klephts. They think they're romantic heroes—the ones who've never run into them, that is. *Klepht* means *thief* in Lokrian, which tells you more than you wanted to know about what Lokris is like. These two looked the part. They had fierce, hawklike faces—lines somewhat blurred by bushy beards—and wore big knives in their belts and bandoleers of crossbow quarrels crisscrossing their chests. I didn't care to quarrel with them, with crossbows or without, even if they also had on those silly little skirts Lokrian men wear instead of pants.

They didn't seem to want any part of us, either. That didn't break my heart. Max's sword could have had their cutlery for breakfast and still been hungry for spoons, which probably had a little something—just a little, mind you—to do with their restraint. They edged warily around the vampire's coffin. They knew what it was, and they didn't like it a bit. I wondered what they'd done to need to go somewhere else in such a tearing hurry.

Better not to know, maybe.

We'd just left the little inlet where we picked them up when a lookout screamed most sincerely and pointed out to sea. My gaze followed his finger. I felt like screaming, too. I'd never seen—I'd never imagined—a sea serpent that big.

VI

Now, don't get me wrong. We have sea serpents in the Suebic Gulf, too. But the northern seas, the seas I grew up with, are cold. That stunts the serpents' growth. They'll eat the occasional fisherman, sure, but they hardly ever eat his boat, too.

This one . . . Well, I've spent a lot of time down in southern climes. Who wouldn't, once he finds out it doesn't have to be cold and nasty and miserable half the year? In Schlepsig, most people don't believe snow can come as a surprise. Poor bastards. I've spent a lot of time in southern climes, like I say, and I've crossed the Middle Sea often enough and then some. I know the nice, warm water grows nice, big (well, big—they *aren't* nice) sea serpents. But there's big, and then there's *big*.

And then there was this one.

When it stuck its head out of the water, the tip of its snout was up about as far as the top of the *Gamemeno*'s mainmast. Now, the smuggler wasn't the biggest ship in the world, and that mainmast wasn't one of the tall firs or spruces that do mainmast duty for all the men-of-war in the world. Neverthenonetheless . . . If that much sea serpent was above the water, think how much had to be below to hold it up.

I did, and I got seasick, or near enough.

Tasos turned green as an unripe olive, so I have to believe he was making the same unhappy calculation. He said something to Stagiros. The weatherworker was minding his own business, which was making the *Gamemeno* go as if somebody'd goosed her. I don't even think he noticed the sea serpent till Tasos told him about it.

Then it hissed. That would have got anybody's attention. The lookout screamed again. Can't say I blame him. Not many live people have ever heard that noise. The ones who did hear it mostly didn't stay alive long, anyhow. Take a bronze statue—a heroic bronze statue, twice as tall as a man. Heat it red-hot. Use some special—and very stupid—sorcery to fly it out over the ocean. Drop it in. The sea serpent sounded a lot like that, only more so.

It was, in its own way, a beautiful creature. Its belly was pale yellow, its back a darker greenish gold. Those back scales were softly iridescent, and the sun also sparkled off the seawater that dripped from it. Like most of its kind, it had a crest of long scales—almost feathers, really, as if serpents were somehow related to birds—along the top of its head. That crest was raised, which meant the sea serpent was interested in something. Probably us, worse luck.

How old was a sea serpent that size? When it was young, had it watched Lakedaimonian and Palladian galleys ram one another in the unpronounceable war that ruined both Lokrian city-states and set up the rise of Fyrom? Had it feasted on philosophers, dined on dramatists, snacked on scholars? I had no way of knowing, and neither does anyone else. What I did know was that those eyes, as big as dinner plates or maybe shields, were more knowing than a serpent's eyes had any business being.

Out shot its tongue, long as a pennant. It was *tasting* the air, wondering what sort of dainties it might find. Unfortunately, I had a pretty good notion where the closest available sea-serpent dainties were.

Even more unfortunately, I was one of them.

That enormous head, graceful as a spearpoint and ever so much more deadly, swung towards us. Tasos said something else to Stagiros. No, let me put that down exactly as it happened: Tasos shrieked at the weather-worker. Stagiros said something in return. Tasos shrieked again, even louder. I don't speak Lokrian, but I didn't need to be philosopher, dramatist, or scholar to translate this dialogue.

Make us go faster!

I'm already doing everything I can.

Make us go faster anyway! Lots faster!

If I were Tasos, that's what I would have said to Stagiros, and you can take it to the bank. The weatherworker went right on raising his wind. The *Gamemeno* skimmed along faster than anything I've ever seen on sails. But were sails faster than scales? I had the feeling we were going to find out. I also had the feeling I might not like the answer. And if I didn't like it, I wouldn't like any that came afterwards, either.

The sea serpent's tongue shot out again, long and pink and questing. When it did, I got a glimpse—just a glimpse, mind you—of the serpent's fangs. I could have done without that, really, thank you very much. Max must have got a glimpse, too, for he said, "Nice to know we're not in a little bit of trouble, isn't it?" Max is always so reassuring.

Then the great beast lowered its head so that about half the upthrust neck, maybe more, went back down into the sea. It started swimming after the *Gamemeno*. It started gaining on the *Gamemeno*, too.

As soon as we were sure about that—which didn't take long, curse it—Tasos wasn't the only one shrieking at poor Stagiros. He was one of the best in the world. So what? If he wasn't good enough to keep us ahead of this mother of all sea serpents (which, given its size and likely age, it might have been), he wasn't good enough. Period. Exclamation point, even.

And he wasn't. He did everything he knew how to do, and he knew how to do more than any other weatherworker I've ever seen. The serpent kept on sliding closer anyhow. The effort Stagiros was putting out, he looked on the point of falling over dead. If he did, we'd all die in short order. And if he didn't . . . we'd all die in short order anyway. That was sure how it looked.

The sea serpent's head came up again. Its tongue flicked in and out, in and out. It was tasting dinner before it even got a bite. The two Klephts started to take out their crossbows and load them with bolts from their bandoliers. The sailors persuaded them not to by sitting on their heads. I would have done more than that—I would have cleft them in twain if I had to. The most they could do, I thought, was annoy the sea serpent, which was just what we needed then.

I wondered if it would come up astern of us and snatch Stagiros off the poop deck. That would have left the *Gamemeno* with nothing but the world's wind, of which there wasn't much just then. The serpent could have snacked on the rest of us at its leisure.

But, however many ancient philosophers the sea serpent had digested, it hadn't digested their wisdom. Or maybe its tongue told it that what it wanted most wasn't back at the poop. So it swam alongside us instead of taking us from behind. Perhaps it wasn't a Lokrian sea serpent after all.

Out went that tongue. In. Out. In. They say small serpents can charm birds so they'll just sit still and be swallowed. Watching that tongue almost charmed me. If I'd had any sense, I would have run below. Then the serpent would have had to smash the ship to get me. Not that it couldn't, mind you. Not that it wouldn't. But it would have taken longer.

Those enormous eyes lit with a cold reptilian satisfaction. Fast as a striking serpent—well, yes, exactly that fast—the great head darted forward. That terrible mouth gaped wide, wider, widest. I can testify that sea serpents have never heard of mouthwash.

And the serpent seized . . . the vampire's coffin. Down that maw it went: wooden box, chains, roses, garlic, and all. Garlic! Maybe that was what the titanic tongue tasted on the air. If it was, I owed the sea serpent an apology for thinking it wasn't Lokrian.

I also spent a moment wondering what would happen to the vampire when the serpent's stomach juices ate through the coffin. How much did being undead matter if you were being dissolved? I didn't have the faintest idea, and I'd bet nobody else does, either. Not even the maddest, most intrepid natural philosopher could arrange an experiment like that.

The vampire would know pretty soon. How long it would know was another question—*the* other question.

How long I would be able to go on worrying about it was another question, too. One vampire, even with coffin, chains, and condiments, was only a bonbon to a sea serpent like that. Its tongue did some more flicking. Then its horrible head descended—toward Max.

Maybe he was just the biggest man on the *Gamemeno*'s deck. Or maybe the sea serpent scented the garlic from our mutton sausage. Never having been a sea serpent, I can't say. But that tongue flicked out right in front of Max's face.

He wasn't charmed, and you can take the word in any of its senses. I must have seen him draw his sword half a dozen times since we set out for the Land of the Eagle. He hadn't done anything *but* draw it, not up till now. But a sea serpent is even less inclined to see reason than Dooger and Cark, which is saying something.

When the serpent's tongue shot out again, Max swung the sword. The sailors didn't have time to sit on his head. The blade sliced right through one of those forked tonguetips. Blood spurted. The sea serpent let out a gigantic-sea-serpent-sized hiss of astonishment and pain. What could be worse than an uppity breakfast? Imagine you've bitten down on your roll, all nicely spread with honey—and discovered the hard way that a bee was as interested in the honey as you were.

No, I've never done that, either. I said *imagine*. If you have trouble with that, use some transcendental floss to clean some of the grime from your mind, then try again.

I wondered whether the sea serpent would smash the *Gamemeno* to pieces with its thrashing. It *was* annoyed—yes, just a bit. But, Eliphalet and Zibeon be praised, it didn't. It swam off instead, looking for food less inclined to stand up for its rights.

Max turned to the closest sailor, who was staring at him all goggle-eyed. "May I please have a rag?" Max asked in Hassocki. "I want to clean the blade before the blood makes it rust."

Moving like a man in a trance—and not one caused by the sea serpent—the man handed Max his pocket handkerchief. But Max didn't have the chance to use it, not right away. Captain Tasos had been standing there on deck, as astonished as any of his sailors. Now he suddenly came back to life. He bellowed like a bull that was suddenly made into a steer and folded Max into an embrace that proved the difficulties of bathing at sea. He almost spitted himself on Max's sword, but he didn't notice that. I don't think Max noticed, either, or he might have made the accident real, not potential.

Tasos bubbled and squeaked in Lokrian, which neither one of us understood. It sounds like sticky wine pouring out of a jug, glub glub glub. After a few paragraphs—like most Lokrians, he liked to hear himself talk—the skipper realized his mistake. He switched to Hassocki: "You are heroic! You are magnificent! You should have been born a Lokrian!"

Max's editorial eyebrow said two out of three wasn't bad. I wondered how long it would be, once Captain Tasos had dropped us off at Fushe-Kuqe, before he started claiming *he'd* wounded (or more likely killed) the fearsome sea serpent. If he needed more than ten days, he had more character than I gave him credit for. He *was* a character, but not the kind of character whose chief characteristic is character.

I went back to Stagiros. "You did everything you could," I said quietly in Hassocki. "Everyone knows it."

The weatherworker shrugged. "It would not have been enough," he answered in his fluent Schlepsigian. He was a man of parts, was Stagiros. "Everyone also knows that. Your friend was very brave or very foolish."

I glanced up the deck toward Max. He'd finally managed to disentangle himself from Tasos, with luck without getting his pocket picked in the process. Even the Klephts were congratulating him. This once, in honor of the moment, I gave him the benefit of the doubt.

Lokris' southern peninsula is shaped like a hand or a plane-tree leaf or anything else with a broad base and several projections sticking out from it. A few islands only mildly meddle with the simile. Down and around went the *Gamemeno*. We saw no other sea serpents. Even more to the point, no other sea serpents saw us.

We did see every little cove and inlet along the way, or so it seemed. Something would go off the ship—the Klephts got off at one little inlet. Something would come on. Some silver would stick in Tasos' pockets, I had no doubts.

One thing—no more coffins came aboard. I don't know whether other Lokrian vampires had some sharp (one might even say *pointed*) questions for our intrepid skipper. I would guess not, for they might have found an answer on the order of *Well, look inside a sea serpent* somewhat less than satisfying. But this is only a guess. All I do know is, no vampires bothered me or Max. That we ate garlic whenever we could, that we festooned our cabin door and porthole with it, that we carried a couple of peeled cloves wherever we went—all this could be merely a coincidence. That we were not inclined to take chances . . . is nothing but the truth. And can you blame us?

We rounded the last stubby finger or leaf lobe or whatever you please and started up the east coast of the peninsula. We did all this sailing around, remember, instead of just sailing through the canal. If we'd sailed through the canal, Tasos wouldn't have been able to scatter contraband all over the Lokrian coastline. Max and I wouldn't have had the chance to meet the vampire or the sea serpent. And we wouldn't have run into the pirates, either.

The pirates. I was just coming to them. I really was.

Now, the Mykonian Sea has islands the way a dog has fleas. They're all over everywhere. The Tiberian Sea, between Lokris and Shqiperi and Belagora and the Dual Monarchy on the one hand and Torino on the other, isn't like that. It has islands, yes, but they all cling to the coastline that runs north from Lokris. Hardly any at all on the Torinan side. I have no answer for why that's so. Till I started talking about it, I didn't even know I had a question.

I will say one thing for the islands in the Tiberian Sea. They're *shaggier* than the ones farther west. They haven't had all the trees chopped down, so their mountains have bearded cheeks. Laertes' son came off one of those islands (Aiaia, it was) back in the ancient days—you know, the fellow whose wanderings were an odyssey in themselves. He was a man who could work wood: remember the bed back in his palace, and remember the boat he built with not much more than an axe and an adze.

Some people say he was a pirate, too. To tell you the truth, I wouldn't be surprised. The men who live on those islands nowadays can still work wood with the best of them. And the whoresons are still pirates, too.

Oh, the Lokrian Navy *tries*. Why, there must be three or four sloops and frigates along the east coast of Lokris that do nothing but hunt pirates . . . and go after smugglers and keep Shqipetari and Torinan fishing boats out of Lokrian coastal waters and help Lokrian fishermen who get in trouble and go after sea serpents and do a little fishing themselves (the tunny in those waters are very fine) and run cattle and sheep from the islands to the mainland and survey the rocks around the islands and show the Lokrian flag and look impressive.

So there we were, coming up alongside one of those islands—Aiaia itself, as a matter of fact, and making kind of heavy going of it, because the world's wind lay dead against us. Stagiros was doing everything he could, but when the wind he called up had to fight something not far from a gale, the *Gamemeno* lost a lot of the speed she'd shown up till then.

We might have been the only ship on the Tiberian Sea trying to make headway against the world's wind. Some fishing boats sat more or less in one place, their anchors out to hold them there. Others scudded south, using the wind instead of working against it. If they wanted to go north again, they could either tack into the teeth of the gale—which was even slower than what we were doing—or wait till the weather got better.

Tasos didn't seem altogether displeased. "No one can chase us down," he said. "The Lokrian Navy has no ship that could chase us down." The Lokrian Navy certainly had none in those waters. But saying that the Lokrian Navy couldn't do this or that was like saying a mouse couldn't have built the wonderful buildings on Lakedaimon's Fortress Hill. It was true, but so what?

And Tasos, who had such a fine weatherworker, was spoiled by having him. He'd forgotten there were other ways to win a race than by speed alone. He'd forgotten cheating, as a matter of fact, which is an odd thing to have to say about a smuggler. But then, I could say a lot of odd things about Tasos, most of them much less complimentary than that.

I was up at the *Gamemeno*'s bow, looking ahead toward what would be my kingdom. Oh, I couldn't see Shqiperi yet, but the Lokrian coastline I could see wouldn't be a whole lot different. It would have Lokrians and not Shqipetari living on it, but I couldn't see that from however far out to sea we were.

The winds howled and swirled. I stood right where Stagiros' wizardly wind faded and the world's wind grew strong. They fought each other there, now one having the advantage, now the other, now a small twister forming as neither would give way. I hung on to the rail.

A southbound fishing boat darted past us, the four or five men in her staring at us as if amazed we could move in the opposite direction. One of the fishermen pointed back to the north and shouted something. The world's wind blew his words away. It might almost have been jealous of Stagiros and his skill.

When I looked north, I saw another vessel speeding along with the world's wind. This one was bigger than a fishing boat, though a little smaller than the *Gamemeno*. She seemed to be coming right down on us, swelling alarmingly as she closed.

Tasos shouted at her through cupped hands. He shouted at her through a megaphone. He could have shouted at her with Eliphalet's great voice. The world's wind would have flung his words back in his face all the same. The world's wind didn't like us that day.

He shouted again, this time to his sailors. The rudder and the sails took the *Gamemeno* out of the oncoming ship's path. An instant later, that other ship swerved so we were back in her path again. I thought her skipper must have been a clumsy, bungling oaf.

Even I can be naive.

Tasos, who always infested these waters, should have known better. We should have turned away from the other vessel long since. With the world's wind and Stagiros' working together, we could have run away from anything. But we didn't.

And then, when she was almost within crossbow range of us, that other ship ran up the white flag with the black hand. I don't know how long pirates have been flying that flag. If the black hand would grab them all by the throat and choke them, I'd be a lot happier, and so would every honest sailor in the world. I do know that.

Tasos let out a bleat like a sheep that just found out where mutton comes from. He shouted to his sailors one more time. We couldn't just turn around and run away. That takes time and room, and we had neither. All we could do was twist aside. If once we could get the pirate ship downwind of us, we'd be safe. Her weatherworker wouldn't be able to beat back against the world's wind the way Stagiros could. But she had the weather gage on us, and she wasn't about to let go on us.

We zigged. She zigged with us. We zagged. So did she. Her captain made his not too poor but not too honest living outguessing other skippers. Tasos was a pretty good sailor, at least as long as he had Stagiros with him. Nobody, though, would ever have accused him of being long on brains—and there were good and cogent reasons why nobody would have accused him of it, too.

He did have the sense to send crossbowmen forward and to serve out a variety of lethal hardware to the rest of the sailors. My sword was belowdecks, so for my very own I got an iron rod about three feet long. Not an elegant weapon, but one good for a few fractures here and there. Max was already armed and presumed dangerous.

"Don't swallow anybody else's sword, mind you," I told him.

He made as if to bow. "Let me write that down." Eliphalet pickle me if he didn't pull out a little notebook and do it, too.

Crossbow quarrels started to fly. The pirates opened up on us before they should have. The first few shafts fell in the sea. Then they thunked into our planking. Then one of them thunked into a man. He made the most appalling noises. People aren't made to be pierced by sharp steel points traveling much too fast. It happens all the time, but it really shouldn't. Something should be done.

I'd seen fighting with the Hassocki army. I knew what battle was like even then. Since those days, of course, we've seen the War of the Kingdoms, which made what I'd seen—and the Nekemte Wars, too—seem like playground games by comparison. Maybe that was enough to teach us all a lesson. On the other hand, maybe it wasn't. I wouldn't bet anything I could afford to lose.

We started shooting back. Since we couldn't run away, we bloody well had to fight. Pirates are not nice people. If they took us, they wouldn't invite us aboard for tea. The chivalrous rogues of romance are murderous bastards for real. I cheered like a madman when one of them took a quarrel right between his beady eyes.

Much too soon, they lay right alongside us. Grappling hooks flew out and bit into our rail and our deck, locking the two ships in an unwelcome embrace. Our sailors cut a couple of ropes, but they got shot doing it, too. More hooks stuck fast. Pirates began leaping from their ship to ours. Gangplanks thrust out across the narrow strip of sea between us. More pirates crossed on them. I even wished the Klephts were still on board. The pirates had the same motley assortment of ironmongery as we did, but there were more of them and they looked meaner.

They reckoned without Stagiros.

There, by Eliphalet's windy homilies, was a weatherworker in a million! He turned the gale that had been in the *Gamemeno*'s sails on the pirates. Sails are made to withstand such a storm. Pirates aren't. Some of them went to their knees. Some of them got blown over the side. Since the *Gamemeno* and the pirate ship were smashing together and then pulling apart, in the drink between them was not a good place to be. I heard shrieks, a couple of them abruptly cut off as the ships came together again. I was too busy to waste much pity on the poor uninnocents.

The weatherworker's gale affected his shipmates not a bit. He even remembered to include Max and me in that protection. I brought my iron bar down smartly on the head of a pirate who'd been blown to the deck. He groaned and let go of the cutlass he was carrying. Since he didn't seem to need it any more, I picked it up myself. With it in my right hand and the bar in my left doing duty for a shield, I was a fairly formidable fellow.

Someone's head rolled along the pitching deck. I wasn't sorry to see it didn't belong to anyone I knew. Whoever he was, he was making a mess on the timbers. I would have complained, but I didn't think he was in a mood to listen.

Max examined his blade, which was red all the way to the hilt. "I really will have to clean this before I swallow it again," he said, and then went back to the fight.

That didn't last much longer. The pirates abruptly lost their enthusiasm for it. Instead of pushing forward, all of a sudden they were scrambling to get back aboard their own ship. They pulled the gangplanks away from the *Gamemeno*. They might have feared we would follow them. They cut the lines that bound their ship to ours. In fact, they cut them while a couple of their friends were still on our ship. Those friends didn't stay there long, at least not in any state to complain about the accommodations we offered.

The pirate ship put on a full spread of canvas and sped off to the south before the world's wind. Their weatherworker added whatever he could to it. They wanted to get away from us as fast as they could. We held in our grief at the parting.

Two or three of the pirates on our deck were still writhing and moaning. We put an end to that nonsense in short order. After a few whacks with an iron bar, no one moans any more. We threw the bodies into the sea. There were nine of them, not counting the ones who'd gone overboard. We'd lost two of our own, plus another three wounded.

Tasos scraped my face with his unshaven chin as he kissed me on both cheeks, a pleasantry I could have done without. "Thou art a lion!" he cried in Hassocki. "Thou art an eagle! Thou art a very dragon of bravery and might! My withers are wrung with sorrow that I might have lived my days without the boon of seeing thy valor on display!"

Then he pulled Max down to somewhere close to his level and delivered another set of kisses. He gave Max a set of endearments not the same as mine but cut from the same bolt of fabric.

As Max turned away, he spoke in Schlepsigian: "Well, that was fun." I don't know whether he meant the fight or Tasos' congratulations. Either way, I thought I might have scented a whiff of irony in the air along with the iron stink of blood and the latrine reek of bowels loosed in death.

I went back to the poop deck. Whether Tasos knew it or not, Stagiros was the one who really deserved all the praise he could get. "I thought we were dead men," I said. "And we would have been, too, if not for you."

He shrugged. I got the idea praise made him nervous, which only proved him no ordinary Lokrian. "I did what I could," he said. "I am no swordsman or archer. I used the only weapon I know."

"You saved all of us," I said, and I think that's true. "Whatever Captain Tasos is paying you, it isn't enough." Would I have talked like that to somebody I was paying? I have my doubts, but it wasn't my money.

And quite a bit of it evidently was the weatherworker's. With a smile, he said, "I could buy and sell you." From most Lokrians, that would have been bragging. The way he made it sound, he was sorry it was true, but it was anyhow. He was something special, all right.

"Yes, well, look what you'd have once you did." I noticed I still had the pirate's cutlass in my right fist. I had to do some serious talking to that hand before it would let go. "Want a souvenir?" I asked.

"Thank you, but no." Stagiros tossed his head, the way Lokrians will. I wouldn't have been surprised had he shaken it the way most people would. He was the most cosmopolitan Lokrian I ever met. Yes, a smuggler's weatherworker. And he eyed me the way a natural philosopher will eye a nondescript beetle. "Why on earth are you going to Shqiperi? Why would anyone in his right mind go to Shqiperi?"

I struck a pose. The cutlass came in handy after all. "To become King of the Land of the Eagle," I said grandly.

"The Shqipetari will kill you." He could have been taking lessons from Max, except he didn't sound quite doleful enough.

"I'll have fun till they do," I declared.

He looked at me. He looked through me. He might have been the sensible, staid man of Schlepsig, I the wild, excitable Lokrian. "Madness," he murmured.

I bowed. "But a great madness," I said.

We put in at Vravron the next day. Vravron is the Lokrian port nearest the border to Shqiperi. It has other things wrong with it, too. It isn't one of Tasos' regular stops. He went into the harbor for a couple of reasons—to pick up sailors to replace the men he'd lost and because Max and I asked him to.

If it hadn't been the day after the fight with the pirates, I'm sure this strange fit of gratitude would have worn off. Tasos was not a man much afflicted by such sentiments. But he folded both of us into a sweaty embrace and said, "My valiant ones, I can deny you nothing!" To prove he could deny us nothing, he swigged from a flask of anise-flavored spirits and handed it to me.

I would like to know which foundry copper-plated Tasos' gullet and stomach. I'd give them my business any time—they do good work. My own innards, being mere flesh and blood, commenced to smolder when I poured that poison down them. "Delicious," I wheezed, amazed I hadn't incinerated my vocal cords. I passed Max the flask.

He'd lit a cigar. That alarmed me; I feared he'd turn into a human blowtorch. But he survived and gave the flask back to Tasos. Later I found out he'd held his tongue against the mouth of the flask and hadn't drunk at all. I wish I would have thought of that. It would have saved my plumbing some serious abuse.

When we came into Vravron harbor, customs men started buzzing around the *Gamemeno* like flies around a five days' dead rabbit. Like the flies, they scented a feast. None of them ever came aboard, though, and I never saw Tasos hand out even a hemidemilepta. His hand may have been quicker than my eye, of course.

My eye saw Shqipetari—my subjects, though they knew it not. Most of the longshoremen at Vravron harbor, and all of the sweepers and trash haulers, were men who'd come down from the north after more work, and better, than they could find in their mountains. More work they got. Better? Not likely!

In Schlepsig, quite a few miners and quarrymen and busboys and barbers and the like are Lokrians. They do work few Schlepsigians care to do, and they do it for less money than most Schlepsigians would take. They're convenient, even if hotheads do rant about dirty foreigners.

In this corner of Lokris, the Shqipetari were doing work few Lokrians cared to do, and I had no doubt they were doing it for less money than most Lokrians would take. They were . . . convenient. I don't speak Lokrian, but the looks and the tone of voice the locals gave them said they thought the Shqipetari were a bunch of dirty foreigners.

They stood out. Eliphalet knows that's so. They were tall men, most of them, long and lean—half a head taller than the Lokrians, more or less. Some had faces like falcons, narrow and fierce. Others looked more like horses. They let their mustaches droop down past the corners of their mouths, which made them look like brigands, even if, by some chance, they weren't.

They wore white headwraps—not quite turbans because their hair stuck out in the middle, an odd effect. I found out later that they shaved part or all of the scalp that didn't show, which made them look even odder without the wraps. Their shirts had all started out white, too. Over them they wore short fringed cloaks. Tight black breeches embroidered in red and rawhide sandals completed the outfits.

Well, almost. Shqipetari wouldn't be Shqipetari without weapons. On their home grounds, they festooned themselves with swords— curved and straight—and crossbows and boar spears and pikes and morningstars and whatever other charming tools their imagination and their smiths could come up with. They tricked themselves out with silver chains, too, those who could afford them, so they jingled when they walked. To my mind, that made them seem less bloodthirsty, but they didn't seem to care.

Lokrian law frowned on flaunting murder quite so openly. In Vravron, they were limited to one knife apiece. Some—most—of those knives could have done duty for ancient Aenean shortswords. Their hilts and scabbards were chaised (chased?) with silver. If a Shqipetar was somebody, he wanted you to know it.

They eyed Max and me as we got off the *Gamemeno*. I could flatter myself and say it was my good looks, but more likely it was Max's inches. They were big men, yes, but not many overtopped me and none came close to Max.

"You should have worn your sword," I told him, even if wearing it would have been illegal. "Then they would think you were one of them."

"Just what I always wanted," he said.

Finding out where Vravron's crystallography office was proved a trial. None of the Lokrians we ran into admitted to speaking any language but his own, which did us no good. When the Shqipetari talked among themselves, it sounded as if they were trying to choke to death. No country that calls itself something like Shqiperi can be all good.

But I discovered that some of the men from the mountains knew Hassocki, while others spoke bits and pieces of Vlachian. Since Vlachians border them where Lokrians don't, that wasn't too surprising. Thanks to my stints in the Hassocki army, I had Hassocki and bits and pieces of Vlachian myself. We managed. I spread around a few coins, too, to encourage memories. That also helped, and they didn't have to be very big coins. Shqipetari come to Lokris because they're hungry.

As in Thasos, the Consolidated Crystal office in Vravron was an island of efficiency in a sea of, well, Lokrianity. Max and I got in line to send our message, and the line moved. The clerks weren't sitting around drinking little cups of strong, syrupy-sweet coffee or smoking cigars or gabbing about women or the rowing races or whatever they do for fun in Vravron (they must do *something* there, I suppose). They didn't act all high and mighty, either. If CC gets complaints about its clerks, it gets new clerks, and in a hurry, too. The people who work in those offices know it. It keeps them on their toes.

The clerk we got spoke decent Schlepsigian but better Narbonese, so we used that. I filled out forms and paid the fee, and he took me back to a crystallographer. The sorcerer—like the one in Thasos, he wore a homburg—spoke Schlepsigian at least as well as I do, though his olive skin, broad forehead, large, dark, liquid eyes, and narrow, delicate chin said he was a Lokrian. "To whom are you sending your message?" he asked.

"To Essad Pasha, in Peshkepiia, in Shqiperi," I answered.

His eyebrows were a raven's wings. They fluttered in surprise. "Essad Pasha serves a kingdom at war with this one," he said. He couldn't have been listening to the crystallographer in Thasos. I know that. We danced around the same barn even so. He warned that Lokrian wizards would examine the message. I promised it held no hostile intent. This time, un-like in Thasos, I knew the steps to the dance; I wasn't making them up as I went along. When the mage was satisfied, he poised a pen over a pad and asked, "And the message is?"

"You speak Hassocki?" I asked in that tongue.

"Certainly, sir," he replied, also in Hassocki. I'm good with languages, but he was better. You have to be sharp to work for Consolidated Crystal, even in a place like Vravron. Still in Hassocki, he went on, "Please go ahead."

"Here is the message, then," I said. "'Arriving soon at Fushe-Kuqe. Looking forward. Halim Eddin.'"

Those raven's wings fluttered again. "Well, well," he murmured. I hoped he wouldn't gossip. CC discourages that, and not many people have the nerve to do anything CC discourages. I dared hope, anyhow. I also dared hope that by keeping my message simple I wouldn't make any errors to draw suspicion my way.

He had to use a spell to find the eight-digit number that uniquely identified Essad Pasha's crystal—being a prominent official, the Has-socki commandant in Shqiperi had a personal crystallographer attached to him. The man in Vravron murmured the charm and the number to connect his crystal to that one.

Light flared inside the crystal on the CC man's desk. I got a glimpse of Essad Pasha's crystallographer in the depths of the sphere: a plump Has-socki in a fez. With only one client, he didn't need to dress to impress.

"It is accomplished," my crystallographer said.

"I thank you very much," I told him. "You don't know what you've done for Shqiperi."

"To Shqiperi," Max said. I glared at him, but the crystallographer seemed to like his version better than mine.

h, Fushe-Kuqe! Fushe-Kuqe! Some ancient Aenean poet sang of its beauty all those years ago. I presume he had the advantage of not approaching the place in a smuggler.

Actually, it *is* pretty. It sits in a little sapphire-blue bay punched out of the rim of Shqiperi: the only decent harbor the country has. All around the edge of the bay and running a few miles to either side are beautiful beaches of white and golden sand. The rest of Shqiperi's coast consists of an unappetizing mix of rocks, boulders, crags, cliffs, and out-and-out mountains, leaping straight up from the Tiberian Sea as if their shoelaces were on fire. Some of this terrain is thickly wooded. Most of it is too steep for trees; they would have to grow sideways if they grew at all.

The land rises steeply back of the bay, too, but half a mile to a mile back of it. Fushe-Kuqe runs up from the sea to the ridge line. The ancient Dalmatians—the ancestors of the Shqipetari—first fortified the place, but they did a spotty job of it, so Lokrian freebooters were able to capture it. In due course, the Dalmatians took it back, with the usual massacre to celebrate the change of ownership. The Aeneans took it away from them, and celebrated with a bigger massacre. Each new owner added new fortifications, figuring he would be there forever. *Forever* usually worked out to about a lifetime: over the past thousand years, Fushe-Kuqe has changed hands thirteen times.

When Tasos told that to Max, he said, "How lucky." That left Tasos scratching his head—or maybe he did have dandruff with legs after all.

But the Lokrians don't suffer from triskaidekaphobia, even if the name comes from pieces of classical Lokrian.

By then, Max was wearing the enormous Hassocki captain's uniform he'd got from Manolis in Thasos. I had on the colonel's outfit I'd bought there. Some of Tasos' smugglers looked askance at us. I'd never seen a skance before, but lots of skances were flying around as we came into the harbor. If we hadn't fought the pirates alongside them, if Max hadn't curbed the sea serpent's tongue, we might have gone into the harbor, all right, with rocks tied around our feet. But we had, and so, while the skances flew, they didn't light on us.

Stagiros got us up alongside a wharf with his usual elegance. He was the best thing aboard the *Gamemeno*. If not for him, we likely wouldn't have got to Fushe-Kuqe at all. He looked from Max to me and back again. "Good luck—your Majesty," he said in flawless Hassocki.

"North and south, east and west, may good come to you from every direction," I replied. I had to remember all the time from now on that I was a Hassocki, a follower of the Quadrate God.

What a role!

And what a risk! That started to sink in now, when it was too late to do anything about it. If even once I absentmindedly swore by Eliphalet's whiskers or made the sign of the Two with index and middle fingers, I was a dead man, and so was Max. Stagiros gave me a small bow and an even smaller smile. I'd passed the first tiny test.

Down went the gangplank with a thud. My head would make a thud like that if something went wrong. I glanced over at Max. He was smiling, which is not something you see every day. I wondered if our spirits had got up in the wrong bodies this morning. Me worrying? Max cheerful? The cosmic order of things was definitely out of order.

We stepped onto the pier. My worries fell away like fireballs from a dragon. Maybe, as Stagiros said, it *was* madness. Or maybe I realized it was too late to turn back, and I had to go on. Or maybe those two were one and the same. However it was, I knew I was in the ring again. I had my audience out there. And I had to perform.

"Here comes trouble," Max murmured—in Hassocki. He sounded like his old self, too, but his old self in character.

I saw the trouble as soon as he did. Two Hassocki soldiers—a young
lieutenant with a neat hairline mustache and an older sergeant with an
enormous soup-strainer—walked toward the base of the pier. The lieutenant wore only a ceremonial sword. The sergeant carried a pike, had a
much more businesslike sword and a knife on his belt, and no doubt kept
some other lethal implements secreted here and there about his person.

"Let's *go*," I said to Max, and started down the pier toward them. He
followed a pace behind me and a pace to my left: just where a prince's
aide-de-camp should walk. Yes, he'd thought I was crazy for a lot longer
than Stagiros had. But he wasn't about to give me away. Of course, it was
his neck, too. If they decided to kill me, they weren't what you'd call likely
to leave him alone.

The lieutenant looked down at something in the palm of his left
hand, up toward me, then down at his hand again. I couldn't see what he
had there, but I could make a pretty good guess. If that wasn't another
sorcerous reproduction of the portrait that had run in the *Thasos Chronicle* and started me off on this adventure, then I wasn't Prince Halim
Eddin.

Which I bloody well wasn't. Except I had to be.

That lieutenant looked up at me one more time. I stopped. So did
Max. He stopped breathing, too. "Your Highness?" the lieutenant said,
and Max exhaled again. Now that you mention it, I did, too.

If I was going to do this, I was going to do it to the hilt. I looked down
my nose at him and said, "I *expected* to be met by Essad Pasha himself," in
tones that should have frozen the sun.

The lieutenant was swarthy, but I could see him turn red anyhow. The
look on the sergeant's face said, *I told you so.* It also said, *I wonder how much
trouble we're in.* One thing it didn't say was, *He speaks funny Hassocki.* The
way I sounded seemed to satisfy the lieutenant, too. He bowed to me and
said, "Please excuse us, your Highness. We were ordered to escort you to
him."

We were ordered meant, *It's not our fault.* It was cleverly phrased, so much
so that the sergeant smiled at him, and you don't see an underofficer smiling at an officer every day.

"Oh, *very* well." By the way I said it, I'd been planning to take their heads but I supposed—just barely supposed, mind you—it wasn't worth the mess it would make. The sergeant's smile flickered and blew out. I went on, "Escort us, then."

Bowing again—more deeply this time—the lieutenant said, "Yes, your Highness. Just as you say, your Highness. Please come with us, your Highness." His knees weren't knocking together, but they weren't far from it.

I glanced back at Max. My face said, *I could get used to this.* Without moving a muscle, his face said, *You are used to this, and you'd better remember it.* He's even more annoying than usual when he's right. We followed Essad Pasha's soldiers (*my* soldiers now!) into Fushe-Kuqe.

Our guides stopped at an elegant Torinan-style building next to a temple to the Quadrate God. Torino, of course, is just on the other side of the Tiberian Sea. It's been interested in grabbing Fushe-Kuqe and all of Shqiperi for years. This proves only one thing: the Torinans haven't taken a very good look at the country they say they want. If they had, they wouldn't.

Several grim-faced guards stood outside the arched doorway. They looked ready to shoot anything that moved. If it didn't move, they looked ready to shoot it anyway, just to see if putting a couple of holes in it might get it moving—at which point, they would shoot it again.

When they saw me, they stiffened to attention. They banged their heels together—a Schlepsigian style that's caught on in the Hassocki army. "Your Highness!" they bawled, more or less in unison. That done, they goggled at Max, who towered head and shoulders above the tallest of them. He affected not to notice they existed. They were only soldiers, after all, while *he* was an officer. In his own surly way, he was playing his role to the hilt, too.

I, however, was a prince. I had to notice all my people, even if I knew they were beneath me. "At ease," I told the guards, and they relaxed their brace—about a hair's worth. I turned back to my escorts. "Take me to Essad Pasha."

"Yes, your Highness," they said together. The sergeant opened the door. The lieutenant bowed and gestured. Followed by my aide-de-camp—who had to duck to get under the lintel—I preceded him into

Essad Pasha's headquarters. The sergeant came last, and closed the door behind us. That sort of thing was what soldiers were for.

Stepping lively, the lieutenant got out in front of me and led me down a corridor to an airy aerie that gave a good view of the harbor. "He's *here,* your Excellency!" he said, his voice throbbing with excitement.

"Well, then, he'd better come in here, hadn't he?" a gruff voice answered. If it held any excitement, it held it very close indeed. Max coughed. Max coughs too much for his own good, but I knew what he meant this time—something on the order of, *You won't impress this fellow with your high and mighty manners.*

I didn't see it that way. If anything would impress someone like Essad Pasha, it was a prince acting like a prince. I strode into the office and stood waiting expectantly.

Essad Pasha sat behind a businesslike desk I might have seen in an office in Schlepsig. Two ordinary chairs sat in front of it. But so did piles of fringed and tasseled velvet cushions, for those who preferred to recline Hassocki-style.

Like his aerie, Essad Pasha himself was a mixture of modern East and ancient, unchanging West. He wore a dust-brown Hassocki uniform like my own; his had a major general's two golden stars on each shoulder strap. He was about sixty, and built like a brick. I wouldn't have cared to tangle with him, even if I had twenty years on him. His face was broad and square, with deep lines and a fierce mustache only now going gray. His pouchy, hooded eyes said he'd seen everything and done everything, and most of it hadn't been worth seeing or doing. They said I wasn't worth seeing, either. Max hadn't been far wrong.

By his military grade, Essad Pasha outranked me. But I was of the blood royal—or he thought I was—and he wasn't. He should have treated me the way he thought I deserved. When he just sat there, my blood, royal or not, started to boil. The emotion was ersatz, but it felt real. Would Prince Halim Eddin let an underling disrespect him so? Not likely! If I was Halim Eddin, would I?

"On thy feet, dog and son of a dog!" I roared. "Truly thy mother was a bitch, and thou knowest what that makes thee! Thinkest thou thy head shall not answer for thine accursed insolence?"

Now, Essad Pasha could have been rid of us with a snap of the fingers. All he had to do was say to the lieutenant, *Kill them,* and we were dead men. He could have, but he didn't. It never once crossed his mind. As soon as I started shouting at him, the color drained from his ruddy face. I guess he hadn't counted on getting a king who intended to *be* a king. Truly they say the Hassocki is either at your throat or at your feet.

His chair went over with a crash. He sprang upright, probably moving faster than he had in years. "Your—Your Highness!" he gabbled. "Forgive me, your Highness! North and south, east and west, I meant no harm, I meant no insult. Let the God look into my heart and see if I lie."

"North and south, east and west, Essad Pasha, thou hast been too long in this far land," I said. "Thou hast been a warrior, thou hast been a governor, but *thou art not a king.* Wert thou a king, didst thou purpose becoming a king, wouldst thou have summoned *me?*"

Even though I wasn't flinging direct insults at him any more, I kept on using the second-person intimate, which was insulting all by itself to one who was neither a close friend nor a small child. I did it as if I had the right to do it. And because I did it that way, I won the right to do it.

I turned to Max. "Yildirim!" I said, giving him a Hassocki name on the spur of the moment. Maybe I was thinking of the first ship we rode, for it means *thunderbolt.* "Your sword, Yildirim!"

Out it came, the edge glittering. Once again, it did the trick. "Mercy, your Highness!" Essad Pasha wailed. "I abase myself before you, your Highness!" And may Eliphalet turn his back on me if the old bandit chief didn't, going down first on his knees and then on his belly, bending his head and baring the nape of his neck. "Let your man strike now, by the God, if I mean to do you harm!"

Max took one loud, thumping step forward. "Your Highness?" he inquired, as if to say my will was the only thing in the world holding him back.

Executing the man who'd invited me—or rather, my double—here might have caused talk, especially when it would be for no more reason than that he stood up more slowly than he should have. On the other hand, the Hassocki respected shows of willful fury. *I really* could *get used to this,* I thought.

"Put up, Yildirim," I said with a sigh, and his sword slid back into its sheath. I turned back to Essad Pasha. "Rise," I told him. "You are forgiven—this time. There had better not be another."

When he got to his feet, his face was the color of yogurt. Cold sweat beaded his forehead. He breathed in great, hitching gasps. He was used to putting others in fear; it must have been a long time since anyone turned the tables on him. "Truly—your Highness—is a lion—of righteousness," he got out, a few words at each gasp.

I'd been lyin' every inch of the way to get this far. But righteousness? Brother! "Be so good as to remember it henceforward," I said. I hadn't even been crowned yet, but I felt every inch a king.

I suggested to Essad Pasha that I review the Hassocki soldiers in Fushe-Kuqe. I didn't suggest that I would turn Max loose on him if he said no. I let him figure that out for himself. He was a clever fellow; he could do all kinds of figuring for himself.

Gathering the troops together took a couple of hours. It shouldn't have. Essad Pasha should have had them ready for me as soon as I stepped off the *Gamemeno*. I let him hear about that, too. He went pale again: not quite yogurt color, but about the shade of a man's teeth after he's smoked a pipe for fifty years. As long as I kept him worrying about things like his alleged discourtesy and unpreparedness, he wouldn't think to worry about *me*. I hoped like blazes he wouldn't, anyhow.

While we were waiting, he remarked, "I did not look for your Highness to be a man of such, ah, impetuous spirit."

"Life is full of surprises," I said, while Max suffered a coughing fit of truly epic proportions. What sort of man was the real Halim Eddin? A placid fool, someone Essad Pasha had expected to lead around by the nose? Someone who would reign over Shqiperi while Essad Pasha went right on ruling the Land of the Eagle?

Whatever he'd expected, he'd reckoned without Otto of Schlepsig. And, if Eliphalet and Zibeon were kind, he'd go right on reckoning without me, too.

After what seemed much too long, the lieutenant who'd led me here came back to Essad Pasha's office to report that the men were drawn up in a square not far away. "About time," I muttered, and Essad Pasha squirmed. I gave the lieutenant my fishiest, most carping stare. "Take me there, and be quick about it."

"Y-Y-Yes, Your Highness." The junior officer needed three tries before he got it out. He'd watched his ferocious boss crumble before me, and that was plenty to turn him from rock to sand.

As he led us toward this square, Max bent to murmur in my ear: "Do you know what the demon you're doing?"

"Trust me," I whispered back, which for some reason only set him coughing again.

"I fear your aide-de-camp may be consumptive, your Highness," Essad Pasha said, looking up and up and up at Max.

"Oh, he consumes a good deal, being the size he is, but he's worth it," I answered blandly. Essad Pasha lifted his fez to scratch his head. Confusing him was almost as good as intimidating him.

Row upon row of soldiers in dust-brown uniforms, all stiff and straight, all with eyes front. A bugle blared out a flatulent note. "Salute the illustrious nephew of his Majesty, the Hassockian Atabeg!" Essad Pasha cried. His voice held a certain urgency. *Do a good job, or you'll watch my head bounce in the dirt.* Someone once said, *Nothing so concentrates the mind as the prospect of a six-foot-eight swordsman with an evil-tempered master.* Perhaps I paraphrase, just a little.

"Highness!" the soldiers roared, all together: a great blast of sound.

Not even Halim Eddin could have found anything to complain about there, and so I didn't. I strode forward and started the review. Max started coughing again. But here, for the first time since I got to Fushe-Kuqe, I really did know what I was doing. No, I'd never reviewed troops before. But I'd *been* reviewed, standing in those rigor-mortised ranks. Some of my reviews were less than flattering, too. This is bad in the theater. It's worse in the army. Say what you will of the theater, but it has no dragonish platoon sergeants.

Now things were different. Now I was the one who went through the ranks making sure buttons were shiny and crossbow quarrels sharp. When I stopped in front of one man, I saw the poor fellow's sergeant's neck bulge, almost as if he were a cobra spreading its hood and getting ready to strike. And he would have struck, too, if I'd found anything wrong with the man's gear or person.

But I didn't. All I asked was, "Where are you from, soldier?"

"From outside a little town called Adapzari, Highness," he answered, blinking to find that the likes of me could speak to the likes of him. "You won't have heard of it, I'm sure."

"I know Adapzari," I said, and I did—I'd been stationed there. Even by Hassocki standards, the place is a dreadful hole, and Hassocki standards in such matters are exacting. I didn't say that to this poor youngster. How could I, when he came from there and now found himself stuck in *another* dreadful hole? What I did do was wink and poke him in the ribs and ask, "Did you ever visit the Green Panther?"

His eyes lit up. "North and south, east and west, your Highness, you *do* know Adapzari!" he exclaimed. Then he went on, "I've been by the place, but I was never in it." That didn't surprise me. The Green Panther is the best joyhouse in Adapzari—not that that says much—and you need piasters in your pocket to get past the door. This poor fellow likely wouldn't have had two coppers to rub together before he got sucked into the army.

I clapped him on the back. "When you go home again, you'll have plenty to spend there." Then I turned to that venomous-looking sergeant. "This man is a good soldier, yes?" I hoped he was. He looked too ordinary to be a shirker or a thief, but sometimes looks will let you down.

To my relief, the underofficer nodded. "He is, Highness," he replied, and his neck shrank till it was hardly more than half again as thick as an ordinary mortal's. He wouldn't want to admit he had a shirker or a thief in his squad, either.

"Good. I'm glad to hear it. I'm sure part of the reason is that he has solid men set above him," I said. The sergeant's neck swelled again, but this time from pride rather than fury. I could tell because it didn't turn so red.

Continuing on through the ranks, I stopped and talked with two or three other men. I didn't find anything wrong with any of them. A reviewer who does that kind of thing has a cruel streak in him that I lack. Essad Pasha would have done it in a heartbeat, for sport.

I nodded to him when my inspection was done. "They're fine men," I said. "I'm sure I'll get good use from them."

"Your Highness?" he said doubtfully.

"Good use from them," I repeated. I think Essad Pasha would have scratched his head again if he hadn't been out there in front of the garrison. I looked at the soldiers—yes, at *my* soldiers. Some of them still stared straight ahead at nothing. But others had a gleam in their eye that hadn't been there before. Prince Halim Eddin made a leader they would sooner follow than Essad Pasha.

Yes, I know this is like saying *tastier than an oyster stew that's gone bad*. But think how downcast I would have been if they'd found me *less* inspiring than their current commander!

Essad Pasha sighed. "Well, your Highness, I am glad the soldiers are to your liking," he said. "You may be right—you may get use from them after all. Considering Vlachia to the west, considering Belagora to the north, considering the wild Shqipetari of the mountains . . . Yes, you may indeed."

More slowly than I should have, I realized he hadn't just bought his wrinkles and lines in a shop in Fushe-Kuqe. He'd come by them as honestly as you can, from cares and worries. And he'd had plenty to worry about—and still did, for the Nekemte Wars dragged on here, and Belagoran troops were laying siege to Tremist, up in the north. They actually wanted a chunk of Shqiperi, which made them all but unique among the kingdoms of the earth. Not even the Shqipetari were enthusiastic about Shqiperi, or there wouldn't have been so many of them living in Lokris.

But, such as it was, it was mine, and I aimed to keep it. Soldiers seemed a good start.

Once the review was over, Essad Pasha had his revenge on me. He proved himself a cruel, implacable Hassocki after all. No, he didn't stake me out in the hot sun with trails of honey leading ants to my tender places. He didn't sharpen a stake and stick it up my . . . Since he didn't do that, I won't go into detail about what he might have done. I don't care to dwell on it.

No, his vengeance was subtler, more refined—and more vicious. After the review, Essad Pasha threw me to the scribes.

I wouldn't have thought that particular breed of pest thrived in Shqiperi's rugged, bracing climate. Few Shqipetari can read or write anything, let alone journals. Considering the way (or rather, ways, for there is no one standard school—yet another proof of lack of civilization) they spell their own barbarous jargon, it's a wonder any of them can read or write at all.

But the vermin to whose tender mercies I was now exposed were foreigners embedded on the countryside—rather like ticks, as a matter of fact. Some had come to write stories proving the Hassocki were villains and monsters in the Nekemte Wars, and that the Belagorans, Vlachs, Lokrians, Plovdivians, and even Shqipetari were valiant, righteous heroes. Others—a smaller number—had come to write stories proving that the Belagorans, Vlachs, Lokrians, Plovdivians and Shqipetari were villains and monsters, and that the Hassocki were valiant, righteous heroes. A few freelancers had come to write stories that could go either way, depending on which journal decided to buy them.

A plump Albionese named Bob wore one of the most pathetic excuses for a wig I've ever had the misfortune to see, and on the stage and in the circus I've seen some astonishing specimens. He asked me whether I wasn't ashamed to belong to such a bloodthirsty pack of murderers as the Hassocki. I was glad he gave me so much trouble figuring out which camp he belonged to.

He asked me, of course, in Albionese. The islanders expect everyone to speak their language, and never bother learning anyone else's. Now, I do speak Albionese, but I had no reason to believe Essad Pasha did. I bought a little time by asking Bob to translate his question into Schlepsigian. If a Hassocki will speak any foreign language, that is the one.

But he couldn't, to my not very great surprise. Someone did it for him. "Ah," I said, as if understanding him for the first time. "No, I am proud to be what I am. Any man should be proud of his kingdom. I hope the Shqipetari will be proud of their kingdom once it finally comes into being—and of their king, too."

Once that was translated into Albionese, Bob said, "How can they be proud of their king when you aren't of their people?"

Again, waiting for his words to be turned into Schlepsigian gave me time to think. "Your King of Albion comes from a line that springs from a Schlepsigian principality, doesn't he?" I answered. "I don't hear of people rioting in the streets because of it."

When Bob was made to understand, he exclaimed, "Oh, but that's different," by which he meant, *That's Albion.* He had a point, of sorts. Albionese will put up with a good deal of nonsense that would cause street fighting in Narbonensis, revolution in Tver, and civil war in Lokris.

"May I ask you a question?" I said to him in Schlepsigian. Once he had that rendered into his language, he nodded. His jowls wobbled. So did his wig; he made as if to tug at his hair to settle it back in place. I had to betray a little knowledge of Albionese to ask, "How is it that you have your name? I thought a bob was the float they use in these newfangled privies."

Bob the scribe turned very red. I had the feeling that question would not appear in whichever journal he worked for. His colleagues laughed loud and long. They hunt in packs, scribes do, but you can tell them from wolves because they're the ones who will also turn and devour their own kind.

"How will the new kingdom look toward Torino?" a Torinan scribe asked in Schlepsigian. The two languages are as different as wine and sauerkraut, so his accent was fierce, but he made himself understood, which was more than blundering, blustering Bob could do.

I gave back my blandest smile. "Why, sir, I expect we will look east across the Tiberian Sea, and there it will be."

That got me another laugh. If you can make scribes like you, half your battle is won—more than half, in fact. I learned that early on. They usually write what they feel, not what they think—just as well, since most of them are none too good at thinking anyhow. An evening telling jokes over coffee or brandy—over coffee *and* brandy, usually—will win you more good reviews than a sterling performance.

"But when you look across to Torino, what will you see?" this fellow persisted.

"A neighbor. A good neighbor, I hope," I answered, bland still.

"Shqiperi stands between Vlachia and the sea," a Schlepsigian scribe said, proving he could read a map. "How do you feel about keeping Vlachia from gaining ports?"

Good, I thought. But that might have proved impolitic—a pity, but true. What I did say was, "Shqipetari live in Shqiperi. Vlachs don't." That was mostly true. I added, "Quite a few Shqipetari live in Vlachia, though." That was most definitely true. The province of Polje, in southern Vlachia, holds more Shqipetari than Vlachs.

This is curious, because the province of Polje is the next thing to sacred ground to the Vlachs. There, more than five hundred years ago, the Hassockian Atabeg crushed their army and brought them under Hassocki rule. If he'd slaughtered that army to the last man instead of leaving a few survivors, they would probably still reverence him instead of Eliphalet and Zibeon. Vlachs are peculiar people.

"How do you like being king?" that same scribe asked.

"I'm not king yet—I haven't been crowned. I'm sure Essad Pasha, having kindly invited me here, is making arrangements for that now," I said. Essad Pasha hastily nodded. His jowls wobbled when he did, but not nearly so much as those of Bob the Albionese. I went on, "Besides, if I'd stayed in Vyzance, I never would have become the Hassockian Atabeg. I get to start my own dynasty here."

What was it like for the real Halim Eddin? There he was, in that ancient city, with his father's older brother with a crown on his head. One of his first cousins would have it next. The only thing he would ever have was a mantle of suspicion. He was lucky he still had his father. Quite a few Hassockian Atabegs had massacred their brothers as soon as they claimed the throne. This was called not taking unnecessary chances. Maybe the present Atabeg was milder than some of his predecessors— though from what I knew of the old reptile, I doubted it. Maybe Halim Eddin's father was too much of a rabbit to be dangerous.

Maybe I was spinning stories out of moonshine. I didn't know the real Halim Eddin, and I hoped I never made his acquaintance.

That Schlepsigian scribe was persistent. He must have thought getting each day's trivia down on paper mattered in the bigger scheme of things. We all have our illusions; who could get through life without them? "After you are crowned, what do you intend to do?" he inquired.

"Live happily ever after, and try to see that my subjects do, too," I said.

That got me yet another laugh. Scribes are jaded. They mostly make their living off other people's misfortunes. Someone living a long, quiet, prosperous life . . . Who could get a story out of *that*? But when there's a battle or a flood or a scandal, you can talk about it for days—and then spend more days talking about what you've just talked about. And the wizards in the press room use the laws of similarity and contagion to run off sheets by the tens of thousands, sometimes till they fall over from weariness, and people in the street buy those copies as fast as they can.

I wonder if scribes aren't related to vampires. They suck sorrows the way vampires suck blood. But garlic and roses won't keep them away, and you can never drive a stake through a lying story's heart.

"You will rule a small kingdom in a troubled part of the world," another scribe said—he was looking for disaster even before it happened. "How will you keep your kingdom free?"

"North and south, east and west, the world is full of troubles," I said, and the sorry old world has done nothing to prove me wrong in the years since, however much I wish it would. I also reminded them—and myself—that I followed the Quadrate God. "If troubles come here, I'll do my best to drive them away. The Shqipetari love freedom. They will stand beside me."

Most of the Shqipetari are entirely indifferent to freedom, save perhaps the freedom to plunder their neighbors. The Hassocki had ruled the region by holding the towns and killing anybody who got out of line. Not subtle, maybe, but more effective than any other way that's been tried in those parts. Long ago, the Aeneans found the same recipe. It worked for them, too, for a while.

"Thank you very much, gentlemen," I said. Two thousand years ago, some Aenean Emperor was probably telling his scribes the same thing. No doubt it meant then what it means now. *Go away, you nuisances. You've bothered me long enough.* The Aenean Emperor could have made heads roll if his scribes hadn't listened to him. All at once, I realized I could do the same.

But my pack did go away. Life is full of disappointments. There are, I suppose, bigger ones. I suppose.

Where I watched the scribes go with a certain bloodthirsty regret, Essad Pasha knew nothing but relief as they headed down toward the Consolidated Crystal office. "You handled them very well, your Highness," he said. "Better than I expected, in fact."

"Oh?" I said, and the air around me got ten degrees colder. Maybe fifteen. Up went my left eyebrow. That expression looks like I've practiced it in the mirror. There's a reason for that: I have. I've practiced it for a reason, too: it works. "And *why* is it better than you expected, your Excellency?"

He went pale again. Nice to know he was convinced I meant business. "Me-Me—Meaning no offense," he finally got out. "But they—they are infidels and foreigners, out to trip you up."

He wasn't wrong, though they would have been just as ghoulishly gleeful to trip up a follower of the Two Prophets. I said, "If we Hassocki are not more clever than foreign infidels, the Quadrate God will not smile upon the four corners of our land." By the way the Hassockian Empire has been shrinking for the past 250 years, the Quadrate God hasn't smiled much lately. I forbore from mentioning that.

And Essad Pasha, out here in what had been the remotest corner of the Empire and now would have to sink or swim on its own, nodded till his jowl-wobbling really did rival Bob's. "Every word a truth worthy to be inscribed in letters of gold," he said. When the compliments turn flowery, you know you've got your man just where you want him.

Knowing that, I changed the subject: "When had you planned to hold the coronation ceremony?" Behind me, Max inhaled sharply and started to cough.

Not being acquainted with my comrade (save as someone who almost took his head: a limited and one-sided relationship), Essad Pasha didn't know that meant Max thought I was getting onto thin ice. "Your Highness, I had thought to bring you into Peshkepiia in two or three days' time for the ceremony, with perhaps a dragon hunt in the hills beforehand, if that should please you," he said.

"A dragon hunt would please me well enough," I said—not the smallest understatement of my career. There aren't many places outside the Nekemte Peninsula—and not so many in it, not in these modern times—where you can hunt dragons in the wild. That the dragons are also hunting you adds a certain spice to the sport. But I couldn't let Essad Pasha off easily, and so I asked, "Why the delay?"

Now *he* coughed, with a delicacy Max couldn't have matched. "Please forgive me, your Highness, but it was only yesterday when I learned you were arriving. I confess to not yet having fully recruited the requisite royal harem."

"The—royal harem?" I echoed, and Essad Pasha nodded. A pace behind me and a pace to my left, Max didn't cough, but his breathing picked up. I said, "Well, in that case, your Excellency, I think the small delay may be excused."

Essad Pasha bowed. "You are gracious." His smile had a certain I-don't-know-what about it. Well, actually, I do know what. It was a leer.

Now, harems are right out as far as followers of the Two Prophets go. Eliphalet had only one wife. Zibeon had only one wife. The Goddess is only one Wife. I don't see how the rule could be any plainer than that. Rule or no rule, though, my coreligionists have been doing what they wanted to do and what they thought they could get away with doing for a good many years—or should I say a good many centuries?

If I'd spoken to a prelate, I think I could have got a dispensation. I was, after all, impersonating a personage who followed the Quadrate God. His followers have silly, cumbersome rules of their own, but not about wives. Their only rule there is if they can afford it, they can do it—and do it, and do it, and do it.

To this very day, the Hassockian Atabeg's harem is legendary for the beauty and variety of its inhabitants. Every so often, some madman inflamed by lust will try to sneak in. The Hassocki don't kill such adventurers when they catch them. No, indeed. They let them go—minus a few important bits. Nobody tries to sneak into the harem more than once.

I didn't suppose Essad Pasha could find me that sort of quality in this backwoods excuse for a kingdom. But I did want to make sure he would be diligent. "I look forward to, ah, evaluating the recruits," I said.

"I shall do everything I can to give satisfaction, your Highness. And so will the girls, I assure you." Yes, Essad Pasha definitely leered.

"You lucky bastard," Max hissed when the erstwhile governor of Shqiperi turned away. My mother and father were married. To each other, in fact. Except for that, I wasn't inclined to argue with him.

VIII

Along with a suitable escort, I rode out of Fushe-Kuqe with Max and Essad Pasha the next morning. The Shqipetari in the port seemed remarkably indifferent to their new sovereign's departure. Well, one sweeper did wave as I rode by. I think he waved. He might just have had something in his eye.

The Land of the Eagle has some stunningly majestic scenery. Shqiperi is not a very large kingdom. The landscape is large, though, large enough to dwarf mere mortals and their works. Roads seem nothing more than thin lines drawn across that immensity. Well, the fanciest roads in Shqiperi are narrow, rutted dirt tracks, which has something to do with it. But the fanciest modern Schlepsigian carriageway would seem lost and tiny amongst those mountains.

They rise row on row, tier on tier, climbing halfway up the sky and more. Till their midsections, they are the pale green of meadows and grainfields. Then the dark green of pines and firs takes over, then the gray of bare rock, and then dazzling white snow. That that snow on those jagged peaks reminds one—this one, at least—of a shark's teeth is perhaps better not dwelt upon. I certainly tried not to dwell on it, but I didn't have much luck.

No wonder dragons live in those mountains. The country is made for them. The wonder is that people live there. North and south, east and west, men with crossbows were watching us. I couldn't see them, but I could feel their eyes on the back of my neck.

"You must not be sorry to walk away from rule over a land like this," I remarked to Essad Pasha.

He gave me an odd look. Of course he was sorry to walk away from rule. To his way of thinking, only an idiot wouldn't be. He would cheerfully have thrown me in that group if I hadn't cowed him. After a couple of heartbeats, he took the meaning I'd intended. "Yes, the Shqipetari can be difficult," he said. "They would have stuck more knives in our backs if they weren't so busy stabbing one another."

His wave encompassed that awe-inspiring landscape. Despite the sunfire flash off the jewels in his rings, he made me see the mountains and, here and there in the distance, the villages that perched on them like scabs on a mangy hound. Every house was a fortress, not to ward the men and women from the ravages of the Hassockian Empire—of which there were plenty—but to protect them from their own kind.

Shqiperi is the land of the blood feud. Lokrians have things they call blood feuds. So do Torinans. The Hassocki claim them, too. But they're all amateurs. The Shqipetari, now . . . The Shqipetari mean it.

If someone from your clan has killed someone from my clan, my whole clan has an obligation to kill someone from your clan for the sake of vengeance. It can be—it often is—someone who hasn't the least idea some hotheaded distant cousin of his has landed him in a small-scale war. That doesn't make him any less dead when my clansmate happens to come upon him on a road or lies in wait for him behind a rock. And then, of course, his clan being the most recently injured party, *my* kinsmen go in fear by day or night till one of them lies bleeding—or sometimes two or three.

These feuds go on for years, for generations, for centuries. I wouldn't be surprised if some of them go back to the days before the ancient Aeneans brought the Dalmatians to heel. Conquerors come and conquerors go, but feuds drag on forever.

"I should do something about that," I said.

Essad Pasha laughed out loud. I glowered at him. Max coughed and touched the hilt of his sword. Essad Pasha stopped laughing more abruptly than he'd started. "I crave your pardon, your Highness," he said. "And I wish you good luck."

The blood feud flourishes in Shqiperi to this day. But then, I—alas!—am king there no more. Who knows what a golden age the Land of the Eagle lost in me!

After a couple of hours in the saddle—long enough for me to begin to feel how little riding I'd done lately—Essad Pasha waved again. Blinking against the refulgent glitter of those gemstones, I needed a moment to realize the castle toward which he pointed wasn't one of the many the Shqipetari had built to protect themselves from themselves. This one was of rather better design, and had evidently gone up to protect foreigners from them.

"My shooting box," Essad Pasha said with becoming immodesty. I raised an eyebrow. I waited. Max didn't even have to cough. Essad Pasha made haste to correct himself: "*Your* shooting box, your Highness."

"Thank you," I replied, as if I'd expected nothing less. "I look forward to shooting dragons." Max coughed then. Looking back on it, I suppose he had just a bit of reason for coughing, too. Yes, just a bit.

As those things go, the shooting box was comfortable enough. Despite the Albionese name, it did not have an Albionese cook, for which I thanked the Two Prophets and the Quadrate God impartially. Any kingdom that will boil bacon doesn't deserve to be allowed anywhere near a fire.

Instead of an Albionese, the cook was an elderly Shqipetari woman with, I regret to report, a mustache not much smaller than mine. Her methods had peculiarities of their own. The salad she gave us, with olives and crumbled white cheese, was not much different from what we might have got in Lokris, though the dressing, with pungent wine vinegar and a strong infusion of mint, had a tang I'd never met anywhere else.

After that . . . Well, how do I explain it? Where an Albionese will throw anything this side of his mother into boiling water, a Shqipetar will fling it into bubbling oil. Maybe this has to do with how the two folk fought off besiegers in years gone by. Or maybe the Shqipetari try to imitate the wild dragons of their mountains. I don't know why they do it. No one can doubt that they do it.

It's not all bad. Fried capon, such as we had that night, can be quite tasty. (It can also come dripping enough grease to keep a carriage from squeaking for a year.) Fried beefsteak, on the other hand, is the first step toward making leather, and the less said of fried mutton, the better.

No one will complain of fried potatoes with plenty of salt. The Shqipetari prefer bread made from coarsely ground maize flour to the usual sort made of wheat. They fry that, too, after baking it. The result would ballast a three-masted ship of the line. It stays with a mere mortal for days, if not for weeks.

They fry okra. Having said that, I draw a merciful veil of silence.

Our supper came with a bottle of brandy made from mountain plums and, by the potency, a good helping of mountain lightning, too. Essad Pasha ceremoniously poured glasses of the stuff for himself, Max, and me. I waited to see if he would take care of that the usual way. Followers of the Quadrate God may have as many women as they please, but they aren't supposed to drink. To my mind, this demonstrates the fundamental falsity of their faith. Name me a man with as many women as he thinks he wants who doesn't *need* to drink now and again.

Of course, some who reverence the Quadrate God are no better than they have to be. (I might say the same of some who reverence the Two Prophets. I might, but I won't.) Essad Pasha handled things with catlike aplomb. He crooked the little finger of his right hand like an Albionese taking hold of a teacup. Then he dipped the crooked finger into his glass. He brought up one sparkling drop of brandy on the end of his finger and ceremoniously flicked it away: no, he wouldn't drink that drop. The rest? Well, the rest was between him and the Quadrate God.

You don't always see that ritual. In the lower ranks of the Hassocki army, as in the lower ranks of any army, soldiers drink first and worry— or, more likely, don't worry—about it later. My own pinkie, and Max's, also bent, also dipped. We flicked. We drank.

After the first sip, my eyes crossed. Lightning in a bottle indeed. I eyed the glass respectfully, wondering why the brandy hadn't charred through it.

Max, however, sent Essad Pasha a reproachful stare. "You ought to fire your cellarer," he remarked in his usual sepulchral tones.

"Oh? For what reason, Captain?" Essad Pasha sounded wary.

"Why, for watering the spirits, of course." Max drained his glass without so much as a blink. It was not a small glass. No, not at all. He wasn't pretending here, the way he had with Tasos.

Essad Pasha goggled. Then he tried to do the same thing. He choked. He spluttered. He sprayed brandy down the front of his uniform tunic. Max took it all in stride. Why not? He pours *swords* down his throat, by the Prophets' curly whiskers. Pretending not to notice Essad Pasha's problem, he poured himself another glass and drank that down, too.

I love Max. Whenever I can stand him, I love him.

I also know better than to get into a one-downsmanship contest with him. Aside from his scarred gullet, there's more of him to soak up the spirits than there is of me. There's more of Max than there is of almost anyone. A glance will tell you this. A glance should have told Essad Pasha. But no. Something—perverse pride, I suppose—made him try to drink along.

He did stop spraying spirits down his front. In short order, though, he started spilling them down his front instead. I hoped he would change his tunic before we went hunting the next morning. Any dragonfire within miles would send him up like a torch if he didn't. For that matter, I was glad he didn't choose to smoke.

He tried to tell me something. He raised his right hand, index finger extended as if to make a point. But his eyes glazed over and he started to snore. I wondered what to do with him. He wouldn't be happy if he woke up in the dining room. Then again, after what he'd poured down, he wouldn't be happy no matter where he woke up.

While I was still wondering, three stalwart Shqipetari silently slipped into the room. One took each booted foot; the third dealt with Essad Pasha's forward end. They lugged him away with an ease that bespoke considerable practice. Maybe he didn't need Max for an excuse to drink himself into a stupor.

One of the Shqipetari returned. "If the noble lords will please come with me . . . ?" he said in oddly accented Hassocki.

I had no trouble getting up and walking: I'd been at least moderately moderate. Max ambled down the corridor without eight or twelve

Shqipetari hauling him along, too. We shared a bedchamber. As he was my aide-de-camp and, presumably, bodyguard, I wasn't surprised that the servants at the hunting box had arranged things so. I was surprised they'd found him a bed without a footboard. That saved him the trouble of sleeping curled up or diagonally, which he usually has to do.

"Well, between us, we've put Essad Pasha in his place," I remarked as we undressed for the night.

"Ah, but will he remember in the morning?" Max replied.

"He won't remember anything in the morning," I said. "And what he does remember, he'll want to forget." Max scratched his head at that. After a moment, I scratched my head, too. Not even the (still un-crowned) King of Shqiperi could make meaning appear out of nothing-ness. I could make sleep appear, though. I lay down—and there it was.

Essad Pasha poured down cup after cup of thick, sweet, strong, muddy Hassocki-style coffee. It did wake him up, which only made him more poignantly aware of his state of crapulent decrepitude. His hand shook. He didn't spill coffee on his tunic, though—he had a napkin draped over it this morning.

Max also seemed somewhat the worse for wear, but did manage to eat his—inevitably—fried eggs. I enjoyed mine. Essad Pasha's sat on his plate, staring up at him. The whites of his eyes were almost as yellow as their yokes. He belched softly. Sometimes, among the Hassocki, a belch shows you've enjoyed a meal. Essad Pasha's showed that his insides were as rebellious as the kingdoms of the Nekemte Peninsula.

"North and south, east and west . . ." he began, and belched again. He shuddered. "In any direction, in every direction, I am unwell."

"Perhaps the hair of the dog that bit you," Max said. After a moment, he added, "Perhaps the hair of the dog that bit me, too."

"'Twas no dog bit me—'twas a viper," Essad Pasha said. But then he brightened all the way up to suicidal. "Perhaps the scale of the snake would serve."

He shouted to the servant who'd brought in breakfast, but flinched from the sound of his own voice. More quietly, he put his request to the man. In due course, a bottle and three glasses appeared. After flicking away the ritual drop, Essad Pasha and Max proceeded to have several scales apiece. I drank a bit, too—just to be sociable, you understand, and as a digestive aid.

Essad Pasha's cheeks regained some color. Up till then, he'd looked as if he'd been staked out for vampires. He even toyed with his eggs, though he didn't actually eat much. He said, "Now when we hunt the dragons, I may hope we catch them, and not the other way round." Maybe he really had been suicidal, then. If a dragon caught him, he might not go out in a blaze of glory, but he would certainly make an ash of himself.

After breakfast, he showed us our weapons. No clockwork mechanism on these crossbows—they were hand-cranked, the way they all were till fifty years ago. With these, if we all shot our bolts and missed, it would be the dragon's turn for quite a while after that.

On the other hand, the quarrels we shot would take the quarrel out of a dragon or anything else if they struck home. They were large and stout and heavy: rather like shooting Essad Pasha out of a crossbow, as a matter of fact, though they weren't so blunt.

He sent me a sidelong glance as I picked up my crossbow and rather dubiously stared along it. "Your Highness' marksmanship is renowned all through the Empire," he remarked. "We shall rely on you today."

"Of course we will," Max said. What he didn't say was, *Now look at the mess you've got me into—and yourself, by the way.* His eyebrows and the corners of his mouth were uncommonly eloquent, however.

If you can keep your head while all around you are losing theirs, you probably don't understand the situation. Here I at least thought I did. I'd never shot this particular heavyweight monstrosity, but I did know what to do with a standard military crossbow . . . and the Hassocki Army had taught me. My marksmanship might not have been renowned all through the Empire, but I generally managed to frighten what I aimed at.

Then again, aiming at a dragon frightened me.

Essad Pasha pointed northward. "Do you see, your Highness? Dragons in their courting flight."

By the way they spun and skipped and tumbled through the air, I had taken them for ravens. If they were that much bigger, then they were that much farther away—where *that much* meant *a demon of a lot.* And they *were,* for I saw one of them swoop *behind* a mountain peak. I could make a pretty fair guess about how far away that peak was. That made the dragons even bigger than I'd thought. Oh, joy, as Max would say.

Out tottered a white-mustached Shqipetari shepherd, a man who'd seen a better decade or six, leading a sheep with very little to look forward to. He tied it to an iron stake set securely in the ground, gave it a couple of tender pats on the head, and then cut its throat. Somehow, that spoke volumes to me about the way Shqiperi works.

The shepherd stumped away. The sheep lay there, twitching and bleeding. I suppose things could have been worse. If they hadn't left it out for dragon bait, they probably would have fried its wool and served it up to Max and me as a delicacy of the countryside.

Another Shqipetar came out, this one a good deal younger and sprier. He bowed to me, then to Essad Pasha, and then to Max. That done, he began a chant of a sort I'd run into before. The language was different, but the rhythms were the same as the ones I heard whenever I put to sea. Eliphalet fry me for sheep's wool if he wasn't a weatherworker.

He knew his trade, too. He wasn't as good as Stagiros, but who is? He was plenty good enough to send a strong breeze wafting northward.

Why he was wafting a strong breeze northward, I couldn't have said. Essad Pasha could, and did: "We'd better take cover, your Highness. The dragons will scent blood soon."

"Oh," I said after a pause that, if not pregnant, was certainly out long past its bedtime. Everyone hears stories about how keen dragons' noses are. In the days when knighthood was in flower, knights would have smelled even more like fertilizer than they did anyway if they hadn't bathed before they hunted dragons. Their ladies, no doubt, would have appreciated that more if they'd bathed very often themselves. But foul hide seldom won fierce dragon, as someone probably didn't say.

Still . . . Those dragons fluttering around that peak had to be miles away. Could a weatherworker send the scent of one sheep's blood that far? Now that you mention it, yes. Watching, I could tell exactly when thoughts of courtship ended and thoughts of breakfast began. It was when the dragons started flying straight toward me.

"I really think we ought to take cover, your Highness," Max said, in lieu of screaming, *If we run for our lives now, maybe the dragon will eat the sheep instead of us.*

A lot of what gets called courage is fear of looking like a coward in front of other people. Soldiers mostly don't go forward because they're wild to slaughter the bastards on the other side. They know the bastards on the other side are getting it in the neck from their generals, the same as they are themselves. But they don't want to let their pals down, and they don't want to be *seen* letting their pals down. *Death before embarrassment!* may not sound like an earth-shaking motto, but it's won more battles than *Eliphalet and no quarter!* I ought to know. I'm no braver than I have to be; the proof is, I never had the nerve to run away.

And so, instead of doing what any sensible human being would do with several dragons bearing down on him—which is to say, vacating the premises as fast as ever I could—I hunkered down behind some boulders that would have done fine as cover against crossbowmen but were essentially useless against anything that could flame from above. They call this sport. I have another name for it—several other names, in fact. The mild ones are hotter than dragonfire. They go up from there.

"You have the privilege of the first shot, your Highness," Essad Pasha murmured.

I was proud of myself. All I said was, "Thanks."

One thing did go right in the next few minutes. Between their mountain and ours, the dragons had a disagreement about who would eat the sheep they'd scented. Being dragons, they settled it by fighting. People would have formed committees and alliances and taken much longer to come to the same conclusion: the largest, meanest one got to do what he wanted, while the rest flew off dreaming of being the largest, meanest one the next time they smelled something good to eat.

The winner was an impressive beast, silvery below and a metallic blue-green above. His wings were the wings a bat might have if a bat were the size of a dragon. The size of a big dragon, I should say—this fellow was to dragons as Max is to ordinary mortals. I wished I hadn't thought of it quite that way; it made me feel much too ordinarily mortal myself.

As the dragon drew closer, I got a good look at his red, glowing eyes.

What I saw there was a nasty blend of raw hunger and old sin. I looked over to my left to make sure Essad Pasha hadn't suddenly sprouted wings. But no, there he sprawled beside me. What I saw in *his* eyes was a nasty blend of raw nerves and old sin. We could kill the dragon. Oh, yes. But the dragon could kill us, too. And the closer it got, the more forcefully it reminded me of that.

"Soon, your Highness," Essad Pasha murmured.

Much too soon, I thought, but no help for it. If I didn't try to shoot the great worm, I would be reckoned a coward till I got flamed and eaten—a brief but unpleasant interval. If I shot and missed, I would be reckoned a thumbfingered dunderhead till I got flamed and eaten—a brief interval that also left something to be desired. There was one other possibility— if I could bring it off.

When I popped up from behind the boulders, the wind from the dragon's wings all but knocked me off my feet. He was a weatherworker of sorts himself. He was also wise in the ways of men. He wouldn't have grown to that size without being hunted before.

His head swung toward me. His great jaws fell open. He was going to flame. He was going to, but I squeezed the trigger first.

That cursed crossbow came closer to knocking me off my feet than the dragonwind had. Any crossbow worth the name will kick. You don't shoot a bolt without its pushing back at you. This miserable weapon shot an extra heavy bolt, and shot it especially hard. I felt as if a mule or a Shqipetar or some other stubborn creature with hard feet had booted me in the shoulder.

As I staggered back, Essad Pasha and Max sprang to their feet. They were going to do what they could to keep me breathing so they could call me a thumbfingered dunderhead at their leisure. When I didn't hear their crossbows snap, I thought we were all doomed.

Then Essad Pasha cried, "Well shot, your Highness! Oh, well shot!" He threw himself into my arms and kissed me on both cheeks.

I recovered my balance and tried to recover from Essad Pasha. The dragon was thrashing its life away on the mountainside. It never even got a taste of the sheep. I hadn't seen where my quarrel hit. I still couldn't see where it had hit.

"Right down the throat," Max said, sounding more than suitably impressed. Considering what he knew of right down the throat, I liked his accolade better than Essad Pasha's kisses.

"In my time, I have seen many marvelous things," Essad Pasha said, though his eyes denied it. He went on, "I don't believe I have ever seen anything to match a dragon slain so. People will talk of this for the next hundred years. North and south, east and west, they will."

I'd come to Shqiperi to give people things more interesting to talk about than any mere dragon. Telling Essad Pasha as much, though, struck me as . . . inexpedient. Instead, I waved toward the dragon as if I'd practiced that shot for years and brought it off twice a day in Vyzance. "Let's wait till it stops wiggling, and then we'll see what we've got."

"Just as you say, your Highness, so shall it be." Essad Pasha was eating out of my hand now. A less attractive picture would be hard to imagine. I surreptitiously wiped my palm against my trouser leg.

Waiting for a dragon to die takes almost as much patience as waiting for Dooger and Cark to smile while they pay back wages. I wondered whether the other flying worms would pay us a call while this one perished, but they kept their distance. Maybe the scent of its death agonies reached them and persuaded them they might do well to shop at another meat market.

Slowly, slowly, the fire in the dragon's eyes went out. I hoped the same held true for the fire in its belly. Its blood smoked on the ground. When at last it lay still, I stepped out from behind the sheltering boulders. Essad Pasha and Max followed my lead.

As I walked past one of those smoking patches, I stooped and dipped my finger in the dragon's blood. "What are you doing, your Highness?" Essad Pasha asked, curiously but respectfully.

Max's cough was anything but respectful. Witte is a Schlepsigian grand duchy; he'd grown up on the same legends I had. Who doesn't remember the story of What's-his-name, the fellow they made the opera about, who tasted dragon's blood and could suddenly understand the speech of birds and beasts?

The dragon's blood was burning my finger. "Just—wondering," I told Essad Pasha, who'd grown up on a different set of legends. I brushed my finger against my mouth. The dragon's blood burned my lips and tongue, too. I didn't hear any squeaky or hissy or chirpy voices.

I'll never go to that opera again. A vole or a starling probably hasn't got anything interesting to say anyhow.

"Take a trophy, your Highness," Essad Pasha urged as we walked up to the enormous, twisted corpse. *A trophy?* I wondered. In Leon, they fight bulls. They don't give the bulls swords, so the fights aren't what you'd call even, but they do fight them. And if the human fighter (*the killer*, he's called in Leonese, an uncommonly honest language) does well, they award him the bull's ears and its tail, those being its most useless parts. (I don't know what they give a bull that kills its man—his brains, probably.)

Dragons have no ears. This one did have a tail, of course, but it was about three times as long as Max. I drew my belt knife and worried off one of the metallic blue-green upper scales. It was not quite the size of the hand Essad Pasha was eating out of (I wished that hadn't occurred to me). I held it out to him, saying, "Have a mount set in the back of this. I will wear it over my heart henceforward, in memory of the day." Insults aren't the only place where Hassocki overwrite their dialogue.

He bowed as low as his years and his belly would let him. "It shall be as you say, your Highness," he told me.

I'd heard things like that more often since coming to Shqiperi than in my whole life before then. I knew exactly what that meant. It meant I should have decided to become a king a long time ago.

Instead of feeding the dragon, that sheep gave us supper. Fried mutton again, with fried parsnips to go with it. They didn't fry the wool; I will say that for them. They didn't fry the coffee, either. I wonder why not. Because they hadn't thought of it, I suppose. If a copy of my tale ever gets back to Shqiperi, it may give them ideas.

Just what they need.

We didn't drink so deep as we had the night before. Two debauches like that in a row, and I think Essad Pasha could have donated his liver to medical magecraft. As things were, he kept praising me. "I've never seen a shot like that," he said. "Never, not in all my hunts. Never heard of one

like that, either. North and south, east and west, I don't think anybody's
ever heard of one like that."

I was modest. "Nothing to it," I said.

He choked on his liquid fire. Max almost did, but not quite. But then,
Max has heard me before. Essad Pasha was still getting used to his new
sovereign. "Tomorrow," he said, "we go on to Peshkepiia for your coronation."

"The harem is arranged, then?" I hoped I didn't sound too eager.

"Your Highness, it is," Essad Pasha assured me, "and I apologize again
for the delay. In a way, it's almost a pity. I'd like to see that shot again."

So would I, I thought: one more thing Essad Pasha didn't need to know.

I was getting out of my clothes and into my nightshirt when a
scrawny cat wandered into the bedroom. The shooting box was full of
mice. Several cats ambled through it. If they didn't catch mice, they
didn't eat. They were all on the skinny side, as if to say, *I'd rather be free than
work hard.* Cats are cats, all over the world.

This one gave me a green-eyed stare and said, "Call *you* a king? Ha!
Not likely!"

I heaved a boot at it. Even a cat may look at a king, but the proverb
doesn't say one thing about badmouthing him.

We rode for Peshkepiia, all five syllables of it, the next morning. The
horses didn't have a thing to say. Maybe I'd imagined the snide crack from
the cat the night before. Maybe I had—except I hadn't. I could still feel
the sting of the dragon's blood on my lips and tongue.

When the fellow in the legends heard animals talk, they told him
things he needed to hear. What did *I* get? Some mouse-breathed, mangy
feline with an overblown sense of its own importance. (Is there any other
kind of cat? Give me leave to doubt it.) Just my luck.

If the horses were quiet, Essad Pasha wasn't. He kept going on about
what a splendid coronation it would be and how many diplomats would
be there from the great powers and the powers that wished they were
great. Listening to that was a lot more pleasant than getting the glove
from a cream-stealing tabby.

We rode into a village at midmorning. Essad Pasha shouted to the locals in Hassocki. "Do you speak Shqipetari?" I asked him.

He looked at me as if I'd asked him if he ate with his fingers. No—he looked at me as if I'd asked him if he picked his nose and then ate with his fingers. "Those barbarous gruntings and mooings and fartings? I should hope not!" he said, sounding as insulted as the cat about my becoming king.

Still . . . "If I'm to rule them, I suppose I ought to learn to talk with them in their own language," I said.

"Suit yourself, your Highness. I've ruled them for years, and I never did." Pride clanged in Essad Pasha's voice. "I rule. They are ruled. Let them learn my speech."

These Shqipetari, at least, understood Hassocki and spoke it well enough. One of them led us to the village square. That was a lovely little place, shaded by plum and pear trees, with a fountain laughing in the middle of it and one of the Quadrate God's low, modest shrines off to one side. Men with bushy mustaches and spotless white headscarves sat on backless benches and drank coffee from a shop by the temple—you could smell the roasting beans—and passed the amber mouthpieces of water pipes from one to the next. Unsanitary, yes, but charming.

Our guide found a bench for us. Then he shouted in Shqipetari. A woman fetched us black bread and honey and yogurt with fruit stirred into it (a Hassocki dish originally, now it's popular all through the Nekemte Peninsula) and small cups of Hassocki-style coffee and even smaller cups of brandy distilled from plums and lightning. Nothing fried. I could hardly believe it.

The locals already in the square let us eat in peace, proving they'd never had anything to do with scribes. Only after the woman had taken away the tray on which she'd brought our lunch did one of them approach us. He looked like a bandit who'd done well enough at his trade to retire from it at a fairly early age, and stood waiting with dignity for me to acknowledge him.

I nodded, I hoped politely. "You wish?" I asked.

"You will be king? King of all Shqiperi?" By the way he said it, all Shqiperi might have been a great and grand place, not a couple of wrinkles on the Nekemte Peninsula's hairy backside.

Max coughed. I knew what that meant. The villager, fortunately, didn't. I nodded again. "That's so, yes."

He looked me up and down. His eyes were as hard and shiny and un-winking as a bird of prey's. "By what right should you be king?"

Max coughed again, this time in some alarm. Essad Pasha growled like an angry bear. I held up a hand and murmured to him. He raised an elegantly pruned eyebrow, then reached into his belt pouch and handed me the dragon scale. I held it up so the Shqipetar could see exactly what it was. He still didn't blink, but those hard, dark eyes widened a hair's breadth. "By this right," I told him as I rose from the bench. "And by this right as well." I flipped forward and started walking on my hands.

He hadn't expected that. He said something harsh in his own lan-guage, then went back to Hassocki: "North and south, east and west, why do you do such an undignified thing?"

"To show you I will turn Shqiperi upside down if I have to, to make this kingdom go the way it should." From my own upside-down vantage point, I saw all the men in the square gawking at me. A man who would be king sitting around drinking coffee and brandy was one thing. A man who would be king waving his boots in the air was something else en-tirely.

I bounced to my feet again. This takes a push with the arms and a snap of the legs—and a deal of practice as well, with luck on a soft mat. You *will* fall the first time you try it, and the fifth, and probably the tenth, too. But once you have it down, it's a striking effect. I brushed my dirty palms on my trouser legs.

"You are . . . not an ordinary prince," the Shqipetar said.

"Indeed not." I struck a pose. "I am an extraordinary prince, a much su-perior type." Max coughed again, but I can't for the life of me fathom why. In all the history of the world, has there ever been a prince more extraor-dinary than I?

If I hadn't convinced the Shqipetar, I'd confused him, which often serves just as well. He bowed and withdrew, as one might withdraw from the presence of a large and possibly dangerous animal. I smiled after him. For some reason, that only made him withdraw faster.

In a low voice, Essad Pasha said, "I didn't know you could do that, your Highness."

I smiled at him, too. "Well, your Excellency, now you do," I said. Let him make whatever he pleased of that. He didn't make anything of it, which pleased me.

The prosperous ruffian who'd come up to take my measure sat down with his cronies and started talking. Every so often, he would look over toward me. I always knew when he did, and was never looking in his direction then. There is a knack to keeping an eye on people without letting them know you're doing it. I had the knack. He didn't. The more he talked, the more impressed he seemed. I smiled once more, this time only to myself.

After that, my party rode on toward Peshkepiia, the capital from which I would rule Shqiperi. More than one traveler from Peshkepiia to Fushe-Kuqe, seeing so many armed men riding toward him, took us for a bandit troop and fled. More than one herdsman in the fields and meadows did the same.

That made Essad Pasha smile. "Already fear of your might goes before you, your Highness," he said.

"Only evildoers should fear me," I said, and glared so hard at Max that he didn't let out a peep.

I puzzled Essad Pasha, who said, "But, your Highness, anyone who opposes you is an evildoer by the very nature of things."

Anyone who opposes you is an evildoer—not because I was always right, but because I was always king. No wonder kings get an exaggerated sense of their own importance. *Anyone who opposes you* . . . Yes, I liked that as much as any other king would have.

With the sun setting ahead of us, Essad Pasha pointed to the city its golden rays illuminated. "There is Peshkepiia, your Highness. May your rule be long and glorious."

"May it be so," I answered. At last, at last, I was coming into my own!

IX

Yes, I was coming into my own. And, once I had come into it, I found it was my own . . . dump. Oh, the site is pleasant enough. Peshkepiia sits at the foot of the Dajti Mountains, near the edge of the most fertile plain in Shqiperi. It sits there, yes, rather like something your horse might leave behind.

Peshkepiia may boast ten thousand souls. Then again, it may not: an inauspicious beginning for a town aspiring to be the capital of the free and independent kingdom. To make up for its small size, it is very ugly. Most of the houses are one-story boxes of mud brick. The shops are built of mud brick and sticks and stones and whatever else the proprietor found to throw together and hope it would stand. The goods they sell are every bit as fine as the shops themselves.

The main street—Shqyri Berxholi, it's called—is cobbled, quite badly. When I rode into town with Max and Essad Pasha and my retinue, we splashed through puddles nearly deep enough to drown our horses. A dead cat floated in one of them. Without a word, it said as much to me as that snooty beast back at Essad Pasha's shooting box. And what it said was, *What the demon are you doing here?*

Peshkepiia does boast one four-domed fane to the Quadrate God that is said to be rather fine. I suppose it is. Still, to anyone used to the sky-leaping grandeur of temples dedicated to the Two Prophets, any fane belonging to the Quadrate God will seem . . . well, squashed. I shouldn't complain about this one, though, not when I was crowned in it.

But, as the writers of cliffhanger stories are fond of saying, I anticipate.

When I rode in, Peshkepiia gave me a typical Shqipetari greeting. It yawned. Of course, what it saw was a troop of Hassocki horsemen riding in—only that and nothing more. Hassocki horsemen Peshkepiia was used to. A large fort with thick walls of dun mud brick stood across the square from the Quadrate God's fane. Hassocki sentries paced along the top of the wall.

I've seen sentries pace where pacing is just routine. I've been a sentry on that kind of duty. You might as well be asleep. Even though you walk their beat, anybody could sneak past you. Not these fellows. They were on their toes. They knew that for half a counterfeit copper some Shqipetar would knock them over the head and steal everything they owned, right down to their bootlaces.

If Essad Pasha thought he was going to stow me in that fortress till he plopped a crown on my head, he would have to do some fresh thinking. I'd spent more time in Hassocki fortresses than I ever wanted to. Amazing what a hungry man will do to keep eating, isn't it?

But I was spared that quarrel, anyhow. He took me to the Metropolis, purportedly a hostel. In any town in Schlepsig, the Municipal Board of Health would close the place at once. In Thasos or Lakedaimon, it would be a dreadful dump. In Peshkepiia, it's the fanciest place in town. For all I know, it might be the only place in town.

"You will want to make the acquaintance of the diplomatic community, eh, your Highness?" Essad Pasha said.

I was surprised he thought I would want to do any such thing. I was even more surprised to learn there *was* a diplomatic community in Peshkepiia. Service in Shqiperi has to be the diplomatic world's equivalent of performing in Dooger and Cark's Traveling Emporium of Marvels. Since I'd been doing exactly that, I decided these so-called diplomats deserved me. After I met them, I wondered what I'd done to deserve them. But, again, I anticipate.

At the time, all I said was, "I'd be happy to, your Excellency." As happy as a blizzard is black—you can use that proverb several ways.

Max looked back over his shoulder. "By—the four directions"—a hasty save; he must have barely swallowed something like, *By Eliphalet's beard*—"we've been followed."

I looked back over my shoulder, too, with a certain amount of apprehension. There have been times in my life when hearing a sentence like that would send me diving headlong out the nearest window. There have been times when hearing a sentence like that *did* send me diving out a window—and a good thing, too. I needed a moment to realize nobody in Shqiperi knew me well enough to follow me for reasons like that. It had to be something much less important.

It was the pack of scribes from Fushe-Kuqe, which proved me right.

Bob the Albionese called out, "How does it feel, now that the crown of Shqiperi is about to descend on your head?" I'd never heard anyone this side of Max make a coronation sound so much like an execution. Bob called out the question in Albionese, forgetting I was pretending not to speak that language.

Fortunately, I didn't forget I was pretending. "What does he say?" I asked in Schlepsigian. "Maybe I will be able to understand him better once he gets his hair on straight."

The other journalistic jackals smiled. Some of them snickered. A man with an ill-fitting toupee should not ride hard. Beneath that disarrayed mop of improbably black hair gleamed a wide expanse of improbably pink scalp. Bob himself was blissfully unaware he'd come undone, which only made it sweeter. I had the feeling Bob was blissfully unaware of quite a few things.

Someone translated his foolish question into Schlepsigian, which I admitted to speaking—I spoke it like a native, in fact. It didn't sound any less foolish than it had before. "It feels good," I told him. "I wouldn't have come to Shqiperi if I didn't want to go through with this coronation ceremony."

That should have been obvious. But nothing is obvious to scribes. If things were obvious to them, they would have chosen a different line of work.

When my reply was rendered into Albionese, Bob asked (still in that language), "What will you do after you are coronated?"

Yes, he said that, in his own allegedly native tongue. It was, I suppose, logical, as scribes reckon logic. What happens at a coronation ceremony? Why, someone is coronated, of course. Someone is, I should say, if you don't bother to think before you open your mouth.

However much I felt like crowning Bob—Albionese can be a noble tongue when spoken well—I couldn't even react till somebody turned his foolishness into Schlepsigian. The translation actually made sense. Any time a translation improves things, you have a pretty good notion how bad the original is.

"What will I do? The best I can," I answered; I wasn't quite so foolish as Bob, but I did seem to be making an effort.

"What will your policy be toward Vlachia and Belagora?" another scribe asked.

I looked out at the swarm of them. "Why are you asking me the same questions you asked me in Fushe-Kuqe?"

"Because you're in Peshkepiia now," they chorused. The frightening thing was, they meant it.

"Well, I hope to be in the bathtub soon," I said. "I probably won't change my mind between now and then, but I promise you'll be the first to know if I do."

Essad Pasha smiled; he enjoyed irony, especially when the sharp iron in it wasn't piercing him. Max coughed, which could have meant anything. And the scribes, both Prophets pray for them, wrote it down.

"To the bathtub," I told Essad Pasha.

"If the place has one," Max said.

There was a cheery thought. "We'll find out," I said.

We found out. The Metropolis didn't have a bathtub. The Metropolis, for that matter, didn't even have a lobby. When we walked inside, we walked into the dining room—and into what seemed like a street fight. Waiters were screaming at one another in Shqipetari. When people start screaming in Shqipetari, you always have the feeling knives will come out any minute. Most of the time, you're right.

A fat man with an enormous mustache was screaming at a customer in Narbonese. The customer was screaming back in Schlepsigian. That by itself might have been enough to make knives come out. Narbonensis keeps trying to strangle Schlepsig's legitimate political and territorial aspirations. Any good Schlepsigian patriot will tell you the same. Ignore Narbonese fanatics' lies.

A little farther back, behind a low counter that could double as a breastwork, the cooks were screaming, too. They already had knives out. They also had serving forks big enough to skewer Max, red-hot frying pans full of sizzling oil, and, if all else failed, burning brands from their cookfires. I rather hoped they would start throwing those around. Burning down the Metropolis would have been the best thing that could happen to it.

For some little while, everyone was so busy shrieking at everyone else, nobody bothered to notice us. I began to feel affronted—when would we get our fair share of abuse? Well, we didn't have long to wait. The fat man must have got tired of screaming in Narbonese, for he came over to us and started screaming at me in Hassocki: "Who art thou, who pollutest the peace with thy presence?"

"I am thy king, thou roasted ox with a pudding in thy belly!" I roared into his startled face. "Down on thy knees, wretch, and see if thou hast the strength to rise again thereafter."

He *did* go down on his knees, and got up brushing at his breeches. Among the other amenities the Metropolis lacked was any flooring fancier than rammed earth. When he arose, he was a different man: one who might possibly know something about keeping a hostel. "Oh, yeah— heard you were coming," he said, his voice casual if still much too loud. "I'm Hoxha. I run this joint."

Somebody yelled at his broad back in Torinan. He answered hotly in the same tongue. By all appearances, a hosteler in Peshkepiia must be able to revile anyone in any language at any time. In that respect, at least, Hoxha seemed perfectly suited to his job.

"Could I trouble you to take me to my room, please, and to get me some hot water for washing?" I asked. I didn't bother inquiring if the Metropolis boasted running water. The smell of sewage in Peshkepiia told me the only running water in town lived in the belly of a running man.

Hoxha went right on yelling abuse in Torinan. I might have disappeared. Something told me politeness won few friends in Shqiperi.

Very well, then: the direct approach. I grabbed him by the shoulder and spun him back toward me. "Thou poxed and scrofulous knave!" I screamed at him from a distance of perhaps two inches. "Thou unlicked whelp of a rabid jackal bitch! A room! Hot water! Or thy head answers for it!"

"All right already," he said, as if I'd asked him the way I had the first time. Then he yelled, "Enver!" Enver looked like Hoxha back in the days when Hoxha was half as old and half as wide. Hoxha crackled out something in Shqipetari. Since I don't speak Shqipetari, I can't prove it was inflammatory, but I wouldn't have wanted anybody saying anything that sounded like that to me.

Enver took it in stride. He'd surely heard worse. "You come with me please, your Highness," he said in passable Hassocki.

Before I could, the Schlepsigian gentleman who'd been shouting at Hoxha came over to me. So did another man, a dapper, clean-shaven fellow with a hairline black mustache: surely a Narbonese. They eyed each other with perfect mutual loathing. The Narbonese spoke first; Narbonese, in my experience, generally speak first. In nasally accented Hassocki, he said, "Your Highness, I am Sous-vicomte Jean-Jacques-Pierre-Roland." He had more names and titles than ruffles on his shirt, which is saying something. "I have the distinct honor and high privilege to be the Kingdom of Narbonensis' commissioner in Shqiperi. I look forward with great eagerness to your coronation."

Of course he did. There would be a feast afterwards, to which he would be invited. And he would be able to write a report that said something besides, *Sat here today gathering dust again. Please let me come home! Whatever I did, I promise not to do it again—or if I do, I promise not to get caught.*

I gave him my second-best bow. "Honored to meet you, your Excellency." I extended my hand. He took it. A corpse has a limper handclasp, but not much.

When Jean-Jacques-Pierre-Roland started to say something more (as Narbonese will, and will, and will), the Schlepsigian who'd been waiting there with exemplary patience got leave to speak with an expedient elbow to the pit of the sous-vicomte's stomach. Clicking his heels, he said, "Hail victory! I am told you speak Schlepsigian, your Highness," in his own language, which also happened to be mine.

I nodded. "I do," I said.

"Good. Then we will continue to use it," he declared, with the decisiveness typical of our countrymen. "I am Untergraf Horst-Gustav of Wolfram, the mighty King of Schlepsig's representative to this . . . place. I present myself." He bowed stiffly from the waist and clicked his heels again.

"Honored, Your Excellency," I said. With Schlepsigian exuberance, Horst-Gustav tried to crush my hand.

"You will please note, Your Highness, that the Schlepsigian son of a sow is too ignorant to speak Hassocki," Jean-Pierre-Jacques-Roland said. "You will also notice that the mighty King of Schlepsig did not think it worthwhile to send a man here who understood either Hassocki or Shqipetari." To show he spoke the latter, he said something to Hoxha. I wouldn't have wanted anyone saying anything that sounded like that to me. By the gesture the gracious hosteler used, he didn't want anyone saying it to him, either.

Untergraf Horst-Gustav's scarred face reddened as the Narbonese and I conversed in a language he couldn't follow—the sous-vicomte was right about that. "We must make alliance, Schlepsig and Shqiperi," he burst out in Schlepsigian. "Each of our kingdoms will gain room to live and will take its natural place in the sun."

"When a Schlepsigian says he will take his natural place in the sun, he means he will take yours, too, and then blame you for mislaying it." Jean-Jacques-Pierre-Roland wasn't shy about slandering my birth-kingdom.

Horst-Gustav looked more and more worried that all this talk in what he thought was my native tongue would seduce me. Had it really been my native tongue, he might even have been right. "Narbonensis is Vlachia's patron!" he burst out. "The Vlachs in Vlachia and Belagora oppress Shqipetari every chance they get. You can never trust Narbonensis—never!"

Jean-Jacques-Pierre-Roland yawned. "This man does not speak. He merely breaks wind with his mouth."

The King of Schlepsig's representative really didn't know any Hassocki, or he would have broken the Narbonese commissioner in half. "I should like to rest and to bathe," I said. "Matters of state can wait until I wear the crown. Enver, please take me to my room." Hoxha's probable son seemed not to hear me. "*Enver!*" I shrieked, and that got his notice.

Another man came into the dining room at the same time as Max and

I were leaving. He had slicked-back hair, a mustache waxed into spikes, and a shirtfront covered with enough medals to make a pretty fair set of scalemail. As soon as I saw that blinding refulgence, I knew he had to come from the Dual Monarchy. They pin a medal for steadfastness on you if you get out of bed on time three days running, a medal for valor on you if you swat a fly, and a medal for heroism on you if you cut yourself shaving.

What with all the brasswork and glass paste and ribbons on the fellow's chest, I almost didn't notice that he had the coldest gray eyes I've ever seen. He looked at me as if he'd just found me on the sole of his patent leather boot: yes, a man of the Dual Monarchy, sure as sure.

"Take no notice of Count Rappaport, your Highness," Essad Pasha said. "You may rest assured no one else does."

But that wasn't quite true. When Count Rappaport shouted at Hoxha, he, like Jean-Jacques-Pierre-Roland, shouted at him in Shqipetari. And the hosteler, though he shouted back, didn't scream back, which, I thought, betokened a certain unusual respect.

"Your room, your Highness," Enver said after we'd walked down the hall a bit.

It had a door with enough bars and locks and bolts to keep out a horde of invading Kalmuks. Of course, there were no Kalmuks for several hundred miles; they've finally been bundled back onto the steppes of Tver, and a good thing, too, says I. Whether the door would keep out your average, ordinary, everyday burglar was liable to be a different question.

Enver had enough keys on his belt to make a pretty fair pianoforte. He used six or eight of them, and had another in his hand when the door swung open, seemingly of its own accord. He sidestepped smartly so it didn't clout him in the head, and turned the sidestep into a gesture of invitation. Enver would go far, probably with the gendarmerie in hot pursuit.

Before stepping in, I held out my hand. He set those six or eight keys in my hand. When Max coughed and dropped his own large hand to the hilt of his sword, Enver added the key he'd been about to use. That struck me as a good idea. You never could tell.

Oh, yes. The room. Well, it had that door, a window with stout iron bars across it, four walls, and a ceiling. It also had the same rammed-earth floor as the dining room, though a profusion of brightly patterned Hassocki rugs and cushions covered most of it. Hoxha no doubt saved on furniture that way. Since I was playing a Hassocki-style prince, however, I could scarcely object to Hassocki-style quarters.

The only non-Hassocki article in plain sight was the homely thunder-mug in one corner. That, like most such from Caledonia to Vyzance and beyond, was of Albionese manufacture. One family has made what must be a sizable fortune from our earthiest needs, and tied its name to them forever. Or haven't you used a Chambers pot any time lately?

"I hope all is well." Enver turned to go.

"Hot water and towels," I said. When he took a step away from me without replying, I seized an arm to prevent his escape and bellowed in his ear: "*Hot water and towels!*" I was learning.

"Just as you say, your Highness," he promised, and I let him go. He took it in good part. That is simply how people do business in Peshkepiia. Imagine the most charming characteristics of Lokrians and Torinans blended together. Now make everyone carry knives—and swords, and crossbows—and revel in using them.

Now multiply by a dozen or two. You commence to have the beginning of a start of an inkling of a notion of what Shqiperi is like. My very own kingdom!

"I shall leave you to your own devices here for the time being, your Highness," Essad Pasha said. "Towards evening, I shall escort you to the fortress for a reception, and the coronation ceremony should be tomorrow."

It had better be tomorrow, I thought. But the best way to hatch anxiety in others is to show you feel it yourself. Ask a lion-tamer if you don't believe me, not that you're likely to be able to ask a lion-tamer who let his beasts know he was nervous. I inclined my head to Essad Pasha: regally, I hoped. "Until evening, then, your Excellency," I said.

Essad bowed and took his leave. A moment later, two elderly attendants came into the room. One carried an enormous cotton Hassocki towel—large enough for an ancient Aenean to have wrapped himself in it for a mantle. The other bore a tiny basin of water ever so slightly warmer than its surroundings.

"More water. Hotter water," I told him in Hassocki. He looked blank. I tried Schlepsigian. Nothing. I didn't want to admit to speaking any other tongues, and the attendant probably wouldn't, either. So I turned to Max and said, "Captain Yildirim?"

By Eliphalet's holy toenails, the sweet *wheep!* of Max's sword leaving its scabbard was a sound I was coming to know and trust, a sound that promised all in the world would soon be made right. The world is sometimes a peculiar place, I grant. Had Max not been the putative aide-de-camp to a putative sovereign and crowned head, that *wheep!* would have been the sound of a man about to be arrested for assault with intent to maim. But things are as they are, not as they might be, so I smiled when the sword sprang free. I felt confident good things were about to happen, and they did.

"Thou!" Max snarled at the water-bearer. "Thou shalt fetch us more of thy stock in trade, and quickly, lest we use it to seethe thy worthless bones for stew!" He rounded on the other gray-mustached lout, the one with the towel. "Thy partner in sloth shall be hostage against thy speedy return."

"'Twill do you no good, for he likes me not," the towel-bearer said, apparently despairing of his life.

"Thou speakest our tongue!" I exclaimed. The towel-bearer bit his lip in shame and mortification; this was something he should never have admitted, yet fear of death unmans the best of us. I went on, "Put our words into Shqipetari, then. Tell thine accomplice and partner in crime what we require of him."

He spoke in Shqipetari. The water-bearer replied volubly, and with considerable warmth. Giving a guest in the hostel what he actually wanted and required must have violated some basic Shqipetari commandment. Sometimes, though, there is no help for a situation. With a sigh that spoke volumes about the abomination he was committing, the water-bearer withdrew, to return only a little more slowly than he should have with only a little less water than we needed, water only a little less hot than it might have been.

Having done so, he hung about with an expectant look on his face. "How now?" I inquired, hoping against hope that . . .

But no. "My tip?" he said in perfectly intelligible Hassocki.

"Oh, of course," I told him, and turned to Max. "Captain Yildirim, if you would be so kind . . . ?"

The water-bearer left in some haste after that, so he didn't get the tip of Max's sword after all. Too bad. Not even a king, I discovered, can have everything he wants all the time: in the confusion, the towel-bearer also made good his escape.

"Well," I said, "let's wash." And we did.

Evening approached. Someone knocked on the door. When I opened it, Essad Pasha stood in the hallway, his uniform almost gaudy enough to have come from the Dual Monarchy. "Your Highness." He gave me a most proper bow.

"Your Excellency." I returned it, not quite so deeply.

"I hear from the good Hoxha that you have shown yourself to be every bit as, ah, masterful here as you, ah, did in Fushe-Kuqe," he said.

"The good Hoxha?" I raised an eyebrow. "The only man by that name I know is the villain who runs this hostel."

Essad Pasha wheezed laughter. "North and south, east and west, you will find worse," he said, which was probably true. "Will you accompany me to the reception in your honor?"

"I wouldn't miss it," I replied. The last reception in my honor I remembered was arranged by the father of a nicely curved little blond girl I'd been seeing. That one involved a horsewhip, among other tokens of his esteem. I hoped this occasion would prove more, ah, festive.

When we first left the Metropolis, I must confess I wondered. In Peshkepiia, evening is the time when the flies go in and the mosquitoes come out. Now, I have met a good many mosquitoes in a good many miserable places. Shqipetari mosquitoes, however, are in a class by themselves. I think some of their grandmothers must have cavorted with the dragons of the mountain peaks. If they didn't breathe fire when they bit, it wasn't from lack of effort.

Max must have been thinking the same thing I was—rather an alarming notion most of the time—for he said, "I wish I had a teeny-tiny crossbow." No sooner were the words out of his mouth than he slapped at the back of his neck.

I did some slapping of my own, then wiped the palm of my hand on my trouser leg. "It wouldn't help," I said mournfully. "They can bite faster than you can reload." The buzzes and whines all around us were nearly as frightening as those from near misses by crossbow bolts.

Essad Pasha stolidly stumped along ahead of us. The mosquitoes didn't seem to bother him at all. At the time, I put this down to professional courtesy. Now I wonder if the odor of camphor that wafted from him might not have had something to do with it.

Most Shqipetari were off the streets and out of the square. Whatever their flaws, they had sense enough to stay behind netting after it got dark. As for me, I'd set out from the hostel a prince, but I wondered if I'd get to the fortress as anything more than a perambulating lump of raw, bloody meat.

Torches blazed by the entrance. Hassocki sentries came to stiff attention as we approached. "Your Excellency!" they called to Essad Pasha. "Your Highness!" they called to me. They didn't call anything to Max, but their staring eyes took his measure—and quite a lot of it there was to take, too. As befit a prince's aide-de-camp, he looked through them rather than at them.

They smelled of camphor, too. That might explain how they could stand out there without being reduced to boots and uniforms by the time the morning came. Something had to. Otherwise Essad Pasha would have used up an uncommon number of sentries, enough for the duty to have become even less popular than it usually is.

"This way, your Highness," Essad Pasha said, pointing toward the only brightly lit building inside the fortress. I think—I hope—I would have figured out all by myself that that was where the reception would take place, but Essad Pasha counted on no man's intelligence but his own.

We passed through seven veils on our way into the reception hall. Some mosquitoes passed through them with us, but not too many. Inside, people could mostly talk without leaping into the air with a curse or rubbing their ears as if those had begun to ring. Mostly.

"I have the high honor and distinct privilege," Essad Pasha said in a booming voice, "of presenting his Highness, Prince Halim Eddin of the Hassockian Empire, soon to become his Majesty, King Halim Eddin of Shqiperi. Long may he reign!"

I took a bow. I don't know how else to describe it. Everyone applauded—well, almost everyone. Count Rappaport sent me another of his cold gray stares. The Dual Monarchy does like to dress its functionaries in comic-opera uniforms. They often have comic-opera manners, too, bowing and smirking till you're tempted to think they couldn't possibly conceal a working brain anywhere about their person. This is a mistake, as the other Powers have often found to their sorrow.

With so many people cheering me, though, I could afford to ignore the iron-faced count—or so I thought, anyhow. Afford it or not, ignore him I did. And so did Essad Pasha, who waved for the small band in one corner of the room to strike up a sprightly tune.

Over the years, I've grown used to Hassocki music. To those accustomed to the styles of Schlepsig and Torino—or even to those of Narbonensis and Albion—Hassocki music sounds like what happens when you throw two cats, a chicken with a head cold, and a small, yappy dog into a sack, tumble the sack down a flight of stairs, and then set it on fire. As a matter of fact, it sounds that way to me, too. But I've learned to distinguish the notes each tormented animal—er, musician—makes, if not always to appreciate them.

This, however, was Hassocki music as played by Shqipetari—I suppose in honor of my impending coronation. Far more than Count Rappaport's menacing gaze, it made me wonder just how big a mistake I'd made in coming here. I had never heard sounds like that before; nor, except once when a crowded coach overturned on an icy road, have I since.

One of the song butchers thumped irregularly on a drum. One sawed and scraped at a fiddle. One plucked away on what might have been a lute if it hadn't had too many strings and too long a neck—it looked like a lute the way a camel looks like a horse, in other words. And if the mustachioed villain cradling it in his lap had been plucking a camel instead, more melodious noises might have emerged from it.

A small chorus accompanied the alleged instrumentalists. The men's voices were too high. The women's voices, on the other hand, were too low. No two of them seemed to my untrained and startled ear to be per-petrating the same tune at the same time. Each one was trying to out-shout all the others, too.

Essad Pasha beamed. "Is it not marvelous?" he said.

"That's one word," I more or less agreed. "I will remember it forever." And so I have, most often in the small hours of the morning. Usually, though, the nightmare doesn't come back when I fall asleep again.

A man in a wolfskin jacket suddenly appeared beside Essad Pasha. The newcomer's face might have been a wolf's, too, with its hungry mouth, sharp muzzle, golden eyes, and rough-trimmed gray hair. Beam-ing no more, Essad Pasha said, "Your Highness, here is the Grand Boyar Vuk Nedic, Vlachia's representative in Peshkepiia."

"Your Excellency." I bowed.

"Your Highness." So did he, all the while eyeing me as a wolf might eye a juicy joint of beef in a butcher's window. But it wasn't me he was hungry for, it was my kingdom. In throatily accented Schlepsigian, he went on, "Fushe-Kuqe should be Vlachian. Vlachia should have— Vlachia must have—a port on the Tiberian Sea."

I bowed. "I have two things to say to that. The first one is, the Powers have agreed that there is to be a Kingdom of Shqiperi, with Fushe-Kuqe as its port, and I am going to be King of Shqiperi. Of all of it, to be plain."

Vuk Nedic had teeth almost as sharp as a wolf's, too. He bared them now, as if to prove it. A small strain of lycanthropy? Not unknown among Vlachs—no, indeed. I wondered how charming he would be when the moon came full.

"That agreement was not just—Is not just," he growled. No Vlach will ever be persuaded that anything giving him less than his wildest de-sires is just. And since Vlachs' desires are often wild indeed . . . They are a people whose charm is perhaps best appreciated at some distance.

I bowed again. "The second thing I have to say is, I suggest you take that up with Count Rappaport over there."

Vuk Nedic's eyes blazed so you could have lit a cigar at them. One of the reasons the agreement made sure Vlachia came away without a sea-port was that the Dual Monarchy insisted on it. Since the Dual Monar-chy has Vlachia on its southern border, it doesn't enjoy the luxury of appreciating Vlachs at a distance. As a matter of fact, the Dual Monarchy doesn't appreciate Vlachs at all. It's mutual.

It would have made an interesting confrontation: the fop in the gaudy uniform and the hemidemisemiwerewolf. But Vuk Nedic was the one who had no stomach for it. Vlachia could huff and puff till it blew the Nekemte Peninsula down, but it would never be more than a third-rate kingdom. The Dual Monarchy was a Power: a Power that had seen better centuries, true, but a Power nevertheless. If reminded of that forcibly enough, it could make Vlachia very, very unhappy.

And Vuk Nedic knew it. He stomped away. Stomping isn't easy on a rammed-earth floor, but he managed. He poured a tumbler full of brandy and knocked it back at a gulp. Vlachs follow the Two Prophets (even if they are benighted Zibeonites), so he didn't have to not drink even a single drop.

"Nicely handled, your Highness," Essad Pasha murmured.

"That bugger'll scrag you if he gets even half a chance, your Highness," Max murmured.

"Thank you," I murmured to both of them. Why not? As far as I could see, they were both right.

I got some brandy of my own, and some fried meat. I had just begun to eat and drink when Essad Pasha introduced me to a certain Barisha, the royal commissioner from Belagora. Belagora has its own king, but it's another kingdom full of Vlachs. Barisha fit the part, even if his outfit didn't. If you can imagine a werewolf in a getup that probably made Count Rappaport jealous, you have him to perfection.

He was every bit as friendly as Vuk Nedic, too. "The borderline in the north of Shqiperi is mistaken," he said without preamble. "That is really southern Belagora."

"I intend to stick to the agreement as it is down on paper," I said.

"The agreement may be down on paper," he replied, "but Belagoran soldiers are on the ground. They will stay there, and they will take Tremist and the rest of the ground we claim."

"Not if I have anything to do with it," I told him.

"If you go looking for trouble in the north, I promise you will find it," Barisha said. "And I promise it will find you."

I switched from Schlepsigian to Hassocki:"Thou art as false as water. May thy pernicious soul rot half a grain a day!"

He understood me. I'd thought he would. Nearly everyone in the Nekemte Peninsula knows enough Hassocki to curse with. "As thine uncle was beaten, so shalt thou be, thou pus-filled carbuncle on the arse of mankind."

I bowed. "Please to give my kindest compliments to thy father, should thy mother chance to know which of her customers he was."

After the exchange of compliments, we parted company. "You have shown him you are not to be trifled with," Essad Pasha said. "He will re-member it, as I do." He sent Max a furtive glance.

My aide-de-camp had a different prediction:"He'll give you one in the ballocks, the second he figures he can."

"Not if I give him one first," I replied. This sentiment met Essad Pasha's approval.

I met Sir Owsley Owlswick of Albion, who couldn't possibly have been as clever as he looked (and wasn't); Baron Corvo of Torino, who couldn't possibly have been as effeminate as he seemed (and, again, wasn't: his numerous bastards prove it); and Count Potemkin of vast and frozen Tver, who couldn't possibly have got that drunk that fast every night (but, from everything I saw, did).

And I formally met Count Rappaport. His Schlepsigian had a whipped-cream-in-your-coffee, strudel-on-the-side juiciness that went with his uniform but not with his eyes. He looked me up and down, not once but twice. "By the Prophets," he said, "I don't believe you're Halim Eddin at all."

X

Have you ever stood too close to a lightning strike, so that your heart forgets to beat for a moment and every hair on your head—and in more intimate places than that—stands out at full length? If you have, you will know some small part of what I felt just then.

Whatever I felt, I showed none of it. I was born in a carnival wagon, and I've been exhibiting myself to make my living ever since I got big enough not to piddle on the stage. If Max coughed a couple of times, then he coughed, that was all. Count Rappaport didn't know what it meant, even if I did.

"Go tell it to the scribes," I told him. "They always need something new to write about, and I don't think any of them has come up with that yet." By Eliphalet's curly whiskers, I hoped not!

"Scribes are donkeys," Count Rappaport said, in three words proving himself a man of uncommon common sense. He raked me with those eyes again, chill and sharp as the edge of an iceberg. "What you are, on the other hand . . ."

" 'What you are, on the other hand, *your Highness,*' " I prompted.

I do believe Rappaport's waxed and spiky mustaches gave his sneer a certain superciliosity it wouldn't have had without them. Be that as it may, I've seldom seen one that could approach, let alone match, it. "If you were Halim Eddin—" he began.

"North and south, east and west, he is none other," Essad Pasha broke in before the man from the Dual Monarchy could go further—and before I had to say a word. "On this, your Excellency, I will take my oath."

Count Rappaport's arctic stare swung his way. "Why?"

"By his looks, first of all. I have met his Highness before, as he doubt-less will recall. . . ." Essad Pasha raised an eyebrow in my direction. I in-clined my head, as royally as I could. He went on, "Further, did my memory falter, he is the spit and image of the portrait of the veritable Halim Eddin. Or will you doubt that, too, your Excellency?"

"A tolerable resemblance—but only tolerable, in my view," Rappaport replied. "And to my ear, he speaks Schlepsigian like a native and speaks Hassocki like a native—Schlepsigian."

"Thou art a fool, an empty purse," I said in my very best and sweetest Hassocki. "Not a catapult made could knock out thy brains, for thou as-suredly hast none."

"The liar paints the honest man with his own brush, which is his chiefest shield against the truth." The count seemed to dislike speaking to me at all, and was plainly glad to turn back to Essad Pasha. "You said his looks were your first reason for accepting this man at the value of his face. A first reason implies a second, which is . . . ?"

Before answering, Essad Pasha fortified himself with a glass of spirits. After disposing of the one drop he was not allowed to drink, he gulped the rest. It was a good-sized glass. He went red—not altogether from drink, as it proved. In a low, furious, embarrassed voice, he said, "He mas-tered me, your Excellency. Do you hear? Do you understand? He *mastered* me. He came to me in Fushe-Kuqe, set his will against mine, and pre-vailed. I obey him. I can do nothing else, sir, for he is a veritable Hassocki prince, and soon to be a king. North and south, east and west, did I reckon him some low Schlepsigian mountebank, I should have fed him to a dragon. Instead, I watched him slay one with as fine a feat of archery as ever I have been privileged to see."

Max coughed again. To tell you the truth, I felt like coughing myself. I wondered how long I would have lasted inside a dragon. Not as long as that vampire lasted inside the sea serpent, I suspected. Of course, under those circumstances, *not* lasting seemed preferable.

Essad Pasha bowed to me. "Here, your Highness, set in silver and on a silver chain, is the scale of the great worm you slew." I bowed in return, and slid it down under my tunic. I wear it to this day.

Count Rappaport made a noise down deep in his throat: a low growl I would have thought to hear from Vuk Nedic. Rappaport's silly uniform and sugary voice said one thing, his eyes and his manner something else again. It is often so with officials of the Dual Monarchy. If they were as foolish as they seemed, their kingdom empire would have crumbled to dust long, long ago.

"I shall have to make out a full report for my government," the count said, in the tones of a judge passing sentence.

"When you do, make sure you write in it that I will be crowned to-morrow," I said. "By all means come to the ceremony, your Excellency."

"I would not miss it." Count Rappaport bowed stiffly. He clicked his heels (he did a much smoother job of it than Untergraf Horst-Gustav, too). And then he did the best thing he could have done: he went away.

"I am sorry you were subjected to that, your Highness," Essad Pasha said. "Please accept my apologies."

"Your Excellency, you did nothing wrong," I told him. "As for the Narbo"—a word the Hassocki will use for anyone who follows the Two Prophets and believes Eliphalet more sacred than Zibeon, whether actually Narbonese or not—"I will tread the unbolted villain into mortar, and daub the wall of a jakes with him."

"May it be so. North and south, east and west, may all his plans stumble and fall." Essad Pasha's fuming could hardly have been more visible if he'd puffed on a pipe. "You, a Schlepsigian! The very idea!" He threw back his head and laughed.

"A ridiculous notion," Max agreed. He wouldn't unbend far enough to seem relieved Essad Pasha thought so, but he did sound less ironic than usual.

"It is indeed, most valiant Yildirim," Essad Pasha said. "One might as well suspect *you* of coming from Schlepsig, eh?"

"Me? I would sooner cut my throat." Max drew his sword. Instead of slicing it across his neck, he swallowed a goodly length of the blade. Essad Pasha's pouchy eyes bulged. All around the chamber, talk dried up as people turned to stare. Max might have created a bigger sensation by dropping his pants. On the other hand, he might not have.

With all eyes on him, Max withdrew the blade, conscientiously dried it on a napkin, and sheathed it once more. Then he took a skewer of chunks of fried meat. Everyone in the large room inhaled at once. I was glad to be quick; otherwise, there might not have been any air left. He pulled off the first gobbet with his fingers and popped it into his mouth. Everyone exhaled, a bit regretfully. The show was over—for the moment, anyhow.

"Truly, your Highness, your aide-de-camp is a man of parts," Essad Pasha remarked in the much too calm tones a man will use only when trying his best not to show how shaken or impressed he is.

"I would not deny it for a moment, your Excellency. Some of those parts, however, are wont to be more useful than others." If the slightest of edges came into my own voice, well, who could blame me for that?

Max bowed low, first to me and then to Essad Pasha, as if we'd paid him undoubted compliments. "I seek to show what any who oppose his Highness may expect," he said.

Essad Pasha bowed almost as low as Max had, which, considering the belly hindering him, wasn't easy. "That is well said," he boomed. "North and south, east and west, that is very well said." He turned to me. "You are fortunate in your servants."

"Yes, I know," I said blandly. Max coughed. I hadn't expected anything else. "Good thing you didn't do that with the sword in there," I murmured.

"Not like I haven't done it before," he answered, and I knew that was true. "I spit red when it happens, so I don't spit for a while then, that's all."

"Such a gentleman," I told him. His bow was even deeper than the last one.

Count Potemkin came shambling up to me then, a glass in each hand, his eyes glittering, his earth-apple of a nose as red as if it grew on a tree. "You gave the lout from the Dual Monarchy his comeuppance," he said in elegant, accentless Narbonese. Most Tverski nobles are fluent in it, which is fortunate, for it saves other people the bother of learning their language. Tverski has more cases than Caledonia Yard, and a battery of choking and gargling noises that make a man speaking it sound as if he's trying to strangle himself.

I speak good Narbonese myself, so I understood him. Halim Eddin, however, was more limited. "Do you speak Schlepsigian?" I asked Count Potemkin in that language.

"Only if I must," he answered grumpily. In Schlepsigian, he had a Tverski accent, and a strong one. He translated his comment. It sounded much ruder than it had before. Maybe it lost—or gained—something in the translation. Or maybe Narbonese puts a veneer of false politeness on almost anything. Not by accident is it the language of diplomacy . . . for now. As a good Schlepsigian patriot, I dare hope a change is coming.

But that is by the way. I had to find some diplomatic (oh, well) way to respond. "I am who I am," I said, with which not even the bibulous Potemkin could disagree. "I have the duty to defend myself and what is to be my kingdom."

"Your kingdom? Pah!" Count Potemkin said. Some Tverskis make a sport of being rude. Maybe Potemkin was one of those. Or maybe he was drunk. Then again, maybe he'd seen more of Shqiperi than I thought and was giving his honest opinion. You never can tell. Whatever the answer to that riddle, he went on, "Leave Vlachia and Belagora alone, and Tver will not trouble you."

"How generous!" I exclaimed, wondering if he could recognize sarcasm (at that moment, I wasn't altogether convinced he could recognize himself). But that sounded like something the Poglavnik of Tver's representative would say. Tver thinks of itself as the big brother of the Plovdivians, the Vlachs (in both Vlachia and Belagora), and the Vlachs' close cousins the Hrvats. They all speak related languages, and they're all Zibeonites except the Hrvats, who have the good sense to accept Eliphalet's primacy.

Using this big brotherdom as an excuse, Tver has fought a lot of wars with the Hassockian Empire, and won most of them. Since Tver would have to charge all the way across the Nekemte Peninsula to get at Shqiperi, I wasn't too worried about Potemkin's threat, if that was what it was.

Count Rappaport probably wouldn't take such a relaxed view of it. There is no Kingdom of Hrvatsk. There hasn't been one for centuries, ever since the Hrvats suffered through their disastrous vowel famine. The Hrvats live in the Dual Monarchy. So do some Vlachs. So do some

Torinans. So do the Yagmars. So do most of the Schlepsigians who don't live in Schlepsig. So do the Voslaks and the Voslenes, who are not the same (though only they care). So do the Prahans, who aren't quite the same as the Voslaks (or is it the Voslenes?), either. So do some Dacians, and all the Gdanskers who don't live in Schlepsig or Tver (no more Kingdom of Gdansk, either, which is what you get for ending up stuck between Schlepsig and Tver and the Dual Monarchy). So do . . . I could go on.

It's a complicated place—or, if you'd rather, just a bloody mess.

So when Tver appoints itself the Hrvats' big brother, the king-emperor of the Dual Monarchy is just as Not Amused as the late Queen of Albion. I don't mean she was Not Amused at the Hrvats; I'd bet money she never once heard of them. But I suppose she had other things not to amuse her.

Potemkin was thinking. It took a while. You could watch the wheels turn, like the ones on a milk wagon pulled by a lazy horse. In due course, he said, "You trouble our friends, we trouble you."

I put my hand on the blue velvet sleeve of his jacket. "I wouldn't dream of it, my dear fellow," I said. I might do it, but I had better things to dream about.

"Don't touch the coat!" He shook me off. "You listen and you listen good, or you be sorry." Yes, he was what Tver calls a diplomat.

"I'm all ears," I assured him. "North and south, east and west, I am nothing but ears. Even my eyes are ears. Even my toenails are ears."

Those wheels inside Count Potemkin's head slowly started turning once more. This time, I watched them stop: Potemkin gave up thinking as a bad job. "You listen," he said again. "Maybe you lucky, coming out here to middle of nowhere. When Tver takes Vyzance, no room for Hassocki princes there no more."

He could have said it better in Narbonese, I'm sure. Bad grammar aside, what he meant was plain enough. Tver has always lusted after the capital of the Hassockian Empire the way a callow boy lusts after a stage actress. She might be a clapped-out old whore—Eliphalet will testify Vyzance is—but he doesn't know that, or care. All he knows is, he wants her.

I yawned in Count Potemkin's face. "The Tverski who will lay hold of Vyzance has not been born, nor has his grandfather's grandfather." Switching to Hassocki, I went on, "So take thyself off, thou infinite and endless liar, thou hourly promise-breaker, thou owner of no one good quality."

"Whoreson mandrake, thy pisspot kingdom is the canker of a calm world and a long peace, and thou provest thyself fit to rule it," he retorted in the same language, and lumbered away.

You just can't tell with some people, that's all.

Taken as a whole, I suppose the evening at the fortress was a success. Nobody challenged anyone else to a duel. And no one except Barisha and the delightful Potemkin threatened to go to war. (As if anyone who didn't have the influence to escape being consigned to Peshkepiia *would* have the influence to send his kingdom to war!) Even more to the point, as far as I was concerned, no one except Count Rappaport doubted I was who I said I was, and no one seemed to take him seriously.

When I went to the Metropolis' dining room for breakfast, a pack of ministers semiplenipotentiary and another pack of scribes set upon me. I wished they would have found satisfaction in one another. Jean-Jacques-Pierre-Roland, for instance, talked enough to keep any four men or eight scribes happy. But no. I was the man of the hour, and they all were either mad to talk to me or to hear me talk.

"Just what you always wanted, our Highness," Max said with a sour smirk in his voice. That would have stung had it held less truth. Being the man of the hour *was* what I'd always wanted. Be careful what you want, then—you may get it.

You may also eventually get breakfast. None of Hoxha's cooks challenged any of the others to a duel, either, though they constantly seemed on the edge of it. Coffee, fried fowl, fried eggs, fried bread (which surprised me by proving tasty), fried sausage (which surprised me by proving even nastier than I expected, and I thought I was braced for the wurst). Everyone kept on telling me things or shouting questions at me while I ate. I wasn't king yet, so I couldn't even order people beheaded.

For that matter, I didn't know where I would be crowned (or even coronated—yes, Bob was there). I didn't know where my palace was, either. Peshkepiia didn't seem the sort of place that had palaces hidden away up back alleys.

I headed for the fortress to find Essad Pasha. And I did: he was heading for the hostel to find me. "Your Highness," he said, bowing low.

"Your Excellency." I bowed back. Essad Pasha's bodyguards and Max bowed to one another. It was all very polite. When men carrying a variety of lethal hardware meet on the street, politeness is to be admired and desired. I went on, "I was coming to ask you about the coronation ceremony."

"Well, good, because I was coming to tell you about it." Essad Pasha looked as affable as a senior officer in the army of the Hassockian Empire was likely to look unless he was plotting something really nefarious. "What would you like to know?"

"Where will it be, to begin with?" I said. "And where will I dwell once I wear the crown?"

"And will his Majesty's harem dwell there as well?" Max added. "He is too much a gentleman to speak of such things on his own, but naturally it is a matter rousing some curiosity on his part."

Rousing, indeed. If it didn't rouse some curiosity on Max's part, and if I didn't know which part of Max was roused, I would have been very surprised. None of which meant my sword-swallowing aide-de-camp was mistaken. Those questions did rouse my curiosity, among other things.

And Essad Pasha seemed to find all the questions reasonable enough. "You will be crowned, naturally, in the Quadrate God's fane," he replied. "That way, your mystical affinity with the land you are to rule will spread north and south, east and west, over the entire kingdom. So may it be."

"So may it be," I echoed. After two terms in the Hassockian Army, I thought I knew enough about the Quadrate God's rituals so I wouldn't give myself away.

"As for your residence," Essad Pasha went on, "if you would be so kind as to come with me . . ."

Off we went, into the back alleys of Peshkepiia. We strode through a market square that had some of the sorriest meat and vegetables and leather goods and, well, everything else, too, that I'd ever seen. It also had the largest assortment of coins passing current that I'd ever seen—probably that anyone has ever seen. Most likely because Shqiperi doesn't coin for itself, everyone's money is good here. You see everything from Hassocki piasters to Albionese shillings and even shekels from Vespucciland across the sea. If someone came out of the mountains after digging up a hoard of Aenean silver, that wouldn't have fazed the merchants. They all had scales—and, no doubt, all had their thumbs on them whenever they thought they could get away with it.

Peshkepiia's sewage system is largely a matter of rumor. I was repeatedly glad Hassockian Army uniform includes knee-high boots. We did considerable squelching. Some of the things we walked through . . . Well, I didn't get a good look at them, and I can't say I'm sorry I didn't.

Essad Pasha paused. "Behold, Your Highness—Your Majesty very soon to be—your palace. I hope it pleases you."

May Eliphalet's curse smite me with boils if it didn't. There it was: a real palace—a little one, but without a doubt a palace—right where I'd never dreamt there could be any such thing. It was charming, even elegant, in the sinuous Hassocki style. And if there was a wigmaker's shop across the muddy street and a horseleech's establishment next door—somehow that added to the charm instead of taking away from it.

"How did it get here?" I asked. I probably would have asked the same question the same way if I'd seen a daffodil sprouting from a cow flop. Given Peshkepiia's general atmosphere, that was more likely than this.

"I believe a governor built it some years ago for his lady love," Essad Pasha answered. "So I was told when I came to Shqiperi, anyhow."

"Why were you living in the fortress and not here, your Excellency?" Max asked: a much more bluntly sensible query than the one I'd come up with. Max is a useful fellow. You never need to think the worst of anyone while he's around, since he'll do it for you.

Essad Pasha coughed once or twice himself—he doesn't do it as well as Max—and sent me what might have been a look of appeal. I pretended either not to notice it or to misunderstand it. "Yes, why were you?" I asked, as if that were simply the most interesting question I'd ever heard in my life.

He thought about telling some spun-sugar fairy tale. Then, of themselves, his eyes went to Max's sword. Max's hand wasn't on the hilt, but it wasn't far away. Conscience doth make cowards of us all, as an Albionese poet once said, conscience being the still, small voice that tells us someone may call us a damned liar. That last definition comes from a Schlepsigian actor, acrobat, showman, soldier of fortune, and—briefly—king.

Instead of spinning the fairy tale, Essad Pasha said, "I judged the fortress more secure. But, with a proper guard contingent and with popular goodwill, your Highness—your Majesty soon, as I say—should be more than safe enough here."

More than safe enough for whom? I wondered. The only thing Essad Pasha knew about popular goodwill was that he'd never had any. "The harem is already installed here?" I asked him.

He brightened. "Oh, yes, your Highness. The quarters are admirable for the purpose. That governor may have built this palace for one favorite, but he entertained the possibility of entertaining more here." He sent me a manly smirk.

I also pretended not to notice that. For once, I found a relevant question ahead of Max: "The royal treasury is already installed here?"

Essad Pasha looked as if my intrepid aide-de-camp had just sliced off the first two inches of his manhood and was poised to take more (assuming he had more). Again, he seemed poised to lie. Again, he decided lying wasn't a good idea; I would have no trouble checking. "Ah, not yet," he said in slightly strangled tones.

"You will attend to that at once, your Excellency, won't you?" I bore down on the last two words. I didn't say what would happen if Essad Pasha failed to attend to it at once. Sometimes it's better to let a man use his imagination. Even someone like Essad Pasha, seemingly born without any such thing, can, when pressed, form the most remarkable pictures in his mind.

"Yes, your Highness." He sounded resigned if not transported with delight.

"Good," I said. "For if I am to be king here, I *shall* be king here. North and south, east and west, this land and all in it are mine. And it *will* have a proper coinage." I scratched at my mustaches. I rather fancied my face on silver and gold, I did. Instead of saying so, I went on, "A proper Shqipetari coinage would go a long way towards insuring popular good-will, eh? *And* towards insuring a proper guard contingent here, I shouldn't wonder."

"Er—so it may." Now Essad Pasha sounded distinctly less than over-joyed. He must have got used to the idea that Shqiperi's treasury was *his* treasury. To have a stranger announce that the kingdom was going to use it—and that the stranger wanted to get his own hands on it—couldn't have sat well.

I pondered. If I said he could keep some, he would hold on to more than I said he could. He would also think me weak for yielding to him in any way. That was dangerous. If I tried to cut him off without a piaster, I ran the risk of a knife in the kidneys or ground glass in the breading of whatever the Shqipetari cooks fried next. That was also dangerous. More dangerous? Less? How could I judge?

Audacity. Audacity again. Always audacity. Some Narbonese politician said that. If memory serves, he got his head bitten off a couple of years later, but if you're going to fret about every little thing. . . . Besides, he was just a fool of a Narbonese (but I repeat myself). If I hadn't had more audacity than I knew what to do with, I wouldn't have been moments away from becoming one of the crowned heads of the world. And so— on with it.

Besides, I had a really demonic thought. "I will tell the scribes you're making the transfer," I said. "I'm sure they'll be interested in watching it and writing about it. Aren't you? They'll probably want to peek into the chests to see all the gold and silver. You should let them, to make sure no-body has any doubts about anything."

I waited. The longer I waited, the less patient my face got. The longer the silence stretched, the closer Max's hand drew to the hilt of his sword—in a polite sort of way, of course. Why, certainly!

Essad Pasha looked at me. He took another long look at Max's right hand. And then he surprised me. He threw back his head and laughed like a loon, or perhaps like a scribe. "Your Highness—your Majesty—I think serving under you will be a real privilege. And I would like to see the face of the first fellow fool enough to try to cross you. North and south, east and west, there will be no escaping your wrath." He laughed again, even more raucously. "And that whoreson malt-horse drudge who styles himself a count of the Dual Monarchy! That poor inch of nature proves himself of no account whenever he opens his mouth to speak. Fond witling, to imagine you some sort of mad Narbo. No infidel Schlepsigian dog would have the wit to stymie me—*me!*—at every turn. See? I speak frankly and openly. I own myself stymied."

Max coughed. I smiled, doing my best to make my teeth seem sharper than they were. *Audacity. Audacity again. Always audacity.* "Any man who admits to being stymied—who brags of being stymied—surely has some scheme to stymie the stymier. When I come back to the palace after my coronation, the first thing I aim to do is examine the treasury. If anything seems wrong in even the slightest way, Essad Pasha, north and south, east and west, there will be no escaping my wrath. Is that plain enough, or shall I speak more clearly?"

"That is very plain," Essad Pasha answered. "And I have no such scheme. Of that you may rest assured. May my head answer if I lie."

He'd just put his scheme back on the shelf. Of that I might rest assured. If he came up with another one he thought he could get away with, he would use it. Of *that* I might rest assured, too. "Shall we go back down to the hostel and the fane?" I said. "It should be about time for the ceremony to begin. And I do need a moment to tell those scribes about the transfer of the treasury. Watching all the sparkly things move is bound to fascinate them."

"No doubt it will, as with any jackdaws," Essad Pasha said with a martyred sigh. "Well, your Highness—your Majesty—you are right. It is time to return to the hostel and the holy fane. And of course you may tell the scribes whatever brings your heart delight." He sighed again. "After all, if I tried to stop you, you would anyhow."

I did tell the pack about the treasury. That yielded even more chaos and commotion and entertainment than I hoped it would. All the scribes tried to figure out how to be two places at once. Since even demons have trouble with this, to say nothing of the greatest sorcerers of our age and every other, it handily defeated the gaggle of second- and third-rate scribes who'd come to this fourth-rate town hoping for a first-rate story.

My story.

Some of them rushed off to the Consolidated Crystal office (yes, even a fourth-rate town like Peshkepiia has one—CC is *everywhere*) to file both stories before either one of them happened. This would have been a miracle, if not necessarily one of rare device.

Other scribes proved perfectly suited for the Nekemte Peninsula, where perhaps the commonest sound in the land is that of one hand . . . washing another. They formed quick impromptu teams. One man would keep an eye on the treasury transfer while the other kept an eye on me. Each would write a story. Both would file both stories. Not quite a miracle, but something that would look like one for the home crowd. Very often, that's more than good enough.

And then there was poor Bob. None of his countrymen wanted to team with him. No doubt they'd seen him in action—or inaction—before. He couldn't team with anyone from a different kingdom, because he spoke only Albionese. By the way he spoke, he didn't have much command of his allegedly native tongue, either.

"What would you do in my fix, your Highness?" he asked lugubriously.

Run away, change my name, and try to pretend the whole thing never happened, I thought. *Or maybe I'd just slit my wrists.* But, since Halim Eddin didn't speak Albionese, I didn't have to understand him. "North and south, east and west, thy fame hath gone before thee," I told him in Hassocki. He followed not a word of it, but Essad Pasha laughed and Max very nearly smiled.

I had no royal robes to don. With the Hassockian Empire at war with so many of its neighbors, no one thought my colonel's uniform out of place. Considering what the members of the diplomatic corps were wearing, I was among the most modestly attired men going into the Quadrate God's fane. I'd thought the diplomats were gaudy the night before—and I'd been right, too. They were even gaudier now.

Jean-Jacques-Pierre-Roland wore black jacket, black cravat, black trousers, and white shirt. But the shirt, as was usual for a Narbonese, was a sea of ruffles. He had a scarlet sash draped from his right shoulder to his left hipbone, a glowing turquoise sash draped from his left shoulder to his right hipbone, and an iridescent green sash doing duty for a cummerbund.

Vuk Nedic of Vlachia wore wolfskin dyed purple—spectacular, but not a success. Barisha of Belagora had on a uniform of golden watered silk that should have made a lovely evening gown for a lovely lady. Inside the fancy clothes, he himself remained a Vlachian semisavage. And Count Rappaport still found a way to upstage him. The noble from the Dual Monarchy looked as if he'd killed and skinned a candy cane, or possibly like a barber pole with legs and enameled decorations. However ludicrous the getup, his eyes still saw everything and believed nothing.

After I saw him, I stopped paying attention to the other diplomats. I assumed no one could outdo that uniform (if something so obviously one of a kind could be dignified by the name), and I was . . . almost right. I'd reckoned without the Quadrate God's votary.

He wore cloth of gold heavily encrusted with pearls and precious stones. His robes must have weighed more than a good suit of chainmail; I marveled that he could walk at all. His curly gray beard, which tumbled down as far as the bottom of his chest, hid some of the mystic symbols on the front of the robe. His long, flowing locks, tumbling down under a miter as massive as a battle helm and far shinier, covered up whatever ornamented his shoulders and upper back.

He smelled strongly of himself (votaries of the Quadrate God bathe once a year whether they need to or not, and I'd say his time was just about up) and just as strongly of sandalwood. The latter scent warred with but failed to defeat the former. Behind him, less gorgeously robed acolytes swung thuribles north and south, east and west. Their scented smoke was spicy with the exotic odors of frankincense and myrrh. But what came from their censers failed to censor what came from the votary (and the acolytes' hides hadn't met soap and water any time lately, either).

"If they put a perfumery next to a place where they pour fertilizer into sacks . . ." Max whispered.

"That's holiness you smell," I said.

"Well, they ought to keep it on ice in the summertime," Max said. "It's gone off."

A horrible noise burst from a set of risers to our left. No, they weren't throwing cats into bubbling oil there, even if it sounded like that. It was a chorus of Shqipetari boys, singing my praises. So they told me afterwards, anyhow. I hate to think what they would have sounded like if they'd disapproved of me.

One boy wore a red robe, the next a black, and so on. The boy on the next step up wore a robe of the color opposite the one just below him. If you can imagine a singing checkerboard . . . Well, if you can imagine a singing checkerboard, I'm sorry for you, but we had one there. They also told me red and black were the colors of the Kingdom of Shqiperi. Since there wouldn't *be* any Kingdom of Shqiperi till that odorous priest plopped a crown on my head, I wondered how they knew, but I didn't ask them.

The song of praise ended on a truly alarming high note. I later found out one of the boys chose that moment to goose another, one he didn't like. At the time, I assumed it was part of the song. The silence that fell afterwards seemed slightly stunned, but any silence was welcome then.

It didn't last. How many welcome things do? The votary began to pray, first in Hassocki and then in Geez, the ancient holy language worshipers of the Quadrate God use. They seem to think him too ignorant to understand any more recent tongue. To me, this is not flattering to a putatively all-powerful deity, but the Quadrate God's followers have never sought my opinion on the subject.

Every so often, the votary would pause and look my way. I would throw in a "So may it be" or a "He is wise and he is just" or a "North and south, east and west." I spoke Hassocki, which was all right; not being a votary or acolyte, I didn't have to know any Geez. And, as I say, I'd been to enough of these services to have a pretty good idea what to drop in when. I didn't make any mistakes bad enough for the votary to start screaming, *This is a filthy Narbo masquerading as a Hassocki prince! Boil him in tartar sauce!*

When the prayers finally finished, he looked at me again. This time, he looked into me. It was an alarming sensation. He Knew. If you travel with a circus, even a run-down outfit like Dooger and Cark's, you get to recognize that look. It does people who Know less good than you'd think.

So what if you Know the answer, when you can't find the right questions to ask? If Knowing mattered, those wizards and fortunetellers would be rich and comfortable and maybe even happy, not stuck performing for wages a bricklayer would scorn.

This holy man didn't find the right question, either. When he looked inside me, he didn't try to see anything like, *Why is this filthy Narbo masquerading as a Hassocki prince?* or even, *Why is he thinking in Schlepsigian and not Hassocki?* He must not have noticed that, though I think I would have. But what he wanted to find out was, *What kind of King of Shqiperi will he make?*

By the way his eyes widened, even that seemed lively enough. "Five," he spluttered, and then repeated it—"Five!"—in even more astonished tones. And then his eyes didn't just widen. They rolled up in his head, and he fell over in a faint.

Someone splashed him with water, possibly holy, possibly not. Someone else, more practical, put a flask to his lips. He slurped noisily. I hope he left one drop in there, keeping with the letter of his faith if not the spirits, but he was so thorough sucking up those spirits that I couldn't be sure.

"Are you better, your Reverence?" one of the acolytes asked. "What did you see?"

"He will be a strong king," the votary declared. He was pretty strong himself, but you didn't hear people telling him about it.

Out of the corner of my eye, I saw Essad Pasha nodding. I really had convinced him I was what I said I was. Of course, as long as he believed that, he didn't have to believe he'd let a Schlepsigian mountebank play him for a jackass. Believing me the genuine article made him feel better about himself. Since it also went a long way toward keeping my head on my shoulders, I didn't mind a bit.

Essad Pasha gestured. At a wedding in a country where the bride and groom follow the Two Prophets, a ringbearer brings up the ring on a velvet cushion. Here, a crownbearer did the same duty. He was a pretty little boy, except that his eyebrows grew together above the bridge of his nose. In Shqiperi, though, this is accounted a mark of beauty among men and women alike.

The votary lifted up the crown. He set it on my head. It was heavier than I'd expected—gold has a way of doing that. "It is accomplished!" the votary cried. "Behold the King of Shqiperi!" He meant me. People cheered. They meant me, too. Acting on the stage? Forget it! I acted before the world—and the world applauded!

XI

What is your first command for your subjects, your Majesty?" Essad Pasha asked.

I paused a moment to strike a pose. The scribes poised pens and pencils above notepads. A sketch artist recorded my likeness in a few quick strokes. Before long, the laws of similarity and contagion would send my image all over the civilized world. I wondered how many weeks or months it would take to reach the outlying districts of Shqiperi.

"Hear me, my subjects!" I boomed. Fanes to the Quadrate God don't have the acoustics of temples to the Two Prophets, but a performer learns how to make his voice fill up the space he plays in. "Hear me! I order you to live joyfully all the rest of your days! Any who fail to obey will be severely punished!"

A brief silence followed. Some were working that out. Others were translating it for those who had no Hassocki. Only after a few heartbeats did people laugh and clap the way I hoped they would.

Essad Pasha bowed. "Indeed, a command worthy of a king!"

"North and south, east and west, may it be so," I said grandly.

Bob the Albionese scribe was frowning. "But if he punishes them, how can they live joyfully?" he asked whoever was sitting beside him. He spoke much too loudly, a common failing of Albionese. And he wasn't bright enough to get the joke, a common failing of scribes.

I fear Untergraf Horst-Gustav also looked puzzled. Brighter Schlepsigians have no doubt been born. Not even my kingdom would waste a capable man on Shqiperi when he could be doing something useful somewhere else. Count Rappaport got it. His only problem was, he didn't think it was funny. He seemed too competent to belong in a backwater like this. But then, it would be just like the Dual Monarchy to send skilled diplomats to pestholes like Peshkepiia and giggling nincompoops to posts that really matter.

"For my second command . . ." I waited. Essad Pasha suddenly stopped breathing. If I wanted to get rid of him, if I wanted to blame him for everything that was wrong with Shqiperi, I could. I could likely get away with it, too. Although I knew much more was wrong with Shqiperi than even Essad Pasha was to blame for, I could buy myself popularity by nailing his head over the gate to my palace. "For my second command . . . I declare this, the day of my accession, a holiday with special rejoicing throughout the land, and I order it to be celebrated each year from now on."

More applause, the most enthusiastic from Essad Pasha. Maybe the old villain thought I couldn't do without him. Maybe he was even right. We never quite got to find out. Essad Pasha is dead himself these days. And I . . . I am the victim of an unfortunate usurpation, a king without a kingdom. Life can be very sad sometimes.

I'm getting ahead of myself again. You, dear reader, don't know how—
And I'd better not tell you just yet, either.

What I had better tell you is that I left the fane to the acclamations of the assembled dignitaries (except for Count Rappaport and a couple of other spoilsports) and to the absolute indifference of the people of Peshkepiia. Sooner or later, I thought, I would have to learn more about these turbulent people I now ruled. And they would have to learn more about me, too. Once they did, how could they help but love me?

Guards stood outside the palace—the *royal* palace, now. People stood in the street staring at the palace. This I took for a good sign; no one had paid any attention to it before. Only one reason for the change sprang to mind.

"The treasury is here?" I asked Essad Pasha.

"But of course, your Highness," he answered. Max coughed significantly. Essad Pasha thought it was significant, anyhow, and thought he knew the significance. "But of course, your Majesty," he amended.

One of the basic rules in performing is that anyone of your own sex who calls you *darling* hates you. Anyone of any sex who says *but of course* is likely to be lying through his—or even her—teeth. Somehow, I didn't think statecraft was all that different. By Max's eyebrow semaphore, neither did he.

"Let's see it," I said.

I waited to see what happened next. If Essad Pasha had being difficult in mind, he would tell the guards something interesting—something like, "Kill them," for instance. In which case I would not only be the first King of Shqiperi but also very possibly the last, and certainly the one with the shortest reign. Not a set of records I really wanted to hold.

I told myself that, in the event of my sudden untimely demise, Essad Pasha's departure from this life would be every bit as abrupt. I hoped Max was telling himself the same thing. You never know with Max till something happens—if it happens.

Was Essad Pasha making the same calculations from the other side, as it were? If he was, he made them in a hurry. "Yes, Your Majesty," he said, and nodded to the guards.

Waiting inside was . . . Well, if it were a squad of crossbowmen, I wouldn't be writing this reminiscence, for the puncture is mightier than the sword, and Max and I had only blades. But the Shqipetari butler or majordomo or whatever he was—flunky, I suppose, will do well enough—bowed low and cried, "Your Majesty!" in accented Hassocki.

The palace—my palace—was as perfect inside as out. Soft carpets lay on the floors. Some of the walls were plaster painted with scenes of the forest and the hunt. Some were tiled in floral patterns climbing gracefully to the ceiling. The beams up there were cedar; they would last forever, barring fire. The governor who'd built this place had simple tastes: nothing but the best.

"Here is the strongroom, your Majesty," Essad Pasha said. It looked strong to me. It had more bars than a harbor district, more bolts than a linen mill, and more locks than all the salmon smokeries in Schlepsig. Essad Pasha produced a key ring and handed it to me. "The first opens the topmost lock."

One after another, I undid them. One after another, Max opened the bolts and took down the bars. I pulled on the knob. The door silently swung open; the hinges gleamed with grease. Inside stood four stout chests. They were festooned with chains and more locks.

Without even looking at Essad Pasha, I held out my hand. *Clank!* He handed me another key ring, this one with even more angled and twisted brass on it than the other. He pointed to the chests to show in which order the keys opened the locks. I wasted no time testing them. They passed the test.

My heart pounding, I opened the first chest. It hadn't moved when I shoved against it. I liked that. Silver is nice and heavy, gold even heavier. Up came the lid. "You see, Your Majesty?" Essad Pasha sounded smug.

I saw, all right. Piasters, leptas, thalers in silver and gold (the Dual Monarchy hasn't minted gold thalers for a hundred years, but you find them everywhere in the Nekemte Peninsula), krams, dinars, livres also in silver and gold, shillings and florins, a fat silver shekel (with IN THE PROPHETS WE TRUST under the eagle), precious stones . . . I wanted to chortle like a miser over his fortune. I wanted to run my hands through the money for that sweet clinking-clanking sound. I wanted to jump in the chest and swim around.

Otto of Schlepsig would have, too, by Eliphalet's strong right arm. Prince Halim Eddin, though—King Halim Eddin, I should say now— would have seen treasures of his own in Vyzance. Since I was supposed to be Halim Eddin, I couldn't cackle like a laying hen, no matter how much I wanted to. I gave Essad Pasha what I hoped was a calm, serious nod. "I see, your Excellency," I said . . . calmly, seriously.

"Examine the other chests, by all means," Essad Pasha said. "You will see I have not cheated. North and south, east and west, treasure from the whole kingdom is here."

Any time someone goes out of his way to tell you how honest he is, watch your wallet. I opened the other chests, one by one. Max stirred a couple of them to make sure the money and jewels weren't hiding rocks or lumps of lead. They weren't. I'd never seen so much—much—in one place before.

I glanced towards Essad Pasha. He was just a little tighter and tenser than he might have been. "This is very good, your Excellency," I said. He relaxed, ever so slightly. If he hadn't, I would have decided I was imagining things. But since he did, I casually asked, "And when do you plan to bring over the rest of it?"

He jerked. I might have stuck him in the rear with a pin. "How did you know?" he said hoarsely. "You showed me you were formidable, but *how did you know?*"

He wouldn't have understood if I told him he reminded me of Dooger and Cark. Or if he did, that would have been worse. Dooger and Cark got as much pleasure from cheating a poor performer in their troupe (as if there were any other kind!) out of half a day's pay as Essad Pasha did from hiding who could guess how much treasure. Essad Pasha got more money, though.

"Have I not lived in Vyzance?" I said, trying to sound indulgent and amused. "Have I not seen ministers? North and south, east and west, will ministers not try to line their own pockets when they can?" Then I wasn't so amused any more. "This is all very well, as long as they realize the game has an end. We have come to the end, Essad Pasha. Bring the rest of the treasury here within the hour. If you hold out on me this time, your story will not have a happy ending."

There was, I judged, at least an even-money (and money was indeed at the root of it) chance he could still order me killed and get away with it. Instead, he went to his knees and then to his belly, knocking his forehead on one of those elegant rugs. I'd intimidated him, all right. "Mercy, your Majesty!" he wailed with that wild tremolo only Hassocki can achieve. "Mercy! I meant no harm!"

Certainly not to yourself, I thought. "The sand flows through the glass, your Excellency," I said. "I suggest you make haste."

"Yes, your Majesty! Of course, your Majesty!" Essad Pasha was all but babbling.

I discovered I liked *Yes, your Majesty!* even better than *Yes, your Highness!* "Captain Yildirim!" I said.

"Yes, your Majesty?" Max said. Oh, I *did* like that!

"Please accompany his Excellency to the fortress and make sure everything goes smoothly when my soldiers bring the rest of the treasury back here," I said. They were, in fact, Essad Pasha's soldiers. But as long as I gave him no chance to remember that and do something about it, I was fine. (And, if the first King of Shqiperi came down with an acute case of loss of life not for being proved an impostor but for acting every inch a king, Essad Pasha would have a demon of a time finding anybody else to play the part. So I told myself, anyhow.)

Max saluted. A Hassocki drill sergeant would have screamed at him. Like any other critics, drill sergeants scream whether the performance rates screaming or not. Essad Pasha noticed nothing amiss, and he was the only audience that mattered. "Yes, your Majesty!" There! Max said it again!

Off they went. I turned to the Shqipetari flunky. "What's your name?" I asked him.

"I am Skander, your Majesty," he replied.

"Well, Skander, let's get these chests locked up." I handed him some of the keys as I continued, "We'll leave the strongroom open till Captain Yildirim comes back with the rest of the treasure. Once it's closed up again, I would like to meet the women of the harem." Again, I didn't want to sound as if I were drooling on the carpet. Back in Vyzance, Prince Halim Eddin would have had plenty of women with whom to amuse himself. Back in Vyzance, Prince Halim Eddin no doubt still did. Here in Peshkepiia, so did I.

Skander bowed. "Hearkening and obedience, your Majesty." There was even a step up from *Yes, your Majesty*! Who would have imagined such a wonderful thing? Skander went on, "The chief eunuch says your ladies are also eager to meet you. Naturally, I have not presumed to enter the women's quarters myself."

"Naturally," I agreed in what were probably abstracted tones. Halim Eddin would be used to eunuchs. His household doubtless had several. He wouldn't have the urge to clutch at himself at the mere thought of the most unkindest cut of all. And, because I was he, I wouldn't either. Or, if I did, I wouldn't show it.

We waited. After a bit, Skander called to a lesser servant and spoke to him in Shqipetari. The underling nodded and hurried off. He came back with a tray with a large goblet and a small one. Skander took the small one, leaving the larger one for me. "Fruit juice, your Majesty," he said. "Improved fruit juice."

Did I need a food taster? In Vyzance, Halim Eddin probably did. As the Hassockian Atabeg's nephew, he was lucky to have lived long enough to grow up. Here, I didn't think I did. Murder in Shqiperi looked to be very straightforward. The sword, the knife, the crossbow quarrel—those were worries. Poison? No.

Skander politely waited for me to drink first. I raised the goblet. "Your good fortune, and Shqiperi's," I said, and sipped. I had all I could do not to cough. They'd, ah, improved that fruit juice with strong spirits till it had hair on its chest. I flicked out a drop with my little finger.

"Your Majesty is pious." Skander imitated my gesture. He didn't bat an eye when he drank.

"Have we got a court wizard?" I asked.

"How could we, your Majesty?" he said. "Up till a few days ago, we didn't have a court."

"We'll have to do something about that," I said. "How many wizards are there in Peshkepiia?"

"Always plenty of hedge-wizards," Skander said. That was true. It was true everywhere. It was also useless: what one hedge-wizard could make, another could unmake. He went on, "Wizards of a quality to serve your Majesty? Perhaps four, perhaps half a dozen."

That was perhaps two, perhaps four, more than I'd expected. Skander probably had lower standards than I did. Were his standards lower than Halim Eddin's? There I wasn't so sure. In the past hundred years, wizards from Schlepsig and Albion, from Narbonensis and Torino, and from Vespucciland across the sea have turned the world upside down and inside out. It's not the same when we're old as it was when we were young. Take Consolidated Crystal. In a lifetime, it's spread everywhere. Now anyone can talk to anyone else. Whether he'll have anything interesting to say is a different question, worse luck.

"Bring one of these wizards before me in the next few days," I said. "If he suits me, I'll use him. If not, we'll try another."

Skander bowed. "Of course, your Majesty."

In about an hour, Max returned with sweating soldiers, with three more treasure chests, and with the keys to open them. When I did, I saw they really were full of money, with the odd bit of jewelry in there for variety's sake. I could live with variety like that. "Is this the lot of it?" I asked.

"It's everything Essad Pasha coughed up," Max answered.

His eyebrows said he thought the local governor had more squirreled away somewhere. Mine said I thought Essad Pasha did, too. But what could I do about it? Short of turning him on a spit over a slow fire and rendering him down for lard—which might get me talked about even if he did yield several gallons—not much. I decided that could wait. Maybe I didn't have all the treasure in Shqiperi. I had plenty for a thousand ordinary men, plenty even for a king.

Which meant . . . "The harem," I said.

"The harem," Skander agreed.

People who've never lived in kingdoms where they follow the Quadrate God have funny notions about harems. Painters—mostly Narbonese— use them as an excuse to paint pretty naked women. Far be it from me to deny that any excuse is a good one, but harem girls don't lounge around naked all the time. For one thing, it gets cold. For another, the master of the harem mostly isn't in. Do they show off for each other, then?

In the Hassockian Atabeg's harem, maybe they do. He has more women than he knows what to do with. Well, no—he knows what to do with them, but with most of them he doesn't do it very often. He has his favorites. The rest make do with one another, or with the eunuchs. Some eunuchs can keep a woman happy with what they have left, and she never needs to worry about having a baby. The ones who can't do that have other ways.

But in most harems the women work when they're not summoned to, ah, entertain. They spin. They sew. They weave. They raise children— and the only people who say that isn't work are the ones who've never done it.

The door to the harem was barred from the outside. The king's chosen women weren't about to go off on their own. After I took down the bar and leaned it against the wall, I discovered the door was barred from the inside, too. Nobody was going to sneak in there and fool around, either. Well, I didn't need to sneak. I knocked on the door: a loud, authoritative knock.

Max coughed. He does that every so often, whether he needs to or not. Sometimes it doesn't mean anything. Sometimes it does. You have to know which is which, and how to translate. I had no trouble this time. *If you think you're going to be the only one in there having a good time, you're out of your tree*—that was what he was telling me.

I was tempted to think, *Too bad for you, pal.* Something told me that wasn't a good idea. Most plots against kings start with their nearest and allegedly dearest. I couldn't promise Max his share in Hassocki. Skander would have been scandalized. I couldn't do it in Schlepsigian, either. Skander would have wondered why I switched languages, and I didn't know he didn't know mine. So I tipped Max a wink. That did the job.

The door opened. A eunuch bowed to me. A lot of eunuchs are fat; some are immense. This fellow was skinny enough to make up for three of them. He looked mean—and who could blame him? He bowed."Your Majesty," he said, his voice somewhere in that nameless range between tenor and contralto."I am Rexhep, your Majesty."

"Pleased to make your acquaintance, my good Rexhep," I said. My good Rexhep's eyes, black as the inside of a bear, said he wasn't one bit pleased to make my acquaintance."I have come to meet the women of my household."

"Of course, your Majesty," Rexhep said, while those glowing black eyes said something else altogether. I got the feeling Rexhep couldn't do a woman any good with whatever equipment he had left. Was that why he looked mean? Lots of people are curious about such things. Me, some details I'd rather not know.

I walked through the door. The eunuch closed it after me. He barred it from his side, and I heard Skander bar it from the other. I knew that was the custom, but it made the hair stand up on the back of my neck anyhow. Was I King of Shqiperi or a prisoner?

As long as I acted like a king, I was one. If I'd learned anything coming from Dooger and Cark's Traveling Emporium of Marvels in Thasos to the royal harem in Peshkepiia, that was it. When people think you believe it, they'll believe it, too. If you want to tell me I'm wrong, think about Essad Pasha. He'd fought Vlachia and Belagora to a standstill, to say nothing of running a province full of Shqipetari for years. But he knocked his head on the ground to a down-at-the-heels Schlepsigian acrobat—*because he thought I was a king.*

Then there was Count Rappaport. The less said about him, the better. So I won't.

Inside the harem, the air smelled of sandalwood and cinnamon and rosewater and spikenard and musk. Just breathing was enough to make your heart race. Poor Rexhep! Even if his heart did race, much good it did him. We turned a corner. There on couches set in a grassy courtyard waited the women Essad Pasha and his underlings had chosen for their king.

Before I set eyes on them, I thought they might be beauties who would dazzle me with their exotic loveliness. Then again, they were Shqipetari. The old joke goes, first prize is a week in Shqiperi; second prize is two weeks in Shqiperi. Maybe they wouldn't be worth seeing at all.

Truth dwelt in the middle. Truth usually does. One end or the other, those are the places where madness lies. Think of the fools who conjured up a bolt of lightning to murder the last Poglavnik of Tver but one. They thought that would somehow set the peasants free. Or think of some of Count Rappaport's colleagues, who figured the best way to keep the Dual Monarchy safe was by slaughtering all the Vlachs. From the Vlachs I've known, the sentiment has its points, but most of those people haven't done anything to anybody. So . . . the middle.

I wouldn't have minded a couple of dozen ravishing beauties. I wouldn't even have minded ravishing them. But a couple of dozen hags? I could have done without that.

Some of these women were very pretty indeed. Some weren't much above plain. I think any man who saw them would have said the same. Some other man might not agree which ones were pretty and which ordinary, though. No doubt about it, there was something here for every taste, or for everyone to taste, or—well, you get the idea.

All of them, pretty and plain alike, wore silk blouses and the baggy bloomers stage shows call harem trousers. In the stage shows, those are as transparent as the tailor can arrange and as the local laws allow. Here, they were of plain cotton—not a smooth thigh or a rounded rump on display. Such is life.

I stood among them and bowed in the four directions. "North and south, east and west, I greet you, my ladies," I said. "I hope you all speak Hassocki?"

"Yes, your Majesty." Their voices made a sweet chorus. I looked around to make sure they'd all answered. As far as I could tell, they had. Some of them had strong accents, but that was all right.

Out of the corner of my eye, I saw Rexhep gesture. I don't think I was supposed to. All the harem girls got down from their divans and prostrated themselves before me. They were a lot more graceful than Essad Pasha. Saying that doesn't do them enough credit. A few days with a dancemaster and they could have earned their keep in any theater in Schlepsig or Narbonensis or Albion.

"Get up, get up," I told them. "No need to stand on ceremony here, or even to fall down for it."

Some of them smiled as they straightened. Others looked puzzled. I needed a moment to figure out why. When I did, it made me sad. You'll always find people who want other people to shout at them and tell them what to do. That way, they don't have to figure it out for themselves. I'd be lying if I said I understood this—I've been making my own way ever since I got old enough to ignore what my mother and father told me, which didn't take long. I don't understand it, but that doesn't mean it's not real. Some of the girls wanted a king who'd roar at them the way a mean taverner keeps his barmaids in line.

I wouldn't have minded roaring at the minister from Belagora. As a matter of fact, I intended to—what else was Barisha for? But I have better things to do with pretty girls (or even with girls not much above plain) than roar at them.

"What are your names?" I asked them.

"Strati." "Lutzi." "Hoti." They rained down on me. I was once in a troupe with a memorious man—Funes, his name was, from Leon. He taught me a few of his tricks: only a few, mind you. I don't have a memory like his—Eliphalet's whiskers, who does?—but I'm good with names.

Inside a few minutes, I had them all straight. Pick something about the person and associate it with the name and you won't go wrong. Strati had straight hair. Lutzi stirred up lust in me—I think she was the prettiest of them. Hoti seemed hot; she dabbed at her forehead with a handkerchief. And so on. It isn't magic, not the kind that uses the laws of similarity and contagion, but it seems sorcerous to people who don't know how it's done. Funes was a master. With any kind of stage presence at all, he would have been rich and famous, not a sideshow performer. I don't have a quarter of his skill, but I can sell what I do.

And the harem girls had to be the easiest audience I ever faced. If I'd roared at them, they would have thought they deserved it. Since I didn't, they thought I was sweet. They'd never dreamt I would bother learning their names, let alone that I could do it so fast. They crooned and sighed and stared at me as if I'd fallen from heaven.

Sometimes—too often, most of the time—you can't get one woman to fall in love with you. Here I had a couple of dozen all doing it at once. It would have been embarrassing if I hadn't enjoyed it so much.

Every once in a while, I glanced over at poor Rexhep. Once, he caught me doing it. That *was* embarrassing. "May I speak with you a moment, your Majesty?" he asked in that strange, epicene voice.

"Of course," I said, and then, to the harem girls, "I'll be with you in a moment, my sweethearts." I was sporting with them. Some of them, I think, realized as much. To others, the play was real. The Shqipetari sequester their women in Hassockian fashion—how not, when they learned it from the Hassocki? That only makes it easier for the girls to grow up naive and trusting.

Rexhep drew me far enough aside to keep the harem girls from overhearing—and don't think they didn't want to, the little snoops! "Are you a wizard, your Majesty?" the eunuch asked.

"Not a bit of it," I answered. "I've only been a king for a couple of hours. Wizardry will have to wait. Why do you ask?" Maybe the girls weren't the only naive ones; maybe he thought those tricks of memory were real magic, too.

That turned out to be close to the mark, but not on it. "Because you've ensorcelled your harem, that's why," he said. "Before you came in, half of them were angry at being plucked from their homes, and the other half were frightened. Now look at them! They want to have more to do with you." He sounded as if that were the nastiest perversion he could think of. All things considered, it probably was.

"I don't want them angry. I don't want them frightened. I want them friendly. I'll want them very friendly tonight," I said. "So I try to make them like me. What's so strange about that?"

He couldn't see it. He thought it was a trick if it wasn't magic. I wondered what sort of harem he'd kept before, and what kind of hellhole it was. By the look of sour bafflement on his face, he knew no more of affection than a blind man knows of sunsets. A pity, no doubt, but I couldn't give him what he'd lost.

I went back to jollying the girls along. Rexhep went back to trying to figure out what I was up to. He wouldn't believe what I told him, even when it was true. He needed complications, poor soul, whether they were real or not.

After a while, I turned to go. The girls sighed in disappointment. Rexhep looked relieved and suspicious at the same time—an expression only a eunuch's face could manage. I told the girls, "Some of you will be summoned to my chamber tonight. If you aren't summoned to my chamber tonight, it doesn't mean I don't love you. I'm only one man, and not quite so young as I wish I were." Some of them giggled. Others had no idea what I was talking about. They really do raise them innocent in Shqiperi. I went on, "If I don't summon you tonight, I will summon you another night, and one not long from now. I know you will all delight me, and I'll try to please you, too. Meanwhile . . ."

Several girls tried to follow me out toward the doorway to the outer world. Only Rexhep's scowls restrained them. Rexhep's scowls, I think, could restrain anything up to and possibly including a dragon. As far as gloom goes, he gives Max a run for his money. Rexhep, of course, has the advantage—if that's the word I want—of a real grievance against the world. No denying Max does well without it.

Rexhep unbarred the door on this side of the wall. Skander unbarred it on *that* side. I passed from one side to the other, from one world to another. Both the head eunuch and the palace majordomo made haste to separate those worlds again. As soon as the door closed, two bars thudded into place at the same time.

"Have you thought of a wizard for me?" I asked Skander. "I'd like to use his services this afternoon."

"The very best in Peshkepiia, I believe, is a certain Zogu," Skander said. "He dwells not far from the palace. If it would please you that he be summoned . . ."

"It would please me very much," I said. I hoped it would, anyhow. Skander bowed and hurried away.

I went to the throne room. It was, to put things kindly, still a work in progress. That might have been gold foil pressed on the arms and legs and back of the Shqipetari royal seat. It might have been, but it looked more like the wrapping paper for nameday gifts you can buy in smart shops from the Dual Monarchy to Albion. Stranger things than a smart shop in Peshkepiia may have happened, but I can't think of one lately.

Above the throne hung the royal emblem: a black two-headed eagle on a red background. It might have seemed more impressive if it hadn't looked like a small rug woven for the even smaller tourist trade. A label was attached to the bottom corner of the royal emblem. PRODUCT OF ALBION, it read—so that really was a small rug woven for the tourist trade.

When I rested my arms on those of the throne, the shiny gold crackled and crunched. It *was* wrapping paper, then. I thought of the treasure in the strongroom. One of these days, Shqiperi would *be* a kingdom, I told myself, not just try to look like one.

Ah, well. We all make promises we can't keep.

After about half an hour, Skander returned with another Shqipetar, presumably Zogu. The wizard had a sharp nose, a bristling mustache, and a pancake of hair on top of his head, the rest of his scalp being shaved. "Your Majesty," he murmured, bowing toward the makeshift throne. "How may I serve you?"

"As you know my rank, you will know the privileges accompanying it," I said. "You will also know the obligations accompanying it. And you will know that some of the privileges, if taken to extremes, become obligations. They can even become obligations a man is, ah, impotent to meet."

I waited. Zogu *looked* clever. If he had not the wit to figure out what I was talking about, though, I wanted nothing to do with him. He didn't disappoint me. Laying a finger by the side of his nose and winking, he said, "You want to screw your way through the harem like you were seventeen again."

"Better than that, I hope—when I was seventeen, I was a clumsy puppy," I said. Zogu laughed—reminiscently, I suppose, for who isn't a clumsy puppy at seventeen? I went on, "I would like to be able to go as often now as I did then."

"I can help you," the wizard said. "The formulary will serve you well for a night, or two nights, or three, or maybe even four. Use it too long, though, and you will soon find you are a man of years not far removed from my own." His chuckle had a wry edge. "Do I know this from experience? North and south, east and west, your Majesty, I do."

"A few such nights should suffice," I assured him. "By then, I shall have made my point."

Zogu laughed merrily. "And I'm supposed to keep you pointing, eh? Well, just as you say, just as you say."

Was he too clever for his own good? Men of that sort often are. "I rely on your magecraft," I said, "but I also rely on your discretion. If your spell fails, I will do the best I can on my own. If your discretion fails, Zogu, north and south, east and west, the world is not wide enough to hide you from me. Do you understand what I tell you?"

"Oh, yes, your Majesty. Oh, yes. I have served . . . others who relied on my discretion. If I were to name them, they would have relied on it in vain," he said.

"Good," I said, for the answer pleased me. "Carry on, then—and I will carry on later."

He chuckled again, and bowed. "May it be just as you say."

At his feet sat a carpetbag. Had I met him in Schlepsig or the Dual Monarchy, I would have taken him for a commercial traveler with the worst haircut in the world. He began taking sundry stones and herbs and animal bits from the carpetbag. "You have everything you need?" I asked.

"Oh, yes," Zogu answered easily. "When Skander summoned me, I thought on what you might require. I was not sure I knew—he gave me no time for a proper divination—but this possibility did cross my mind."

"Get on with it, then," I said.

He smiled and bowed and did. He was one of those wizards who like to explain things. I always let such people ramble on. You never can tell when you'll hear something worth remembering. "This we call here the eagle's stone, your Majesty," he said. It was about the size and shape of an eagle's egg, or half an egg sliced lengthwise. The inside was lined with glittering white crystals, but otherwise hollow. "Its property is the engendering of love betwixt man and woman."

"Engendering is what I have in mind, all right," I said.

Zogu put some seeds into the eagle's stone and brayed them with a pestle. "These come from sweet basil," he told me. I didn't know who Basil was, but I wanted the girls to think me sweet. More seeds. I recognized these from their smell before Zogu said, "Anise." It goes into Lokrian spirits, and they'll rouse anything this side of the dead. The wizard added more bits of vegetable material. "Rocket," he said. Since I wanted to up, up like a rocket, if not so fast, I nodded.

Next came some scraps of what looked like thin parchment. "What's that?" I inquired.

"The shed skin of a *long* snake." Zogu winked at me. I grinned back.

After that he put in some small blue pills and used the pestle to crush them to powder. "What are those?" I asked.

Zogu winked again and powdered another couple of pills. "My secret ingredient, you might say."

"Well, well," I said. Since he talked about so much of what he did, what he wouldn't talk about must have been potent indeed.

"Set the eagle's stone under your bed before you summon your lovelies," Zogu told me after chanting over it in both Hassocki and Shqipetari. "You will rise to the occasion, and may you win a standing ovation."

"My thanks," I said. "And your fee for the services rendered?" When he named it, I didn't scream, as I would have in my private capacity. How could I, when he was increasing my privates' capacity? I just paid him. It's good to be the king.

XII

Several hours still lay between me and sunset. I suppose I could have begun in broad daylight, but that might have scandalized the harem girls. And, as I soon discovered, a king's life is not an idle one. Anyone would think a man with a crown on his head ran a kingdom or something.

No sooner had Zogu departed the palace, his belt pouch clinking with silver, than Skander came up to me and said, "Your Majesty, Barisha of Belagora would have speech with you."

"Oh, he would, would he?" I said. About the only people less welcome in the throne room would have been Count Rappaport and a dentist. But Skander nodded. I didn't suppose I could summarily dismiss the representative of my northern neighbor, however much I wanted to. With a sigh, I nodded. "Let him advance and be recognized."

Recognizing Barisha, I must confess, was seldom a problem. Each uniform he wore was more garish than the last. This one was of thick, shimmering blue silk, with a gold sash running from northeast to southwest. I wondered if he'd won it from Jean-Jacques-Pierre-Roland at dice. Medals and ribbons bedizened his chest. I also wondered what they were. The Belagoran Award for Gloriously Getting Up on Time Two Days Running? The Grand Star of the Illustrious Order of Horseleeches? The Medal for Proficiency in Stealing Chickens, Second Class? I shook my head. Barisha, no doubt, was a first-class chicken thief.

All the medals clanked and jingled as he grudged me a bow. "Your Majesty," he said, and then, even more grudgingly, "My congratulations on your accession."

"Thank you," I said. "I hope Shqiperi and Belagora long remain at peace."

"May Zibeon grant it be so." Even Barisha's agreement was insulting. He rubbed Halim Eddin's nose in his following the Two Prophets rather than the Quadrate God. And, though he didn't know it, he rubbed Otto of Schlepsig's nose in his following Zibeon rather than Eliphalet.

Because I had to be Halim Eddin and not Otto, I rubbed back as a proper worshiper of the Quadrate God would have: "North and south, east and west, let peace prevail."

"In the south, in the east, in the west, peace will indeed prevail, as far as Belagora is concerned," Barisha said. "In the north . . . In the north, your Majesty, we do not recognize the border the Powers have declared. Now that the Hassockian Empire has lost the Nekemte Wars, that border should and must become more rational."

"By which you mean more the way you want it," I said sourly.

"But of course." He was a very smug and self-satisfied chicken thief—he didn't even take the trouble to deny it.

"This is my land now. You may not steal it," I said.

"How do you propose to stop us?" he sneered. "I told you before—we have the men on the ground. Tremist will be ours, and soon."

"Hassocki soldiers still in Shqiperi will obey me," I said. Barisha went right on sneering. I added, "And we will create a proper Shqipetari army as soon as possible." I had some hope he would take that seriously. Shqiperi had no true soldiers except for what was left of the Hassocki garrisons—no denying that. But the custom of the blood-feud means every male Shqipetar who shaves goes around armed all the time. I'd never seen so much deadly hardware on display as I did here.

Barisha remained unimpressed. "And what hero from ancient days has been reborn to command your fearsome host?" he inquired.

That question struck much too close to the bone. Most Shqipetari acknowledge one master and one master only: themselves. This makes them excellent raiders, excellent ambushers, excellent hunters—and terrible soldiers. Men in an army need to act together. Shqipetari do as they bloody well please. They might obey a hero from ancient days—or they might decide he was an old fool and ignore him, too. Any modern leader would have his hands full.

Even more than in the rest of the world, in the Nekemte Peninsula to back down is to admit weakness. If I yielded so much as a clod of Shqipetari soil to Barisha, he would be back demanding more day after tomorrow. Vlachia and Lokris would scream for their share, or more than their share, too. Other kingdoms would want to do the same, but only those three border Shqiperi. Well, I suppose the Torinans would take a seaside bite, too. And so . . .

"The old border will stand," I said.

"It will not," Barisha answered.

"We shall resist with force any attempt to change it," I said.

"We do not seek to change it. We seek to set it right." Barisha proved himself a hypocrite and a liar in the same breath—no mean accomplishment.

"If you do not take your soldiers back across the old border, we will make them sorry," I said.

Barisha bowed. "What is ours is ours."

"And what is ours is also yours? Is that what you are saying, your Excellency?"

"I am saying the Hassocki soldiers still in Tremist occupy land that should always have belonged to Belagora. We must correct this unjust and immoral situation."

"And I must tell you that it looks fitting and proper to me," I answered. "We shall not let our kingdom be abridged before it is well begun. The old Hassocki province of Shqiperi, on whose borders the Powers have agreed, shall be the new Kingdom of Shqiperi, and there is nothing more to be said."

"Oh, but there is," Barisha said. "For one thing, your Majesty, your so-called kingdom is a joke, a land full of goatherds and cattle rustlers. For another, Belagora has its legitimate rights, and will protect them by force of arms as necessary."

I remembered my earlier ruminations on Barisha's medals, and a joke I'd once heard. "Do you know how to make Belagoran chicken stew, your Excellency?" I asked.

Barisha's bushy eyebrows made his frown something less than a thing of beauty. "Why, no," he said—he made an admirable straight man.

"First, steal a chicken . . ." I began.

He turned a color no doctor would have cared to see in a man of his age and weight. "You insult me! You insult my kingdom!"

"You enjoy it more when you insult mine, don't you? Well, I am here to tell you that that arrow can shoot both ways," I said. "And I am also here to tell you that we will fight you if you do not withdraw. Is that plain enough, or should I draw you pretty pictures to color in?"

Barisha went an even less appealing shade of purple. It clashed badly with his uniform. Before I could point this out to him, he said, "Do you presume—do you dare—to threaten the mighty Kingdom of Belagora with war?"

"I dare not to be redundant, which is more—or rather, less—than you can say," I answered. "And if you want a war in the north, you can have it. I don't just threaten Belagora with war. I declare war on your robbers' nest of a kingdom. As of this moment, your not very Excellency, you are *persona non grata* in Shqiperi." I raised my voice to a shout: "Skander!"

He appeared as if from a trap door. "Your Majesty?"

"Give this person"—I pointed at Barisha with the index finger of my left hand, an insult Skander understood and the Belagoran, unfortunately, didn't—"a horse, and aim him in the direction of his kingdom. If he is not out of Shqiperi in three days' time, let him be declared fair game."

From what I knew of the Shqipetari, there was at least an even-money chance they wouldn't wait three days to descend on Barisha. From the look on his face, he knew the same thing. He did his best to bluster: "I shall return to this piddlepot hole in the ground at the head of an army that darkens the sun with—"

"The flies that hover over it," I finished for him. "If you Belagorans bathed once in a while, you'd have fewer troubles along those lines."

Barisha must have had some chameleon in him, probably on his mother's side. He did a very creditable imitation of an eggplant. "Let it be war, then!" he cried, and stormed away.

A couple of minutes after he left the throne room, Max ambled in. "Um, your Majesty, what have you done?" he asked.

"Declared war on Belagora. Why?"

He laughed. Getting a laugh out of Max isn't easy. I laughed, too, at the look on his face when he realized I wasn't joking. "Well, there's a record!" he said. "You haven't had a crown on your head more than a few hours, and you've already started a war? I can think of a lot of kings who'd be jealous, I can."

"Your Majesty!" Skander sounded scandalized. "Is this—this personage allowed to speak to you so?"

That made Max laugh again. "You try and stop me, pal!" A warning of this sort from an officer six feet eight inches tall and armed with a sword does carry a certain persuasiveness. Skander sent me a look of appeal.

"My aide-de-camp means well," I said, and don't think that didn't made Max laugh one more time. "Sometimes I find it useful to employ a man who enjoys full freedom of speech." Sometimes, even before I was royal, I found it a royal pain in the fundament, too. But I didn't tell that to Skander.

"Yes, your Majesty." My majordomo's tone suggested that I was eating with my fingers and didn't know any better. When I showed no sign of ordering Max drawn and quartered and placed outside the palace as a warning to others, Skander threw his hands in the air and stalked off. All things considered, he made a better exit than Barisha had.

"You really declared war on Belagora?" Max said. I nodded, not without pride. He, by contrast, shook his head. "How are you going to fight it?"

"Don't be silly," I answered. "Nobody can fight a proper war in those mountains. The Belagorans and the Hassocki have just spent months proving it. Why should things be any different now?"

"Because you're in command instead of old Essad Pasha?" Max suggested. "What you know about running an army doesn't exactly fill up the *Encyclopaedia Albionica.*"

All at once, drawing and quartering Max looked much more attractive. I thought about calling Skander back. If he knew a reliable wizard, he probably knew a reliable executioner, too. But thinking of Zogu and his magic made me decide to try to distract Max instead. Execution is so . . . permanent.

I told Max about the sorcery, adding, "I'm going to have Rexhep bring some of the harem girls to the royal bedchamber tonight."

"*Are you?*" Max said. That got his attention, all right.

"Of course I am. What else would a king do? Insult the poor dears by leaving them lonely? What sort of cad do you think I am?" I held up a hasty hand; Max was liable to answer that. Having forestalled him, I went on, "Rexhep may fetch more girls than even a king can handle, all in one night."

"You expect me to take care of your leftovers?" Max asked haughtily.

"Well, unless you'd rather not," I replied.

Now he was the one holding up a hand. "I didn't say that. I didn't say anything like that." He got sensible mighty fast. Somehow, I thought he might.

"All right, then," I said. "We'll see how that goes after the sun sets."

I waited to find out what happened next. What happened was that Max, realizing which side his bread was buttered on, bowed very low. "Thank you, your Majesty," he said. All of a sudden, he didn't care so much about war with Belagora.

And do you know what else? Neither did I.

I don't remember much about the rest of the afternoon. After war and the harem, not much seems important. I think Jean-Jacques-Pierre-Roland called on me. I can't begin to tell you why. Narbonensis is a long way from Shqiperi. Any civilized kingdom is a long way from Shqiperi. And Narbonensis is friendly toward Vlachia and Belagora, which only goes to show all its taste is in its mouth.

Maybe he wanted to tell me not to go to war against Belagora. That makes as much sense as anything else, and more sense than a lot of things I can think of. I can't prove it, though. And if Jean-Jacques-Pierre-Roland had any sense to start with, what was he doing in Shqiperi?

Not long before supper, I heard screams and the clash of cutlery—I hoped it was cutlery, not swords—from the kitchens. I sent Skander off to see who'd murdered whom, and why. When he came back, he reported, "Nothing to worry about, your Majesty. Only a disagreement. No blood."

"No, eh? By the noise, I expected you'd be wading through it up to your knees." My answer was punctuated by more shouts and the ringing of steel on steel. With a sigh, I said, "You must have hired the cooks from the Metropolis."

"How did you know, your Majesty?" I think it was the first time I impressed Skander as myself and not as King of Shqiperi.

Supper was . . . what you would expect with a bunch of Shqipetari cooking it. Fried chicken, which again wasn't bad—though fried chicken feet were something I'd never tried before. (And, remembering my little love fest with Barisha, I kept wondering where the fowl came from.) Fried potatoes, once more pretty good, even if we'd be likely to boil them in Schlepsig. Fried squash, which was—well, better than it sounds, anyway. Fried lettuce, about which I draw a merciful veil of silence.

By Eliphalet's beard, if they had ice cream in Shqiperi they would fry that. They've never heard of it, proving mercy still does stream down from on high.

As the meal came to its greasy conclusion, I turned to Max and said, "Captain Yildirim!"

"Yes, your Majesty?" Max gives nothing away, not even to himself.

"Attend me in my quarters, if you would be so kind," I said. "We can smoke a pipe together and study the best way to drive the Belagoran curs off our soil." I got that out with a straight face. I really did.

"Yes, your Majesty." Despite the uniform he wore, Max was and is about as military as your cat. Soldiers make other people swallow their swords. Max swallows his own. Need I say more? But, again, no one who didn't know him would know that. Skander and the servants who cleared the table looked very impressed.

One of the servants, in fact, was so busy sneaking glances at Max that he knocked over a goblet he should have picked up. It fell off the table and smashed. The servant turned pale. So did his friends. They muttered in Shqipetari.

"Mercy, your Majesty!" Skander begged. "Mercy!"

What was I supposed to do, cut off his hand? Cut off his head? By the fear in their eyes, maybe I was. I started to laugh and tell them not to worry about it. I started to, but I didn't. Shqiperi is the kind of place where they see kindness as weakness. "Take it out of his pay," I told Skander. "It had better not happen again."

"No, your Majesty. Of course not, your Majesty. Thank you, your Majesty," Skander said. The servant bowed very low indeed. I did it right.

I nodded to Max. "Shall we go, Captain?"

"Certainly, your Majesty," he said. "You are as merciful as you are kind." I've never known a man who could pay a more venomous compliment.

Have you ever seen a sorcerous print of one of those Narbonese paintings that imagine what the Hassockian Atabeg's bedchamber looks like? They're all carpets and cushions and silks and gauzy curtains and polished brasswork and bright colors and clashing patterns. I don't know what the Hassockian Atabeg's bedchamber really looks like; the authentic Halim Eddin may, I suppose.

Mine looked like . . . one of those paintings. Not one of the good ones, where everything seems elegant and expensive, but the tasteless kind, where all the furnishings look as if they're one step—and a small step, at that—up from what a whorehouse would have. All that was missing were the naked girls.

They weren't far away, though.

Max looked around as if he couldn't believe what he saw. I didn't blame him; I had trouble believing it, too. He waved. "How are you supposed to sleep with all *this* going on?"

"This place mostly isn't for sleeping," I answered.

"Well, how are you supposed to do *that* with all this going on?" he said.

I tucked the eagle stone stuffed with Zogu's, ah, condiments under the bed. "I have hopes of finding out," I told him. "And you may rely on it that there are plenty of girls in the eunuch's care for both of us."

"Ah." Max brightened, as much as Max ever brightens. "You mean you didn't ask me here to help you figure out how to fight your stupid war against Belagora?"

"If I ever need a general bad enough to look to you, my kingdom is in more trouble than it knows what to do with," I said with dignity.

"If it's got you for a king, your kingdom's already in more trouble than it knows what to do with," Max retorted.

"Thou cowardly hind, thou art the veriest varlet that ever chewed a tooth," I said. I love Hassocki . . . endearments.

"Oh, be still, thou flea, thou nit, thou winter-cricket thou!" Max said. Oh, yes, I love Hassocki endearments—except when they come back at me.

We slanged each other for a while. Then we smoked pipes together: the long Hassocki-style pipes called chubuks. After we'd smoked a bit, I stopped caring whether we'd been throwing darts back and forth. Whatever we were smoking, I don't think it was just tobacco. In the Hassockian Empire and other western lands, they will sometimes mix hemp or hashish in with their smokables. I resolved to ask Skander if he'd done that for me. Somehow, I never did.

I kept forgetting.

I didn't forget the harem girls, though. Whatever we were smoking, it didn't bother that side of things at all. On the contrary, in fact—or maybe Zogu's magical stone, now that it was in place in a bedchamber—was starting to do its job. After some searching in that garish room, I found a closet. Right behind the door, it held half a dozen iridescent silk robes, which clashed with one another and with everything around them—not easy, but they did it.

The closet also held Max, even if he had to duck to get in. "Now stay there till I let you out," I told him.

"All right," he said, "but if you think you can get away with diddling the girls while I listen, *your Majesty*, forget it."

Yes, I'd thought about that again, but I tossed it aside the same way I did the first time it crossed my mind—I can't imagine a better excuse for an assassination. So I said, "No, no," as if the idea had never once—let alone twice—occurred to me. "I didn't bring you here to screw *you*, Max." That seemed to mollify him. I closed the closet door, which all but disappeared, and I called for Skander.

"Yes, your Majesty?" As he had in the throne room, he seemed to come out of nowhere. One thing I will say: when you wanted him, you didn't have to wait around for him.

"Go to the harem door. Tell Rexhep to bring me Lutzi and Maja and Bjeshka and Varri and Zalli and Shkoza."

"Certainly, your Majesty. Are you sure they'll be enough for one evening?"

If I'd ever thought Skander a man without sarcasm, I had to revise my opinion. The only way to top him was to pretend I didn't notice he didn't mean what he said. In my blandest tones, I answered, "Well, if they're not, Rexhep can always bring me a few more, eh?"

Now Skander had to figure out whether I meant it. He couldn't. I was a performer in front of an audience, and that was all I needed to hold up a mask to the world. Balked there, Skander started a new hare: "Where is Captain Yildirim, your Majesty? Did he leave your chambers?"

Just when you wish things would be simple once in a while . . . "Of course he did. He's not here, is he? He must be back in his own rooms by now."

"I'd better check," said the conscientious—the much too bloody conscientious—Skander. "You wouldn't want him sneaking into the harem while Rexhep brings you your ladies, would you?"

"No, I wouldn't want that." *I want to share them with him right here.* "But I don't think he'd do anything like that."

"You never know," Skander said darkly. "Let me go see. I'll be back directly." And away he went.

I couldn't even tell him no. He would wonder why if I did. No proper Hassocki gentleman, let alone a high Hassocki nobleman like Halim Eddin, would have protested even for a moment. Those who follow the Quadrate God take the harem seriously. If I was going to be Halim Eddin, I had to . . . pretend, anyhow.

The much too bloody conscientious Skander returned almost as fast as he'd promised. "I am glad to be able to tell you, your Majesty, that you seem to be right," he said. "Captain Yildirim did not respond to my knock, but, as his door is barred from the inside, I have no doubt he is indeed in the room. After all he ate at supper, he must have decided to turn in early."

Barred from the inside? Max is a resourceful man, but how the demon had he managed *that?* "All right, then," I said, a remark that means nothing but bought me a heartbeat or two to think. Even after whatever I'd smoked, I knew what I was supposed to be thinking about, too. "Go speak to the eunuch. You do remember the women I asked for, don't you?"

"Lutzi and Maja and—" He bogged down. "I am so sorry, your Majesty."

"Don't worry about it." I could afford to be magnanimous, because I was showing I was smarter than he was. "Lutzi and Maja and Bjeshka and Varri and Zalli and Shkoza." I brought out the string of names with no hesitation. I'm not in the same league with the memorious Funes, but I'm pretty good.

"Bjeshka and Varri and Zalli and Shkoza. Bjeshka and Varri and—" Skander repeated the names over and over to himself as he walked down the hallway. I hoped he wouldn't forget Lutzi and Maja. I especially hoped he wouldn't forget Lutzi. She wouldn't have been a sovereign's mistress in the Dual Monarchy or Narbonensis, but she might well have been a duke's.

Nothing to do but wait and hope Zogu's spell lived up to my anticipation. Not knowing just when Rexhep would appear, I couldn't go to the cleverly concealed closet and ask Max what he'd done and how he did it. *A time for everything*, I thought.

When Rexhep led the girls to my room, they were veiled and cloaked against men's prying eyes. "Here you are, your Majesty," he said in that cool, sexless voice. "Do you require anything else of me?"

I wondered what he was thinking. No, looking into his eyes, I didn't wonder—I knew. The question wasn't whether he hated me, but how much. "No, that will be all for now," I told him. "I'll summon you when I need you to take them back." I just wanted him to go away. Can you blame me? Thinking about eunuchs at a time like that? Thanks, but I'd rather not.

Rexhep didn't want to be there as much as I didn't want him there, maybe more. "Very well, your Majesty," he said, and withdrew. It wasn't very well, not for him. Nothing would ever make it very well, either. Away he went, tall and thin and proud—and damned, or as near as makes no difference.

I closed the door to the bedchamber and barred it from the inside. (How *had* Max done that?) Then I bowed to the girls. "No one here will have to do anything she doesn't enjoy doing," I promised. "The idea is for us to have a good time—for all of us to have a good time. Do you understand?"

"Yes, your Majesty," chorused Lutzi and Maja and Bjeshka and Varri and Zalli and Shkoza.

"Good." I smiled at them. They had to be nervous. The only way they had to my heart wasn't through my stomach, but by a more direct route. They didn't know what strange tastes I might have. For that matter, they might not know which tastes were strange and which weren't. Had Essad Pasha recruited a couple of dozen true maidens for me? I'd find out. I smiled again. "You may unwrap yourselves, my dears. Nobody"—well, almost nobody—"here but us."

And so they did. What they had on under those cloaks was a good deal skimpier and more transparent than what they'd worn when I called on them in the harem. Maja and Zalli were either natural blondes or thorough. I didn't care which, not a bit.

"May I ask you something, your Majesty?" Lutzi said.

I bowed again. "Of course, sweetheart. In a little while, I expect I'll ask you something, too."

She blushed. With what she was almost wearing, I could watch the blush travel a long way. I don't know when I've had a more pleasant contemplation. She said, "One of you and six of us, your Majesty?" All the girls leaned forward to hear what I'd say about that. They seemed to have some notion of what was what, anyhow. That was nice.

"Do you think I can't do you all justice?" I asked.

"Oh, no, your Majesty!" "Of course not, your Majesty!" "You are the king, your Majesty!" They all denied it: much squeaking and twittering, many artfully shocked expressions. What they meant was, You haven't got a prayer, your Majesty.

Maybe they were right. No—certainly they were right, even with Zogu's spell. But I had something better than a prayer. I had a friend. I said, "My loves, my aide-de-camp and I go back a long time together. We've guarded each other's backs through years of dangers." That not only sounded good, it had the added virtue of actually being true. I went on, "He having shared danger with me, the least I can do is share my reward with him. And so I have the honor and privilege to present to you . . . the valiant Captain Yildirim."

I opened the closet door. Max came out and bowed. Lutzi and Maja and Bjeshka and Varri and Zalli and Shkoza all squealed. For one thing, as I've said, Max is very, very tall. For another, while in the closet he'd contrived to rid himself of anything he wouldn't need later: his uniform, for instance. He emerged wearing nothing but a smile.

It occurred to me that I was the only one wearing anything significant—surely the only one wearing anything beyond the decorative. I didn't need long to divest myself of the problem, to say nothing of my pants. After a bow of my own, I waved grandly toward the broad, inviting bed. "Well, my lovelies, here we are. We have one another, we have all that room, and we have plenty of time. Shall we make the most of them?"

We did our best. You will have seen a kaleidoscope, I suppose. They're clever little toys. All the wizards I know insist they're not magical, even if those clever mages can't tell me how they *do* work. The little chunks of polished stone and colored glass inside them move, and when you look through the other end you watch the colors and the pretty patterns shift.

You will have seen a kaleidoscope, yes. But have you ever imagined being *part* of a kaleidoscope display, making pretty patterns and shifting from this one to that one to the next one as the whim—or the next beckoning partner—takes you? I've done some interesting, enjoyable, and complicated things in my time. Nothing I've ever done comes close to that evening for being all three at once.

Every so often, I would pause for a moment to admire what was going on all around me. I wasn't the only one, either. I think we all had the feeling this was something very special, or could be if we made it so. I think we all tried harder than we would have if we enjoyed such sport every night, too. And I think I would have soon collapsed from exhaustion— happy exhaustion, but exhaustion even so—if not for Zogu's sorcery.

I amazed myself. I might have been a bunny. I kept going and going and going. . . . Well, actually, I kept . . . The magic lived up to its promise, I will say that.

Max held up his end of the bargain. By the sighs and moans and murmurs that came from that part of the kaleidoscope picture, his end held up quite well indeed, thank you very much.

And the girls were even better than I'd hoped they would be, which is saying a lot. I don't know how much experience they had. That's not the sort of question a gentleman asks. I am sure a couple of them, though they did seem to know a good deal about some other things, hadn't had one particular experience before. Cold water would get the stains off the quilt.

I'm also sure they didn't have enough experience to let any of what we did embarrass them. They accepted it as natural and enjoyable—and by thinking it ought to be that way, they helped make sure it was.

Lutzi lived up to what her name sounded like. Bjeshka proved shapelier than I thought she was back in the harem; maybe her outfit there hadn't fit her well. Varri had a very talented mouth. Maja was almost as limber as dear Ilona. Shkoza enjoyed being rolled onto her stomach. Zalli . . . I don't remember anything remarkable about Zalli, but I'm not complaining, either. Oh, no.

Everything passes, everything perishes, everything palls.

So said some dreary, world-weary Narbonese, allegedly a sage. All I can tell you is, he wasn't there in that bedchamber that night. I never wanted it to end. I don't think any of us wanted it to end. And, for a long time—longer than I ever would have expected—it didn't.

But, even with the best will in the world (and with what had to be somewhere close to the best magecraft in the world), the time comes when all you can do is all you can do. We sprawled here and there on the quilts and cushions, and on one another. We were all tired. We were all sweaty. We were all grinning like high-grade idiots.

"Well," I said lazily, "I'll have to thank Essad Pasha after I sleep for a week."

"He told us it was our duty," said one of the girls—Maja, I think it was, but I'm not sure. By then, they all ran together in my mind. Whoever she was, she went on, "I never thought doing my duty could be so much fun."

A chorus of agreement followed. It wasn't a very energetic chorus, but that was all right. I wasn't very energetic myself just then.

I thought I ought to say something, so I did: "If a king can't make his subjects happy, what's the point of ruling?"

That won more agreement. I felt . . . statesmanlike. But then Max asked, "What about the grannies with mustaches? For that matter, what about the granddads with mustaches?" Even at a time like that, even in a place like that, Max *would* be difficult.

"Well, what about them?" I said. "Let them console each other. As for the king"—I ran my hand along the sweetly curved length of Bjeshka (I think it was Bjeshka)—"doesn't he deserve the best the kingdom has to offer? And haven't I got the best, right here with me?"

"And we have the best, right here with us." Was that Zalli? Was it Varri? Was she looking at me? Or did her eyes wander over toward Max? I was too happily sated to care.

"The rest of the charming ladies in the harem deserve a trial, too," I said, wondering if my heart would stand the strain. Zogu *had* warned about overusing his charm. Well, what a way to go! Who wouldn't want such a . . . patriotic ending?

"Wait till the others hear about our sport!" Was that Lutzi? I hope it was Lutzi. I did want to make her happy. And I know, with memory yet green, how happy she made me. She went on, "They won't be able to wait for their turn to come." The others all nodded, except for—I believe—Shkoza, who'd dozed off.

I gently shook her awake. Then I said, "I'm afraid, my dears, it's time for you to put on your cloaks and your veils and go on back behind the door for a while. I'll call for you again as soon as I can. North and south, east and west, I promise you that."

They sighed, but they obeyed. Alas! Only the Two Prophets can see ahead of time how and whether what a man says will come to pass. I intended to keep that promise. I was, ah, firmly resolved to keep that promise. But—alas!

I nodded to Max. "Captain Yildirim, you might do well to disappear while we go through the boring formalities." He went back into the closet—and no, not like that. But I didn't want Skander and Rexhep spitting rivets. The girls sighed when he closed the door. I reminded myself they'd taken pleasure with me, too. I had to remind myself rather loudly, I fear.

I also had to remind myself to get dressed again. I was the last one out of my clothes, and the last one into them again. With a sad sigh of my own, I opened the door and called for Skander. He was yawning when he got there. What time was it? I'd had other things on my mind. "Be so good as to summon Rexhep to escort the ladies back to the harem," I told him.

"Of course, your Majesty," he said, stone-faced. "I trust everything went well?"

"Oh, *yes!*" That wasn't me. That was Lutzi and Maja and Bjeshka and Varri and Zalli and Shkoza. They sounded so convincing—and so convinced—that Skander retreated in disorder.

Rexhep came and took the girls away without a word. Did he hate me more because I'd satisfied them? For that matter, did he hate me more because I'd satisfied myself? I didn't inquire. Yes, some few things are better left unknown.

Max emerged from the closet neatly sheveled (the opposite of disheveled, yes?) once again. "How do you propose to get back into your room if it's barred from the inside?" I asked. That, I did want to know.

"I'll pull strings," he said. The reply made no sense to me, but then, a fair amount of what Max says makes no sense to me. The only thing saving him from complete incomprehensibility is that, unlike a lot of people I could name, he doesn't talk too much.

On the way to Max's room, we passed Skander in the hallway. Skander gave one of the better double takes I've seen on noting the redoubtable Captain Yildirim out and about. Put it on the stage in Schlepsig or Albion or even Narbonensis and it would stop the show for a couple of minutes: it was *that* good.

I wondered if my majordomo would follow us. That could have been awkward. But he didn't. Maybe he didn't trust his own eyes. If not, he was foolish: if you think you see something Max's size, you probably do.

When we got to Max's door—also tall—he reached up and yanked on a bit of string up near the top. No one less uncouthly tall would have noticed it or could have reached it. "I put the bar on a pivot," he murmured. "All I need to do is pull down here, and up it comes." And it did. He opened the door and went into the room where Skander thought he'd been all along. "Sweet dreams, your Majesty."

Well, I obliged him there. Oh, didn't I just!

XIII

orry—no Chapter XIII. It's unlucky.

XIV

Yes, I know this is the thirteenth chapter. But it's not Chapter XIII. There's a difference. If you don't believe me, ask the next tall building you happen to meet.

When I woke in the morning, I had some trouble remembering where I was and who I was supposed to be. But I didn't have any trouble at all remembering what I'd been doing. I smiled. Traces of cinnamon and rosewater and sandalwood still lingered in the air. My smile got wider.

Had it been only the morning before when I was crowned King of Shqiperi? By Eliphalet's curly whiskers, so it had! This would be my first whole day as a sovereign among sovereigns, equal in rank (if not in might) to the lords of Schlepsig and Torino and Leon.

In something over half a day's worth of kinging it, I'd started a war and started an orgy. I wondered what I could do to top that, given a day with the full complement of hours.

First things first. I looked under the bed. Zogu's stuffed eagle stone was still there. He'd warned me about overusing it, but he had said I could get a few days out of it. You never know how much till you try. It would, I told myself, be purely in the pursuit of knowledge. Can you deny that carnal knowledge is knowledge like any other kind? Can you deny it's more fun than any other kind?

Didn't think so.

I walked over to the closet to see what all was in it when it wasn't holding Max. Besides those incandescent robes, it turned out to have some specimens of Shqipetari national costume. What Shqipetari wear is more attractive than, say, Lokrian clothes: no short skirts, no pompoms on the shoes. Past that, I don't have much to say for it. One of these days, I might have to put it on anyway, to show I was at least pretending to be a jolly Shqipetar like the jolly Shqipetari I ruled. (More often than not, a jolly Shqipetar either has something wrong with him or he's just killed someone, but that's another story.)

Along with the white shirts and tight trousers and clumsy cloaks and horrid headgear (and those robes, which even Count Rappaport would have disdained), the closet held several sensible, comfortable Hassocki caftans. Evidently I was allowed to recall the land I came from as well as the one I now inhabited. A caftan and a crown go together oddly, but I donned them both. Maybe I would start a new trend.

The faithful—I hoped—Skander wasn't far from the door when I came out. If he saw anything odd about my outfit, he didn't mention it. "Good morning, your Majesty," he said. "How may I serve you today?"

"Coffee," I said. "Breakfast." A king has to have his priorities straight. I thought about asking for another helping of harem girls, too, just to see the look on Skander's face. But I couldn't do them justice right then, and my mother always taught me not to ask for anything I couldn't use. So I tried a different question instead: "Who wants to see me this morning?"

"Several scribes, your Majesty—they seemed quite insistent," the majordomo replied. "And Essad Pasha—he seemed quite upset. And Untergraf Horst-Gustav—he seemed quite . . . well, quite hung over."

"I'll deal with all of them," I said, though the prospect of dealing with scribes made me wish I were hung over, too. Considering some of the katzenjammers I've had, that tells you how much I love scribes. I couldn't face them on an empty stomach. "Coffee," I repeated. "Breakfast."

The coffee was Hassocki-style, thick and sweet and muddy, the way it always is in the Nekemte Peninsula. It was also strong enough to pry my eyelids apart despite my sweaty exertions the night before. If I had been hung over, the curses and clashing cutlery in the kitchens would have driven me to despair. As things were, they helped wake me up.

Fried eggs. Fried blood sausages. Fried mush, which looks like something from the wrong end of a cow but actually tastes pretty good. The cooks didn't fry the strawberries. If they had, I might have ordered my first executions.

Max staggered into the dining room when I was about halfway through breakfast. He looked even more bedraggled, or possibly bed-raggled, than I felt. "Coffee," he croaked in piteous tones.

"Yes, your Excellency." Skander bowed deeply. "At once, your Excellency." He acted a lot more deferential toward Max than he had the day before. He must have decided Captain Yildirim was a powerful wizard along with being my aide-de-camp. How else could the redoubtable captain have got out of a locked room? Not for anything would I have told Max's secret.

I lingered over coffee, and smoked a cigar to stretch things out still further. It seemed to distress Skander. Shqipetari, I learned later, reckon anything but a pipe unmanly. This doesn't keep some of them from smoking cigars and cigarettes. It does give the rest an excuse to sneer at the ones who do. And Skander couldn't very well think me unmanly, not after the night before.

Bless the girls, anyhow!

At last, though, I had to face the evil moment. Captain Yildirim at my side, I went to the throne room to do it. Maybe the royal trappings would impress the foreign scribes (there were no Shqipetari scribes, proving the kingdom did have something going for it after all). Or maybe not—the trappings didn't much impress me.

In swarmed the scribes, pens poised above notebooks. They shouted questions in half a dozen languages, only two of which I was supposed to understand. I glanced over to Max, who stood behind and to the left of the throne. "Captain Yildirim," I said.

Out came the sword, the blade glittering in the torchlight. "Show respect for the royal dignity!" Max bawled in Hassocki.

Not many scribes knew Hassocki. That was all right. When a very large man bares his blade and shouts angrily, even some journalists will pay attention—enough to lessen the racket, anyhow.

Bumbling Bob of Albion wouldn't have noticed the sword if it cut off his head, and probably would have gone right on talking afterwards. Losing his head wouldn't have affected his brainpower much. In Albionese—of course—he asked, "Why did you declare war on Belagora?"

He didn't know I spoke Albionese. He thought I didn't, in fact. But, poor sap, he didn't speak anything else. Eventually someone translated the question into Schlepsigian, which I could admit I understood. *Because Barisha wears silly uniforms and ridiculous medals.* No, I didn't say it. It was true, but I didn't say it. Ah, diplomacy.

"Because Belagora does not respect Shqiperi's northern border. Because Belagora has soldiers on our territory"—my very first royal we!—"and refuses to remove them." That was also true. It had the added virtue of being polite, or as polite as you can be when you declare war on somebody. It had the vice of being dull.

The scribes didn't care. They solemnly wrote it down. One of them asked, "What will you do if Vlachia declares war on you?"

"Why should I care about the Vlachs?" I said grandly.

"Because they just beat the stuffing out of the Hassockian Empire?" the scribe suggested. "Because most of your soldiers are Hassocki leftovers?"

As a Schlepsigian, I had nothing but scorn for Vlachs. As I'd pointed out to Barisha, they're born chicken thieves. They also have a certain talent for murdering their betters from ambush. But the idea that I should take them seriously struck me as absurd.

As a Schlepsigian . . . I had to remember that, to these hovering vultures, I was no Schlepsigian. I was Halim Eddin, prince of a folk who, as the scribe was blunt enough to remind me, had just got ignominiously beaten by the Vlachs. How should I—I as Halim Eddin—react to that?

I decided that neither I as myself nor I as Halim Eddin could stomach knuckling under to the Vlachs. "If they want a fight, let them come. We will give them all they ask for, and more besides. They didn't beat our army here in Shqiperi during the Nekemte Wars, and they won't beat it now."

More furious scribbling from the scribes. "Do you trust Essad Pasha as a general?" one of them called.

Now *there* was an interesting question. I didn't trust Essad Pasha to empty my Chambers pot. Deceit was his middle name. I'd put the fear of the Quadrate God—or at least of Captain Yildirim—in him, but how long would that last? Long enough for me to let him command an army when he wasn't right under my eye? Max's cough said he didn't like the idea. Neither did I. But if he let the Vlachs beat him, he wasn't just risking my neck. He was risking his own even more.

"Essad Pasha is a very valiant warrior," I said after those calculations swallowed perhaps two heartbeats. I might not even have been lying. And I knew that, whatever I told the scribes, Essad Pasha would hear of it in short order. I went on, "Thanks to his courage and brilliance, Vlachian aggression in Shqiperi went nowhere during the late wars."

I might not have been lying about that, either. I didn't say anything about my new kingdom's impossible geography. You can't make a hero out of swamps and mountains. Yes, I admit that making a hero out of Essad Pasha is just about as unlikely, but all the same. . . .

I also hadn't said whether I trusted him. I wondered if the scribes would notice. There went some wasted worry. Scribes get paid to write down the obvious, and to try not to put their readers to sleep while they do it. The better ones can more or less manage that. The rest? Well, if someone like Bob can still get work, the standards of the trade could be higher.

"How did you like your harem, your Majesty?" somebody asked.

All the scribes leaned forward. *There* was the sort of story they were made to cover. They didn't have to think, which was lucky for most of them. They only had to be sensational. They could handle that, all right. Some semipornographic drivel their editors could tone down—or spice up, if they were Narbonese—later on was just what they had in mind.

As Otto of Schlepsig, I might have given it to them. As Halim Eddin? No. In the matter of harems, Halim Eddin was a worldly-wise man of experience, where the scribes were panting boys with drool running down their chins. So I said, "The girls seem pleasant enough. They fully measure up to the ones I knew in Vyzance."

"How many of them do you know?" someone shouted.

"I made a point of introducing myself to all of them yesterday afternoon," I replied. "Summoning women I had not met would be most impolite."

"How many of them did you summon?" a scribe asked, while another one called, "Did you summon them all at once or one at a time?"

I looked severe. At least, I hoped I didn't just look exhausted. "Gentlemen, I don't ask you what you did in the nighttime."

Once that was translated for Bob, he said, "I did nothing in the night-time."

"Thou lying dog," Max said behind me in Hassocki. I don't think any of the scribes heard him, which was probably just as well.

"We're not the King of Shqiperi," a journalist said. "We haven't got a harem."

"And you don't want your wives hearing what you did do?" I suggested. That produced laughter and nudges and winks. Nobody denied it.

Well, next to nobody. "I did nothing in the nighttime," Bob repeated plaintively. He was an old man. It might even have been true.

"You will have to draw a veil of silence around the harem," I told the scribes, "for I do not intend to think of it further." The real Halim Eddin would have been proud of me. The real Halim Eddin might even have assumed that, since I didn't say anything more about the harem, the scribes wouldn't write any more about it.

If so, the real Halim Eddin would have proved himself a naive, innocent Hassocki. I knew better. If I didn't talk about the harem, the scribes would put words in my mouth. If they didn't, their editors back in Albion or Narbonensis or Schlepsig or Torino would. They had to sell journals, after all. If the King of Shqiperi wouldn't give them the copy they wanted, they'd come up with it some other way. After all, what could he do about it?

Declare war?

What a tempting thought! But Belagora lay within my reach. The idiot scribes of Narbonensis and Albion? I'm afraid not. If I could have marched a Shqipetari army through the streets of Lutetia and sacked the editors one by one, dividing all of their gall into three parts . . . Even more a fantasy on my part than the journalists' slavering visions of a harem were on theirs.

"Anything else, gentlemen?" I asked, stretching a point.

There wasn't. After war and women, they weren't very interested in other matters. Now that I think about it, they had a point.

After the scribes trooped out, gabbling among themselves, Skander brought Essad Pasha into the improvised throne room. The former governor of Shqiperi bowed low to the master he had summoned. "Your Majesty," he murmured.

"Good morning, your Excellency," I said. "How are you today?"

"I am well, thank you." Essad Pasha's heavy features worked. "Your Majesty, did you really declare war on Belagora?"

"I'm not making this up, you know," I said. "I most assuredly did. Why?"

"Because they'll slaughter us!" he said.

"I doubt it. They didn't slaughter you in the Nekemte Wars. Why should they start now? They're only Belagorans, after all," I said. "North and south, east and west, are there any greater cowards in all the world?"

"Well, there are the Shqipetari," Essad Pasha said with a laugh.

Skander, hearing this, did not laugh. He quivered like a hound taking a scent and then aimed himself at Essad Pasha like that same hound getting ready to spring. Shqiperi is the land of the blood feud. Any little insult can bring it on. Essad Pasha had just insulted all the people in the land, and not in any little way. I wondered if he would get out of the palace alive. I wondered if I wanted him to.

With some reluctance, I decided I did. "Perhaps you might think about rephrasing that," I said.

"Why should I?" Essad Pasha fleered. Then he noticed the tension in Skander's body and the terrible intensity in the majordomo's eyes. Like a pricked bladder, Essad Pasha's bravado collapsed. He realized he'd stepped over a line. Now the problem was to step back without making himself out to be a worse coward than he'd called the Shqipetari.

"You might have been hasty," I suggested.

"Mmm." That wasn't a word, just a noise in the back of Essad Pasha's throat, as if to suggest he needed oiling. "Mmm." He made it again. This time, it turned into a word: "Mmmaybe. I suppose I put it badly. If the Shqipetari were properly drilled and led and disciplined, they would be brave enough. As things are, with all their quarrels and ambushes, they don't really get the chance to show what they could do."

He waited. I waited. Behind me and to my left, Max waited. Skander hadn't said a word before. He didn't say anything now. He'd tensed all in a moment. He didn't relax the same way. Instead, the tautness left his body inch by inch. At last, he stopped staring at Essad Pasha as if about to fling himself at the older man in the next instant.

Essad Pasha breathed then. So did I. I hadn't realized I'd stopped till I started again. I hadn't realized how long I'd stopped till I found out how much I needed that new breath. Life in Shqiperi is often squalid, sometimes downright nasty. It is rarely dull.

In Schlepsig, even in Narbonensis, you can go for years without being threatened with sudden and violent death. Is dullness one of the great unheralded virtues of civilization? I wouldn't be surprised.

"Shall we get back to the northern frontier?" I asked, and Essad Pasha nodded jerkily. Since he'd just acted like a jerk, that seemed altogether fitting and proper. I went on, "Now that I'm King of Shqiperi, have the mountains up there flattened out? Have the roads got better? Have the dragons got friendlier?"

"Give me leave to doubt it, your Majesty. You are a great and mighty lord"—Essad Pasha had a certain low talent for sarcasm himself—"but you are not the Quadrate God. Or if you are, the incognito is remarkable effective."

He could say that. If I agreed with it, even in jest, I blasphemed. I knew enough of the Quadrate God's cult to understand as much. "No, no. I am only a man," I said, and passed the test. "So what can the Belagorans do past making a nuisance of themselves? They're already a nuisance, yes?"

"That they are." Essad Pasha sighed. "I suppose the biggest worry is that Vlachia will jump into the fight, too. Vlachia lusts after Fushe-Kuqe, having no port of its own."

Only people who've never seen Fushe-Kuqe could possibly lust after it. "You held them off before. I'm sure you can do it again," I said, and Essad Pasha, no more modest than he had to be, nodded. So much for his worries, then.

One of Skander's assistants came in and murmured to him in Shqipetari. Skander turned to me and raised an eyebrow, showing he wanted to be heard. I nodded. He spoke in Hassocki: "Your Majesty, his Excellency Vuk Nedic of Vlachia urgently requests an audience with you at your earliest convenience."

"What about Horst-Gustav?" I asked.

More back-and-forth in Shqipetari. "He appears to have gone back to the Metropolis," Skander reported. "He seemed unwell."

"I see," I said. "Well, you can send the werewolf in, then." That sent

Skander into gales, torrents, cloudbursts of laughter. He never explained why. Maybe he thought Vuk Nedic was one, too, but was too polite to say so out loud. Or maybe the idea hadn't occurred to him till I used it. Wherever the truth lay there, he liked it. I asked Essad Pasha, "You can defend the kingdom a while longer?"

"A while longer, yes," he replied. "Do please try not to declare war on Vlachia right this minute, though, if you'd be so kind." Maybe Max's coughs meant he thought that was a good idea. Maybe they just meant he had his usual catarrh. I didn't inquire.

"I'll try," I told Essad Pasha. "North and south, east and west, he deserves it, though."

"Most of us deserve a great many things, your Majesty," he replied. "If we're lucky, we don't get all of them."

Now there was a nice philosophical point. It almost made me wish I had time to discuss it. "Anything else?" I asked Essad Pasha. He shook his head. I gestured to Skander. "Show in the Vlachian."

"Yes, your Majesty." He'd got control of himself. Now he started giggling softly again.

Essad Pasha stumped out of the throne room as Vuk Nedic strode in. They glared in passing. Each man's hand fell to the hilt of his sword, but they both kept walking. Looking more lupine than ever, Vuk Nedic bowed before me. "Your Majesty!" he barked.

"Your Excellency," I said. "What can I do for you this morning?"

He ran his tongue across his lips. It seemed exceptionally long and pink and limber. When he reeled it back into his mouth, his teeth looked uncommonly large and sharp. No ordinary man should have had those golden-brown eyes. "You have declared war on Belagora," he growled.

"That's true," I said. "So what?"

"Vlachia is Belagora's ally," he said. "Why should we not declare war on you?"

"Because you wouldn't get very far?" I suggested. "Because if you could have got very far, you would have done it in the Nekemte Wars? Because there would be no point to it except killing soldiers who don't urgently need killing?"

He blinked. With those odd-colored eyes, the effect was particularly startling. My guess was, he'd never imagined soldiers might *not* need killing. "We could tear the throat out of this miserable excuse for a king-dom," he snarled.

"I doubt it," I said.

He waited. Skander waited. Even Max seemed to be waiting, though I couldn't see him. But I'd said everything I intended to say for the moment. It was Vuk Nedic's turn. He bared those impressive teeth again. They weren't impressive enough to scare me off my throne. After a pack of scribes, what was one possible werewolf?

And I hadn't even begun to find out what fangs scribes have!

Vuk Nedic growled again, down deep in his throat. "Count Rappa-port is a blundering fool," he got out at last.

Well, well! We'd found something on which we could agree! Who would have imagined it? "Why do you say so?" I asked. Always interesting to hear someone else's reasons for despising a man you also dislike.

"Because if you were not a proper king, you would never have the nerve to defy grand and mighty Vlachia," Vuk Nedic replied.

I didn't laugh in his face. I don't know why not. I merely report the fact. Max didn't cough, either. In an experimental mood, I pulled a coin from my pocket: a good, solid silver Schlepsigian kram. I tossed it to Vuk Nedic, saying, "This for your courtesy."

Most of the time, if you toss a man a coin, he will automatically catch it. If you toss a man who is at least part werewolf a silver coin, he will auto-matically catch it—and will then be sorry he has. That was what I wanted to see: whether Vuk Nedic would be sorry he was holding a silver coin.

But I never found out. The Vlach made an awkward grab for the kram, but missed it altogether. It bounced off the front of his wolfskin jacket and fell to the floor, where it rang sweetly. Before bending to pick it up, he pulled from his pocket a pair of thin kidskin gloves, which he swiftly donned. Only then did he retrieve the coin.

"I take this as one man takes a present from another," he said. "I do not take it to mean that Vlachia is in any way obliged to Shqiperi. If my king decides to go to war alongside Belagora, you may be assured I will fight at the fore."

"I would not doubt it," I said, and then, "As one man takes a present from another, yes." I'd had my question answered, all right, if not quite in the way I thought I would. As soon as Vuk Nedic stowed away the kram, the kidskin gloves came off and likewise disappeared.

After that, we didn't seem to have anything else to say to each other. The Vlach departed. I couldn't help wondering if the skin from which his jacket was made came from anybody he knew.

"Your Majesty." Zogu the wizard bowed before me. "I hope my little preparation gave, ah, satisfaction last night." He was bold enough to tip me a wink.

"I'm not complaining," I said dryly. Max coughed once or twice. Zogu's clever eyes slid toward him for a moment. Did the wizard know my aide-de-camp had shared the bounty? More to the point, did Zogu know what a good idea keeping his mouth shut was? I suspected he did. Mages who blab only encourage their clients to turn other mages loose on them.

"I'm glad you were pleased," he said now. "If you were, then I take it you summoned me for some other reason?"

"You might say so," I told him. "You will have heard the kingdom has gone to war with Belagora?"

"I think everyone in Peshkepiia will have heard it by now," Zogu replied. "It will not hurt your name in this kingdom. Shqipetari are always at war with Vlachs, whether they have fancy proclamations or not. But what has this got to do with me?"

"The mountains in these parts are full of dragons," I said. "I haven't been north to the Belagoran border, but I assume it's the same up there. Am I right?"

"I should say you are, your Majesty," Zogu said. "And so?"

"And so there will be columns of Belagoran soldiers marching through those mountains," I said. "Dragons might find columns of soldiers tasty any which way. Can you use your art to make sure they find columns of Belagoran soldiers especially tasty?"

He didn't answer right away. Instead, he cocked his head to one side, studying me. "You don't think small, do you, your Majesty?" he said at last.

"I wouldn't be a king if I did," I said, which was—I hoped—truer than he knew. "Can you do this?"

"Not right here in the throne room," Zogu said. "I'll need a dragon scale and a Belagoran uniform even to begin the spell. Compelling dragons is a dangerous business. No one does it without the greatest need. Hardly anyone gets the chance to do it more than once. Coaxing them is commonly wiser."

"You will know your own business best, I'm sure," I said. "But may I ask you a couple of questions before you go about it?"

Zogu smiled. "You are the king. How can I say no?"

"Easily enough, I suspect," I said, which made the smile wider. "If you work this magic, dragons will look to columns of Belagoran soldiers on the far side of the border, not just on ours?"

"Certainly, your Majesty," the sorcerer said. Yes, indeed—amusement, or perhaps deviltry, danced in his dark eyes. "I presume that doesn't disappoint you?"

"Not a bit. North and south, east and west, not a bit," I answered. "The Belagorans are bad neighbors. One way to make a bad neighbor leave you alone is to convince him you're a worse one. Which reminds me—do you suppose you can get your hands on a Vlachian uniform, too?"

Now Zogu laughed out loud. "I think I might be able to do that, yes." But before I got too happy, he went on, "Most of the border with Vlachia is swamp country, not mountains. You won't see dragons so often in those western parts."

"Too bad," I said, and then, "Could you make some arrangement with the leeches, maybe? They ought to be fond of Vlachs—like calls to like, after all."

Zogu didn't get it—and then, all at once, he did. As he wagged a forefinger at me, he made a choking noise that said he was holding in more than he was letting out. He bowed very low. "Ah, your Majesty, surely the imp of trouble dwells in your heart."

"Surely," Max murmured in back of me. I couldn't even tread on his toes. The indignities a king must put up with sometimes!

"One matter we have not discussed, your Majesty," Zogu said: "the price."

"What?" I drew myself up straight on my rickety throne. "You would not undertake this as a patriotic duty to your kingdom?"

By the look in Zogu's eye, if I wanted somebody to undertake something, I should talk to an undertaker—and I should talk to him about my own funeral as long as I was there. "Your Majesty," he said in a voice all silky with danger, "wizards have to eat no less than other men."

"Put your feathers down," Max advised him. "He's joking."

Was I? Had I been? I couldn't very well call my aide-de-camp a liar, not without starting an unseemly row. "Name your price, magical sir," I said to Zogu, "and we'll see how loud I scream."

Zogu didn't answer right away. His calculations, I daresay, were twofold: how much the magic would really cost him, and how much the traffic would bear. I, the traffic, waited apprehensively. Once he'd added up the numbers, he did name his price.

I screamed loud enough to bring not only Skander but half a dozen lesser flunkies to the throne room on the run. I hadn't thought I could hit that high note without being treated the way poor Rexhep was. Some of the servitors had paused to snatch up implements of mayhem before they got there. Shqipetari are always ready for brawls. Sometimes, if they can't find one, they'll start one for the sport of it.

Skander looked around wildly—for spilled blood, I believe. "Are you all right, your Majesty?" he panted.

"I could be worse," I said. "The only place I'm wounded is in the pocketbook. This optimist"—I scowled at Zogu—"thinks I bleed gold."

"Ah." Skander paused to digest that. By his expression, he didn't find it especially digestible. "Your Majesty has . . . an odd way of haggling."

"Thank you," I said. He blinked. One more time: if you can't confound them, confuse them. He and the other servitors withdrew—in confusion. I nodded to Zogu. "Where were we?"

"I believe we were trying to cheat each other." The wizard was refreshingly frank. "What price would you consider reasonable, your Majesty?"

"About a quarter of yours," I answered.

"I see." Zogu bowed. "Well, if I were to scream now, it would only upset your servants twice in the space of a few minutes, and for no good purpose. You may, however, take the thought for the deed."

"Try another price, then," I said. "Try one that doesn't make me want to shriek."

He did. I opened my mouth again, melodramatically but, I confess, silently. Max coughed. Max always thinks I overact. This, from the greatest ham not sitting on a dinner plate! No one gets the respect he deserves.

Zogu appreciated my performance, and he was the intended audience. Mirth sparked in his eyes. "Your Majesty is not the common sort of king," he said, something of which for one reason or another I was often accused during my reign.

I did my best to look regally severe. "And with how many kings have you consorted?" I asked.

"I'm not interested in consorting with them." By the way Zogu said it, he could have had tea with monarchs every day if he cared to. He went on to explain why he didn't: "The King of Belagora is a bore, and the King of Vlachia is a boor."

"You left out the King of Lokris," I said.

"Excuse me. You are correct. The King of Lokris is—a Lokrian. I shall say no more." And Zogu didn't, not about that. Shqipetari love Lokrians even more than Lokrians love Shqipetari. You think it couldn't be done? Well, I thought so, too.

We eventually settled on a price that, I'm sure, made both of us want to scream: the proof of a hard-fought bargain. Then we started haggling all over again, over how much Zogu should get before he cast his spell and how much should wait till word of its effectiveness came back to Peshkepiia. Not surprisingly, he wanted to get it all in advance. Just as not surprisingly, I didn't want to give it to him that way.

Reaching an agreement there that dissatisfied us both also took its own sweet time. Nothing in the Nekemte Peninsula happens as fast as a civilized person, or even a Narbonese, wishes it would. You haggle. You have coffee. You have spirits. You have little cakes, or possibly fried mutton on skewers. You smoke a pipe. In Schlepsig, by Eliphalet's purse, a price is a price. You pay it or your don't, and you go on either way. Hereabouts, a price is negotiable. Hereabouts, everything is negotiable (except a blood feud—a blood feud is serious business). And the dickering is as important as the price you finally settle on.

To a Schlepsigian or any other sensible person, this all seems utterly mad. I had to remind myself again and again that I was not a Schlepsigian. I was Prince Halim Eddin, and I was used to haggling for the fun of it. If I hadn't done those tours in the Hassockian Army, and if I hadn't spent more time than I ever wanted in the Nekemte Peninsula with outfits like Dooger and Cark's, *and* if I weren't a damned fine actor (Max to the contrary notwithstanding), I never could have brought it off.

Seeing the royal treasury again as I got the money to give Zogu his first installment helped cheer me up. Taking the money out of it didn't. But there was still plenty left. I consoled myself with that. Zogu, no doubt, consoled himself with what I gave him.

Not an earth-shaking day, perhaps—of which there are too many in literal truth in those parts—but a right royal one even so.

And a right royal night as well. Once again, Max contrived to leave his room seemingly locked from the inside and to find himself a waiting place in the royal bedchamber. I ordered another half-dozen girls brought from the harem, and hoped Zogu's spell wouldn't, ah, let me down.

When Rexhep brought the girls, they were bubbly and giggly and eager, from which I concluded that Lutzi and Maja and Bjeshka and Varri and Zalli and Shkoza (you see?—I remember them all) had given me a good report. The eunuch looked as if he loathed me more than ever, from which I concluded the same thing. Poor fellow! I had a hard time blaming him.

After a few high-pitched grumbles, he went on his none too merry way. I closed the door behind Shinasi and Urani and Xharmi and Flisni and Kalla and Molle (yes, I remember them, too) and barred it. "And now, my sweets, the night is ours," I said.

They were polite. I was the king, after all. Still, their newly unveiled faces fell. I think it was Xharmi who got up the nerve to ask, "But, your Majesty, where is the Thunderbolt we heard so much about?"

Lutzi and Maja and—well, you know the rest by now—hadn't given just *me* a good report, then. Oh, well. I don't suppose I should have expected anything different. You will recall that Thunderbolt, in Hassocki, is Yildirim.

I went to the closet and opened the door. "Will you join us, Captain?" I said sweetly. "Your presence—among other things—has been requested."

Join us Max did. As he had been the night before, he was dressed, or undressed, for the occasion. The girls exclaimed in admiration or apprehension or possibly both at once. Max looked as smug as a man with a vinegar phiz can.

Well, I won't bore you with the details. (And if the details of such things don't bore you, I'm sure you can invent your own. They'll probably be even juicier than what went on while the two of us and the six of them . . . But I wasn't going to bore you with that, was I?) Suffice to say that if Zogu's sorcery against the Belagorans worked half so well, the dragons would devour every man wearing that uniform by the morning after he launched that spell. And speaking of devouring—but no, that's one of those details, I'm afraid.

By the time—a very pleasantly long time—Max and I couldn't hold up our end of the bargain any more, everyone in that bedchamber was happy enough, or maybe a little more than happy enough.

"I was afraid they were fooling us," said Molle—I think it was Molle, anyway. "But no. They meant it." By the way she sighed, she was glad to be mollified, too.

Maybe even kings who follow the Two Prophets should be allowed harems. It might give them something to do besides starting wars. But then, considering how many the Hassockian Atabegs have started, and considering that I'd just started one myself, it might not, too. What a shame.

XV

There are people who believe Eliphalet and Zibeon personally presided over the discovery of crystallography. (Quite a few of them work for Consolidated Crystal.) Me, I don't belong to that school. In case you hadn't noticed, I also can't stand scribes. Yes, my story deserved to be in the journals—do you think I became King of Shqiperi just for the sake of the Shqipetari? But I didn't need all the trouble the story got me.

Scribes in the Nekemte Peninsula, like scribes everywhere, are out for the splashiest stories they can find. And so the sensation-stealers who'd followed me from Fushe-Kuqe to Peshkepiia wrote the loudest, gaudiest reports of my coronation that they could. For them, my story was a found feast, you might say. They sent their blitherings off to their journals, which duly ran them. Nothing else nearly so interesting was coming out of the Nekemte Peninsula just then, if I do say so myself.

Why am I so unhappy? you ask. Didn't I want my name—well, Halim Eddin's name—on everyone's lips?

Almost everyone's. Almost, but not quite.

The trouble was, before long the story of Halim Eddin's coronation got to Vyzance. The Hassocki are backward, but they aren't *that* backward. Consolidated Crystal has offices in Vyzance. Consolidated Crystal has offices everywhere. I sometimes think that, if wizards ever figure out how to master apportation and let men rise to the moon, the first travelers there will walk over to a CC office so a crystallographer can send word back to a waiting world.

In Vyzance, then, word of the coronation naturally came to the Hassockian Atabeg. Why couldn't he have been disporting himself with *his* harem when it did? And, I supposed, word of the coronation also reached the authentic, the veritable, the actual, the genuine Prince Halim Eddin, who was sitting by the Silver Trumpet—for such they style the main harbor of Vyzance—innocently smoking his long, picturesque Hassocki-style pipe.

I can imagine the scene. In spite of the chaos gripping the Hassockian Empire on account of the Nekemte Wars, in spite of everything else that was wrong with the Empire—a subject on which I could write volumes (and many men have)—the whole business must have seemed something past a joke to the Atabeg.

He would have sent a message to the real Prince Halim Eddin: "North and south, east and west, what the demon are you doing in Shqiperi?"

And the real Halim Eddin would have sent a message back: "North and south, east and west, your Most Sublime and Magnificent Awfulness, the last time I looked I was right here. As far as I can tell, I still am."

And the Hassockian Atabeg would have said, "Well, those Schlepsigian and Narbonese and Torinan journalists—to say nothing of Bob, the half-witted Albionese—all put you in Shqiperi."

"If Bob has me there, that's the best proof in the world that I'm really here," Halim Eddin would have replied.

Now, the Hassockian Atabeg is not the brightest and most perceptive of men; Eliphalet knows that's so. But even he would perceive that his nephew had advanced an argument of weight. He would have said, "Why don't I come over to your little palace and have a look at you for myself?"

"Come ahead, your Most Supreme and Appalling Splendor," Halim Eddin would have told him. "If you discover that I'm not here, I will confess to being very surprised."

And the Hassockian Atabeg would have gone to look. And, I daresay, he would have seen the authentic, the veritable, the actual, the genuine Prince Halim Eddin with his very own eyes. They might even have innocently smoked together a couple of long, picturesque Hassocki-style pipes.

In due course, the Atabeg would have returned to the imperial palace in Vyzance. And, in due course (just how due the course depending on the precise mix those long, picturesque Hassocki-style pipes were charged with), he would have issued a statement of his own, saying no

one in Vyzance had thought at all about sending Prince Halim Eddin—
or any other Hassocki prince—to Shqiperi. Since neither Prince Halim
Eddin nor any other Hassocki prince was in Shqiperi, no such worthy
could possibly have become King of Shqiperi. The news to the contrary,
then, had to rest on an error. And it was probably Bob's fault for getting
things wrong.

You will please understand I was not in Vyzance while all this was going
on. I was in beautiful (Eliphalet, no!), picturesque (Eliphalet and Zibeon,
no!) Peshkepiia, much more pleasantly occupied. I cannot prove how the
Hassockian Atabeg came to make his unfortunate statement. I can only
imagine, as I say, and reconstruct.

But I can prove that he did make the statement. And I can prove it
was unfortunate. For me, worse luck.

On the third day of my reign I appointed Captain Yildirim minister
for special affairs. The title seemed fitting to us both. Aside from a round
dozen—a very nicely round dozen—of the harem girls, we were the only
ones who knew just why it fit so well. To the outside world, it was just
one of those mostly meaningless handles by which officials so often come
to be known.

I also announced I would name the rest of my cabinet the following
week. Alas! The full administration of the Kingdom of Shqiperi under
the rule of that brilliant and enlightened potentate, King Halim Eddin
I—otherwise Otto of Schlepsig—will never be known. I'm sure it would
have performed better than any has since in that unhappy realm. I'm just
as sure it could scarcely have performed worse.

Having made the initial appointment, then, I sent the intrepid minister for special affairs out to wander through Peshkepiia and learn what he
could in the bazaar and the fortress. "Be inconspicuous," I told him.

For some reason or other, he chose that moment to suffer one of his
coughing fits.

I threw my hands in the air. Some people *will* insist on being unrea-
sonable. "Oh, *all* right!" I said. "Be as inconspicuous as a six-foot-eight
man in a fancy uniform can be, then."

"Yes, your Majesty." The intrepid minister for special affairs, Captain

Yildirim—otherwise Max of Witte—nodded in somber satisfaction (not at all the sort he'd shown the past two nights). "Always nice to get orders I have some hope of following."

"Heh," I said, and then, "Heh, heh. As if you ever cared about following orders!"

"I do," he said with dignity. "If I'm not going to follow an order, I want to have fun not following it."

If he hadn't been having about as much fun as a man could without falling over dead right afterwards, he disguised it very well. But then, Max was always good at disguising enjoyment, even from himself. "Just go," I said. "Come back in the afternoon and tell me what you hear."

While he was going up and down in the city doing his job, Skander announced a caller who surprised me: Count Rappaport, from the Dual Monarchy. "Send him in. By all means, send him in," I said. "What do you suppose he wants?"

"Something that will do him good," Skander replied. "Whether it will do Shqiperi any good is bound to be a different question." He might have made a good foreign minister. Being able to see the obvious put him quite a few lengths ahead of several men holding the post in older, larger kingdoms.

Into the throne room strode Count Rappaport. The phalanx of medals on his narrow chest outshone the (I admit it) tawdry show of finery we'd been able to arrange on short notice. The Dual Monarchy had centuries of practice at that kind of thing. They were good at it. It is, I often think, the only thing they were good at. Count Rappaport bowed. "Your Majesty," he said.

"I thought you didn't believe in me," I replied.

"Your *de facto* Majesty," he said with legalistic precision, and bowed again. Some of the metalwork pinned to his shirtfront clanked. "Since you've declared war on Belagora, I find myself willing to be agnostic, at any rate. Our interests may march in the same direction."

"You're trying to tell me you want my interest to march with yours," I said.

His narrow mouth got narrower. They didn't much like obvious truths in the Dual Monarchy. They had reason not to like them, too, for one most obvious truth was that the Dual Monarchy had no business stumbling on into the modern era. But he knew the right words to say here: "We are no more enamored of Belagora than you are, and we do not love Vlachia, either."

"How dangerous *is* Vuk Nedic when the moon comes full?" I murmured.

"An interesting question," said Count Rappaport. "Did you try to cross his palm with silver? Is rumor true?"

"Yes, your Excellency, it is." I told him how the Vlach handled his money with kid gloves.

"Well, well," said the nobleman from the Dual Monarchy. "I still have no idea who you are, your Majesty. My opinion remains the same: you are no more Halim Eddin than my grandmother's cat is. But I do believe Shqiperi and the Dual Monarchy can do business all the same. We have enemies in common, and the enemy of my enemy is. . . ."

Is like as not another enemy, for different reasons, I thought. *That's how it works in the Nekemte Peninsula, anyhow.* I almost laughed out loud, there on my foil-wrapped throne. Barisha of Belagora and Vuk Nedic of Vlachia were sure I was Halim Eddin, sent from Vyzance to rule Shqiperi. Yes, they were sure I was the genuine article, and they hated me on sight. But, though Count Rappaport knew I was a fraud—damn him!—he was ready to act as if I were authentic, and to help me poke the Vlachian kingdoms in the eye. Even for this part of the world, that struck me as perverse.

Which didn't mean I wouldn't take advantage of it if I could. Perversions can be enjoyable; they wouldn't be so popular if they couldn't. A couple of nights with the harem girls and the redoubtable minister of special affairs had proved remarkably instructive on that score. Count Rappaport was offering a different pleasure, but not one to be despised on that account.

"The enemy of my enemy," I said, "can share his short ribs. With pepper sauce."

Count Rappaport . . . smiled.

Max—Captain Yildirim—my new minister for special affairs—the sword-swallower—my old friend—came back to the palace looking like a man who'd seen a ghost: his own ghost. Now, Max is not one of the more gleeful-looking people in the world. He never has been. He never will be. Even when he's happy, he mostly seems sad. When he's sad, he seems appalled. And when he's appalled . . .

When he's appalled, he looks a lot more cheerful than he did just then.

He was doing his best *not* to seem horrified, too, the way a man who's just lost an arm will tell you it's only a flesh wound. The arm is still gone; Max's best was miles from being good enough. He staggered into the throne room a few minutes after Count Rappaport departed.

"Could we speak in your chambers, your Majesty?" He sounded as bad as he looked, which is saying something.

Skander saw and heard it, too. "Shall I send for a healer, your Majesty?" he asked.

I had the feeling a Shqipetari healer does to health what a Shqipetari cook does to food. I also had the feeling I needed to hear what Max had to say. So I told Skander, "Maybe later," before turning back to the minister for special affairs and saying, "Of course, your Excellency. Come with me."

Even in his state of poleaxed dismay, Max raised an eyebrow at that. He'd never been *your Excellency* in his life before; I'm sure of that. *You dead-beat son of a whore* was much more his usual style. (And mine, oh yes—and mine. But I was learning how to play the king.)

We chased a sweeper out of my bedchamber. I barred the door behind us. Then I said, "Well, what is it?" Even behind a closed door, I spoke Hassocki, not Schlepsigian: the sound of my voice might get out into the hallway even if words didn't.

"I—" Max paused to try to gather himself—without much luck, I'm afraid.

I handed him a jug of plum brandy. He didn't bother flicking away a drop before he drank. His throat worked: worked overtime, in fact. After he'd poured down a good slug, he seemed a new man. The new man wobbled a bit on his pins, but you can't have everything.

"I went down to the Consolidated Crystal office to see what I could find out," he said. "A lot of the scribes don't know I can understand 'em, so they just blather away like nobody's business."

Most scribes blather away regardless of whether anybody understands them, but that's a different story. "Good thinking," I told Max. "Might as well find out how the journals are looking at us. Until the reviews come in, who knows how the show will do?"

"So I was mooching around listening to all their foolishness, but then a message came in instead of going out." Max paused portentously. "A message from Vyzance."

"Oh," I said. A ship can sail along happy as you please, the weather-worker filling the sails with wind, everything calm, everything serene— and if it tears out its belly on a rock lurking just under the surface, everybody on board will drown. And it will strike all the harder because it was going so well before. I had to gather myself to get out more than the one word, which is not like me at all. "What—what did it say?"

"What would you expect a message from Vyzance to say?" Max answered. "It says the Atabeg's bloody surprised to find out his nephew's King of Shqiperi when good old Halim Eddin's really back there being useless the way a proper Hassocki prince is supposed to. And what do you think about that, good old Halim Eddin?"

"The message was for Essad Pasha?" I asked. Max nodded, then reached for the jug of brandy again. I grabbed it first—I needed it, too. Once I got a healthy snort inside me, I felt better, or at least number. I pointed an accusing finger at my minister for special affairs. "Why didn't you waylay the messenger?"

"I tried," he said morosely. "Little bastard gave me the slip. It's his town, and it isn't mine. What are we going to do, O sage of the age? I mean, besides getting our heads cut off and spears rammed up our backsides, probably not in that order?"

I had to think fast. I took another slug of brandy. Maybe it would lubricate my wits. If it didn't, maybe I wouldn't care. *Something* worked in there. "It's a lie," I told Max.

"What's a lie? That the Atabeg sent the message? That Essad Pasha's cursed well got it? Don't I wish it was, *your* Majesty." Max made my title positively poisonous. "I was there, I tell you."

"Yes, yes," I said impatiently. "There's a real message, but it's a real lie, too."

"In a pig's posterior!" Max said. "You're as much a Hassocki prince as I am a camel."

"The way you've been humping the last two nights, you might be," I said. "Shut up and listen to me. The Hassockian Atabeg has to deny that I'm really his nephew—even though I am, of course."

"Oh, yes. Of course." Max gives the most disagreeable agreement I've ever known.

I ignored him. It's not easy, but I have practice. "He has to deny that I'm Halim Eddin. What just happened to the Hassockian Empire? It just got the snot kicked out of it in the Nekemte Wars. If it hadn't, Shqiperi wouldn't be a kingdom. It would still be a Hassocki province, right?"

"I suppose so," Max said. "But what's that got to do with—"

I went right on ignoring him. Brandy helps. "Listen, I tell you. The Hassocki tried to sneak a fast one past their neighbors and the Great Powers by sending me here. I'm their stalking horse. I'm the key to their holding on to influence in the eastern part of the Nekemte Peninsula."

"You're out of your mind," Max said. "I knew it all along. You really are."

"You're just jealous," I said, which had the distinct virtue of making him shut up. That accomplished, I went on, "What other choice have we got? We've jumped on the dragon—we can't let go of its ears now."

"Of course we can't. Dragons haven't got ears. And you haven't got any brains."

"This is not the time to revoke my poetic license. You know what I mean," I said. "What do we do if this crystal message from Vyzance isn't a stinking lie, eh? Do we paste on sheepish grins and go, 'Sorry, we were just playing a little joke on you people. I guess we'll be running along now'?"

"Don't I wish!" Max exclaimed. "I'd love to. Only thing is, I don't think Essad Pasha's laughing right now."

I didn't think so, either. Essad Pasha is one of those people who will laugh till the tears come while he's watching his enemies' beards burn after he's soaked them in oil and touched a match to them. His sense of humor does go that far. When it comes to seeing a joke on himself, though . . . "If you want to live to spend any of the money in the treasury, if you don't want to wind up envying Rexhep—"

"What's the eunuch got to do with it?" Max broke in.

"Well, for one thing, if they find out we're just a couple of performers from Schlepsig, they may want to cut our balls off on general principles," I said. "But they may not need general principles, not when they've got specific ones. How many Shqipetari maidens have you debauched the past two nights?"

"Debauched, my left one. They loved every minute of it." But Max looked worried about his left one, and his right one, too.

"To the Shqipetari, that only makes things worse. They aren't supposed to enjoy it here. You're not supposed to enjoy anything here except the cursed blood feuds." Now that I think on things, that made Essad Pasha a pretty fair governor for Shqiperi, didn't it? I had more urgent worries just then, or I would have seen it sooner. I went on, "So that message has to be a lie. The best thing we can do is make everyone think it is. The worst we can do is buy some time."

"Time to get out of here," Max said. "Eliphalet's beard, it *is* time to get out of here!"

"Don't talk about Eliphalet, even in Hassocki," I told him. That proved good advice, because a moment later someone knocked on the door. Max jumped like a cornered sword-swallower pretending to be an aide-de-camp to a cornered acrobat pretending to be a king. Quite a bit like that, in fact. As calmly as he could, the cornered actor pretending to be a king opened the door. There stood Skander, not pretending to be a major-domo—and not even knowing he was cornering us. "Yes?" I said—regally.

"Excuse me, your Majesty, but his Excellency Essad Pasha is here. He would like to see you for a moment," Skander said.

Max didn't jump again, but he definitely twitched. Skander already suspected my minister for special affairs of being in two places at once. Now Max seemed not to want to be any place at all. I felt a certain sympathy for that; I didn't much want to be any place in Peshkepiia myself. But if I had to be any place in Peshkepiia, the palace was the best one.

"Tell his Excellency I will meet him in the throne room in a quarter of an hour," I said. Skander bowed and scurried away.

You'd be surprised how much brandy you can drink in fifteen minutes. Or maybe you wouldn't, in which case the Two Prophets have mercy on your liver.

At the appointed time, I sat myself down on the cheap, tawdry throne. The two-headed Shqipetari eagle (made in Albion) hung on the wall in back of me, looking symbolic or absurd, depending on your attitude toward such things. Behind me and to the left of the throne stood the mostly faithful Max, otherwise Captain Yildirim, otherwise my new minister for special affairs.

If Max swayed as he stood there, if my eyes were glassy, you can blame the fifteen minutes just past. And if Max seemed steady enough, if I looked the way I usually do—well, you can blame a lot of other sessions with a lot of other jugs and bottles. In which case, the Two Prophets have mercy on our livers.

"His Excellency, Essad Pasha!" Skander cried, as if the Kingdom of Shqiperi were as venerable as Albion or the Dual Monarchy.

In stumped the man who was the former military governor of Shqiperi, the man who'd decided Shqiperi needed a king, the man who'd decided he knew exactly which king Shqiperi needed, and the man who'd thought he'd got the king he'd decided on. Made quite a procession for one fellow, didn't he?

He stopped at the prescribed distance from the throne. He bowed the prescribed bow. "Your Majesty," he said: the prescribed phrase. Except he didn't say, "Your Majesty." He said, "Your Majesty?" He admitted the possibility of doubt that I *was* his Majesty.

Doubt is not a good thing. Doubt subverts faith. If you don't have faith in me on this score, ask a priest. It doesn't matter whether he's a sedate Eliphilatelist, a wild-eyed Zibeonite, or a votary of the Quadrate God. He will tell you the same thing. Doubt *does* subvert faith. If you could find a priest who serves the old Aenean gods nowadays, he would tell you the same thing, too. But you can't find one of those priests any more. They're as extinct as unicorns (or is it virgins?). Doubt *has* subverted their faith.

"Your Excellency," I said. *I* didn't sound like a man who had doubts. Well, I daresay the brandy helped. "What brings you here today, your Excellency?"

Like I didn't know! Scribes!

"Your Majesty?" There it was again, that cursed question mark, hanging in the air. And if Essad Pasha didn't get his punctuation revised, Max and I might end up hanging in the air, too—by our necks, or perhaps in some fashion even less pleasant than that.

"Yes?" I said, as portentously as a sozzled sovereign could. I didn't doubt that I was King Halim Eddin—or if I did, no one else ever knew it.

Essad Pasha gathered himself. I was glad to see he needed to gather himself. He wasn't sure I was Halim Eddin. But he wasn't sure I wasn't Halim Eddin, either. Good. That gave me something to work with. After coughing a couple of times (which made me stare at him to see if he'd suddenly turned tall and lean: he hadn't), he said, "Your Majesty, I have received a peculiar, a most peculiar, report from the offices of Consolidated Crystal."

"Have you?" I said indifferently—or maybe I was just drunk. "Well, what report is this?"

He sounded hesitant. He sounded apologetic—better that than sounding apoplectic, I suppose. But I heard from him what I'd already heard from Max: that the Hassockian Atabeg, Eliphalet smite his scrawny arse with boils, had the infernal gall to deny that I was the authentic Prince Halim Eddin, just because I wasn't.

"Oh, that," I said, more indifferently still. "Well, weren't you expecting that?"

"Your Majesty?" Now Essad Pasha sounded like he doubted which end was up, and, unlike some people in the throne room I could name, he wasn't even pie-eyed—or I don't think he was. "I don't understand, your Majesty."

"Obviously." I piled on the scorn the way Shqipetari cooks pile on the grease.

It worked, too. I could all but hear the gears grinding inside Essad Pasha's head. An impostor who knew he'd been found out should have trembled like an aspen leaf in fall. I didn't act the way a terrified fraud should have. I acted every inch a king, or at least a prince.

"Perhaps your Majesty would be gracious enough to explain?" Cautious wasn't a bad way for Essad Pasha to sound, either.

"Perhaps he would." I don't think I'd ever talked about myself in the third person before. It's even more fun than the royal we. "Perhaps he wouldn't have to if he were served by men who could see past the end of their nose."

Behind me, Max coughed. Well, it might have been the two-headed eagle on the wall, but I suspected the doubtable—to say nothing of redoubtable—Captain Yildirim. Essad Pasha looked wounded. He wouldn't have bothered with an expression like that for a man he didn't believe in. He would have gone about wounding the pretender instead. "North and south, east and west, my ignorance is wide as the sky, deep as the sea, black as blackest midnight," he said. "Would your Majesty grant his slave the boon of enlightenment?"

When a Hassocki goes all poetical on you, he's either being insulting or you've got him on the run. Essad Pasha wasn't being insulting. I smiled . . . to myself. Then I fed him the same farrago of nonsense about why the Atabeg couldn't publicly admit I was who I was that I'd rammed down Max's throat.

Max did what any normal human being would do: he gagged. Essad Pasha swallowed the whole thing. He didn't even choke. He must have been eating Shqipetari cooking for a long time.

"I see, your Majesty," he breathed when I was through. "Indeed, that makes most excellent good sense."

Yes, maybe it was the two-headed eagle that coughed. When I looked back at Max, he wasn't doing it. I knew what he was thinking, though: that it made no sense at all. I was thinking the same thing. Then again, in the Nekemte Peninsula things that make no sense often prove perfectly sensible, while what would be sensible anywhere else turns out to be the height of folly.

An actor in a down-at-the-heels circus would be most unlikely to claim the crown of Albion, for instance. He would be even less likely to find it plopped on his head.

I graciously inclined my head to Essad Pasha. "Now that you see where the truth lies"—and the truth was lying as hard as it could, believe you me it was—"perhaps you will be so kind as to take it back to your junior officers, to avoid any unfortunate outbreaks of excessive zeal."

To keep them from coming over here and murdering me, I meant. I happen to think it sounded much nicer the way I put it.

Essad Pasha bowed. "As your Majesty commands, so shall it be." He did a smart about-turn and marched out of the throne room. I looked down at my hands. I felt like a successful surgeon. And so I was: I'd just amputated Essad Pasha's question mark, and without even numbing him beforehand.

"My hat's off to you, your Majesty," Max said. May Eliphalet beshrew me if he hadn't doffed it when I looked around.

"If a man knows the truth when he hears it, he will do what is right," I said, which sounded good and had nothing to do with anything. Essad Pasha couldn't tell the truth from saltwater taffy. As for doing what was right—he was doing what I wanted, which was even better.

Having removed or at least reduced Essad Pasha's inflamed interrogative, I thought the world was my oyster. And maybe it was, but I forgot something essential: oysters don't keep. No sooner had Essad Pasha departed than Skander bowed to me and said, "Your Majesty, a woman wishes to appeal her sentence as a witch."

"Oh, she does, does she?" I wasn't so sure that sounded appealing to me. "Can she do that?"

Skander shrugged. "It is for you to decide. You are the king."

So I was. For the first time, I wondered if I wanted to be. Romping through the harem was fun. Declaring war on Belagora was fun, too. So was arranging things so the mountain dragons decided Belagoran soldiers made even better snacks than sheep (to say nothing of shepherds).

But hearing a possible—probably a probable—witch's appeal? It sounded much too much like work. Worse, it sounded like boring work. I didn't want to admit that to Skander. I didn't much want to admit it to myself, either. Not wanting to admit it, I asked the majordomo, "What is the Shqipetari custom? I am not of your blood"—Eliphalet be praised!—"and I do not wish to offend by accident or ignorance."

He only shrugged again. "We have not had a king for many, many years. The custom is what your Majesty chooses to make it. Once your Majesty makes it, we will uphold it with all our might."

"What will they do with the woman if I don't hear her appeal?" I asked.

"Burn her, I suppose. Or else stone her," Skander said indifferently. "Give her what she deserves, anyhow."

"I see." And I did. So much for Skander's faith in her innocence. Maybe I could enlighten the Shqipetari. By all appearances, they needed it. "Fetch her in. I will hear her," I declared in ringing tones.

"Before you do, though, call Zogu the wizard to the palace," Max put in. "Just on the off chance she is what everybody thinks she is."

I thought that sentiment shockingly illiberal. Skander evidently thought it sensible. He bowed first to me, then to my minister for special affairs. "Yes, your Majesty. Yes, your Excellency." He hurried away.

That Peshkepiia was a small town had its advantages. No more than a quarter of an hour later, Zogu stood before me. "At your service, your Majesty," he said. "Which mangy trull has decided to try her luck with you?" He didn't seem to have much faith in her innocence, either, did he?

"I didn't hear who she was," I confessed. "Skander?"

"She is called Shenkolle, your Majesty." He pronounced the name with fastidious distaste, almost as if he were Rexhep.

Zogu laughed and laughed. "And she says she's not a witch? Next you'll tell me the joyhouse girls aren't whores!"

"She is entitled to her appeal," I said stiffly. Zogu thought that was funnier yet. I nodded to Skander. "Bring her in. I'll listen to what she has to say."

"Yes, your Majesty." He sighed, but he obeyed.

When I got a look at Shenkolle, my first thought was, *She sure looks like a witch.* She was old. She was bent. She was homely. She had a long nose and a sharp chin with a wart on it. If she hadn't been conjured straight from the pages of Hans Eliphalet Andersen and the Grim Brethren, she should have been.

"Do you speak Hassocki?" I asked her.

"Oh, yes, your Majesty." She didn't sound like a witch. She sounded the way you wish the girl of your dreams sounded. She turned your blood to sparkling wine.

Zogu was immune to that . . . purr. I don't know how, but he was. If I hadn't believed he was a strong wizard before, I would have now. "What do they say you were up to this time, you old she-devil?" he asked Shenkolle.

"I didn't do anything, your Majesty." She ignored Zogu and concentrated on me. Listening to her, I would have been putty—well, perhaps something than stiffer than putty—in her hands. She went on, "I am innocent. I am nothing but a poor woman wronged."

"You're the richest poor woman in Peshkepiia, that's dead certain," Zogu said. "How many big, fat silver shekels from Vespucciland did you bury in your garden week before last?"

"Why, you sneaky old crow!" Shenkolle screeched. When she wasn't talking to me, or maybe when she was angry, she sounded the way she looked. Then her voice—magically?—softened again. She batted her red-tracked eyes at me. "It's a lie, a foul, evil lie, your Majesty."

When she spoke directly to me, I believed. Well, no: it wasn't quite that. When she spoke directly to me, I didn't care whether she was telling the truth or not, any more than I cared that she looked like my granny's wicked cousin. I glanced over at Max. By the way he was staring at Shenkolle, she'd ensnared him, too.

But not Zogu. He laughed some more. By all the signs, he was having the time of his life. "Prove you're not a liar, Shenkolle," he said. "Swear by the Quadrate God that you're telling the truth. Come on—you can do it. 'North and south, east and west, I am telling the truth.' "

She tried. I watched her try. The words wouldn't come. Her eyes snapped with fury. Her face turned as red as a drunkard's nose. But the words would not come. All she could get out was, "Have mercy, your Majesty!"

She still sounded as seductive as ever. But if failing to take the oath didn't break the spell, it did dent it. Max sighed, a sad little noise. That was just how I felt. I asked her, "Do you really have those shekels in your garden?"

"Why, yes, your Majesty," she said sweetly, though the glare she sent

Zogu was anything but sweet. Then she remembered she had to aim at me. "Do you want them? If you do, of course they are yours. Anything you want of me is yours."

Even after looking at her, and even after two wild nights in the harem, the sheer promise in her voice tempted me to . . . I don't know what. But, with her charm dented, I was able to say, "I don't want them for myself. If you pay them to the people you wronged, will it buy you forgiveness?" Before she could answer, I turned to the majordomo and asked, "What do you think, Skander?"

"How much silver do we speak of?" Skander asked. Zogu told him. Shenkolle screeched, which had to mean Zogu knew what he was talking about. She sounded like a sawblade biting into a nail. Skander considered. "That much silver would settle a blood feud up in the mountains. It should be enough to atone for her crimes here. Settling is better than slaying—most of the time, anyway."

"All right, then." I pointed to Shenkolle. "Those shekels—all of them—to your accusers today will buy your life—this once. If you come before me again, though, nothing will save you. Do you understand?" She nodded. "Do you swear you will pay the price today, then?" I asked.

"North and south, east and west, I will pay it today." She had no trouble with that oath. She seemed surprised. Zogu smiled to himself.

I sent Shenkolle away. "If she doesn't . . ." I said to Zogu.

"Don't worry, your Majesty," the wizard said. "She will." And she did.

XVI

Thethi, Dashmani, Shala, Ragova, Kiri, Toplana. Yes, my minister for special affairs and I stayed busy that third night. And either Zogu was an even better wizard than he claimed to be or we were even better men than we thought ourselves to be, for we had no trouble keeping up our end of the bargain, you might say.

From certain encounters I have had since, I am inclined to give the wizardry at least some of the credit. Max will tell you he would have done as well if we'd never heard of Zogu. But then, Max will tell you any number of things. Some of them almost anyone can believe without seriously endangering himself. Others, however, should be heard only after consulting a physician, and are definitely unsafe for invalids and those in delicate health.

At last, after our strenuous efforts to establish friendly relations with the locals were crowned with success, I sent the girls back to the harem. Once Skander and Rexhep led them down the hallway, I let Max out of the closet again.

"You see?" I told him. "You can get away with anything, as long as you put up a bold enough front."

"We're not dead yet, so you must be right," he answered. "I wouldn't have believed it. When the Atabeg said you weren't who you said you were, I thought for sure they'd tear us to pieces."

I shrugged. "Essad Pasha doesn't dare believe I'm not Halim Eddin. If he did, he would have to believe he was a fool. Nobody wants to do that."

"Even so, we're not out of the woods," Max said. "Some of Essad Pasha's officers may decide he's a fool, whether he thinks so or not. And if they do . . ." He made a horrid gurgling noise.

"How can you sound so gloomy after what we've just been doing?" I asked.

"I'd like to stay able to do it," Max said. "You were the one who talked about losing bits and pieces of ourselves if things went wrong."

"Nothing will go wrong," I assured him. "You'll see in the morning. Why don't you head back to your room and get some sleep? After tonight, after the last three nights, you ought to sleep like a baby—a tall baby, but a baby even so."

"I don't want to sleep like a baby. Piddling in the bed and spitting up? Thanks, but I'd rather not."

I shoved him out the door. "Go on. You're lucky I'm a kind and merciful king, or I'd give you what you deserve for that. Everything will be fine in the morning. You'll find out."

But everything wasn't fine in the morning. I found out. And I very nearly *was* found out. It happened like this.

Trouble usually strikes at the most inconvenient times, when you've shaved half your face or just stepped out of the tub or told her that of course you weren't married. Here, though, everything seemed fine. I'd drunk my coffee. I'd eaten my fried mush. I thought I was ready to park my fundament on the throne again and act royal. I even thought I was getting pretty good at it.

Skander came up to me and bowed. "Excuse me, your Majesty, but Colonel Kemal and Major Mustafa are here to see you."

"Are they?" I said innocently. I don't know if I'd convinced Max everything was fine. Max is not easy to convince of such things. I do know I'd convinced myself. "Well, I'd be glad to see them."

There I sat, on the throne, happy and kingly, Max standing a step back and to the left, where he belonged. There they came, two of Essad Pasha's officers in dust-brown uniforms. Neither of them had missed a meal any time lately. Major Mustafa had a big black mustache. Colonel Kemal had an even bigger gray one. Major Mustafa's fez and shoulder straps had one jewel. Colonel Kemal's had three.

They didn't bow. They didn't say, "Your Majesty." They just looked at me, not quite as if they'd found half of me in their apple but as if they'd like to give me to a Shqipetari cook for some intimate acquaintance with hot grease.

I did my best not to notice. To tell you the truth, I didn't want to notice. I said, "Gentlemen, it's good that you're here"—which only shows how much I knew. "Tell me your specialties. I'll want to get the best use out of you when the fighting with Belagora heats up."

They just kept staring at me. After a little while, I started not to like that very much. At last, Major Mustafa said, "How can you be who you say you are when the Atabeg says you aren't who you say you are?"

I waited for Max to cough. He didn't bother. He evidently figured I could see this was trouble all by myself. Max is so trusting. "You must not have heard. I explained that to Essad Pasha just yesterday," I told the officers, and went through my song and dance again. Really, I should have had an orchestra accompanying me. I finished, "So you see, all this silly fuss should die down in a few days," and waited for the applause from my adoring audience.

Only it wasn't adoring. If the major and the colonel were carrying rotten rutabagas, they would have thrown them. Since they didn't, they contented themselves with shaking their heads. They were out of synch with each other, which struck me as most unmilitary. Major Mustafa said, "We did hear that yesterday."

"We don't believe it," Colonel Kemal said.

"The Hassockian Atabeg would never sully himself by telling a lie," Mustafa declared.

I almost had a laughing fit, right there on the throne. There hasn't been a Hassockian Atabeg for the past five hundred years who wasn't a lying reptile. It's essential for living long enough to get halfway good at the job. And I couldn't tell them so. If I did, they would decide I was insulting their sovereign, and I couldn't possibly be the lying reptile's nephew.

I was, plainly, going to have to be a lying reptile myself. Well, if working for Dooger and Cark prepared me for anything, it prepared me for that. I rose from the throne, a smile still on my face. "Gentlemen, I have to tell you you are mistaken," I said. *Or at least right for the wrong reasons.* "Let's talk about it, shall we? Captain Yildirim, why don't you come along with us?"

"Yes, your Majesty." Max had to be wondering if I wanted him to murder the two Hassocki. I don't blame him; I was wondering the same thing myself.

We ambled through the palace. I went on explaining how I really was Halim Eddin and always had been, even as a small child, although the lying reptile in Vyzance (whom I couldn't call a lying reptile) couldn't admit it. Colonel Kemal and Major Mustafa went on not believing me. I started to get angry, though I didn't let it show. Anyone would have thought from their attitude that I was deliberately lying to them!

In due course, we reached the front entrance. The soldiers standing guard there sprang to stiff attention. Whoever was in charge of them seemed imperfectly trustful of my popularity; he'd posted a couple of squads' worth of men there to protect me from my beloved people. "At ease," I told them.

"Yes, your Majesty," they chorused, and relaxed from their brace.

They thought I was King of Shqiperi. And if they did . . . "Men," I said, "arrest these officers! They plot to remove me from the throne!"

It was as easy as that. The soldiers seized Colonel Kemal and Major Mustafa. After a moment's shocked paralysis, the officers raised a horrible fuss. It did them exactly no good. A king outtrumped a major and a colonel put together. "What shall we do with 'em, your Majesty?" a sergeant asked once the loyal dimwits, uh, soldiers had laid hold of Kemal and Mustafa.

"Take them to the dungeons," I said grandly. Kemal and Mustafa cursed and moaned even louder than they had before. I paid no attention to them. To my vast relief, neither did the palace guards.

"Uh, your Majesty, where *are* the dungeons?" the sergeant asked: a reasonable question, under the circumstances.

"I don't know," I admitted. "They're in there somewhere, I suppose—

how can you have a palace if you don't have dungeons?—but I just got here myself. I haven't found 'em yet." I went back to the doorway and shouted down the hall: "Skander!"

"Yes, your Majesty?" I don't know how he kept appearing out of nowhere like that, but he did. Maybe Zogu had something to do with it.

"We have a couple of gentlemen here who require incarceration," I said. Colonel Kemal and Major Mustafa vehemently denied it. Skander didn't listen to them, either. "Noisy, aren't they?" I remarked. "Would you be so kind as to show the soldiers to the dungeons so they can lock these rascals up? I hope the doors are thick—that way, their racket won't bother anyone else."

"The doors are very thick indeed, your Majesty," Skander said. He nodded to the sergeant. "Come this way, if you please." Mustafa and Kemal did their best not to go that way. Their best wasn't good enough. I don't believe the soldiers did anything in persuading them that wouldn't heal in a few days.

All the palace guards trooped along with the loud, boisterous officers. The more Kemal and Mustafa tried to fight, the more men joined in to make sure they couldn't. Max and I stood by ourselves at the entrance. "Well," I said brightly, "*that* was interesting."

"There's one word," Max said. He used several others, most of which would set the page on fire if I tried to write them down.

"Did I get out of it or not?" I asked him. "Did I get away with it or not?"

He didn't want to say I had, but he couldn't very well say I hadn't. "You've got the balls of a burglar," was what he did say, "and if you don't watch out, you'll get 'em chopped off just like Rexhep."

"Oh, rubbish," I said, and hoped like anything it was.

When the guardsmen came back, it was without Colonel Kemal and Major Mustafa. The sergeant didn't look happy. "Whoever designed those dungeons didn't know what he was doing. No dripping water, no bad smells . . . I didn't see a single rat. North and south, east and west, there are hardly any cockroaches, even."

"They'll have to do for now," I said. "Later on, maybe, we'll fix up something properly nasty."

"I should hope so!" he said. "Back in Vyzance, now, you'll be used to doing it right. Filth, vermin, water, gloom, easy access for the torturers . . . They don't fool around back there." If I ever did decide to renovate my dungeons, here was a man with ideas.

I had an idea of my own. It turned out not to be a *good* idea, but I couldn't know that when I had it. "Come with me," I said to Max. "The people of Peshkepiia should get to know us. Let's go to the market square and see them at their earnest endeavors." Yes, *Let's watch the quaint natives* was what it boiled down to. I should have known better, even then. Shqipetari are too confounded ornery to be quaint.

Not that a Shqipetar gave me trouble. Oh, no. But I'm getting to that.

If a Schlepsigian public-health mage got a look at the market square in Peshkepiia, he would close it down on the spot, fall over dead from a fit of apoplexy, or more likely both. Flies buzzed everywhere. They settled on meat and vegetables and stallkeepers and customers. Sewage ran in the gutters and puddled here and there, which helped account for the flies. Consumptive beggars held out bowls and coughed on passersby.

Another difference between civilization and Shqiperi that I've already noted is, people were haggling wherever you looked. When I went on the road, I needed a while to understand this. In Schlepsig, there is a price. That is the price. The seller tells you what it is. You pay, or you don't. This is the natural way, the sensible way, to do business.

It's not the way they do business in the Nekemte Peninsula. There is no deal in those parts without a dicker. The seller would be offended if you took his first offer. He would think you despised him, or he would think he set his price much too low. Since no one ever takes a first offer, his honor and his sense of his own cleverness meet no danger.

In Shqiperi, where every man usually carries as many weapons as he can afford and as many as he can wear and still walk, dickering takes on a whole new dimension. A bargainer will think nothing of drawing a dagger or swinging a sword or letting the flat of an axe blade crash down on a tabletop. Shqipetari treat a haggle like the prelude to a blood feud. Every now and then, it is.

So when Max and I saw—and heard—a knot of shouting, gesticulating people in the market square, we didn't think much of it, not at first. Shqipetari shout and gesticulate as naturally as Schlepsigians take orders. It doesn't necessarily mean anything; it's just part of who they are. It doesn't necessarily *not* mean anything, either, though, as I was about to discover.

In fact, Max, being so uncouthly tall, discovered it before I did. He could peer over the crowd and discover why it *was* a crowd. I had to peer through people, which is harder; they refuse to go transparent when you most want them to.

"Uh, your Majesty, we have a problem here," he said.

"What kind of problem?" I asked. The Shqipetari not only stubbornly stayed opaque but got more excited by the minute. And they said it couldn't be done!

"You know the emblem of this kingdom?" Now Max, Eliphalet bless his pointed little head, was being opaque, too.

I thought of the bicephalous eagle (made in Albion) tacked up behind my makeshift throne. "Personally, no," I answered, but I was wrong.

Max proceeded to point this out: "If that emblem were a man, he'd be in the middle of that crowd right now."

A horrid suspicion ran through me. "Tell me anything you please, O most excellent Minister for Special Affairs, anything at all. But north and south, east and west"—even in my extremity, I did remember not to swear by the Two Prophets—"tell me that's not José-Diego in there."

But it was, or they were, depending on how you look at things. Dooger and Cark's flyers went right on showing a two-headed man, even though we didn't have one in the company any more. José-Diego was the one we didn't have any more. The reason we didn't have him—them?—any more was that the two heads couldn't get along with each other, not even a little bit, which meant he, or they, didn't have an act.

I finally got my own glimpse of him, them, whatever. He, they, whatever, hadn't changed a bit since the last time I saw him/them. José, the right-hand head, wore a full beard. Because he did, Diego was clean-shaven. Diego, the left-hand head, let his curly brown hair fall almost to his shoulders—I mean, shoulder. Because he did, José shaved his scalp.

Just to make matters worse, José controlled their left arm and leg, Diego their right, and not the other way around. Sometimes they—he?—couldn't even walk, because the right leg didn't know what the left leg was doing.

It gets worse. José was a reactionary. Diego was a radical. José ate meat—adored it. Diego was a vegetarian. José liked girls. Diego liked boys. Whether they ever managed to make like lucky Pierre, I'm afraid—or rather, glad—I can't tell you.

And it gets even worse than that, because José-Diego saw me, too. Actually, I suspect José-Diego saw Max first. Max is almost as noticeable as José-Diego, and under some circumstances even more so. And after the two-headed man spotted Max, he didn't need long to spot me with him. He waved to us and headed our way.

That was about as bad as it could get. He knew we were Otto of Schlepsig and Max of Witte. He *didn't* know we were supposed to be King Halim Eddin and his more or less faithful aide-de-camp, Captain Yildirim. He knew we followed the Two Prophets. José followed them, too, with the fanatical devotion of most Leonese. Diego was a free-thinker. Neither of them knew we were affecting to reverence the Quadrate God. Even if for different reasons, they both would have been appalled.

Giving José and Diego something to agree about was *not* what I had in mind.

"What are you fellowth doing in thith Prophetth-forthaken plathe?" Diego asked. Yeth, uh, yes, he talked like that. No, he wasn't being effeminate. José spoke Schlepsigian with the same lisping Leonese accent. José was a lot of things, starting with bad-tempered fool and rapidly going downhill from there, but no one would ever accuse him of effeminacy.

Max did his best to tip José-Diego off to what we were doing. Drawing himself up to his full height—which takes a lot of drawing—he spoke in severe tones: "Have a care how you address Halim Eddin, King of Shqiperi."

That got both heads' attention, but not in the way we wanted. "Whose leg are you pulling, Max?" José asked. I'm not going to write the lisp any

more. I'm just not. But it was there. You can hear it in your mind's eye, if
you want to, or see it in your ear.

"Otto's no more a king than I am," Diego added.

"You're no king. You're a cursed queen," José said. I told you they didn't
get along.

They switched from Schlepsigian to Leonese about then. I don't
really speak Leonese, but I do speak Narbonese and Torinan, which are
its cousins, so I can follow it after a fashion. Diego said something rude
about José's mother, which is strange, since she was Diego's mother, too.
José said something very rude about the only kind of meat Diego ate.
Diego screeched and tried to hit him. José blocked the punch.

The crowd watched in fascination. As long as the two heads were
shouting at each other—as long as José-Diego was shouting at himself?—in Leonese, everything was fine, or near enough. Hardly any
Shqipetari understand it. But if and when José-Diego went back to
Schlepsigian, all my troubles came back, too. Even in Peshkepiia, which is
every bit as Prophets-forsaken as José-Diego said (why else would he, or
they, have ended up there?), quite a few people know Schlepsigian, the
language of Culture.

José stamped on Diego's foot. That didn't do either one of them any
good, since they both felt it. They howled the polyglot curses anyone
who's done time in a circus uses.

José did go back to Schlepsigian, and I felt like cursing him. "Seriously,
Otto, what are you doing here?" he asked.

And then, at my elbow, someone spoke to me in Hassocki: "Excuse
me, your Majesty, but is this, uh, person bothering you?"

May I turn into a Shqipetar if it wasn't the sergeant of the guard. He
and his men had put Mustafa and Kemal away, and then they'd come
after me to make sure I was all right. Such devotion is touching; it almost
made me wish I really were Halim Eddin. "He's . . . getting there," I answered. "Tell me—do you or any of your men speak Schlepsigian?"

"No, your Majesty," the sergeant said. "I'm sorry, your Majesty."

"Don't be," I told him.

José-Diego gave me two suspicious stares. "What are you yattering
about, Otto?" José said irritably. It wasn't just Diego he couldn't get along

with; he had trouble with the whole world. "Talk a language a thivilithed man can underthtand."

"He'th going to thcrew uth," Diego thaid—uh, said. I said I wouldn't do that any more, didn't I? Well, I'm trying. "He's going to screw us to the wall." There, that's better.

And I did aim to screw them to the wall, too. I'll tell you something else—I enjoyed doing it metaphorically much more than I would have enjoyed it physically. I nodded to the sergeant. "This fellow is a trouble-maker, I'm afraid. Why don't you take him, uh, them, to the dungeon to cool down for a while?"

"Yes, your Majesty!" All at once, the sergeant sounded enthusiastic. He nodded to his troopers. "Grab the monster, boys!" I have no doubt that members of the Society for the Advancement of the Rights of Individuals with Multiple Necks will be distressed by the crudity, prejudice, and discriminatory nature of his language, and I apologize for the infliction of any such distress. I do not editorialize here; I merely report.

Apparently untroubled by higher feelings of brotherhood, the Hassocki soldiers grabbed the monster. José-Diego tried to fight back. In less time than it takes to tell, he—they—had three black eyes and two bloody noses. If it wasn't pretty obvious that I wouldn't have approved, he would have lost two heads.

"For Eliphalet's sake, Otto, call the authorities!" José howled.

"You don't seem to understand. I *am* the authorities," I said, and then, to the sergeant, "Take him away!" If you're going to be a tyrant, *be* a tyrant!

"Yes, your Majesty!" Away José-Diego went. He was still making a dreadful racket. Fortunately, he was doing most of it in Leonese, which the bystanders couldn't follow. Now that I look back on it, that might have been lucky for him as well as for me. If they had understood some of the things he was calling them, he might not have made it to the dungeon.

"Keep him away from Mustafa and Kemal," I called after the soldiers. "They don't need to listen to his ravings." Could you hold a two-headed man in solitary confinement? A nice grammatical and philosophical question, isn't it?

The sergeant waved to show he heard me. I wasn't sure whether the

Hassocki officers spoke Schlepsigian. I wouldn't have been surprised, though. If they did, they would have found out some things I didn't want them knowing. They would have been able to tell the palace guards about them, too. That could have proved . . . awkward.

As things were, *Take him away!* worked just fine. No wonder tyrants enjoy being tyrannical. Not many bigger thrills than telling people what to do and actually having them do it. Some, yes (I wondered if Zogu's aphrodisiac preparation was good for one more night), but not many.

The market square slowly went back to normal—which is to say, dull. I turned to Max. "Well, I'm glad that's over with," I said. "We don't want any more two-faced dealing around here."

My esteemed minister for special affairs looked revolted if not outright rebellious. But he said, "I guess you did about as well with that as you could. Out of sight, out of mind."

"Don't be ridiculous," I said. "José-Diego is out of his mind— minds—even when he's in sight."

Max didn't try to tell me I was wrong—a good thing, since I was right. "I wonder what he was doing in Peshkepiia," he said.

I shrugged. "This is a place for losers. Where else would somebody like José-Diego show up?" There aren't many like him—and a good thing, too, I say.

"What are we doing here, in that case?" Max inquired.

"Don't be difficult," I told him. "I'll say this—what we're doing here is a lot more profitable than haggling for vegetables in the market square. More fun, too. By tonight we'll have tried out the whole harem."

"A point," Max said. When Max doesn't argue, you know it's a good point, too.

Peshkepiia, royal harem and royal treasury excepted, was rapidly running out of good points. Chief among the not so good points was the Consolidated Crystal office. Given any encouragement from me, Max would have haunted the place like a jilted ghost in one of those castles on the crags above the river that are so beloved of Schlepsigian romance-writers of the female persuasion.

Even without encouragement from me, the intrepid Captain Yildirim went back to the CC office. When he returned to the market square, his face was longer than the road between Dooger and Cark's and a good circus.

"Well, what is it this time?" I asked. Maybe if he got it out of his system all at once, as if from a purgative . . .

"It's the Hassockian Atabeg, that's what," said my minister for special affairs. "Really bellowing like an angry dragon now. He says the fellow who has the unmitigated gall to pretend to be his Highness, Prince Halim Eddin, should get exactly what he deserves, and another twenty piasters' worth besides."

Now, I've always thought of my gall as being on the mitigated side. "Twenty piasters piled together aren't worth a good Schlepsigian kram," I said.

Somehow, this observation failed to calm Max. "That still leaves you getting what you deserve," he said. "It leaves me getting what you deserve, too, for which I thank you *so* very much. What the Atabeg thinks you deserve would keep a team of torturers busy for weeks."

"You've been getting what I deserve the past three nights, too, or half of it, anyway," I said. "When you thank me for that, you can sound like you mean it."

Max ignored that thrust, despite all the thrusting he'd done on those three memorable nights. "Wait till this fireball gets to Essad Pasha," he said dolefully. "Just wait. He can't pretend he doesn't believe it, the way he did with the last one."

"No. He really didn't believe that one," I said. I had a certain amount of trouble believing Essad Pasha would disbelieve the Atabeg's latest. Since I had trouble believing it, I didn't waste my time trying to persuade Max. Trying to persuade Max of anything good is commonly a waste of time. I did want to persuade him to keep quiet, so I added, "Essad Pasha hasn't complained about my jugging Colonel Kemal and Major Mustafa."

"Not yet," Max said. "No, not yet. But he hasn't heard the latest, either. When he does, he'll probably complain about your jugging José-Diego, too."

Now he'd gone too far. "Nobody could possibly complain about jugging José-Diego," I said with great certainty. "North and south, east and west, even José thinks Diego wants jugging, and conversely."

"And perversely, you mean," Max said. "Curse it, we're in trouble, Ot— uh, your Majesty."

"You worry too much," I said. "For all you know, this latest mumble from Vyzance won't even get to Essad Pasha. Why should it?"

"Your Majesty!" That was Bob, the bewigged Albionese attempt at a scribe. Who else would shout at me in a language he didn't think I spoke? Still in Albionese, he went on, "What do you think of the Atabeg's latest statement, your Majesty?"

"*That's* why," Max said, fortunately in a low voice.

"Oh, shut up," I told him, also quietly. I nodded to the scribe with Bob, a man possessed of some sense. The other newshounds, I noted, made a point of not letting Bob wander around by himself. I suppose none of them was really eager to be the one who had to identify his body. "What does he say?" I asked in Schlepsigian.

The other scribe translated something I understood into something I admitted understanding. "I also would like to know this, your Majesty," he told me.

I'll bet you would, I thought. No matter how foolish Bob was, not all of his questions were. Perfect idiocy, appearances to the contrary notwithstanding, seemed beyond him. "I am afraid the Atabeg feels acknowledging my presence here would be an embarrassment," I told the other scribe, and embroidered on that theme for some little while—the same story I'd given my dear Max and my not so dear Essad Pasha.

As I talked, Bob hopped up and down in an agony of impatience. He tugged at the other scribe's sleeve like a little boy with no manners. "What does he say?" he asked, as I had. But he did it over and over again. "What does he say? What does he say?"

Had I been that other scribe, I would have hauled off and decked him. But the other man showed admirable patience—what was he doing in his line of work, anyway? He even did a good job of translating what I'd told him. When he finished, Bob nodded, as if in wisdom. "Well," he said, "that makes sense."

I sent Max a slightly superior smile, one that said, *You see? They're still buying it.* I didn't want to be too blatant, for fear the other scribe would notice me reacting to things I wasn't supposed to be able to follow. Bob I wasn't worried about. Bob noticed nothing, as he proved by believing me.

The other scribe sent him a pitying smile, as if he still thought Eliphalet drank the extra mug of beer people put out for his name day. "It's a crock of crap, Bob," he said in Albionese. "This guy's lying through his teeth. Either he is or the Atabeg is, anyway, and the Atabeg sounds too cheesed off to be blowing smoke. Something's screwy somewhere. You wait and see."

I wasn't supposed to be able to follow that, either. By my expression, you'd never know I did. I glanced over at Max. I wasn't expecting a slightly superior smile from him, and I didn't get one. Max doesn't waste smiles like that. I'd never imagined anybody frowning a slightly superior frown, but there it was. Max's face is made for expressing subtle shades of disapproval.

"Are you really the Atabeg's nephew, your Majesty?" Bob asked. He had a childlike faith that, because he was a scribe, nothing he said could land him in trouble. Or maybe he was trying to prove he was a perfect idiot after all; I don't know. I do know his keeper turned a shade of chartreuse that didn't go at all well with the dark green jacket he was wearing.

"What does he say?" I asked again, as innocently as if I were innocent.

Instead of answering me, the other scribe spoke to Bob in a low voice. I really couldn't follow all of that. What I could follow was . . . entertaining. Bob's keeper wasn't telling him all the different kinds of fool he was; he'd still be standing there in the Peshkepiia market square talking if he tried it. He did seem to make a judicious selection.

"What does he say?" I asked again after a while.

"Never mind, your Majesty. He's decided he doesn't really want to ask that question," the other scribe said in Schlepsigian. "*Haven't you, Bob?*" he added in ominous Albionese.

"It really would be interesting to find out," Bob said. "Add a bit of human interest to things. Make a good story—do you know what I mean?"

"Yes, and the story right after it would be how an Albionese scribe got his nose cut off because he couldn't keep from poking it into dark corners with knives hidden in them." His keeper had some basic grasp on reality. The man switched to Schlepsigian to tell me, "Bob really and truly doesn't want to ask that question."

Bob really and truly did, but I wasn't supposed to know it. So I smiled and nodded and let the other scribe lead the ineffable Albionese out of danger. Out of danger from me, anyhow—I had the feeling Bob would keep on putting himself in danger wherever he went and whatever he did. And he wouldn't even know he was putting himself in danger, which would be all the more dangerous for him.

"Your Majesty." By the exaggerated patience with which Max said it, he didn't think I even knew I was putting myself in danger. "Your Majesty, it's unraveling. It's coming to pieces. Don't you think we ought to get out while the getting's good? Don't you think we ought to while we still can?"

I sighed and reached up to pat him on the back. "Go if you want to, old fellow. I won't say a word about it. But I'll miss you tonight, I really will. Even with Zogu's charm under the bed, I don't know if I can handle six of them all by myself. Oh, well. I'll just have to try my, ah, hardest. It's my patriotic duty, after all."

Max walked back to the palace with me. I'm sure his patriotic duty was the uppermost thing in his mind. Max always was a very patriotic fellow.

Strati. Hoti. Rruga. Jeni. Zarzavate. Silnif. The last of the harem. Thinking that made me sad. There wouldn't be any more first times for me and Max. Ah, well. Some things don't get boring even with repetition.

By that fourth night, Skander had given up asking the whereabouts of my distinguished minister for special affairs. He assumed Max was in the room where he belonged. I assumed Max belonged in the room where he was. Skander's assumption satisfied him—and presumably Rexhep. Mine satisfied me.

Max seemed quite capable of satisfying himself.

Between the two of us, we seemed quite capable of satisfying Strati and Hoti and Rruga (roll those first two r's as hard as you can) and Jeni and Zarzavate and Silnif. Yes, Zogu's magic helped. But we knew what we were doing, and we did several different things. If we'd just done *that*, we never could have managed, even with a helping hand from the wizardry.

"*Oh*, your Majesty!" Zarzavate said at one point in the proceedings. I think it was Zarzavate. Whoever it was, I don't believe I got a more heartfelt compliment in my whole reign.

But all good things must come to an end, which is another way to say you can't keep coming forever, no matter how much you wish you could. We sprawled across the bed and across one another, worn out but happy.

"Which of us did you like best, your Majesty?" asked Hoti—I do believe it was Hoti.

"All of you," I said. I might not be a politician, but I'm not an imbecile, either. I sounded sincere, too.

The girls laughed. Even Max unfrowned a little. But Hoti—*was* it Hoti?—didn't want to leave it alone. She pouted prettily. "Yes, your Majesty, which of all of us?"

Well, I had an opinion. I had it, and I was bloody well going to keep it to myself. The Atabeg's torturers couldn't have torn it out of me. So I say, anyhow, never having made the acquaintance of those illustrious gentlemen.

"All of you," I repeated. "I can't imagine how any king anywhere in all the world could be happier than I am right now." And I could imagine the harem wars if I didn't stay evenhanded. I could, and I didn't want to.

None of the girls felt combative just then. I liked the way they felt just fine. "We'd do anything for you, your Majesty," Strati said. I'm almost sure it was Strati. "Anything at all." If she was the one I thought she was at one particular moment—exactly who was who when blurred a bit—she meant every word of that, too.

"And for you, brave Captain Yildirim," Silnif added. Well, let's say it was Silnif. "We don't want you to feel all alone, now." She giggled. My minister for special affairs might have felt a lot of things right then, but he was most unlikely to feel alone.

A little later, Max did his amazing, astounding, never to be equaled disappearing act: he went back into my closet. The girls sighed with regret. I restored myself to something resembling decency. They sighed about that, too, which did ease my mind. Then they got dressed, which gave *me* something to regret.

I summoned Skander. Skander summoned Rexhep. The eunuch took the girls back to the harem. "You've made yourself remarkably popular, your Majesty," Skander said, for all six of them went right on sighing. "Remarkably." He knew something was going on, but he didn't know what. A good thing he didn't, too.

That was the end of my fourth night as King of Shqiperi.

XVII

On the fifth day, things fell apart.

I might have known they would. By Eliphalet's fuzzy whiskers, I *had* known they would. I'd tried not to admit it, even to myself. I'd tried not to admit it, especially to myself. That didn't make things any better when they did fall apart. Yes, I admit it. If I'd had any sense . . .

If I'd had any sense, I would have stayed in Thasos. I never would have become King of Shqiperi. I never would have browbeaten Essad Pasha. I never would have slain a dragon on the way to Peshkepiia. I never would have declared war on Belagora. I never would have made the acquaintance of so many lovely—well, reasonably lovely—Shqipetari maidens.

That was the good side. I'd savored every instant of it.

The bad side was, once things started falling apart, everybody else in Peshkepiia savored the notion of killing me in as many ingenious ways as possible. Even Essad Pasha showed a regrettable tendency not to stay browbeaten. I certainly regretted it, let me tell you.

He came to the palace while I was still eating breakfast. Given the general greasiness of Shqipetari breakfasts, most of the time I wouldn't have minded having mine interrupted. Most of the time. This particular morning, though, he came with a sorcerous copy of the portrait of Halim Eddin, the very portrait that had launched me on my kingly career.

He looked at me. He looked at the portrait. He looked at me some more. He looked at the portrait again. Apparently, I was expected not to notice this. If I'd played by the rules, I wouldn't have been sitting in the royal palace of Shqiperi eating an indifferent breakfast in the first place. "Is something troubling you, your Excellency?" I inquired.

Essad Pasha looked at me. He looked at the portrait. This could have grown tedious. It could also have given him a crick in the neck if he'd kept it up much longer. "You *look* like his Highness," he said grudgingly.

"And what do you suppose the most likely reason for that is?" I said. "A man often resembles his portrait—if the artist has half a notion of what he's doing, anyway."

"But *is* that the most likely reason?" Was Essad Pasha asking himself or me? Himself, for he went on, "The Atabeg says you are not Halim Eddin."

"I've already explained to you why he has to do that," I said with such patience as I could muster. A man does get tired of telling the same lie over and over.

And a man does get alarmed when the fellow who most needs to believe that lie starts wondering about it. "Yes, but the Atabeg seemed quite emphatic, even impassioned, in his latest denial," Essad Pasha said. "I shall have to investigate further."

He didn't really disbelieve me, or he never would have let me hear that last. "Investigate all you please," I told him. "You will find it is just as I say." The only *sure* way he could find it wasn't was by sailing to Vyzance and looking at the veritable Halim Eddin there with his own eyes. If he was determined enough to do that, at least he would give me plenty of time to make my getaway.

Or so it seemed to me. But once things started unraveling, they came unknotted and unknitted faster than a cheap mitten. "Where are Colonel Kemal and Major Mustafa?" Essad Pasha asked.

If he didn't hear it from me, he would from someone else. That would only make him more suspicious, if such a thing was possible. "In the dungeon here," I answered. "They presumed to doubt my royal status, too." I couldn't very well jug Essad Pasha, no matter how good an idea that might seem. Without him, I had no hold at all on the Hassocki troops in Peshkepiia and the rest of Shqiperi.

Before Essad Pasha could say anything, Skander bustled up to me. "Your Majesty, Zogu the mage would speak to you."

I sighed. I wouldn't have enjoyed my breakfast even alone, not as oily as it was. I might as well not enjoy it in company, then. "Go fetch him," I told Skander, and away he went. *He* still thought I was king.

"If we are going to fight the Belagorans, your Majesty, I need to speak to these officers," Essad Pasha said. "I should like to have them released, if at all possible. They are excellent commanders."

He waited. I wondered if he wanted to persuade them I was the king or if he wanted them to persuade him I wasn't. But I had to act as if I trusted him, or he wouldn't trust me at all. "You may see them," I told him as Skander brought Zogu up to my table. "If they pledge their loyalty to me—and if they make me believe it—they may be released."

"Very well, your Majesty." Essad Pasha bowed and took his leave. He didn't need to ask Skander where the dungeons were. Plainly, he already knew.

He would.

And he hadn't even got to the dining-room door before I realized how many different flavors of fool I was. Colonel Kemal and Major Mustafa weren't the only ones languishing in the dungeons. José-Diego was sitting in one of those cells, too. And José-Diego knew enough about Max and me not just to cook our goose but to incinerate it.

"Zogu!" If fate was kind enough to throw me a straw, I'd try to grab it. "How would you like to put another chunk of the Shqipetari royal treasury in your own pocket?"

"Well, I wouldn't mind," Zogu answered. Somehow, I hadn't thought he would. "What do you need me to do?" He didn't ask about a fee, not right then. I figured that meant he figured he had me by the short hairs. I also figured he was right.

I pointed after Essad Pasha. "Can you arrange it so his Excellency thinks he's hurrying toward the dungeons but he's really not moving very fast at all?"

A light gleamed in the wizard's dark eyes. For all piratical porpoises, I'd just told him I wasn't the rightful King of Shqiperi. If he felt like denouncing me, I'd probably end up envying my breakfast. But he only bowed. "As your Majesty wishes, so shall it be."

If Zogu had to withdraw to his sorcerous lair, Essad Pasha would already have got to the place where I didn't want him to go by the time the wizard set out to stop him. That struck me as an impractical solution to the difficulty in which I found myself. I cast about for one more timely. Tackling the military governor sprang to mind.

But Zogu proved himself a man of parts. And he had all the parts he needed right there with him. He took from his belt something that re-sembled both a curiously mottled fingernail and a much smaller version of the dragon's scale I now wore under my tunic.

"As tortoises grow," he remarked, "they shed the outer layer of the scutes that armor their backs. These come in handy now and again."

I didn't know whether this was now or again. I did know Zogu had better hurry if he was going to take care of what I needed from him. I also knew that, the more nervous I seemed, the more he would charge me when he finished—if he finished in time. I'm not the least accomplished actor in the world. I wouldn't have succeeded even for five days in the role I was playing without a share of the true gift. But staying calm, or seem-ing to stay calm, while Zogu went through the rest of his pouches and pockets was one of the hardest things I've ever done.

After what felt like forever and might have been half a minute, he let out a small, satisfied grunt. The bit of dried, withered greenery he held up put me in mind of nothing so much as . . . a bit of dried, withered greenery. But he seemed pleased with it. "Henbane," he explained—he was an inveterate explainer, was Zogu. "It has the property of blurring that which is and that which seems to be."

"Very good," I said, and could not help adding, "Can you make it seem to move faster?"

His smile told me his price had just gone up. Well, I was past worry-ing about that. What could I buy with the gold and silver in that multi-ply locked treasure chamber more precious than my own neck and its continuing attachment to my shoulders?

Zogu rubbed the henbane to powder between the thumb and forefin-ger of his right hand. He let the powder drizzle down over the shed tor-toise scute, which he held in his left palm. As he did so, he chanted in nasal, braying Shqipetari: an unmusical language at the best of times, which this was not.

I thought I caught Essad Pasha's name in that flood of incomprehensible syllables. I also thought I caught mine. No, not Halim Eddin's—mine. If Zogu didn't say *Otto of Schlepsig* in there—well, then he said something else, that was all. But I sure thought he did. For a moment, I was offended. How could he presume to know who I really was? But he was a wizard, after all. If he set his mind to it, how could he *not* know?

With an abrupt motion, he swept the scute and the henbane dust from his hand. "It is accomplished, your Majesty," he said, with no irony in my title that I could find—and I was looking.

I got to my feet. "All right," I said. "Let's see what Essad Pasha is doing."

Before I could leave the dining room, Max burst in. My distinguished minister for special affairs seemed imperfectly pleased with the world around him. I wondered why. I had the distinct feeling I didn't really want to know.

"Your Majesty—" Max sounded as happy as he looked—which is to say, he thought the end was nigh.

"Captain, the news will wait, whatever it may be," I said.

"No, it won't," Max said.

"Yes, it will," I said in my best royal tones—so soon to be abandoned! "We must discover what our bold and clever mage has accomplished."

"You do me too much honor," Zogu murmured.

"I had better not," I told him. Let him take that as he pleased. Maybe I meant his services were vital, and that I had confidence he'd done what he set out to do. Or maybe I meant his services were vital, and his head would answer if something had gone wrong. A man with a spell is generally stronger than a man with a sword. But a man with a sword can generally use his weapon faster than a man with a spell. Since Zogu was right there between Max and me, he had to be a little thoughtful. . . .

Max seemed about ready to burst. "Your Majesty, you really do need to know— Ow!" Not entirely by accident, I'd done my best to flatten Max's instep. The look he gave me made me wonder if Zogu was the only one who needed to worry about swords. But he did shut up. That was nice.

Each of us thinking his no doubt interesting thoughts, none of us saying anything, we walked out into the hallway. One of the palace servants trotted toward me, calling, "Your Majesty! Your Majesty!"

When I put the crown on five days earlier, I never dreamt I might tire of the title. Just at that moment, though, I rather wished people would forget I was King of Shqiperi. "Yes, Mujo?" I couldn't possibly have sounded as apprehensive as I felt.

But Mujo said, "Your Majesty, Essad Pasha's had some kind of fit! Come quick!"

"You see?" Zogu said quietly.

"I see," I answered, as quietly. Max started to say something. I stepped on his foot again; I don't know how I could have been so clumsy. "Oh, what a pity!" I told Mujo in my normal tone of voice, or as normal as I could sound while shamelessly overacting. "Take me to him right away!"

And the good Mujo did. By what he'd said, I expected to see Essad Pasha thrashing on the floor foaming at the mouth. That wasn't what I'd looked for from Zogu's wizardry. It turned out not to be what I got, either.

There Essad Pasha was, hurrying along toward the dungeons. Every line of his body proclaimed his urgency. Purpose gleamed in his eyes. His mouth was firm and determined.

I walked up to him. I walked past him. I walked around him. I stopped next to him. If I watched for a little while, I could see him moving. If I'd stood around for an hour or so, I might have seen him take another step. At that rate, he would get to the dungeons just a little before Colonel Kemal and Major Mustafa died of old age.

A number of fates might still await me in Shqiperi. Somehow, I didn't think dying of old age was one of them.

"Are you satisfied, your Majesty?" Zogu asked.

"Will you *listen* to me, your Majesty?" Max asked.

"Yes," I said, and then, "No." To Zogu, I went on, "Let's go to the treasury. You've earned your pay." To Max, I went on, "Captain Yildirim, whatever it is, it will keep for a little while."

"They're getting ready to hang you from a lamppost out there, and me from the one next door," Max said.

"Don't be ridiculous," I told him. "Peshkepiia hasn't got any lampposts."

That kept him quiet till we got to the treasury chamber. The guards standing in front of it came to attention. I had the keys to the treasury with me—what better perquisite of kingship? One by one, the locks opened. The bars came off. The door swung wide. We went inside. I unlocked the chests.

"Go ahead," I said to Zogu. "Help yourself."

"North and south, east and west, your Majesty, that is spoken like a king!" he exclaimed.

"Nice of you to say so," I answered. By Eliphalet's holy hangnail, I *was* still a king! I might not have been Prince Halim Eddin, the way Essad Pasha thought I was. But I *had* been properly crowned as King of Shqiperi, no matter who I really was. All hail King Otto I! Long may he reign! Unfortunately, King Otto I was going to have a short reign, and it would have been even shorter if he hadn't been smart enough to realize as much.

Zogu wasn't shy about exacting his fee, but he wasn't greedy—or not too greedy, anyhow. "You put my honor at stake here," he said. "Were you niggardly, I would feel duty-bound to take more."

"If I didn't know you had honor, I wouldn't have spoken the way I did," I replied. One more lie for the road, even if a lie kindly meant. The truth was, right then I didn't care how much he took. He couldn't carry it all away, which was the only thing that mattered to me. But this was a lie that helped me more than the truth would have.

The mage bowed very low, clinking musically as he did. "For your kindness, your Majesty, I will give you a parting gift." He plucked a withered leaf from a pouch on his belt. "Here is a veritable tortoise leaf."

He'd used a tortoise scute before. That I understood, even if I'd never heard the term till he gave it to me. But this . . . "Do tortoises in Shqiperi turn into shrubs, or maybe grow on them?" I asked.

"Not so," Zogu said. "No one knows from which plant the she-tortoise—for it is always a she-tortoise—finds this leaf. She will not seek it if she is followed. But she carries it in her mouth with her. To get it from her, you must build a wall of stones around the nest where she has laid her eggs. The leaf has the property of breaking down any wall or door." He bowed again. "May it prove useful to you."

He still didn't say he knew I wasn't the king Essad Pasha had thought I was. He didn't need to say anything of the kind. He just gave me a present that would help me go on being who I was, even if I wasn't who Essad Pasha thought I was. Zogu might have worn his hair in a cut that looked like a pancake, but he was all right.

I bowed to him in turn. "It shall be a talisman, as long as my reign lasts." No, I wasn't going to admit a thing.

"Good fortune go with you—and with your leaf," he said. One more bow, and he was gone.

"Now," I said to Max. "You wanted to tell me something?"

He eyed the guards outside the door and spoke in a low voice. That didn't make him sound any less, ah, sincere—on the contrary, in fact. "Man, things are getting critical out there! We can't stay here any more, not after those cursed scribes—may demons take them—went and spilled the beans. More and more people know about the denials from Vyzance, and more and more people believe them. If we don't escape right now, we're lost. We'll be shot!"

Shot! Brr . . . That was not a pretty word.

But it was obvious that my good minister for special affairs was right. If it became clear the denials were true, then nothing good would happen to us. Essad Pasha (once he thawed out anyway) and his officers would be in a fine fury because we'd led them around by the nose like that. I could picture it perfectly well in my mind. I didn't want to wait around to see it for real.

And I wouldn't have to wait around very long. One of the palace guards trotted up to the treasury. He saluted me as king and said, "Excuse me, your Majesty, but there are soldiers outside the front entrance who don't seem well-inclined toward you."

How big an understatement was that? Probably bigger by the second. If I couldn't get adulation, chaos seemed the next best bet. I clapped a hand to my forehead. I looked stricken. As I had with Mujo, I overacted like you wouldn't believe. "Traitors!" I cried. "North and south, east and west, traitors beset me! They must be in Narbonese pay, those accursed curs! They'd eat their dead, vomit it up, and howl for more. Hold them off as long as you can. Reinforcements are on the way!"

The soldier saluted. He bowed. He ran back toward the entrance, waving his sword. When you do things like that, people get out of your way. They'd better, anyhow. One of the guards at the treasury door turned to peer in at me, his eyes as wide as saucers. "Your Majesty?" he said.

"Go help the men at the entrance," I told him. "Captain Yildirim and I will protect the treasury till you've beaten back the wicked rebels."

"Aye, your Majesty!" This poor sap saluted and bowed, too. He and his pal hotfooted it down the corridor after the other soldier. I couldn't see if they were waving their swords. It wouldn't surprise me, though. If you're going to act melodramatic, don't do it halfway.

"Narbonese pay?" Max said. "Protect the treasury?"

"Of course, Narbonese pay. You wouldn't expect me to blame a kingdom that's friendly to Schlepsig, would you?" I said. "And you'd best believe I intend to protect the treasury—as much of it as I can carry, anyway." I started filling every pocket and pouch my uniform possessed. I stuffed coins down my boot tops, too.

Max stared at me. Then—I know you'll think I'm making this up, but I am a truthful man—he started to laugh. "By Eliphalet's burgeoning bank account, Otto, you're not crazy after all!" He also loaded up.

Zogu had clinked when he left the treasury. We didn't. We'd packed ourselves too tight with cash to make much noise. The first few steps, I was awkward—I'd gained more than a little weight. I soon got the hang of it, though. Max was less graceful, but Max is always less graceful.

"Aren't you going to close the door?" Max inquired as we exited, stage left.

"Not me," I told him. "Sooner or later"—by the racket out front, it sounded like sooner—"those mean-spirited, misguided, misunderstanding rogues out there are going to break in. Some of them just may prove more interested in an open treasury than in open season on a king—and on his minister for special affairs."

"A point. A distinct point," he allowed. "How much do you think we've got?"

"More than Dooger and Cark would have paid us, that's for sure," I said. "Enough so that I'd sooner not go swimming."

"Urk," Max said, which was more or less what I was thinking. Servants stared at us as we strode past. I don't know what they were thinking. There wasn't really time to ask. They didn't try to stop us. Surely that was a sign of approval of my glorious if all too brief reign. After a bit, Max asked, "Do you have any idea where you're going?"

Surely that was a sign of imperfect trust in one's sovereign. "As a matter of fact, yes," I answered. And I did.

Things were getting quite unpleasantly loud out front when I came to the harem door. "Ah," Max said as I unbarred it from my side. If you want great roars of approval from Max, you'll be disappointed. If you want any sort of approval from Max, you'll mostly be disappointed. I was glad to take what I got.

That door, of course, remained barred from the other side. I pounded on it, calling, "Rexhep! Where are you, man?" The last word gave him too much credit, but better too much than not enough just then.

The pause that followed almost lasted long enough for me to try out Zogu's tortoise leaf, or whatever it was. In due course—much too due—the eunuch peered at me through the grate. "Well, what is it?" Rexhep asked, and then, after another beat, "Your Majesty?"

"I want to come into the harem," I said. "What did you expect? That I wanted to sell you some garlic?"

His cold eyes flicked from me to Max, who was standing behind me. Max couldn't hide behind me—Max can't hide behind anybody I can think of. "You cannot bring Captain Yildirim in with you," Rexhep said.

"What?" I yelped. "Demons take you, I'm King of Shqiperi! I can do anything I please!" If I got into the harem, I might even get away from Peshkepiia with a whole skin. That would have pleased me, all right.

Rexhep shook his head. "I am the chief eunuch of the harem. Captain Yildirim may not come in. No whole man may enter my domain, save only the king. It is the law." He didn't know what kind of entering Max had been up to back in my bedchamber, the Two Prophets be praised.

I started to reach for the tortoise leaf again. I wasn't going to put up with that nonsense, not even for a heartbeat. But then women's squeals and cries of, "Yildirim! Sweet Yildirim!" came from the other side of the door. Rexhep said something in Shqipetari. Whatever it was (I do—somewhat—regret not learning any of the language of the kingdom I ruled), it didn't work. A moment later, I heard the sounds of a scuffle. A moment after *that*, the door opened.

"Come in, your Majesty," Lutzi said.

"Come in, sweet Captain Yildirim," Maja and Strati added. Several of the other girls were sitting on Rexhep. If looks could kill . . . If looks could kill, he would have slaughtered the men who made him into what he was, so I was safe enough there. In I went, *sweet* Captain Yildirim at my heels.

"What do you need, your Majesty?" Hoti asked.

"The back way out," I answered. "I'm afraid there's been a bit of a palace revolution. Some of the Hassocki soldiers in the city want to see me slightly dead—and sweet Captain Yildirim, too." If they were going to make an unseemly fuss over Max (no accounting for taste, is there?), I intended to remind them that his long, scrawny neck was on the line, too.

Lutzi gasped. "Why would anyone want to hurt you, your Majesty? You're so—so lovable!" I liked the way she thought. I liked just about everything about her, to tell you the truth. She'd been pretty thoroughly lovable herself.

"It's a long story." I heard several crashes from out front, and then furious shouts *inside* the palace. None of that sounded good. "It's a long story, and I haven't got time to tell it. The back way, fast as we can go!"

"Yes, your Majesty!" the girls chorused. To them, I was still a king. Some of them led Max and me through the harem. Some went on sitting on Rexhep—one of them had the presence of mind to gag him. Some had even more presence of mind than that. They shut the door between the harem and the rest of the palace and set the alarmingly stout bar in its brackets, which was something I should have thought of.

"They'll notice it isn't barred from the other side," Max said sorrowfully.

"They'll still have to get in," I answered. "By the time they do, we'll have got out." If we hadn't got out by then, we were in even more trouble than I thought we were. And they said it couldn't be done!

I started to reach up and yank the rank badges off Max's shoulder straps. My first thought was that it would make him less conspicuous. My next thought was that painting over a few of a giraffe's spots wouldn't make it a whole lot less conspicuous. Unfortunately, that made better sense than the other did. I wished I'd asked Zogu for a spell to make Max seem shorter. Too late now.

We hustled to the back door. One of the girls looked through a spy-hole to make sure no unfriendly soldiers—there didn't seem to be any other kind just then—were lurking outside, intent on making some royal shashlik. The girls hadn't been in the palace much longer than I had. Did Rexhep tell them about the spyhole? I doubted it; Rexhep wouldn't have told his own mother his name. They'd probably found it themselves, then. They had all sorts of interesting talents.

"The coast is clear, your Majesty," she said.

"Those nasty people haven't broken into the harem yet, either," another girl said.

"You don't have to leave *just* yet, then." Three or four girls said that. I wasn't sure if they were talking to me or to the redoubtable (he was certainly worth doubting more than once) Captain Yildirim.

I also wasn't sure what would—or could—happen next. They'd spent the past four nights draining both of us dry. Worse, Zogu's aphrodisiac was back in the royal bedchamber. I hated to leave the girls disappointed. . . .

And, somehow, I didn't. Neither did Max. We got out a little later than we thought we would, a little tireder than we thought we would, and a lot happier than we thought we would. The back door opened silently, on well-oiled hinges. Had any of the women from earlier harems sneaked out? Had they smuggled any men in? I'd never know, but I had my royal suspicions.

"Farewell, your Majesty," Lutzi purred.

"Farewell, sweetheart." I corrected myself: "Sweethearts. Umm . . . You may be interested to know that nobody bothered closing the door to the treasury after the last time Captain Yildirim and I, ah, checked it."

They didn't forget about Max and me the instant they heard that. I can imagine no more sincere compliment. Out into the alley behind the palace we went. They closed the door behind us. The bar thumped down. *Then* they all squealed—I could hear them through those stout oaken timbers—and then, I have no doubt, they scrambled off for their share of the royal loot.

I hope they grabbed with both hands.

"Well," Max said, "what now?"

"Getting out of Peshkepiia without ending up with more holes than a colander would be nice," I said.

"It would, if we could," Max said. "How do you propose to manage it?"

"If we can get away from the goons around the palace, I think we'll be all right," I answered. "Once we do that, we scurry off toward the eastern gate as fast as our little legs will take us. If we steer clear of the Metropolis and the fortress, we've got a pretty fair chance."

"I don't know what you've been putting in your pipe, but give me some if you've got any left," Max said.

I don't suppose it was lese majesty; I wasn't exactly king any more. I said, "Think about it. Who really knows *I'm* King of Shqiperi? The Hassocki soldiers who were trying to get hold of this place and the foreigners at the hostel. The Shqipetari may know they've got a king, but most of them don't know what he looks like. To them, we're just a couple of Hassocki officers."

"That's not reason enough to knock us over the head?" Max was cheerful as usual.

"Nobody without a stepladder could knock you over the head, my dear," I told him. "And speaking of stepping . . ."

Step we did, and step lively, too. We tried to head east, steering by the sun and doing our best to stay away from what passed for main streets in Peshkepiia. Now, I didn't fall off the turnip wagon yesterday. I know how to find my way around. If you don't understand how to find your way around strange towns, you've got no business signing up with an outfit like Dooger and Cark's.

Peshkepiia was harder to navigate than it had any business being. It's not very big, but the streets double back on each other like you wouldn't believe. They would remind me of a plate of those long, skinny Torinan noodles, only they're slathered in stuff a lot nastier than tomato sauce.

If the Hassocki soldiers caught up with us, though, they'd do their best to turn us into meatballs.

Right then, I didn't think anybody could catch up with us. I thought we might run into ourselves coming and going. It wouldn't have surprised me much; the lanes and alleys and streets were *that* twisty. By the time we walked past the same place that sold secondhand clothes for about the fourth time, I started wondering how anybody ever got out of Peshkepiia, or if anybody ever did.

The old man who ran the place didn't seem surprised to watch us go by and go by and go by and go by. He didn't need to worry about shaving part of his scalp; he was bald as an eggplant, and not a whole lot less purple. He wore a big gray mustache that looked like it was trying to be wings and damn near succeeding.

When we saw him the fourth time, I had an idea: "What do you say we buy some Shqipetari clothes? Uniforms are fine here in town, but out in the countryside we'd do better looking like everybody else."

"You should have thought of that back in the palace. I know every outfit you had in your closet," Max said. I'll bet he did, too. But it was also too late for that. Given his excessive assortment of inches, I figured he was thinking clothes wouldn't unmake the man. But something else was on his mind: "Maybe we ought to just stick around this place. Soldiers will never find it. I'm not sure it's connected to the outside world."

My guess was that he had at least an even-money chance of being right. Whether he was or not, though, we really couldn't stick around. "Maybe new clothes will change our luck," I said. Max made a small production out of his shrug. I made a small production out of not seeing it. Striding up to the fellow who sat at the front of the shop, I asked, "Do you speak Hassocki?"

He paused to puff on his water pipe. He blinked a couple of times. Nothing happens fast in Shqiperi. You'll go mad if you expect it to. That's true all over the Nekemte Peninsula. And if they think you're in a hurry down there, they'll only go slower. Watching foreigners go mad is one of the local sports. Driving them mad is another one.

I waited. And waited. And waited some more. If I was a Hassocki myself, I was supposed to understand how the game worked. When I didn't whip out my sword or try to snatch that amber mouthpiece away from him and either jam it down his throat or up the other way, he eventually unbent enough to take it out of his mouth and grudge me a word: "Yes."

"Will you sell us outfits?" I asked. Whatever Max got wouldn't fit him well. I knew that. But the people looking for us were unlikely to care much about how Shqipetari clothes fit any which way.

The old geezer looked at me. He looked at Max. His eyes were as black and opaque as a tortoise's—and I don't mean a tortoise with a leaf in its beak, either. He gave me another grudging, "Yes."

"As you find the time, then, you might let us see your wares." I yawned and shrugged. "Nothing of great importance, though. I don't know why I asked in the first place. You probably won't have anything we want, anyhow."

All games have their tricks. Acting slower than the other fellow will speed him up. After a last puff on his pipe, the old Shqipetar actually stood up. I'd wondered if he was taking root there. "Come. I will show you," he said.

I'd won the round. I knew it, and he had to know it, too. His shop was even dimmer and darker inside than it had seemed from the street. That turned out not to be so bad. About two minutes after we went in, a couple of squads of Hassocki soldiers clumped by—the place was attached to the rest of Peshkepiia after all. The soldiers didn't look inside the shop. I wasn't sorry they didn't—oh, no, not a bit.

I bought black trousers and a white shirt and a sheepskin jacket and a leather sack to hold my loot; I was abandoning any number of pouches and pockets. I also bought a floppy hat to keep people from noticing I wasn't sheared like a Shqipetar. The breeches Max got were too short, but they were the longest ones the old man had. Max's wrists stuck out of his shirtsleeves, too. He chose a wool cape instead of a jacket: it had no sleeves. His sack was canvas, and his hat was even uglier than mine.

We gave the old Shqipetar our uniforms—all but the boots—as part of the price. They were bound to be worth more than the outfits we were buying, but we couldn't be fussy just then. With the uniform went the last vestiges of my royalty. I was a commoner again: an uncommon commoner, but a commoner even so.

"Which way to the east gate," Max asked, in lieu of something like, *How do we never see this corner again?*

The old man gave us directions. I made him repeat them. We tried them. They really and truly worked. The Two Prophets must have been in the mood to dole out miracles. Thank you, Eliphalet. And thank you, too, Zibeon, but not quite so much.

We had only one bad moment on the way to the gate. We walked right past Bob. He was speaking—in Albionese, of course—to someone who didn't seem to know much of his language. "Yes, the king and his minister appear to have fled," he said. "No one has any idea where they are."

He was looking right at us. The only way to make Max look like anyone but Max would be to chop him off at the ankles. A cowflop of a hat will not do the trick. Bob perceived . . . nothing. He was looking for two men in Hassocki uniforms. Failing to see them, he had no interest in anything or anyone else. Neither my good looks nor Max's height made him give us a second glance.

No one else did, either. The gate guards were counting sheep (for the wool tax, not for the sake of sleep) as we strolled out. One of them nodded to us. The rest went on arguing about the count with Bopip—I think that was the shepherd's name, anyway. I showed the seat of my pants to the seat of my government and headed east.

fter we'd put a mile or so between ourselves and Peshkepiia, Max said, "Well, you haven't got us killed yet. I don't know how you haven't or why you haven't, but I'm still breathing."

"Keep it up," I said. "I noticed you were rather vigorous about it the past four nights."

"I've passed evenings I liked less," he said, and I knew that was as much as I'd get out of him.

"Back to Fushe-Kuqe, then," I said. "Passage on the first ship that's going anywhere. And a story to dine out on as long as we live—and the money to dine pretty well."

"Assuming we live long enough to be able to dine at all." No, that wasn't Max being gloomy. He was looking back along the road we'd just traveled. Only a troop of horsemen riding hard could have kicked up that cloud of dust.

We were standing in the shade of a mulberry tree. "Sit down," I hissed to Max. "That way, they won't need to be as blind as Bob not to notice how tall you are."

"No, but we're still dead if they talked to the old bugger who sold us this clobber," Max said. I never needed to worry when he was around— he was so much better at it than I'd ever be. He sat down even so, and I stretched out beside him.

Up rode the cavalrymen, with much jingling of harness and what have you. They were going at a fast trot, and they paid us no particular attention. "What do we do if we catch this fellow who was calling himself king?" one of them asked.

"Take him back to Peshkepiia." The man who answered looked and sounded like a sergeant. No one was going to get any nonsense past him, not if he could help it. "Then we give him to Essad Pasha."

"Oh, they've got him moving again?" the curious cavalryman said.

"Would he want that other bugger if they hadn't?" Why do sergeants answer questions with questions? Oh, there I am doing it myself. Well, I've been a sergeant, too. I'll tell you, kinging it is better.

"What if—?" I couldn't make out the rest of what the first horseman said; the jingling and the clop of hoofbeats drowned out his words. Then the cavalry troop was gone, riding east.

Max looked after them. "Nice to know they remember you."

"Yes, isn't it?" I sounded as bland as I could.

That wasn't very; Max wouldn't let it be very. "Do you suppose they hired Zogu to thaw Essad Pasha out?"

There was an imperfectly delightful thought. I managed a smile in spite of being imperfectly delighted. "Well, what if they did?" I said. "The only thing better than getting paid is getting paid twice."

"The only thing better than getting paid is getting laid," Max returned.

"Well, we did that, too, by Eliphalet's holy foreskin," I said.

"It wouldn't have done him much good if it wasn't holey." Max is a blasphemous cactus.

I climbed to my feet. I picked up my sack full of silver—and the odd bit of gold, and the occasional jewel. I had only memories to remind me I'd got laid. The sack told me loud and clear that I'd got paid. Max grunted as he hefted his. It might have been heavier than mine. For all I knew, he'd got paid better as a king's aide-de-camp than I had as his majestic Majesty. Was that enough to make him stop grumbling? Not likely!

"On to Fushe-Kuqe!" I said.

But we never got there.

Half an hour after that first cavalry troop jingled and clattered past us, another one rode by. Again, we plopped down by the side of the road and pretended to be lazy, good-for-nothing Shqipetari peasants—but I repeat myself. Again, the Hassocki rode by without giving us a second glance. They were still after King Halim Eddin and Captain Yildirim, not Otto of Schlepsig and Max of Witte, to say nothing (which is about as much as should be said) of Fatmir and Beqiri—or pick two other Shqipetari names that suit you, if you'd rather.

We kept going in spite of that. Half an hour later, though, *another* troop went by. This one was loaded for bear, or more likely dragon. At its head rode Essad Pasha, looking grim. Half a pace behind him and to his right rode Colonel Kemal, looking determined. A whole pace behind him and to his left rode Major Mustafa, looking angry. Directly behind him, on a distinctly spooked horse, rode José-Diego, looking, respectively, furious and murderous.

So they weren't just out for Halim Eddin and Yildirim. They were after Otto and Max, too. But they still hadn't figured out Fatmir and Beqiri. Well, no one's ever figured out the peasantry of Shqiperi.

"Tell me, my dear, dear friend, how do you propose to get around that?" Max can be most difficult when he sounds the mildest. He has other character traits I find more endearing.

"We'll get to the coast somewhere that isn't Fushe-Kuqe, we'll find a fisherman, and we'll pay him to take us across the Tiberian Sea to Torino," I replied.

Max looked at me. "As easy as that, eh?"

"As easy as that," I said.

And so it was—n't.

If we weren't going to lovely, charming Fushe-Kuqe, if we weren't going past Essad Pasha's shooting box—where now we were all too likely to become part of the entertainment, not to take part in it—we needed to leave the main road between Peshkepiia and the port. At first, I reckoned this no great hardship. Indeed, I reckoned it no hardship at all, since in any kingdom that actually *has* roads the one between Peshkepiia and Fushe-Kuqe would be recognized at once for what it is: a horrid, muddy, rutted, winding track long, long overdue for repair, refurbishment (or even furbishment), and restoration.

Once we left it, though, we rapidly found out why it was the main road. All the others were worse. Yes, universally and without exception. No, I wouldn't have believed it, either. But I saw it with my own eyes. I went into it with my own feet . . . and ankles . . . and calves . . . and, a couple of times, knees.

You would think a farmer could find a better place to let his hogs wallow than in the middle of what was allegedly a road. You would think so, if you've never been to Shqiperi. By the time you saw it for the third time, it wouldn't surprise you any more. It wouldn't even infuriate you any more. It would just be—how do I put it?—part of the landscape.

One other thing: hogs in Shqiperi are not the plump, placid pink porkers we turn into hams in Schlepsig. They are one short step, one very short step, up from wild boars. You can't go through their wallows. You would resent it. If you try to go around their wallows, they are apt to resent it—and to come after you. When we bombarded one brazen beast with rocks to keep him from eating us instead of the other way round, his farmer resented it. He shouted loudly and irately in Shqipetari.

"Thou wretched, bloody, and usurping boar!" I replied in Hassocki. "Thou hast a sow for a mistress, and right sorry am I to have disturbed thy brats!"

He understood me. All over the Nekemte Peninsula, people revile one another in Hassocki, even when they don't use it for anything else. This says something about the language and something about the Hassocki—nothing good in either case, I fear me.

"Let vultures vile seize on thy lungs!" he cried. "May thy yard rot off!"

"Thy yard is but an inch!" Max shouted at him.

After a few more such pleasantries, we went on our way. We soon found we hadn't skirted the wallow quite well enough, for its stench went on our way with us. When we came to a small stream, we paused to clean the muck off our boots.

Max wiped at his with a tuft of grass. "This is a pain in the morass," he grumbled.

"Look on the bright side," I said, something he was unlikely to do without encouragement—or with it, for that matter. "Essad Pasha won't find us as long as we keep going down tracks like these."

"Of course he won't." Max threw the clump of grass into the stream. It floated away. "No one could find us here. We couldn't find ourselves here if we went out looking for us."

I started to follow that one through its range of possibilities, then gave it up as a bad job. We climbed to our feet and splashed across the little creek. Several frogs jumped off of rocks and into the water and swam away. They must have taken us for Narbonese.

Perhaps half a mile farther on, things got more complicated. The track we were following stopped. I don't mean it just sort of petered out. It stopped. A considerable gully interrupted it. I considered the gully—unhappily. The track resumed on the far side. Maybe it had been made before the gully was there. Maybe, once upon a time, a bridge spanned the gap. If so, somebody'd bridgenapped it.

I peered down into the gully, wondering if the troll who'd lived under the bridge—if there'd ever been a bridge—could tell me anything. I didn't see any trolls. Maybe he'd been trollnapped. Maybe there'd never been a troll. If there had been a troll, maybe he'd decided he was no homelier than anybody else in Shqiperi and gone off to Peshkepiia. The only thing I was sure of was that he hadn't been in my harem.

"Well, now what?" Max asked.

If we went back, we'd have to go all the way back to the main road. Essad Pasha, Colonel Kemal, Major Mustafa, and José-Diego made that seem less than desirable. If we went forward, we needed wings. Eliphalet wasn't likely to grant a prayer for them. Just on the off chance, I sent one up anyway. Eliphalet was not only unlikely to grant one, he bloody well didn't.

I sighed. "Back to that last farm," I said. "We need some rope."

"Planning to hang yourself?" Max inquired.

"No—you," I said. We glared at each other. I went on, "With rope, I may be able to get across. *You* may even be able to get across."

"And what's that supposed to mean?" he asked.

"I'd kill myself if I tried to swallow your sword," I said. "What kind of a tightrope walker are you?"

"We've been walking a tightrope since we got here. But that isn't what you meant, is it?" Max gave me a large, loose-jointed shrug. "Better to use the rope to get across the gully than to give it to the hangman. He already has plenty of rope to make us dance on air."

"Try not to cheer me up any more," I said. "I may fall over and die of joy."

"You can die of all sorts of things in this Prophets-forsaken place," Max said. "Now that we're out of the harem, joy isn't likely to be one of them."

We walked back to the farm. Since we'd exchanged endearments with the farmer, I wondered whether he would turn his dogs—or, maybe worse, his hogs—loose on us. "Can you sell us some rope?" I called to him in Hassocki.

He looked as much like a bandit as any Shqipetar I'd ever seen, which is saying something. "What do you want it for?" he asked.

"I know a spell that will make it stand up so we can climb all the way to heaven," I answered. The less I told him, the better off I expected to be.

The only trouble with saying what I did say was, it made him raise his price. I suppose he thought any rope that was going to heaven had to be expensive. But what a Shqipetari farmer finds expensive doesn't badly hurt someone who's been pawing through a royal treasury, even a small royal treasury like Shqiperi's (smaller now—oh, yes!).

As we headed back to the gully, he wanted to follow us. Max discouraged him. Max could discourage anything this side of a mammoth, I suspect. The farmer wasn't much brighter than a mammoth, but he was a good deal smaller. He decided he'd have to get to heaven on his own, not on our coattails. I thought his odds poor; even the Quadrate God must be more fussy about the company he keeps than *that*. But the Quadrate God's companions aren't my worry, Eliphalet be thanked.

Several tall trees stood on our side of the gully. Others leaned toward them from the far side, but not close enough—not to someone without special talent, anyhow. Special talent I had—or, at least, I hoped I had.

I handed Max my current share of the royal treasury—and if that doesn't prove I trusted him, obstructive and obstreperous as he was, nothing ever would. I also took off my boots. Barefoot was better for what I'd have to do. That coil of rope attached to my belt, I climbed an oak that had a stout branch sticking out over the gully. My target was an outthrust branch on a tall tree on the other side.

I tied one end of the rope to my branch. Then I let myself down, and then I began to swing back and forth, harder and harder. Each pendulum swing took me farther across the gully. I started to feel like part of the works from one of those elaborate mechanical clocks you'll see in towers all across Schlepsig. That other outthrust branch came closer and closer. I reached and—missed.

Another swing, and then yet another to rebuild the momentum I'd squandered. I reached out—and caught the branch I wanted. I couldn't pull myself up onto it with one arm. I had to let go of the rope with both hands, holding on to it with only my feet. Yes, I was glad I had toes to grip with! I wished I were a forest ape; then I would have come equipped with a couple of extra thumbs.

What I had sufficed. Once I was up on the branch on the far side, I tied the rope to it. Then I stood up and also tied the rope to a branch above it. And then, holding the rest of the coil in my right hand, I started back across the tightrope I'd created. A tightrope made a good enough bridge for me. It wouldn't do for Max, not by itself. But if he had one strand on which to put his feet and another above it to hold on to, I thought that would be good enough to get him across.

Nothing ever turns out to be as simple as you wish it would.

"Grrr! Who's that walking on my bridge? Grrr!" No, the troll hadn't been there a few minutes before, when I looked down into the gully. But then, the bridge hadn't been there a few minutes before, either.

And there he stood, on top of my strand of rope. Or possibly she—it could only matter to another troll. This one had plenty of ugly for both sexes. Green complexion. Warts. Hair. Fangs. Claws. All the standard equipment, including a bad attitude.

He might have been six inches tall.

"Come on!" he roared in a voice ridiculously deep for anything his size. "Come on, you big thing! I'll bite your toes off!"

I didn't like the sound of that. I wasn't sure he could bite a toe off. He had a big mouth for anything his size, but *that* big? Still, when you're on a tightrope, you don't want anything biting your toes, even if not *off*. That could make your day less enjoyable than you'd like.

I thought about imitating the billy goats in the story and asking him to wait till something bigger and tastier came along. But I wasn't convinced Max is tastier than I am. I'm still not, as a matter of fact. And, even more to the point, I wasn't convinced he could knock the troll off the rope—I should say, the bridge—even if he went across it wearing boots.

The burdens of a kingdom still lay on *my* shoulders, even though the kingdom was gone. It hardly seemed fair.

I took a step toward the troll. He gnashed those unpleasant-looking teeth. "Why don't you be reasonable?" I said—reasonably. "If it weren't for me, you wouldn't have a bridge where you could annoy people."

"And so? I've got one now!" The troll rushed toward me. Running along a rope didn't bother him at all.

I had the rest of the rope, though. I snapped it as if cracking a whip. It caught the troll right in his trollish chops. He let out a squawk—this time one of surprise and dismay, not one of bad-tempered rage. And he went flying, nasty little arms flailing uselessly, out and down into the gully. I hoped a ferret would eat him. Just what he deserved, though he'd probably give the beast heartburn.

Of course, I fell off the tightrope, too. You don't make a violent motion like that on a rope without paying for it. But I'd known I would. I caught the rope as I went down, and pulled myself back up onto it. Then I gathered up the second strand again and finished taking it back across the gully.

"Well, that was entertaining," Max said when I got back to the side where he waited.

"So glad you were amused," I said. A lot of things are more entertaining to watch than to do. I would put being attacked by a miniature troll while you're walking a tightrope fairly high on the list. "Now that we've got a length of rope for you to hold on to while you cross, do you think you can make it over the gully?"

"I think I'd better," Max said, which showed good sense. "And I think you'd better carry the money."

"I'll do that," I promised. "You didn't run off with it while I was going across. I won't, either."

"I should say not. Where would you run to?" Max said. "Ah, do you suppose that thing you larruped is likely to come back?"

"I hope not," I said sincerely. "If you want to leave your boots on while you're crossing, maybe you can squash it flat if it does, or at least kick it off again." I didn't believe it, but you shouldn't discourage somebody who may have to try something hard.

And Max nodded in something that looked like approval. Who

would have believed it? "Good idea," he said. "How did *you* come up with it?" He climbed the tree. He is, to put it mildly, inelegant at such pursuits. If there were monkeys in Shqiperi, they would have killed themselves laughing. Maybe there are no monkeys in Shqiperi because they spent too much time watching clumsy tree-climbers and laughed themselves to death. Wouldn't surprise me a bit.

Max was every bit as ungraceful—maybe even disgraceful—edging out across my makeshift bridge. Did he hang on tight to the top strand? Oh, you might say so. Yes, you just might. Did he get from this side of the gully to that one? Yes, he did, and how can you ask for more?

I suspect the nonexistent monkey would have laughed at me, too. You cannot haul two sacks of silver up into a tree and look good while you're doing it. I started across the rope again. I'd got most of the way across when . . .

"Grr! Who's that walking on my bridge? Grrr!"

He'd learned his lines well; I will say that for him. But nobody'd blocked his moves for him. I was almost to the far side of the gully, and there he stood, back in the middle of the rope bridge. I said, "Please don't eat me, Master Troll."

"Why not?" he roared—a damn good roar for his size, I must say.

Because you'd explode if you tried. But no, I didn't tell him that. Since I'd been thinking of it earlier, I gave him the time-honored answer instead: "Because the fellow who's coming after me is much larger and juicier and tastier, that's why."

"Juicy," the troll said, and then, "All right. You can cross. I'll wait for him."

Cross I did. As far as I know, the troll is waiting yet. Oh, it's possible some Shqipetar has tried to cross by the rope bridge. If he did, a grouchy little troll would have annoyed him. But more likely the miserable green nuisance is still standing there. Many good-byes to him.

Max had had the sense to get down from the tree on the far side of the gully before I crossed over to it. When I'd descended, too, he asked, "Well, what now?"

"Now on to the coast," I said, "and let's hope we don't run into any more trolls. That little pest may have some big friends."

I don't think I'll put Eliphalet and Zibeon out of business any time soon, but that was one of the best prophesies I ended up wishing I'd never made.

I didn't have to worry about building my own bridge over this gully. A wooden span that looked as old as time already crossed it. The bridge seemed solid enough, though. It certainly had no trouble bearing the weight of the troll who appeared in the middle of it as soon as Max and I started across.

"Grrr!" he roared. "Who's that walking on my bridge? Grrr!" Yes, the same old tired line. It sounded much more impressive coming from him than it had from the other one, because he was at least as tall as Max and about four times as wide.

"You and your big mouth," Max said to me.

Since I was thinking the same thing, I couldn't even snarl at him. Oh, maybe—probably, even—the troll would have appeared if I hadn't predicted it. That didn't make me feel any better. A six-inch troll was ugly and annoying. A six-foot-eight troll was even uglier and much too likely to be lethal. This fellow had warts the size of his little cousin. I might have resigned myself to those. But he also had fangs and talons about the size of his little cousin. By all appearances, he intended to use them, too.

"Do you suppose he's as smart as the little one was?" Max asked out of the side of his mouth.

I eyed the troll. "I don't think he'll put the Seventeen Sages out of business any time soon, or even Ibrahim the Wise."

Max snorted. "Ah, good old Joe," he murmured, remembering the tubby Torinan who'd worked for Dooger and Cark. "I wonder if his demon's devoured him yet." And then he did something that convinced me he was no threat to the Seventeen Sages, either: he drew his sword and advanced on the troll.

I drew my sword, too, and went after him. I didn't want him to die out there on the bridge by himself, but I didn't really think both of us together could take out that mass of muscles and claws and teeth.

"*Grrr!*" The troll got louder and angrier as we got closer. Any moment now, he was going to charge. That might be . . . unpleasant.

"You're not so tough," Max said, and I wondered if he'd come unhinged. Well, no—I didn't wonder, not even a little bit. I was convinced.

Even the troll seemed surprised. "Who says?" he bellowed. "I'll show you!" By then, we were close enough to be sure he'd never made the acquaintance of a fangbrush—or if he had, he desperately needed a new brand of fangpaste.

But Max just repeated, "You're not so tough." He brandished his blade. "If you're so tough," he went on, "let's see you do *this.*" He threw back his head and swallowed the sword, or enough of it as makes no difference.

The troll's beady, bloodshot eyes went wide. He jumped up and down on the bridge in his excitement, which made those old, old timbers creak more than I wished they would. "Gimme that! Gimme that!" he shouted, and held out a spiked hand. "You'll see!"

Max bowed and handed the troll the sword. Down the creature's throat it went—one great thrust. And we saw. And it wasn't pretty, I'm afraid. After the thrashing stopped at last, Max extracted the sword from the dead troll's gullet. Eyeing the gore on it with distaste, he said, "Well, you were right. He wasn't very smart. But I'll *really* have to get this steam-cleaned before I use it professionally again."

"I'm sorry for you," I said.

Max gave me an odd look. "How's that?"

I said it again: "I'm sorry for you." He still looked odd. He looks odd a good deal of the time, but not odd like that. I explained: "No matter how you cough, now you won't be the first one to cut your throat from the inside out."

"Oh." Max stirred the troll with his foot. It stayed dead. He shrugged. "Well, I'll just have to live with that. And, with a little luck, I'll go on living with it quite a while longer." He stepped over the troll. A moment later, so did I. We crossed the bridge and headed east, toward the coast.

To my relief, we didn't run into any more trolls. The two we did meet seemed like about six too many. If we had encountered another one, there's no guarantee Max's trick would have worked again. I think the odds are decent—trolls, pretty plainly, aren't bright, which goes a long way towards explaining why they don't infest more bridges—but you never can tell ahead of time.

We came down to the Tiberian Sea somewhere not too far south of Fushe-Kuqe. Don't ask me exactly how far, because I haven't the slightest idea. It was still beach, though—a nice stretch of sand—and not rocks. In Narbonensis and Torino and Leon, there's a growing custom of going to the beach, taking off most of your clothes, and baking under the sun. Not in Shqiperi. Nothing there but sand . . . and us.

Well, almost. Someone was walking along the sand. As Max and I got closer, we saw it was the ineffable Bob. No, I don't know what he was doing there. I'm sure *he* didn't know what he was doing there. Interviewing sea gulls and sandpipers, I suppose. I daresay he expected them to understand Albionese, too.

I tried not to pay any attention to him. A couple of fishing boats bobbed (no, I didn't do that on purpose—of course I didn't) not too far offshore. I waved to the nearer one. I hallooed. I didn't think it would take a whole lot of the royal treasury to persuade the skipper to carry Max and me across to Torino.

Somebody on the boat waved back. Somebody else raised the sail. The boat began gliding toward the beach. Bob came up to me. "Good day, your Majesty," he said—in Albionese, naturally. I don't know how he recognized Max and me—maybe somebody'd told him we might be wearing native costume. That would have let him see us when we weren't in uniform.

"Bob, I don't speak Albionese," I said . . . in Albionese.

The breeze gently ruffled his toupee. He frowned at me—something was going on inside his head. I hadn't been sure anything could. But I finally found a standard of comparison for Bob: he was brighter than a troll. Than two trolls, in fact. Maybe even than two trolls put together, though I'd have a harder time proving that. His heavy features worked. "You— You just did!" he said. Point him at the obvious and shove him forward and he might—just might, mind you—flatten his nose against it.

"Well, what if I did?" I replied, still in his language.

"But you didn't before." Bob paused. I don't believe it was in thought—the breeze picked up, and tried to pick up his not-quite-masterpiece of tonsorial artifice. He hastily jammed it back almost into place. Still, that brief gust of wind directly on his pate must have improved the functioning of the brain under it, for he came out with something that came close to counting for insight: "Or you didn't seem to, anyhow." His rheumy eyes narrowed in suspicion.

I nodded in approval of his mental calisthenics. "You're right—I didn't seem to."

"Why didn't you?" Was that a scribe's probing inquiry or a child's blind naïveté? I only ask the questions—you have to answer them.

"Because as far as I know, Prince Halim Eddin doesn't speak any Albionese."

I waited again. You had to wait with Bob; nothing ever happened in a hurry with him. Except for the small language difficulty, he was made for the Nekemte Peninsula. At last, things percolated through. "Then . . . you really aren't Prince Halim Eddin!" he exclaimed.

I set a fond hand on his shoulder. "Nothing gets past you, does it?" I said.

"That must be why Essad Pasha is so interested in finding you!" he added. It's a good thing we have such clever scribes; otherwise no one in the world would have any idea what's going on. Of course, by the evidence no one in the world does have any idea what's going on. Which means . . . Well, you might be better off not dwelling on what it means.

"Oh? Is Essad Pasha looking for me?" I asked, as innocently as only a guilty man could.

"I should say he is," Bob replied. He gasped as a new idea struck him—and well he might have, because such a thing didn't happen every day, or every month, either. "There's a story in this!"

I would have told it to him. I would have been glad to tell it to him. He and the other bloody scribes had already ruined my reign. Thanks to them, I wouldn't be a famous king. Since I wouldn't be famous, being notorious would have to do. Yes, I would have told him everything—except that by then the fishing boat was close enough to hail.

"Can you take two men across to Torino?" I shouted in Hassocki to the gray-bearded fellow at the bow. Bob made a frustrated noise. Why his journal sent him down to Shqiperi when he spoke only Albionese would be beyond me if I didn't know how many of his countrymen are just as provincial as he is.

The fisherman didn't even blink. "Ten piasters apiece," he called in the same tongue. That was cheaper than I'd expected. I wondered if he was a small-time smuggler who went from one coast of the Tiberian Sea to the other all the time. I wouldn't have been surprised. Even though the price was reasonable, I haggled for form's sake—I didn't want him to get the idea that I had so much money, I didn't care what I spent. After a few good-natured curses on both sides, we settled on eight piasters apiece.

In came the boat. It looked a bit large to beach itself to take us aboard. I supposed we would have to wade out a ways and get wet. Max plunged his sword into the sand again and again to scour off the troll's blood. I'm sure he wouldn't have wanted to swallow it again right after that, but at least the blade wouldn't rust.

"I just saw a funny thing."

No, that wasn't Max or Bob or the fisherman. That was a gull that had landed on the beach about twenty feet from me after gliding in from the north. I remembered the taste of dragon's blood by Essad Pasha's shooting box. I haven't talked much since about understanding the speech of birds and animals for a very simple reason: most of the time, birds and animals haven't got anything interesting to say. They might as well be people.

I wouldn't talk about this gull, either, except that a sandpiper asked, "What kind of funny thing?"

The gull flicked a yellow-eyed glance toward Max and me and even Bob. "One of these useless, featherless creatures riding a horse this way, only it had two heads."

I didn't think the bird meant the horse had two heads, even if it could have done a better job of straightening out its syntax. What I did think was, *If José-Diego is riding this way, how far behind is Essad Pasha?* Did I want to find out?

"That damn fishing boat better hurry up, or we're going to have a problem," I told Max.

"How do you know?" he said.

"A little bird told me," I answered. Max may not have known I meant it literally. He didn't taste the dragon's blood himself.

But I had only a couple of minutes' start on him, as things worked out. The gull knew what it was talking about, all right. Here came José-Diego riding south down the beach—and riding hell for leather on catching sight of Max and me. He—they?—shouted something in Leonese. I couldn't quite make out what it was, but it didn't sound complimentary.

Here came the fishing boat. The fisherman was being cautious as he drew close to shore. Bob was standing around scratching his head—carefully, so as not to rumple his rug—and wondering what was going on. Bob spent a lot of time wondering what was going on, poor sap.

Just as the fisherman waved to us to come aboard, José-Diego sprang down from his/their horse. He's usually clumsy—José tells his body one thing, while Diego tells it something else. This time, though, they were both telling it the same thing. For some reason or other, neither José nor Diego was very happy with me. Their body drew a dagger and charged.

"Throw me in a dungeon, will you!" José shouted—I think it was José.

"Lock me up, will you—with no one to talk to but *him!*" Diego screamed—I believe it was Diego.

"You'll pay for that!" they roared together—I'm sure it was both of them.

I started to dodge. With my acrobatic grace, it should have been easy—except I stumbled in the sand. That cursed dagger caught me right in the middle of my chest.

Yes, I'm still here. No, you don't see dead people—I'm not ghost-writing this tale. What happened was, the blade snapped in half. José-Diego howled in horrified disbelief. Me? I smiled more smugly than the circumstances probably justified. But a dragon scale, even without a silver backing, is more than enough to turn any ordinary blade.

Max tackled José-Diego. Down he—they?—went. I jumped on him—them—whatever you please. If I remember straight, Max pounded on José while I beat on Diego, but it could have been the other way round.

After we'd knocked both heads together a few times, their arms and legs stopped paying attention to either one of him. That was what we'd had in mind. We got to our feet, brushed sand off each other, and waded out into the blue Tiberian Sea.

Bob clapped his hands. "My," he said, "that was exciting!" He knelt beside José-Diego. "Would either one of you care to give me your comments in regard to this incident?"

Both José and Diego were too battered to make much sense right then. Besides, I don't think either one of them spoke Albionese. Bob didn't care. Well, maybe he did care, but he couldn't do anything about it, because he didn't speak anything else. The blind misleading the deaf, you might say.

The fisherman reached out a hand and helped us into the boat one after the other. "North and south, east and west, you have a strange foe," he said. "No wonder you want to put the width of the sea between yourselves and him."

"No wonder at all," I said. He held out his hand, palm up. I gave him eight piasters. "You'll get the other half when you put us ashore in Torino," I told him.

"Be it so," he said, not in the least put out. "You will be a man who has traveled with strangers before."

"Now and then," I agreed. "Yes, every now and then."

He shouted to the other three men in the boat. One worked the rudder. The other two trimmed the sails. The boat nimbly spun about and started for Torino. I waved good-bye to Bob. I don't think he saw me. He was kneeling on the sand, still trying to squeeze a story out of José-Diego.

As we neared the Torinan coast, the skipper of the fishing boat—his name was Hysni—asked, "You won't want to come right into a regular port, will you?"

I looked at Max. Max looked at me. We both shook our heads, the motions so nearly identical we would have got a big laugh on any stage. "Well, now that you mention it, no," I said.

Hysni smiled a thin smile. "Didn't think so," he said. A few minutes later, he added, "Bugger customs men, anyway." Since Max and I were carrying as much of the Shqipetari royal treasury as we could, I sympathized with Hysni's enlightened attitude. Officials might have found some really tedious questions about the money; best to avoid all those unpleasant possibilities if we could.

And we could. Hysni put us ashore towards evening on a beach not too far from a town—but not too close to one, either. I happily paid him the other half of our fee. He was so forthrightly mercenary, he made doing business with him a pleasure.

"Good luck," he said. "North and south, east and west, good luck."

"North and south, east and west, may good luck sail with you," I said. He smiled. So did the other fishermen, who were his sons and his nephew.

Max and I splashed up onto the sand. The fishing boat smartly put about and started back to Shqiperi. Watching Hysni and his kinsfolk sail west into the setting sun, Max murmured, "Poor bastards." Max always was so sentimental.

I poked him in the ribs. "Now," I said.

"Now what?" he answered irritably. "And what the demon was that for, anyhow?"

"We went into Shqiperi," I said. "I bloody well ruled as King of Shqiperi. We screwed ourselves silly—sillier—and we got out of Shqiperi. Not only that, we got out of Shqiperi with more than we came in." I nudged my leather sack with the toe of my boot. It clinked softly, as if to remind Max how right I was. "Now I get to say I told you so, that's what, and now you get to admit that I told you so, too."

I waited. I folded my arms across my chest so I could wait in the proper royal style. I still felt like the King of Shqiperi, even if I'd had my reign unfortunately cut short.

"You told me so," Max agreed. Being Max, he couldn't just leave it at that. Oh, no. "And I told you you were out of your mind right from the start, and Eliphalet turn his back on me if I was wrong."

I thought about that. "Well, maybe," I said, "but I got away with it." I poked him in the ribs again. "I had some pretty good help, too, Captain Yildirim."

He poked me back. "Yes, your Majesty." We both started to laugh. No, I'm not making that up. Max really and truly started to laugh. Twice in the space of a few days! What was the world coming to?

After a while, I asked, "Do you want to find a town now, or do you want to spend the night on the beach and find one in the morning?"

"I'd just as soon sleep here," Max answered. "I'm not what you'd call hungry or anything."

Neither was I. Hysni had fed us well on—inevitably—fried fish. "Suits me," I said. "This will do well enough—better than well enough—for tonight. Our clothes will dry out, too."

"We'll need new ones," Max said. "They don't wear this kind of stuff here, and I won't miss it a bit, either. You speak Torinan, don't you?"

"Sure—enough to get by with, anyhow," I said. "They won't think I'm a native or anything, but they'll understand me. How about you?"

"Maybe enough to get my face slapped," Max replied. And how much more of a language than that do you really need, anyhow? We lay down and stretched ourselves out. The sand made a fine mattress, my sack of silver a perfectly lovely pillow.

• • •

"More Shqipetari riffraff," the clothier muttered, peering at Max and me around the promontory of his nose. Torinans like Shqipetari about as well as Lokrians do, and for about the same reasons: men come from the Land of the Eagle looking for work, and they steal if they don't find it (or sometimes even if they do).

I wanted to curse the fellow in Hassocki, but he wouldn't have understood me. The Hassockian Empire never got to Torino, so its oaths and obscenities never got there, either. Torinans have to make do with their own set, which is distinctly impoverished by comparison.

"Do you always try to run customers out of your shop?" I inquired in my best—indifferent—Torinan.

"Customers?" He laughed as if I'd said something funny. "Customers have money. Shqipetari have—" I wasn't quite sure what he said then, but I believe it involved irreverent affection for a donkey.

"No, that was your mother," I said. While he was still gaping, I set enough silver on the counter to make him gape in a whole new way. "Now—are we customers, or do we give our business to an honest man instead?"

He started to reach for the silver. I started to reach for my sword. Max started to reach for his. The clothier's hand suddenly had second thoughts. "You are customers," he allowed, and said nothing more about donkeys. "What is it you want?"

"Civilized clothes," I answered, and said nothing more about his mother. "We went into Shqiperi and we got out again, and now we don't have to look like we live there any more."

"You I can fit with no trouble," he said, and then eyed Max with the dismay clothiers have eyed him with since he was fourteen years old. "Your friend, I am afraid, will take a little longer."

"My friend is a little longer," I agreed.

"He will cost extra, too," the clothier said.

"A little extra, I suppose," I said. "Not a lot."

Torinans think they're good hagglers. Put them next to Schlepsigians or Albionese, who hardly haggle at all, and they're right. In the Nekemte

Peninsula, they'd be picked to skin and bones before they knew what hit them. I was used to playing a tougher game than the clothier. I got the price I wanted without even coming close to mentioning his mother again.

By that afternoon, Max and I looked like a couple of men who'd just bought new clothes in a Torinan provincial town. It could have been worse. We could have gone on looking like Shqipetari.

People gawked at Max when we bought fares on a northbound stage. But people gawk at Max's inches even in Schlepsig, though he did seem to have more of them in Torino, where the folk are mostly shorter. And the fellow who sold us our tickets smiled at my accent. "You are from the north, eh?" he said. "You speak dialect up in that part of the kingdom."

He didn't think I was a foreigner, mind. He just thought I talked funny. Well, I thought he—and the clothier, and everybody else down there—talked funny, too. It's true that the lovely and talented lady (and she was both, dear Annaluisa was) from whom I learned most of my Torinan did come from the north. I was happy enough to follow her lead in whatever she did—you'd best believe I was.

She didn't slap my face, either. I was luckier with her than Max was with the girl from whom he'd learned his little bits of the language.

And I was luckier when it came to the coach. Max eyed it with distaste. "Crammed into another bloody shoebox," he said.

"Would you rather stay in Torino?" I asked him.

"Weather's better," he said, which is true. After you've sailed the Middle Sea, you can never look at the weather in Schlepsig the same way again. But in the end, he shook his head. "No, I'll go home, too."

An hour later than it should have, the coach rattled north. Even though a small woman sat across from him, Max didn't have much legroom. I didn't, either. I don't think anyone else on the coach did. But Max had it worse than the rest of us.

We were all glad to stretch our legs when we got to the next town. This one boasted a Consolidated Crystal office across from the depot. I stretched my legs by walking over there. The crystallographers inside wore turbans. I smiled, seeing myself back in a civilized kingdom.

I sent my message to several leading Schlepsigian journals. *The exiled*

King of Shqiperi returns to his homeland, it said. I hoped that would pique some interest. Scribes had helped bring my reign to a premature end, but I couldn't make my bid for fame without them now. It was like sitting down to supper with a dragon: you know you may be the next course, but if you're hungry enough you have to take the chance.

When I got back to the depot, one of the clerks recognized that my accent was foreign, not just northern. "Your passport, please, sir," he said. Seeing that Max was traveling with me, the clerk asked for his, too. He looked up from them a moment later, his face a dark cloud. "I am afraid you two gentlemen do not have proper Torinan entry stamps. This is a matter of some importance, since flouting our regulations can lead to a fine or imprisonment or both, at the judge's discretion."

"I am devastated!" I cried, and clapped a hand to my heart—Torinans love melodrama. "What can we do?"

After a bit of dickering, we did it. From that time forward, our passports *did* boast proper Torinan entry stamps. Well, they boasted proper-*looking* Torinan entry stamps, anyhow. A forensic wizard might have expressed a different opinion, but how likely was it that a forensic wizard would examine the proper-looking passports of a couple of obviously respectable, obviously innocent travelers?

Not very. I hoped.

When we got up into the north of Torino, I sent the journals in Schlepsig another message, this one letting them know where and when I was likely to come up into Schlepsig. I hadn't wanted to do that before, since travel in Torino is tardy and inefficient enough to come right out of the Nekemte Peninsula, and things in the Dual Monarchy aren't always better.

The turbaned crystallographer who sent my message said, "So you're the fellow who pretended to be the Hassocki prince, are you?"

"That's me." I strutted a little, even sitting down. "So you've heard of me, eh?" Maybe the scribes in Shqiperi were good for something after all. And sure enough, the crystallographer nodded. I showed off a little more. Then I asked, "What do you think of me? What does the world think of me?"

"You must have been out of your mind to try it, and you're lucky you got away with your neck," he answered without the least hesitation.

One good thing, anyhow: Max wasn't along to hear him say it.

Our passports passed muster when we passed from Torino to the Dual Monarchy. The customs official at the border checkpoint added more stamps. "Why were you in Torino?" he asked. Like most officials in the Dual Monarchy, he was of Schlepsigian blood. Like some other Schlepsigian officials I've known, he liked to throw his weight around just because he could.

"I'd just escaped from Shqiperi," I answered.

"And what were you doing in Shqiperi?" he asked, as if I'd just confessed to some horrible depravity. In his eyes, no doubt I had.

"I was being King of Shqiperi," I said, not without pride.

And his whole attitude changed. He pounded me on the back. He clasped my hand. He gave me a knock of cherry brandy from a flask on his belt. He gave Max a knock, too, when he found out I'd had an enormous aide-de-camp. Max drank only with the greatest suspicion. Now that you mention it, so did I. Who ever heard of a customs official acting like a human being?

But this one had his reasons. "You're the fellow who turned the dragons loose on the Belagorans!" he exclaimed. "By Eliphalet's toes, they've been screeching like a bunch of cats with their tails under rocking chairs for the past week!"

I looked at Max. Max was looking at me. Zogu's magic had worked again. He was no lightweight wizard, not Zogu. He was wasted there in Peshkepiia, the way Stagiros the weatherworker was wasted aboard the *Gamemeno*. Both of them—and how many others?—could have done so much more with themselves if only they'd got the chance.

All of a sudden, nothing was too good for Max and me. The Dual Monarchy hated and feared Belagora and Vlachia because even then they were doing their best to lure their relatives inside the Monarchy away from Vindobon and the King-Emperor and into some kind of kingdom with them. The Vlachs weren't fussy over how they went about it, either. And so anybody who'd given the Belagorans a good tweak was a friend of the Dual Monarchy's.

Max and I rode in government coaches fit for a grand duke—which, I suppose, made them more or less fit for a king, too. We feasted at every stop. We got put up at the grandest hostels. No one asked for a thaler from us—or even for a copper thent. I was almost sorry to cross the border into Schlepsig. Oh, and we got there ahead of schedule, which, in the Dual Monarchy, is as near unheard-of as makes no difference.

Crossing into Schlepsig ahead of schedule complicated things for me. I wanted to tell my story, and the stupid scribes hadn't got there to hear it. You just can't rely on those people. They're there when they shouldn't be, they stir up trouble when you don't want them to—and when you really need them, where are they?

And then, at last, they finally did show up. *Took* them bloody long enough, that's all I've got to tell you. But they listened as I told my tale. They listened as Max told his, too. One enterprising journal sent along a sketch artist as well as a scribe. He did my portrait—I still have the original, as a matter of fact. That outfit ran the picture of me next to the one of Prince Halim Eddin that had started my adventure. ONE MAN OR TWO? it said below them.

I was a nine days' wonder. I might have been an eleven days' wonder, except . . . Well, we'll get to that soon enough. Because of all the stories about me, I got offers from three or four of the biggest circus companies in Schlepsig—and, later, after some of the stories were translated, from troupes in Narbonensis and Albion and even Tver, where they take the circus very seriously indeed.

Max also got his share of offers. He got inducted into the Sword-Swallowers' Hall of Fame, too. If you didn't know there was such a thing as the Sword-Swallowers' Hall of Fame, well, neither did I. And, as Max confessed after a few beers one night, neither did he.

The Circus of Dr. Ola has to be the best company in all of Schlepsig. Max and I both signed on there. With what they paid—and with what we'd brought back from Shqiperi—we wouldn't have to worry about money again, as long as we stayed anywhere close to careful. Dooger and Cark's Traveling Emporium of Marvels? I've spent a lot of time—a *lot* of time—trying to forget Dooger and Cark's. I haven't done it yet, but every year I gain a little.

As things worked out, I would have been glad to hire on with the Circus of Dr. Ola if they hadn't paid me a kram. The proprietor's real name is Gunther, by the way, and he's no more a doctor than I am—less, if anything, because I've bandaged wounds on the battlefield. But I don't want to talk about Gunther, however admirable he may be. He *is* a good fellow, but not so good that I would have been willing to work for him for nothing . . . except for Käthe.

If you can imagine Ilona even better-looking, even better-shaped, and—!—even-tempered, you have a good start on Käthe. And I'm glad—and everyone's glad—she *is* even-tempered, too, because she does trick shooting with a crossbow the likes of which the world has never seen the likes of.

That's what the barker says about it, and Eliphalet smite me if he's not right. She'll shoot doves on the wing—behind her back, aiming with a mirror. Yes, I know it's impossible. She does it anyway. Once, before I knew her, she shot a lighted cigar out of the King of Schlepsig's mouth from twenty yards.

"What would you have done if you missed?" I asked when I heard about that, meaning, *What would they have done to you?*

"I didn't even think about it then," she answered, and I believe her— you don't think about what can go wrong when you're doing a stunt, or else it will. You just make sure you do it right. "Afterwards . . ." She didn't go on for a little while. Then she said, "I only did that once."

"Eliphalet! I bet you did," I said.

We didn't fall for each other right away, but it didn't take too long, either. One afternoon when we were getting ready for a show, she said, "We've both done a lot of things, and we've both done them with a lot of other people." I nodded. I already knew she wasn't a maiden, or anything close to a maiden. As if I minded! But she went on, "That was fine then. If we're going to get along from now on, though, we probably shouldn't do those things with anybody else any more."

And I nodded again. And we didn't. And we haven't. And it's a boy and two girls and a fair number of years later, and I haven't missed the variety a bit . . . except every once in a while. And Käthe's never once— never *once*, mind you—said a word about shooting a crossbow quarrel in one ear and out the other (to say nothing of shooting one through some even more tender spots) if I slipped.

I told you she was even-tempered. As for me, I have sense enough to know when I'm well off. Yes, I really do—now. You need to keep a sense of proportion.

Speaking of a sense of proportion, Max fell for a little trapeze artist named Rita. And when I say little, I mean *little*: she's got to be two feet shorter than he is. Of course, all girls are short to Max. I wondered if they could enjoy more postures because of the difference in size, or if it closed some off for them. Before I met Käthe, I probably would have just asked him. Now . . . I'm still wondering. She's—civilized me.

She has. Believe it or not.

Max and I did fine in the Circus of Dr. Ola. We were billed as King Halim Eddin and Captain Yildirim, and performed in costumes garish enough to embarrass Barisha, let alone Count Rappaport.

As I say, we might have been eleven days' wonders in Schlepsig instead of just nine. We might have been, but we weren't. The second round of the Nekemte Wars crowded us out of the journals.

Not a kingdom in the Nekemte Peninsula was happy about what it had stolen from the Hassockian Empire the first time around. Plovdiv wanted Thasos (which Lokris was holding on to) and more of what used to be Fyrom just north of there. Lokris wanted southern Shqiperi and more of Fyrom. Vlachia wanted northern Shqiperi and more of Fyrom. Belagora wanted northern Shqiperi, too. Belagora doesn't come close to bordering Fyrom, but probably wanted some of it anyhow.

Essad Pasha kept hanging on in Shqiperi, even without a king to call his own. He didn't lose any to Belagora, not least thanks to my dragons (and thank you, Zogu!). He didn't lose any to Vlachia, not least thanks to the Dual Monarchy. And he didn't lose any to Lokris, not least thanks to, well, the Lokrians.

Farther west, Plovdiv tried to chase Lokris and Vlachia out of the part of Fyrom the Plovdivians thought should belong to them (which is to say, most of it). How do I put this politely? It didn't work. Lokris and Vlachia thrashed Plovdiv in Fyrom. Dacia, which hadn't even been in the first round of the Nekemte Wars, jumped Plovdiv from the north. And even the Hassocki sallied forth and took back the fortress of Edirne.

So when the dust settled, Plovdiv had to cough up its chunk of Fyrom to Lokris and Vlachia, and some land in the northwest to Dacia, and the territory up to and even past Edirne to the Hassocki again, which must have been even more embarrassing than everything else that happened to her. Now there'd been two rounds of war down there, and everybody— except possibly Dacia—was still unhappy. Of course, the only way to make anybody in the Nekemte Peninsula really happy is to slaughter all his neighbors out to the horizon. They were still working up to that, but they hadn't got there yet.

Then the Powers gave Shqiperi a king whether Essad Pasha—and the Shqipetari—liked it or not. Wilhelm the Weed, I think they called him: a Schlepsigian prince with time on his hands. He went down there, but he couldn't make Essad Pasha or anyone else pay any attention to him. *I* had better luck than that, by Eliphalet's strong right hand.

And then . . . And then . . . Well, how do you talk about the start of the War of the Kingdoms without breaking down and sobbing? How do you talk about the Vlach werewolf who tore out the throat of the Dual Monarch's heir—and the poor prince's wife's, too—before a silver cross-bow quarrel killed him? How do you talk about the Vlach werewolf who had friends at the court of the King of Vlachia?

Once upon a time, I said the Vlachs might huff and puff and blow the Nekemte Peninsula down. The Vlachs huffed and they puffed and they almost—*almost*—blew the world down.

When they didn't do enough to show the Dual Monarchy they were sorry (if they were sorry instead of laughing behind their hands, which is more likely), the King-Emperor declared war on Vlachia. Then Tver declared war on the Dual Monarchy, because Tver was Vlachia's ally. Then Schlepsig, my Schlepsig, declared war on Tver, because Schlepsig was the Dual Monarchy's ally. Then Narbonensis declared war on Schlepsig, be-cause Narbonensis was Tver's ally.

Narbonensis had fortified its border with Schlepsig, clearly with evil intent. To get at the Narbonese, my kingdom had to march its soldiers north of Narbonensis through the little kingdom of Bruges. Yes, years ago an earlier King of Schlepsig signed a treaty promising not to do any such thing. But what's a treaty? Only a scrap of paper! Because of a scrap of paper, Albion, perfidious Albion, declared war on Schlepsig.

All the same, everybody thought we'd beat Narbonensis in a hurry, turn around and give the Tverskis a couple of good ones in the slats, and go home again before the leaves fell. Only . . . it didn't quite work out that way. With help from Albion, and with the Brugeoisie fighting like fiends, the Narbonese held us in front of Lutetia. And we did give the Tverskis a couple of good ones, but so what? Tver is so big, she can take more than anybody else can dish out.

The war dragged on . . . and on. The Hassockian Empire came in on our side. So did Plovdiv. Torino was supposed to, but decided to jump on the Dual Monarchy's back instead. Dacia tried to do the same thing, and promptly got squashed for her trouble.

For a while, the Circus of Dr. Ola toured behind the lines, entertaining troops on leave. So did other troupes. Then more and more of the men started putting on pike-gray uniforms themselves. My own call came when the war was about a year old, just after Käthe had our first.

I speak good Narbonese. They could have sent me east. I speak fluent Hassocki—do I ever! They could have sent me southwest. I speak pretty fair Torinan. They could have sent me south when Schlepsig gave the Dual Monarchy a hand down there. I would have been truly useful in any of those places.

They shipped me west to fight Tver. I have little bits of Vlachian, which is sort of like Tverski. In other words, in that fight I was no more useful than any other soldier, and less useful than quite a few. Did they care? Ha! I was a body. I could shoot a crossbow. That, they cared about.

We could beat the Tverskis whenever we set our minds to it. It did us less good than we hoped it would. I shot a few of the poor bastards. Some of them only had hunting bows. It hardly seemed fair. Then one of the lousy Zibeonites shot me in the arm, and I stopped caring whether it was fair or not.

Max? Max never never did get into pike-gray. Turns out they didn't make uniforms—and especially boots—large enough to fit him. He went on swallowing his own sword all through the war, and never had to worry about anybody else's. Just as well, I suppose. He would have been a demon of a big target.

Thanks to some good medical magecraft, the arm healed fine. I went back to the line—and got shot in the leg. I was evidently a demon of a big target myself.

We managed to knock Tver out of the war while I was laid up the second time, and no, I don't call that cause and effect. But Vespucciland came in about then. The cursed Vesps were getting rich selling Albion and Narbonensis everything under the sun. They wanted to protect their investment, Eliphalet afflict them with carbuncles.

We fought for four years all told, till we couldn't fight any more. Then we threw in the sponge. The king abdicated. There was a short civil war till we got a new one, who's only distantly connected to the old royal house. We lost land. Worse, we lost face.

And at that, we were lucky. Tver had a peasants' revolt, and councils of peasants and artisans are trying to run the place till someone steels himself to put a crown on his head. The Dual Monarchy fell to pieces. All the pieces declared themselves kingdoms of their own or else joined neighboring kingdoms—Great Vlachia got too big for its own britches in a hurry, but it's still not big enough to be a Power. The old dynasty still hangs on in the Eastmarch, which isn't much to hang on to. And the Hassockian Empire also fell apart. Their old imperial family had to run for its life. They've got a tough new Atabeg named Kemal (no, I don't *think* he's the one I jugged) who's trying to whip what's left of them into shape. We'll see what comes of that, if anything ever does.

Shqiperi? Shqiperi's a bloody mess, but then Shqiperi's always been a bloody mess, so it hasn't changed as much as most of the world has. Wilhelm the Weed didn't last—he ran away during the war. Essad Pasha didn't last, either—somebody murdered him right after the war. I wonder how many suspects there were. The whole population of Shqiperi minus about twelve, I suppose.

Last I heard, someone named Zogu claimed to be running things there. *That* Zogu? *My* Zogu? I don't know. If it is, they could do worse. And they probably will.

After the War of the Kingdoms, I half hoped the Shqipetari would call me back to take over again. No doubt Wilhelm the Weed hoped the same thing. We're both still waiting, I'm afraid. I don't know about Wilhelm, but I've given up holding my breath.

"Just as well," Käthe said when I told her that. "Haven't you got enough going on right here?" This was just after we had our third, so no denying she had a point.

Once I came home for good, I needed a while before I started performing again. That isn't just, or even mainly, because I got wounded twice while I wore the pike-gray. Part of it's because, like a lot of soldiers coming home from the war, I was too gloomy and disappointed to care about anything. We'd done so much, we'd suffered so much, and what did we have to show for it? Nothing. Nothing at all. I needed a while to get over that *who gives a damn?* feeling.

And part of it's simply because I'd got out of practice. You don't practice for a day or two and you notice you're off when you go back to it. You don't practice for a month or two and the audience notices you're off. At the front, I didn't practice for much longer than a month or two. If a lot of your performance involves going up there on a tightrope, the audience is like to notice because you fall off and go splat. Not good.

Little by little, I eased myself into it again. I wasn't the only veteran coming back to the Circus of Dr. Ola, and I wasn't the only one who had trouble picking up where he'd left off.

The circus wasn't the same, either. The circuit was smaller, and so was the pay. After the war, they didn't want to watch performing Schlepsigians in Narbonensis or Torino or Albion or Gdansk (yes, Gdansk has risen from the dead—till the next time her neighbors pound a stake into her heart). So we played in Schlepsig and the Eastmarch, with an occasional foray into Yagmaria (whose new king is an old admiral from the Dual Monarchy, which would make more sense if Yagmaria had a coastline).

I knew I wasn't going on any more grand adventures. After you've been king, how can you top that? I found myself doing more behind the scenes than I ever had, too: arranging for coaches and wagons, booking halls and hostels, seeing that things ran smoothly for the circus. I still get out in front of the crowds every so often, but that's mostly when the circus plays near Putzig, the little town where Käthe and I settled down with the children.

You see? I ended up normal, which for me is an even bigger surprise than ending up king. I'm a good citizen. I'm a breadwinner. I'm the father of a family. Sometimes, when the bookings are more complicated than usual, I hurry down the street to the CC office carrying my papers in a briefcase. A briefcase! Me! Normal as you please, no more hijinks for me.

Well, hardly any.

Because I don't tour much any more, I was at home when someone knocked on the front door one mild summer morning. I think I muttered a little as I got up from my desk. A hostel in the Eastmarch had just written to say they couldn't take us after all, and I had to scramble to find the troupe some other place to stay next week. I didn't fancy getting interrupted just then. If it was a peddler, I aimed to send him away with a flea in his ear.

The man at the door wasn't a peddler. He wasn't a neighbor, come to borrow a hammer or scrounge a cigar. I'd never met him before, but he looked familiar. And well he might have.

He was wearing my face.

Close enough, anyhow. After a nervous moment when we sized each other up, I managed a bow and spoke in Hassocki: "Won't you please come in, your Highness?"

Prince Halim Eddin courteously returned the bow. "Thank you very much—your Majesty," he said in excellent Schlepsigian. His voice wasn't really much like mine; it was a bit higher and a lot more musical. I can't carry a tune in a sack, but you could tell just by listening to him talk that he'd be able to sing.

I got him settled on the sofa. I brought him coffee: the thinner brew we make in Schlepsig, but it was what I had. I fixed myself a cup, too. I also brought out a bottle of Narbonese brandy and set it on the table in front of him. "For improving the coffee, if you care to," I said. He did. I did, too. I needed it. He didn't bother flicking away the ritual drop; he just drank. "It's a great privilege to make your acquaintance at last, sir," I told him.

He raised an eyebrow. He didn't pluck them any more. "I was going to say the same thing to you," he answered. "Now that I see you, I see how you brought it off. The resemblance is remarkable, isn't it?"

"It is," I agreed. We looked all the more like each other because he had on a homburg and a sack suit I might have worn myself, even if the suit was cut more conservatively than I favor. I took a big swig of that improved coffee and said, "I daresay I've owed you an apology for a good many years. For whatever it's worth to you now, you have it."

"I don't want it. I don't need it." He was still studying me. "North and south, east and west, how did you have the nerve? Do you know what Essad Pasha would have done to you if he'd realized you weren't me? Have you got any idea?"

"I tried not to think about that," I said.

"I believe it." Halim Eddin poured more brandy into his coffeecup. He took another sip, then eyed me again. "Why?"

"Because it was the grandest role I'd ever have the chance to play," I said. "I was a king. I really *was* a king. For five days, I was. I don't know if that makes any sense to you. . . ."

"Oh, yes," he said softly. "*Oh*, yes. You must remember, you had five more days as king than I ever did. You had five more days as king than I ever would have, even if the dynasty survived. My dear uncle told me he would take a month killing me if I tried to go to Shqiperi. He thought I would rise against him if I did. He thought everyone would rise against him." He let out a harsh chuckle. "And in the end, he was right. Everyone did—not that he hadn't earned it."

I'd never thought my going to Shqiperi might endanger the real Halim Eddin. Truth to tell, I hadn't cared. "What did he do when he heard you—I mean I—was there after all?"

"He came to my home. He had to see me with his own eyes—he had to hit me with his own fist—before he would believe I wasn't in Peshkepiia," Halim Eddin said. "It was . . . an unpleasant afternoon."

I didn't think I wanted to ask him any more about that. Instead, I said, "What do you do these days?"

"I teach Hassocki. I buy and sell. I do well enough. I'm not rich, but I'm not poor, either," he replied. "I live by your customs here. I have one wife, three children. What of you?"

"One wife and three children also," I said. "I'm slowly easing out of performing. After I played your part, none of the others seemed to matter so much. I help keep the circus running smoothly, and I do some gardening out back of the house—I grow herbs and flowers." I shrugged. "It's a hobby."

"We twist the arm of coincidence again," Halim Eddin said, "for I am a gardener, too."

"Would you like to see what I'm up to, then?" I asked.

"Nothing would please me more," he said. As we walked out to my plot, he found a question of his own: "And how did you like your harem?"

"It was a lot of fun for a little while," I answered. "But do you know what? One woman is plenty, as long as she's the right one."

I more than halfway thought he would laugh at me, but he only said, "I have found the same thing. The right one is worth any number of wrong ones." I opened the back door for him. He stepped out, then paused to look at what I was doing. His nod of approval was worth gold to me. "Ah, this is fine. This is fine indeed."

"I'm so glad it pleases you," I told him. Inside a border of roses, some red, some yellow, I grew neat rows of sweet basil and rocket and anise. I was particularly proud of the last, which is not easy to raise in Schlepsig because of the cold winters. Rocks with hollows underneath—placed north and south, east and west—sheltered grass snakes and smooth snakes; every so often, I would find a cast skin. Those crushed blue pills Zogu used . . . I do manage without them. Yes I do.

Halim Eddin nodded again. "Very much. Had you started it when you were younger, it would have been wilder, I think, and I might have liked it that way myself then. Now I prefer things neater and tidier, too," he said candidly. "As we go through our lives, we all must cultivate our gardens as best we can."

"Yes," I said, and we stood there together in the warm sunshine.

HARRY TURTLEDOVE is an award-winning author of science fiction and fantasy. His alternate-history works have included several short stories and novels, such as *The Guns of the South; How Few Remain* (winner of the Sidewise Award for Best Novel); the Great War epics: *American Front, Walk in Hell,* and *Breakthroughs;* the Worldwar saga: *In the Balance, Tilting the Balance, Upsetting the Balance,* and *Striking the Balance;* the Colonization books: *Second Contact, Down to Earth,* and *Aftershocks;* the American Empire novels: *Blood & Iron, The Center Cannot Hold,* and *Victorious Opposition; Settling Accounts: Return Engagement; Settling Accounts: Drive to the East;* and others. He is married to fellow novelist Laura Frankos. They have three daughters: Alison, Rachel, and Rebecca.